SOMETHING TO DIE FOR

"A TRULY PRESCIENT BOOK.
Jim Webb's new novel is a rarity;
it captures both the gritty reality
of modern desert combat
and is a wholly convincing insider's view
of defense policy being made
on the highest level."
W.E.B. Griffin,
author of *Brotherhood of War*

"COMPELLING FICTION . . .
A novelist with something tough-minded to say
that goes beyond wild-blue-yonder,
gee-whiz weaponry."
Seattle Post-Intelligencer

"AS TIMELY AS TOMORROW'S NEWS,
as reflective of today's world
as only a man of deep experience
and scholarly understanding could produce."
John Del Vecchio,
author of *The Thirteenth Valley*

"FASCINATING . . .
Webb's style is like Tom Clancy's . . .
He has something to prove and settles the score . . .
The country continues to be well-served
by this military maverick."
Christian Science Monitor

SOMETHING TO DIE FOR

JAMES WEBB

AVON BOOKS ◆ NEW YORK

AVON BOOKS
A division of
The Hearst Corporation
1350 Avenue of the Americas
New York, New York 10019

Copyright © 1991 by James Webb
Inside front cover photograph by Steve Eisenberg
Published by arrangement with the author
Library of Congress Catalog Card Number: 90-43122
ISBN: 0-380-71322-5

Published in hardcover by William Morrow and Company, Inc.; for information address Permissions Department, William Morrow and Company, Inc., 1350 Avenue of the Americas, New York, New York 10019.

First Avon Books Printing: February 1992
First Avon Books Special Printing: September 1991

AVON TRADEMARK REG. U.S. PAT. OFF. AND IN OTHER COUNTRIES, MARCA REGISTRADA, HECHO EN U.S.A.

Printed in the U.S.A.

RA   10   9   8   7   6   5   4   3   2   1

With love to:

JoAnn
Amy
Jimmy
Sarah
Julia

Acknowledgments

Thanks to the following people, who were more than gracious in their assistance as I prepared this novel.

Captain Oleg Jankovic, USN, for his overall comments regarding many of the matters in the book, as well as his expertise in the area of naval aviation.

Susan Breedlove Kew, for her unfailing willingness to help on many fronts.

Hugh Howard of the Pentagon Library and Caroline "Killer" Krewson, for their research assistance in a variety of areas.

Captain Timothy LaFleur, USN, and the sailors of the U.S.S. *Elliot* (DD–967).

Former Peace Corps members John Herbert and Jack Prebis, for their help on Eritrea.

And Sterling Lord, a valued friend and an agent who has no peer.

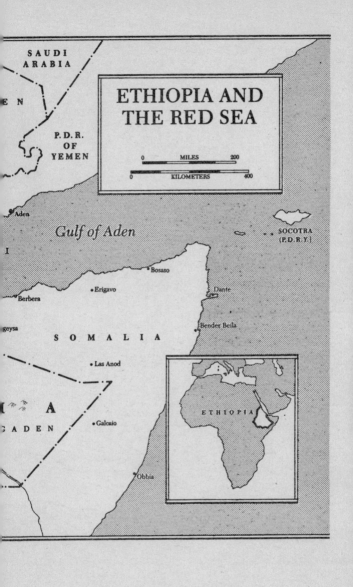

ETHIOPIA AND THE RED SEA

MILES 0 200
KILOMETERS 0 400

SAUDI ARABIA

P.D.R. OF YEMEN

Aden

Gulf of Aden

SOCOTRA (P.D.R.Y.)

Bosaso

Erigavo

Dante

Berbera

Bender Beila

geysa

SOMALIA

Las Anod

A

ETHIOPIA

GADEN

Galcaio

Obbia

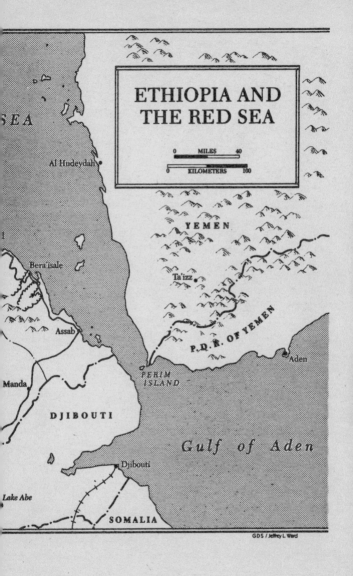

On the wall in his private study at home there was an old black-and-white photograph of his father. The picture was taken on the outskirts of Seoul, Korea, in September 1950, just after the Inchŏn landing. His father had returned to civilian life after World War II only to be ripped from home and family and suddenly flung back into battle when South Korea was invaded five years later. In the photograph his father stood next to the charred remains of an old warehouse, amid piles of rocks and smoldering timber. He was wearing a helmet, a green field jacket, and a set of old combat fatigues that had seen their best days on Iwo Jima. He was standing at attention, eyes lowered, his thin face unshaven, and his hands clenched into fists, as General MacArthur congratulated him for having led his rifle company in an assault that routed a North Korean stronghold.

When Bill Fogarty was five years old, this photograph was not merely a picture of his father, it was his father. He would carry it with him and show it to his neighbors in the small Nebraska town where the family was waiting out the war. He would mimic his father's stoic expression, and the careful curling of his fingers, when he talked seriously with adults. He would keep it next to his bed when he went to sleep at night. This was his father, off in a foreign land as the family waited every day and prayed every night for his return. His father was good and brave and beautiful, and General MacArthur had congratulated him for his courage.

The day his father came home, Fogarty and his two sisters excitedly practiced their welcome for him throughout the afternoon. They were going to sing songs, and do somersaults. Fogarty was going to ride on his back as he crawled like a pony across the small living room floor. Then when his father walked into the house, filling the front door with his size and power, calling to them in a booming, joyous baritone that had been absent for so long, Fogarty had become so stricken by his power, the very realness of this demigod that he had worshiped in his prayers each night for years, that he had run out of the room and hidden underneath the dining room table. His father's presence simply was too overwhelming to be real.

Fogarty could still see the uniformed legs walking toward him as he peered out from underneath the table, so happy and relieved that his father was finally home that he could not bear to face him. And then his father crawled underneath the table and held him there, brushing a whiskered face against his cheeks, joking gently with him and refusing to leave their hiding place until his son took him by the hand and showed him around their home. And when he stood beside his son's bed and saw the photograph at its shrinelike place of honor on a nearby chair, now wrinkled at its edges by the grip of little hands, he pulled Bill Fogarty onto the bed and they both cried for a very long time.

Over the years, during the dark times when others questioned why he had remained in the Marine Corps after gaining a master's degree in business, running a congressional liaison staff in Washington, and having received numerous lucrative offers from businesses and universities, Fogarty had always come back to the picture of his father with the general on the battlefield in Korea. At bottom, he soldiered for the children who sat at home and pondered photographs and prayed that their own fathers might soon return. But he knew that such a motivation seemed even medieval in modern America, and so he covered it with his well-honed talent for cynical humor.

"Hey, I'm good at killing people," he would mutter bluntly while seeking to change the subject. Which was not actually untrue, as Fogarty had distinguished himself numerous times on the battlefield.

When his own time came and he had chosen the infantry, his mother viewed his calling with quiet desperation. He was her only son. But she was of the mountain South. She knew that conflict filled her people's veins, and that she could no more alter the flow of her blood than she could redirect the Tennessee River, which curled past Lookout Mountain near her childhood home, reminding her every day of the Civil War battles that tore at the hearts of her ancestors. She knew her son was part of a continuum, that her people had straddled a paradox for thousands of years, wishing most of all to be left alone, but drawn to fighting as naturally as a bird dog thrills at its first flushed covey of quail.

But Bill Fogarty wasn't so sure anymore. Maybe he had done it too long. Maybe it was the recent assignment in Washington, three years split between working the Congress and serving as an action officer on the Joint Chiefs of Staff. The assignment had unsettled him, opening up his eyes to the sometimes bewildering series of second and third agendas advanced by ambitious top-level executives whenever military force was debated.

Or maybe it was simply that his own son had just turned fourteen, and Fogarty was afraid in a way he had never been before. Because there was another picture, and Fogarty paused before it for a long time as he went from room to room in his home just outside Camp Pendleton, California, performing a secret farewell ritual as he again prepared to go to sea.

The rooms were empty. His wife was at work and his two children were at school. He stopped inside each doorway and tried to memorize the furniture, the clothes, the pennants and the teddy bears. In six months he would return, and go through the rooms again, and try to measure the little, irretrievable moments he had lost—changes in clothing styles, nights helping with homework, family arguments that shaped personalities and bred memories.

The photograph had been taken of him in Lebanon in 1983, a month before the headquarters building had been blown up by Muslim terrorists, killing more than 240 Marines. It showed him in his camouflage uniform, standing on the roof of the building as he pointed toward the Marine positions on the other side of the Beirut airport's runway to a delegation of posturing congressmen. He had sent it home to his wife. And his son, then six, had treasured it in his absence and later framed it.

And then will it be him, serving to honor me, while the rest of the country goes off to business school or plays Nintendo and forgets that his suffering is real?

The U.S.S. *Saipan* seemed to be a gray, living eminence, strapped unwillingly against the quays. His staff car approached the ship and again the sea smells welcomed him. The water seemed yeasty and alive, filled with pierside flotsam that somehow seduced him with the promise of strange things on distant shores. The 820-foot amphibious assault ship purred, straining against this California edge of the great Pacific Ocean, as if it were impatient at pierside, ready to embark. Hundreds of sailors and marines choked the narrow pier along the *Saipan*'s length. Some were saying good-bye to lovers and families. Others were busily making last-minute loadings of equipment and supplies. Still others were testing lines and moorings and electrical hookups, preparing to unleash the ship and let it go.

Fogarty strode heavily up the forward brow and stopped at the quarterdeck, where a young Navy lieutenant was functioning as officer of the day. He first saluted toward the fantail, where the American flag would remain until the ship was officially at sea, when it would be raised above the bridge. And then he saluted the lieutenant.

"Request permission to come aboard."

"Granted. Good morning, sir." The lieutenant pointed toward the stern of the ship. "Sir, your XO is in the aft hangar deck with the sergeant major. You're missing at least one man."

"Thanks."

Fogarty climbed down an internal ladder and entered the shadowed reaches of the aft hangar deck. New smells enveloped him: mess hall food, fuel oil, exhaust fumes, old canvas, sweat and must. Lieutenant Colonel Roger Reid was holding a heavily papered clipboard in the midst of a clutter of netted supplies and busily working marines. Reid saluted Fogarty as the Colonel approached.

"Good morning, sir. We're all accounted for. Only two changes from last night. Bravo Company lost a man to emergency leave. His grandmother died yesterday. Charlie Company has one man in the base hospital. He got stabbed in a bar down in the Tenderloin section last night."

"How bad is he?"

"Multiple lacerations, face and chest. No permanent damage. The doctors want to hold him for a couple days."

"Go get him."

"Sir?" Reid looked at him uncertainly.

"Send somebody over to get him. I'm not having a marine miss a six-month deployment because he got into a fight. We've got doctors on board."

"He took forty stitches."

"He can heal on the way to Subic."

"Aye, aye, sir."

Fogarty walked briskly away as Lieutenant Colonel Reid called to a driver and dispatched a lieutenant to retrieve the missing man. He went forward, visiting the troop spaces to check on berthing arrangements for his men. He inspected the equipment storage, tugging at camouflage netting and dull green straps. He cornered his air liaison officer to ensure that the mix of helicopters and AV-8 Harriers that would fly out to the ship once it was at sea were all "up" and ready to go. He called to the elements under his command that were deploying on other ships, ensuring the remainder of his aircraft and other support units were either on board or standing by to join the battle group when it hit the open sea.

And in thirty minutes, the 51st Marine Expeditionary Unit was locked and cocked, ready to fight. Under Fogarty's direct command were more than twenty-four hundred marines and naval personnel, including an infantry battalion reinforced with tanks and 155-millimeter artillery, a composite aviation element of assault, heavy-lift, and attack helicopters as well as AV-8 Harrier jets, and an extensive service support group providing logistical, medical, and special demolitions assistance. The MEU was deployed on the *Saipan* and three other support ships. In the coming days a total of eight ships would join the aircraft carrier U.S.S. *Roosevelt*, forming a battle group that would sail into the Indian Ocean and points beyond.

Now Colonel Bill Fogarty climbed up a series of ladders, moving toward the flight deck for "quarters," the time-honored way a navy ship said farewell.

San Diego sparkled, new urban growth rimming the waterfront and crowding the dry surrounding hills with all the evidence of burgeoning greatness. Fogarty said a quiet good-bye to all that as the *Saipan* made its way out of the harbor, heading for the open sea. The ship emanated its own personality as it churned against the ocean. It seemed strong and steady, even unafraid, as it hummed and droned and shook. And again the strangely seductive mingling of odors washed over him, kissing the insides of his lungs. And he settled into his six-month prison of a home.

Along the edges of the flight deck the *Saipan's* sailors and marines stood elbow to elbow at parade rest as the ship departed the harbor, making a wide perimeter of white and green. The sight of a thousand seafaring faces staring solemnly back toward the harbor never failed to move him. An electricity had now engulfed the men, a curious mix of anticipation and sadness. On the pier, wives and lovers waved farewell. Some men openly cried as the ship pulled out. But they would recover. They always did. Just as a scout dog assumed a new identity when its handler strapped it with a working collar, the sailors and marines would grow tough and bawdy as the ship traversed the Pacific. Their normal lives were fading in a California fog. The isolation and cramped conditions and unending shipboard regimen would make them different men, cover them with a layer of their very own boilerplate.

By the time California disappeared behind the wake of a gray, misty sea, Fogarty was already covered with his. By the time they had formed the battle group and passed Hawaii, he was bronzed from the sun and spending hours every day going over training plans and operational contingencies. And by the time they eased into the sultry, brackish waters of Subic Bay, he was ready to take Olongapo apart, bar by bar.

The troops would blow it out in Subic, and Fogarty would make no effort to stifle it. Because after that they would be swallowed by the endless expanse of the Big IO, as they called the Indian Ocean. And times were not good in Washington. Fogarty could sense it from little hints on the news that he never would have noticed had he not spent three years learning the doublespeak of government. The more bellicose members of the administration seemed especially antsy of late, spoiling for a reason to use military force.

When the ship pulled into Subic, Fogarty was met by Navy captain George Mathews, an old friend who was now serving on the U.S. Naval Forces staff in the Philippines. Mathews warned him that Admiral Mad Dog Mulcahy had a new grand scheme, and was flying out from Hawaii to spend a few days discussing it with the senior officers of the battle group.

"Mad Dog, eh?" Fogarty had grinned sardonically to Mathews as they stood on the quarterdeck, readying to go on liberty in Olongapo. "Not a good sign. Not a good sign at all."

CHAPTER 1
WASHINGTON, D.C.

Washington is a town whose only industry is the making, shaping, processing, and marketing of words. Words to define how citizens should conduct themselves. Words to direct and limit industry. Words to calm friends and warn enemies. Words to throw at one another in the halls of Congress, or in front of devouring cameras. Words that in the end can kill, or impoverish, or imprison, or empower. And also recycled words—on editorial pages or inside the pages of legal briefs—dissecting other words, assessing implications, making distinctions, arguing their true meaning as if the words were holy writ. Words without poetry or music, whose mastery brings money and authority.

And few had mastered this arcane industry as well as Ronald Holcomb, who at forty-six had become one of the youngest secretaries of defense in history. Physically small and unathletic, his ability to think and speak had always enlarged his presence. As a young boy at Andover preparatory school, Holcomb had learned their power, compensating for his small stature by negotiating his way out of confrontations. At Harvard he had led the debating team.

At Cambridge he had mastered English literature. At Yale law school he had edited the law review. And in only twenty years, he had talked and written his way from a position in the foreign service, to a key post on the National Security Council, to an undersecretaryship of state, and now to the head of the Defense Department. President Everett Lodge loved to hear Ron Holcomb talk. And more important, the President listened to what he said.

Today, as his black limousine drove past the historic buildings and wide fields of the Mall, Holcomb silently rehearsed his lines from his place in the right rear seat of the car. He had two stops to make, and it was his mission to talk the President out of trouble.

Billy Parks, Holcomb's driver, slowed the large car and made a right turn off of Constitution Avenue. It was a steamy summer day, one that recalled Washington's original beginnings as a swamp. Across the street, young staffers and interns were calling to each other in the sultry morning air as they walked along the edges of the Russell Senate Office Building. As always in the summer, the town was filled with tourists. From the back seat, Holcomb had counted license plates from more than thirty different states on cars and vans as he made the journey from the Pentagon to the Capitol. Counting license plates was an old habit, designed by Holcomb's father when he was a child to strengthen his memory. And the young defense secretary had an unbeatable memory.

Parks turned on the flashing red light that was mounted on the dashboard, and slowly eased the limousine past concrete blockades that sealed off the Capitol parking lot. Before the days of terrorism, the lot had been an open thoroughfare named Capitol Street. A potbellied policeman in black trousers and a white shirt stepped out of a gate house and halted the limousine. He peered inside, checking them with a dark, emotionless face that had lost its capacity to trust. Parks turned off the siren light and showed him a government pass.

"Secretary of defense," said Parks. "Here to see the Senate majority leader."

The policeman allowed himself one more piercing look into each man's face, just to be sure. Finally, he pointed inside the lot, next to the Capitol itself. "Alright. Good morning, Mr. Secretary. Park over there."

Parks drove to a reserved area adjacent to the Senate chambers and halted the car. Holcomb stepped gingerly out of the right rear door, smoothing out the wrinkles in his suit and tamping down his hair just above the ears. His senior military assistant, Major General Bear Lazaretti, exited from the left. In a locked briefcase under his left arm, Lazaretti carried a sheaf of papers containing fact sheets and briefing materials.

Sid Rose, the assistant secretary of defense for legislative affairs, had been waiting for them. Now he strutted like a rooster toward the car and stood at the curb. Rose bounced on his toes, constantly scanning the sidewalks and waving to people as they passed: staffers, police officers, janitors, gawking tourists, it didn't matter. It seemed Sid Rose knew them all, and each one had a smile for him. Everybody was Sid Rose's best friend. Even Ronald Holcomb, who rarely thought in terms of friends.

Holcomb walked toward him and Rose took the secretary by the crook of one arm, an act that caused Holcomb to recoil slightly from the unpermitted familiarity. Rose noticed that, and in response became even more familiar. Rose couldn't help it. He was a creature of Capitol Hill. Touch and pat, slap and shake. Those were important tools in the business of seducing support from congressmen and others who lived in a world of shaky, constantly changing alliances.

"Hey, Ron! I really appreciate you coming over here this morning. It's the first time Joe Barksdale's even noticed we existed since June."

They walked under a concrete tunnel that was an extension of the building, and then through a side door, into the

Senate side of the Capitol. The interior of the Capitol was
dark and heavily ornate. With some modification, the building had served American legislators since 1800, with a few
minor interruptions such as its burning by the British in
1814. High columns marked the hallways. Beautiful mosaics covered the towering ceilings. Patterned marble made
the floors. There had been a time when this building alone
had been the very power center of a small but vibrant nation.
In the nineteenth century the entire Congress, as well as the
Supreme Court, had met and kept their offices inside the
central building.

Another policeman checked them at the door, and Rose
steered Holcomb through a bustle of staffers and tourists
toward a nearby elevator. On the way up, Rose briefed him.
"They gave up on the idea of a filibuster on immigration
reform this morning. The bill is going to pass now. Reform,
they call it! We're looking at a disaster, a goddamn disaster!
We may as well make Mexico a state. Not to mention
Salvador, Nicaragua, Honduras, Colombia, Bolivia, hell
you name it. Hong Kong, Taiwan, Korea. The majority
leader sits up late at night talking about the end of the Roman
Empire. He let the filibuster die because he claimed he
wasn't getting any help from the President. Hey, Ron, be
nice to Joe Barksdale, do you hear? He's mad as hell at the
President. And we need a bill. We need to get this thing
passed. He can bring it to the floor with the wave of one
hand. I know he doesn't like you." Rose paused, searching
for an optimistic note. "But that's okay. I mean, he *hates*
the President."

Holcomb rolled his eyes knowingly as the elevator ascended. "So, what does the old guy want?"

Rose laughed, viewing Holcomb with the camaraderie of
a fellow conspirator. "My spies say he's going to hit you
up for a wind tunnel at the University of Mississippi. It's
cheap, Ron! For God's sake, all he wants is his name on
something before he gets too old. 'The Joseph J. Barksdale
Wind Tunnel,' or something like that. You know how these

guys get. They reach seventy and they want to have a legacy in concrete. He's seventy-five, he wants marble.''

"Well, we've already got the Marsha Barksdale Family Center down at Collins Air Force Base.''

"Yeah, but this is for him! Forty-five years he's put into this place. Nine million dollars, Ron. The money's already in the bill. We just haven't made the site selection for the tunnel yet. It could go anywhere, it doesn't matter. And Ole Miss completely qualifies. I checked. Besides, let's face it. Nine million wouldn't make a pimple on the ass of our budget. In fact, nine million could get us three billion once the bill reaches the floor, if he's on our side.''

Holcomb shrugged, ready to do business. "Sounds acceptable. Pork is pork, as they say over here in the pigsty.''

The doors opened at the second floor. They walked down another long, high-ceilinged corridor, bordering the Senate chambers, and finally turned into a door marked S-221, JOSEPH J. BARKSDALE, MAJORITY LEADER. It was a beautiful, lush, historic stroll to S-221. Ron Holcomb felt as if he belonged with the marble and the mosaics. In a way, he felt, he was its clearest inheritor, even though he had never run for office. He knew government. He knew history. He was a part of the continuum, he decided, even more than Joseph J. Barksdale, or Doc Rowland.

Hicks, he thought. Hicks elect hicks, that's the basic truth of democracy. You do indeed get the government you deserve. And then the problems begin. They'd never elect people like me, but they couldn't survive a week without us. Too stiff, they'd say. He can't tell a joke good enough, they'd say. He can't play the fiddle like Robert Byrd or milk a cow like Doc Rowland. He can't sing Hank Williams songs like Sad Joe Barksdale or rap and orate like Ron Dellums.

But who do they run to when the world begins to cave in? The professionals, the people they make fun of at their barbecues, and whose wealth and education they envy. The people who spend their lives keeping the country moving along the canalized banks of its true historical place, no matter what gyrations undulate from the car dealers and rabble-rousers who happen to claw their way by luck or scheme into elected office.

People like me, thought Holcomb as he walked into the majority leader's office.

The majority leader occupied four large rooms inside the Capitol Building, in addition to his regular offices in the Dirksen Building across the street. S–221 was his greeting area. Holcomb, Rose, and Lazaretti languished for five minutes in the outer office, absently studying photographs of former majority leaders on the walls, and feeling the occasional glances from three young secretaries. The office was oppressively quiet as the three women worked. They even seemed to whisper when they talked on the telephone.

Just above the door to Barksdale's inner office was a photograph of Nathan Bedford Forrest, a revered Confederate general who had fought many battles in Mississippi and western Tennessee. On the desk closest to the front of the office, someone had proudly framed a door hinge with a shard of splintered wood still intact. A caption underneath the hinge proclaimed FROM THE BOMB BLAST AT THE CAPITOL, OCTOBER 1983. Holcomb privately found such displays ostentatious, *gauche*. He felt his lips tighten with distaste as he surveyed them. As if the internecine, racist bloodletting of the Civil War should still be celebrated. And as if there had been grave danger, serving here in the Capitol, where once every hundred years or so some kook blew away a door hinge.

Finally a young aide opened the door to the inner office spaces. He was short and cherubic. Bright blue eyes burned at Holcomb from behind designer glasses. He wore four rings on various stubby fingers, and a Rolex wristwatch. His hair was permed. He reminded Ronald Holcomb of a fat young Truman Capote. He spoke quietly, as if he were asking the three men to come view a casket.

"Gentlemen, if you'll come this way, the majority leader will see you."

He led them through a second room, into a conference room. The room was surprisingly cluttered, with papers stacked high on a nearby desk. Pictures of politicians now long dead hung on the wall: Sam Rayburn, Lyndon Johnson, Everett Dirksen, men whose uncoiffed hair and tight-lipped smiles reminded Holcomb immediately of an era that also was long dead, an era that did not consult the pollsters for solutions, one of raw political machinations to be sure, but also of forward movement for the nation.

Barksdale sat at the head of a large, deeply polished table made from an uncut slab of Philippine mahogany, a treasure sent back by General Douglas MacArthur after the reconquest in World War II. For some reason, Barksdale had stacked three old scrapbooks on the table in front of him, replete with the black pages and lick-on tabs of yesteryear. One look at the unkempt room with the dated pictures on the wall, and at Barksdale himself, and Holcomb began to wonder if the majority leader had quietly gone senile.

Holcomb strode across the seemingly endless floor and extended his hand. "Senator, very good of you to see us this morning, sir. How have you been?"

Barksdale did not rise. He froze Holcomb with one glance, as if he had seen so many hundreds or thousands like him that he was nothing more than a photocopy, a bureaucratic clone. "I've been fine. Despite the wildest hopes of many of my friends. Sit down, sit down. Don't mean to be rude but my legs don't feel too good today." But of course Barksdale did mean to be rude, and Holcomb knew it. He and the others immediately sat down at the table.

Holcomb sought to break the ice. "I was admiring your pictures in the outer office. Wasn't that Nathan Bedford Forrest on the wall above your door?"

The majority leader wore a dark double-vented suit and a red tie. He had grown heavy and gray during his forty-five years in the House and Senate. His hair seemed lavender in the room's artificial light. His cheeks looked as soft and full as a woman's. And when he spoke in private, his famous stentorian voice was as gentle and dry as Kleenex.

"Yes, it was." His voice was deliberately flat, as if a display of emotion might be interpreted as advocacy for the Cause of the Confederacy. "Bedford Forrest I think was one of the few American generals who deserve to be called great. Winston Churchill said there were three great generals in the Civil War. Robert E. Lee, Stonewall Jackson, and Bedford Forrest. Did you know that the German high command studied the Battle of Brice's Crossroads, up near Tupelo, when they were putting together their blitzkrieg doctrine? Bedford Forrest whupped more than eight thousand Federal soldiers with three thousand of his own."

And he was a slave dealer who slaughtered a contingent of black soldiers at Fort Pillow, too, thought Holcomb, who nonetheless was congratulating himself on getting the meeting off swimmingly. "What was it he said, Senator? 'Get there the fustest with the mostest,' wasn't it?"

"An ethnic slur, Mr. Secretary, designed to emphasize a great soldier's lack of schooling. But no matter. Beford Forrest didn't have time or money to go to school. His daddy died when he was fifteen, leaving him to raise five brothers and three sisters. He went to the army at forty, and kicked the ass of every West Point general he ever fought." Joe Barksdale stared calmly at Holcomb, as if daring him to say more.

"Rather like Teddy Roosevelt in that respect, wasn't he, Senator? I've always admired the way Roosevelt stepped into the soldier's role, taking on the leadership of the Rough Riders and leading the charge up San Juan Hill."

And now Sad Joe rolled his eyes with open disgust. "Teddy Roosevelt? Come now, Mr. Secretary. A cheap Harvard imitation of a real soldier, although a President of the likes we could use today. It shows the value of connections, doesn't it? Teddy Roosevelt made his name in a battle that was hardly more than a skirmish by any standards. Bedford Forrest fought for four years, in all the bloodiest campaigns. He was the only Confederate leader who refused to surrender at Fort Donelson. Led his whole cavalry regiment out, each man riding double with a foot soldier on his horse while the other commanders gave up. Seriously wounded at Shiloh. The bright star at Murfreesboro and Chickamauga. His little brother, who he had raised as a son, was killed at his side there at Brice's Crossroads. He got off his horse and held his brother for a minute, calling for him, then got back on his horse when he saw his brother was dead and won the battle. Wounded four times. Had twenty-nine horses shot out from under him. Killed at least thirty men in hand-to-hand fighting. And what do we remember? An hour on San Juan Hill.''

The majority leader's voice had not risen once. Now he shrugged, fingering the papers and scrapbooks in front of him. ''But that doesn't matter. That's history. Neither man would make it to the top today. They didn't see the value in blow-drying their hair. I want you all to see something.'' Barksdale carefully turned the pages of one of the scrapbooks, and pushed the open book in front of them. They peered a bit uneasily at a dozen black-and-white snapshots from at least three decades before. Taken with an ordinary Brownie camera, they showed people working on farms and in factories. A few showed smiling servicemen.

Barksdale waited for almost a minute before he spoke again. ''Campaign 1952. People working. America growing. That is what America used to look like, gentlemen.''

An eerie feeling came over Holcomb. He had no idea where the majority leader was heading. He had come to make a deal on a wind tunnel, that was all. Not to look at Brownie black-and-white snapshots from forty years before.

''Yes, sir.''

''Do you know what I'm saying? No, I don't think you do. You know, I used to be pretty good friends with General Marshall. I didn't like the idea of his plan for Europe and

I told him so. And Eisenhower. An overrated man, but harmless. Nice, I guess you'd say. Empty-headed and full-smiled, like too many generals. I told them both it was good to help these other countries in their time of need, but we were fools to just be giving it away. Just *giving it away!*''

Barksdale's soft hands had been fidgeting nervously with the papers and scrapbooks in front of him. Now he gestured toward the pictures again. "Your President *Lodge* says the economy is going good. I know him. I got nothing against him. I helped him when he was a junior senator. But he writes a lot of nice notes and makes thoughtful phone calls, and now he's *President*! I'll tell you, he's selling us down the river! What economy, that's what I want to know? What are we building? Steel's gone. Shipbuilding's gone. Motorcycles are gone. Textiles are going. Hell, we can't even make a damn TV anymore. We're just a bunch of people passing dollars back and forth for doing each other's laundry and booking each other's airplane rides, did you know that? What do you do when you get off the airplane, your hair all in place and your suit all clean? Only thing our corporate bigshots seem to be good at is buying up other companies and selling them off. All our factories gone. Except the ones owned by other countries.''

Barksdale stared evenly at Holcomb, as if the defense secretary were a thoughtless whore. "And what are you doing in the Department of Defense? Last count, somebody told me we had one hundred sixty-one military bases overseas. You all are coming over here, wanting three hundred billion dollars to keep all those bases going. Putting all that money into other countries' economies. What are we protecting? You tell me. Go ahead, read from some article in *Foreign Affairs* and talk about your latest seminar. And then admit the truth. The world's been changing, and all the while we've gone hollow. We've emptied out from the inside. Running around all over the world, protecting other people so they can steal off our business and sell it back to us.''

Barksdale quietly searched their faces. They sat motionless in the power of his presence, almost afraid. The room was silent as he stared. "You may think this is just an old man talking, gentlemen. But I'm telling you, this is the voice of *history* talking to you. The voice by which you will be *judged*."

He slammed both hands, palms down, on the table. "You got your meeting. Now, what do you want?"

The suddenness of his demand caught Holcomb off guard. He looked over and saw the small young aide staring at him with all the dislike that Barksdale's soft, dry words had conjured. Holcomb cleared his throat. "Well, Senator. We're thankful to you for taking the time to see us this morning, and now that the Senate is ready to do business again, we are hoping, quite naturally, that we can get the authorization bill to the floor as quickly as possible. It becomes very difficult to run the department on continuing resolutions after the fiscal year ends, and—"

"You don't want much at all, do you? All you want is three hundred billion dollars of somebody else's money." Barksdale nodded toward his aide. "Call Chairman Stratford. If he's ready, put the bill on tomorrow." He looked back at Holcomb, still without emotion. "That soon enough?"

"Well, that would be fine, Senator. Let me just say that we really appreciate your thoughtfulness—"

"But I want something."

Now Holcomb warmed up. This was more like it. He smiled, leaning forward in his chair. "Weil, sir, that was another thing I wanted to tell you this morning. I'm very pleased to report that we've decided to go ahead with the wind tunnel project at the University of Mississippi. And the President personally asked that it be named in your honor."

Barksdale nodded slowly, his face unchanged, his hands moving again, this time fondling a fountain pen. "That's very gracious of you, and very kind as well. Tell the Pres-

ident thank you for me, if you would. But that wasn't what
I wanted. Let me tell you what I want.''

The aging Senator peered steadily at Holcomb. ''First,
let me say that Doc Rowland is not a personal friend of
mine. Not that I don't like Doc Rowland. It's just that I
never got to know him, with me in the Senate and him over
in the House, and us on different authorizing committees.
And I'll be honest. From what I do know of him, I think
he'd screw a female goat under the right extenuating circumstances. But nobody asked him to be their preacher, did
they?''

It was not the kind of question that Ronald Holcomb could
even attempt to answer. He felt his stomach flutter, and
decided to push it over onto Everett Lodge until he learned
what Joe Barksdale was after. ''Well, the President always
makes a point of mentioning that Doc Rowland has been a
good friend of the administration.''

''Yes he has. Sometimes I think he's been *too* good of
a friend, especially to the Defense Department. I don't recall
him ever voting against you. But now he has an idea that
makes sense. He put in a bill yesterday to stop that bunch
of Japanese crooks from doing business in this country for
three years unless they pay us full damages for selling off
our secrets to the Russians.'' Barksdale turned his head,
seeking help from his soft-faced assistant. ''Nakash—?''

The young aide immediately helped him out, speaking in
a voice just above a whisper. ''Nakashitona Industries. They
sell computer chips, video recorders, electronic systems,
portable computers, and other such devices. Three billion
dollars of trade in this country last year. Chairman Rowland
is scheduling hearings within the next week. There's no
doubt that some members of the corporation have sold the
essential elements of the Iroquois air defense system to the
Soviets, using North Korea as an intermediary. It's a very
serious technology leak.''

''Yes,'' said Sad Joe Barksdale, continuing to stare res-
olutely at Ron Holcomb. ''For more than forty years, we've

played big brother to the people we defeated in that war. We've treated them like we felt sorry for them for having tried to destroy us. We lost hundreds of thousands of fine young boys to their guns, and then we decided to keep our nation on a war footing overseas while they claim they're pacifists, and put their national energy into commerce.''

Sad Joe Barksdale's tone was soft and melancholy, almost as if he were delivering a eulogy. ''Somewhere we made a miscalculation. Somehow this has gone wrong. We've protected them as they developed markets around the world. We've put our boys in the ships and the planes and on the line, ruined our balance of payments, supplemented their economies. And then what do they do? They use unfair trade practices to dump their products on our markets and kill off our own industries. They start buying up our country. They find clever ways to accuse us of being inferior. They sell off our technology to our enemies.''

The majority leader's voice had never risen, never lost its monotone. And yet it transfixed Ronald Holcomb, accused him, dared him to deny the truth of Joe Barksdale's diatribe. And now Barksdale continued, having further chilled Holcomb with a glaring pause. ''If we don't draw the line, Mr. Secretary, you can just pack up your three hundred billion dollar defense budget and hand it over to the Russians. Or maybe to the Japanese. Because we won't be using it to defend ourselves, anyway.''

For a quick moment, Ron Holcomb could not grasp the realization that the majority leader was not asking for a personal favor. Barksdale still had not told him what he wanted, and it would be foolish to guess, lest he make a mistake and Barksdale would decide he wanted that, too.

Holcomb frowned, searching for a safe reply. Finally he began. ''Well, Senator, I can sympathize with those who feel the way you do. Certainly there are merits in that frustration. The international economic environment has become extraordinarily complex over the past few decades, and—''

Barksdale interrupted him with a cold, flat ferocity. "Your President is a smart politician, but this has gone too far. You tell Ev Lodge to stop dragging his feet on this issue. The man ought to be ashamed of himself. You tell him to stop being afraid of the Japanese, and to start being afraid of people like me and Doc Rowland. I am deadly serious, Mr. Secretary. We can do this the hard way, or we can do it the easy way. But we are going to do it. We are going to get a full apology from the Japanese, and full reparations from . . ." Barksdale searched again for his aide.

"Nakashitona."

"Yes," said Barksdale. "Either the Japanese are going to do it, or we are going to do it to them. And your President is *disgracing* himself, claiming in a press conference that the facts aren't clear enough to make a judgment!"

"Well, as you know, Senator, I'll be going to Japan next week, to confer with their minister of foreign affairs on the matter."

"Well, you'd better do more than that. I'm keying on Doc Rowland on this one. You'd better have a solution by the time you get back."

"We will. And in all due respect, sir, the President is not simply a''—he hesitated to use the word pejoratively— "a politician. He's a very careful, but courageous man. And this situation is fraught with delicacy."

"Sure, and what would you know about courage?" Sad Joe Barksdale nodded to his aide, concluding the meeting. "Bring back an apology from the Japanese, and get your President to support reparations, or we are going to have your head. Good day, Mr. Secretary."

Barksdale's anger had surprised him, but Ronald Holcomb was aware that the leak of technology by a few employees in Nakashitona Industries was the most serious problem facing the Lodge administration. And fixing that problem involved the greatest political risk Holcomb had ever faced. He had already scheduled a meeting with Doc

Rowland, the chairman of the House Armed Services Committee. He needed to slow the issue down.

Holcomb had made a career out of slowing things down. And now his instincts told him that despite the vitriol in the speeches on the House and Senate floors, the Congress would eventually back off. The country had lost its leverage with the Japanese. The administration was impotent on the matter. Holcomb and others had already advised the President to tread softly on the Japanese. It could be "worked on the Hill," as Holcomb had gently put it, as long as they could delay a major public confrontation.

Holcomb knew there would be a fount of activity and rhetoric from the Congress. But if it was handled right, the whole thing would go away, just as the Toshiba crisis of 1987 had simply disappeared. The Congress had screamed, sanctions were legislated against the company for having sold milling machines that helped Soviet submarines, and then after the media had been served its ration of raw meat Toshiba's profits had increased by 50 percent in the first year alone. It would be the same with Nakashitona. The public's attention never held on such crises; economic stories were too complex for the evening news unless they dealt with unemployment, and the unemployment numbers looked extremely good, thanks in large part to foreign investment.

And the best way to make sure that attention was shifted away from Nakashitona was to shift their attention *toward* something else. Especially toward an international crisis. The Persian Gulf hostilities had been a rather fortuitous diversion during the Toshiba affair.

And now Ron Holcomb knew of one that involved the Soviets and the Cubans. Conquest, Communists, the possibility of war, Soviet ships and Cuban soldiers off in a place whose name the public would have to learn to say and spell. That was the way to resolve these problems, thought Holcomb, strange as it might seem when stated so baldly. There was only so much space in a newspaper, so much time on the evening news, so much attention span in the average voter's brain. Wars they understood. Military threats they grew excited over, and loved to debate. But an argument over whether or not a corporation sold technology that no one understood to an enemy few believed the United States would ever fight lost its staying power after a while.

Now a military crisis, that was different. Something fresh, dangerous, and yet remote. Something to unite their anger and get their blood going, without causing them any economic or personal discomfort. Something relatively safe, which would nonetheless demonstrate that America would not be intimidated by the Soviets or their allies. Something that would also help justify the defense budget, which Sad Joe Barksdale still held hostage, despite his promise to move it out of committee.

A conflict they could follow as if it were a football game.

And it seemed to Holcomb that his good friend Admiral Mad Dog Mulcahy had found just the right set of circumstances. In the Red Sea, of all places. With the future of the brave Eritrean freedom fighters at stake.

And to top it off, the Soviets needed a crisis, too. The classified photographs that Ron Holcomb was bringing to show Doc Rowland, now locked inside General Bear Lazaretti's briefcase, were testimony to that.

CHAPTER 2
THE SOUTH CHINA SEA

1

The world surrounding the South China Sea at twenty thousand feet was warm and oh so very blue. Bright blue in a clear equatorial sky. Royal blue below, in the endless expanse of the ocean. Deep blue, the color of unalterable sadness, in Admiral Mad Dog Mulcahy's heart. He peered through the large cockpit window of the S-3 aircraft and remembered journeys he had made across these waters as a young man, when heading westward had meant weeks of austere loneliness on South Vietnam's gun line or on Yankee Station in the Tonkin Gulf, followed by days of mad, boozy revelry during port calls at Subic Bay or Hong Kong or Yokosuka.

Gone now, the things he loved best, all the rock and sock of sailing into harm's way. Replaced with the knowledge that in a year or two he would be mothballed just as surely as the first destroyer he had commanded. And with a burning determination that he would not go quietly. That there were scores to settle with enemies, both foreign and domestic. That he would be remembered as more than a fading name scratched into a brass plaque that hung outside the CINC-PAC FLEET office at Makalapa Heights, just above Pearl Harbor. That he had been a man willing to take action, to push events rather than merely reacting to the bland, cow-ardly caution of Washington as if he were a knob on an instrument panel. That one's reward for being an admiral was not the four stars he would be entitled to wear into his grave, but the right to command the movements of warships. That he had been a warrior, and had exercised that right. That he had been a leader. Mad Dog, Mad Dog, the history books would acclaim. The Nelson of the Nineties.

The U.S.S. *Theodore Roosevelt* seemed to coalesce from the sea itself, a faint speck appearing out of nothingness and then growing larger. Lights flashed, as if there were a mirror reflecting the sun. The speck became a narrow rect-angle, grew a superstructure, and finally was recognizable as an aircraft carrier. The S-3 passed it on the starboard side and then turned suddenly to the left, entering the landing pattern, and pulled hard left in a tight circle. Mulcahy saw the fantail of the Roosevelt in front of them, coming up quickly, a gray scar on an emerald sea. The S-3 flitted this way and that as the pilot aligned the aircraft to the carrier. The pilot and copilot talked to each other in clipped sen-tences as they approached the angled portion of the flight deck. And then in a moment the aircraft hit the flight deck at full speed. Mad Dog's body pressed violently against his shoulder straps as the tail hook of the aircraft caught a landing wire, jerking the S-3 to a complete halt within the space of a few feet.

For a moment it was perfectly still. Then they were over-whelmed by a bustle of activity, having dropped onto a city in the middle of the empty sea. Sailors wearing brightly colored jerseys and ear protectors surrounded the aircraft, unhooking it, leading it with hand signals toward the forward catapults, shutting it down and chocking it in. The side door opened and Mad Dog climbed out of the small aircraft dressed in his khaki uniform and a white inflatable life preserver. He pulled off his plastic flight helmet as he walked toward the island on the flight deck. Two rows of side boys dressed in dungarees and colored shirts formed outside the entrance to one door. He walked between the rows of side boys. A boatswain piped him aboard, the side boys saluting, the 1-MC speaker system now ringing four bells and announcing him throughout the ship.

"Commander in Chief, Pacific Fleet, arriving."

Rear Admiral Ward McCormick, commander of the *Roosevelt* battle group, greeted him, along with Captain Tom Shinn, the commanding officer of the aircraft carrier. They shook hands briefly, and yelled at each other through the noise that emanated from the flight deck.

"Good morning, Admiral. Glad you could make it out, sir."

"Hell, are you kidding me? I never miss a chance to go to sea, even if it's only for a few days. Captain, how's the morale?"

"They're just about done with the homesick blues, sir. You know how that is. Hawaii always seems to be the turning point. And once they're west of Subic they get serious."

"Well, I used to get pretty serious about Subic in my younger days. Olongapo, anyway."

Captain Shinn laughed. "That doesn't change, sir. Work hard, play hard, that's what it's all about. This is the Navy."

Inside the superstructure, McCormick and Shinn began climbing the seemingly endless flights of ladders toward McCormick's stateroom. Mulcahy called up to them, halting their movement.

"Where the hell are you going?"

"We've got some briefings arranged for you, sir. I thought we could visit for a few minutes, and then we'd—"

"What is this shit? People see me coming and they want

to break out charts and slides. I know more about what the hell you're doing than you do. I don't need any goddamn briefings! Let's go see your sailors, and then I'll brief *you*.''

Mulcahy jogged expertly down the ladder in the other direction. Captain Mark Van Epps, his senior aide, followed just behind him, and Captain David Mosberg, his intelligence chief, followed after that. McCormick and Shinn raced down to catch them. In a moment Mulcahy was on the hangar deck of the huge carrier. He disappeared underneath an A-6E Intruder, surprising two sailors who were working on one of the aircraft's engines.

"You guys make sure you don't have any parts left over when you button that thing back up, you hear?"

They seemed stunned to be staring, all hot and greasy, into the face of a madly grinning four-star admiral. "Yes, sir! Aye, aye, sir.''

He reappeared on the other side of the aircraft. Near a far bulkhead, a half-dozen sailors were working out on a universal gym. Above him, a workout room was packed full of sailors in gym shorts and T-shirts, pedaling on more than two dozen stationary bicycles. Farther along the hangar deck itself, teams of sailors were working in the bellies and the cockpits of other aircraft—F/A 18 Hornets, F-14 Tomcats, A-6s, and EA-6B Prowlers. Yellow forklifts passed back and forth, carrying supplies and parts. A working party was sweeping down one section of the deck. Others passed to and fro, on the way from noon meal in the mess hall below, or from working spaces that included machine shops, barber shops, a small hospital, machinery spaces, refrigeration spaces, disbursing offices, and the all-important combat information and weapon centers. The *Roosevelt* was a city of more than five thousand young men, and every one of them had a job that was vital.

The nine ships of the U.S.S. *Theodore Roosevelt* carrier battle group were now west of the Philippines, dispersed in a nontactical formation that nonetheless covered hundreds of miles of ocean. In addition to the *Roosevelt*, the battle group included the Aegis cruiser U.S.S. *Chancellorsville*, the amphibious assault ship U.S.S. *Saipan*, a DDG 51 class destroyer, a frigate, two logistic ships carrying oil, ammunition, food and other supplies, and two smaller amphibious ships. The battle group was on a standard six-month deployment, and was scheduled to replace the U.S.S. *Independence* battle group in the western Indian Ocean.

Mad Dog Mulcahy sighed deeply, a hidden admission of his sadness as he stared down the length of the *Roosevelt*'s hangar bay. It had not changed, and it would never change. The energy of a warship's crew at sea was palpable. Mad Dog was proud of every sailor in his vision. More important, he envied them, every one of them. He envied them their youth. He envied them the freedom of their lowly ranks. He envied them their futures. All of this was gone for him, even though he owned it.

Suddenly he burst into motion, calling to four sailors loading boxes onto a forklift. "You guys get your asses over here! Is your division officer taking care of you? Anybody not getting paid?"

2

On the amphibious assault ship U.S.S. *Saipan*, the word passed quickly: Mad Dog had landed on the *Roosevelt*. But Colonel Bill Fogarty had known it was Mad Dog, as soon as he saw the little S-3 aircraft flit past the *Saipan* fifteen minutes before, heading for the aircraft carrier fifty miles away.

And so the aircraft had appeared as a harbinger of lust for glory. To Fogarty, Mad Dog was a man of brilliance, whose career had come down to idiocy. Like a dying virgin who longed for a single night of sin, Mad Dog wanted to direct a fight before he retired. Anywhere, any place, any enemy. Fogarty kept that from his men. It did no good to foster resentment toward more senior commanders. And who knew? Mad Dog might just stumble onto a good reason.

Fogarty had been running laps on the flight deck of the *Saipan* when he saw the aircraft dart overhead and knew that Mad Dog had arrived. It was a doubly unpleasant interruption. Olongapo had awakened old memories, and he had been thinking of the firm, springy skin and the sweet smells of a young Filipina woman named Maria, in whose bed he had spent three nights almost twenty years ago. Maria had been a special treasure. She had gleaming black hair that reached her hips. Her teeth were white and perfectly straight, as if she had once worn braces. She was a deliciously bad young woman.

Fogarty was remembering her mischievous smile, and how her eyes had shone with pleasure as she slowly fitted his condom before they made love. On the second night, he had brought her a box of Godiva chocolates, which she had found even more delightful than his money. And then two hours later he had awakened to find her in the bathroom, sitting on the toilet with her knees underneath her chin, eating chocolates and counting her rosary beads as she prayed.

Fogarty knew that God would understand Maria. Starvation was a powerful aphrodisiac. And although his own motives had not exactly been altruistic, he felt that when it came time for him to talk himself up from purgatory or maybe hell, God would give him credit for the twenty extra dollars he left on Maria's tiny bed table as he soundlessly crept out of her apartment into the wet, dark air of Olongapo.

And where was she now? Probably dead from AIDS, or if she was lucky running a bar somewhere.

The oil from the helicopters made the flight deck smell like freshly laid asphalt. The deck's black tarmac held the heat, making the soles of Fogarty's feet burn through his running shoes. He wore red Marine Corps shorts and no shirt. He was thickly muscled, and deeply tanned. His head was shaved. His gray eyes peered brightly out of a face that was lined from more than twenty years of infantry service.

A trough dug years before by an AK-47 bullet still creased his left shoulder. A half-dozen old shrapnel scars made small, shiny pocks along his legs and lower back.

Unconsciously, he touched his scarred shoulder as he ran, thinking of Mad Dog, who had never suffered wounds, much less been shot at, except from far away as one of his destroyers ravaged some coastline village with five-inch shells. *Here we are, Mad Dog. The Expendables, out here waiting for your latest little plan.*

Over the space of twenty-three years, Fogarty had commanded a rifle platoon and company, a shipboard detachment, an infantry battalion, and now the 51st Marine Expeditionary Unit, better known as the 51st MEU. He knew troops, and it wasn't the quality of his marines that worried him. Having spent three years watching the Wizards of Oz in Washington, he stayed up nights worrying about the uses to which they would be put. The night before he deployed, his father had called from Omaha to wish him well. They had ended up arguing. His father was an optimist who treasured his own Marine Corps memories and equated uncertainty with disloyalty. He had chided Fogarty for criticizing those above him, especially Ronald Holcomb, the secretary of defense. Fogarty had nearly burst with an anger that he had been suppressing for months.

"Let me just say this," he had said to his father. "You can figure it out for yourself. The legislation after World War Two that created the Department of Defense and supposedly ensured civilian control over the military has been a disaster. Do you think I'm kidding? Ask yourself why we won every war before 1947, and we haven't won one since. Civilian control over the military wasn't supposed to mean that every pin-striped, arrogant whiz kid who grabbed a Pentagon job because he wanted to play Napoleon, or run for Congress, or work in the right D.C. law firm after cutting his spurs on the backs of people like you and me should be given the authority of an all-knowing guru."

His father had been silent for a moment, and then had

spoken tentatively. "Are you talking about Holcomb?"

"Holcomb's my age. He doesn't know a base plate from a paper plate. How many times has *he* ever been shot at?"

"You're the warrior, Bill. You've got no call to criticize the secretary for being something else."

"That's not what I'm saying, Dad." He had given up on the argument, but continued, hoping that his father might comprehend his anger even if he disagreed. "I don't need to be protected from our enemies, whoever the hell they happen to be these days. God save me from manipulative bureaucrats in polyester-wool suits, button-down collars and power ties, and the kiss-ass officers who let them get away with it. I don't need to see my men die because somebody cares more about helping the careers of their fellow madrigal singers over in the White House or the State Department than they do about the troops they compromise and misuse in places like Beirut and the Persian Gulf."

"Son," his father had intoned in a voice now warbling with age, "maybe you need to retire."

And maybe he did. But where would that leave the troops? Holcomb and the others wouldn't go away if he left, and at least he knew how to fight. And that was the bottom line, anyway. The better you fought, the less your people bled.

Three and a half laps were a mile. The ship rolled softly in the gentle waves, and a warm wind caressed him as he ran toward the bow. When he ran, Bill Fogarty felt he was ageless, suspended inside the beating of his heart and the exertion of his muscles. He knew he would run like this until the day he died.

I can run all night. And I can run all day.

Not that he wanted to die. You just didn't think about it, because it was out of your hands. It either happened or it didn't.

Around Fogarty's neck, pinched onto a chain that carried an old set of dog tags, was a gold tooth. Twenty-two years before, a young corporal named Castro had pried it out of the mouth of a dead North Vietnamese soldier with a bayonet, and given it to Fogarty as a prize. His platoon of thirty men had been moving all day under a weeping sky that was the color of slate, pushing through wet weeds, crossing low ridgelines and wide rice paddies, wading choked little streams as they fought a company of the Q-83rd Main Force battalion.

Every now and then the Q-83rd held up along a ridge or in the hedgerows of a village and fought the marines. They were not great battles. The Q-83rd was merely slowing the marines down, pushing them away. Its soldiers knew the war would turn around when it grew dark, giving them the advantage. The marines would find a blown-out, unpopulated village or a muddy ridge and would suspend their attack. They would form a perimeter of four-man fighting positions, with their command groups in the center. They would eat quickly heated C rations, sitting unprotected in the rain. Then they would dig deep fighting holes in the mud, put out Claymore mines, and take turns sleeping in the weeds, wrapped inside their ponchos. They would shiver from the rain and from malaria and fear, take their boots off for a few precious moments to massage the numb dying skin of their waterlogged feet. They would agonize over patches of ringworm and jungle sores on their arms and legs. And it would be their turn to try to slow down the Q-83rd, to push them away until dawn. Then at first light off they would go again, hunting down the Q-83rd, which was a very fine battalion of hard little soldiers who knew how to fight and when to run.

Night and day, attack and defend, yin and yang. The harder you tried, the quicker you died.

In the late afternoon Fogarty's platoon had been in an open rice paddy when the Q-83rd began to fire at them from a nearby ridge. His men slogged immediately toward the protection of the paddy dike to their front, up to their waists in the murky paddy water, no longer caring that the water was a haven for leeches and that the paddies were mile-wide cesspools, having been fertilized with human excrement. The paddy dike was a shield against rifle and machine-gun fire. The water would absorb shrapnel bursts from mortars and rocket-propelled grenades. Muck, lovely muck, was their inalterable salvation. For that moment they loved the mud and the cool, coffee-colored water that lapped against their groins.

A dead NVA soldier lay in the water on the other side of the paddy dike. He had been shot in the chest and the neck while firing at the marines from the Q-83rd's side of the dike a half hour earlier. He had curled into the fetal position as his life left him, and was cradling a B-40 rocket launcher as if it were his child. Castro saw the rocket launcher first, and crawled quickly onto the exposed side of the paddy dike as the bullets skipped along the water and splattered mud on top of the dike. He tossed the rocket launcher back to the platoon. Then Castro knelt like a dental surgeon in the rain and the muck, holding the dead soldier's head by a topknot of hair. He dug his bayonet blade into the dead man's jaw and flecked out a prize.

"Here, Lieutenant," said Castro as he slithered back over the paddy dike, chased by AK-47 bullets from the Q-83rd, "you always wanted a gold tooth."

And Fogarty had worn the tooth on his dog tags for twenty-two years. At first he kept it to remember Castro and all the other wild, courageous, doomed teenagers who had given so much as the nation turned its face away from them in embarrassment. But slowly the tooth had taken on a meaning of its own. Next to his heart, Bill Fogarty wore the only remembered remains of a man who had died a violent, unnecessary death and then melted into the mud. An enemy, to be sure. But what had his suffering won? And, as both enemies festered and fought and bled in those remorseless paddies, who indeed had been their friends?

I killed soldiers I did not hate, to fulfill the desires of politicians I did not love. And now what's up?

The South China Sea stretched forever in all directions, a welcoming seducer. The *Roosevelt* battle group was now five hundred miles west of Subic Bay, on its way to the Arabian Sea. Fogarty loved the baking sun on his back as he ran, the flying fish and occasional sea snakes that were visible off the sides of the churning ship, the memories that swayed in his mind like melancholy *wayang* shadow dancers every time he saw the misty jungle forests and the water-laden rice fields along the approaches to Subic Bay. Tomorrow the ship would pass through the Strait of Malacca and enter the Indian Ocean. In a week he would be in the dreadful, sand-filled winds off the Horn of Africa. But for now he had East Asian memories.

They were as recent as the night before. Subic's furnace heat, the air surrounding him as if he were inside a jungle stew, the fetid rot and ferment creating a brackish, cooked odor that told him he was back. Olongapo's choked streets and loud bars, the disco drums beating against his ears and the bar girls calling to him like old friends. His men all over the town, drinking, singing, dancing, screwing. Fogarty himself sitting drunk in a sleazy bar, filled with uncertain fear and the memories, watching a naked young stripper do the splits over a banana. She stood back up, her face smiling proudly and her round breasts glistening from a spotlight in the dim bar, and left the banana on the bar, cut in four equal sections by the muscles of her vagina. And he had joined the others in throwing dollars her way, a reward for her tawdry skill.

The memories now spanned more than half his life. Some of them were mawkish, some were beautiful. Some had even changed him. As he ran, Fogarty recalled a cold Chicago morning twenty-three years before, saying good-bye to Ilona, his fiancée. She was a tall woman just out of college. She had blond, ratted hair and a look of tragedy on her face. It was freezing and the wind, which the local blacks had come to call the Hawk, was blowing down from Canada, taking his breath away as he walked from their car into the airport terminal. Ilona was wearing a miniskirt and a heavy wool coat. Men openly admired her long, graceful legs when she entered the terminal. She was crying. She did not want Fogarty to go to Vietnam. She was telling him that she could not live without him. But within three months he received a letter, saying she was in love with another man. *How very American*, thought Fogarty as he held the letter with muddy hands while sitting shirtless on a broken gravestone near a village called Le Bac (3). *I am like plastic: indispensable one day, and into the garbage pail the next.*

Fogarty's mind blinked and a new memory appeared. It was six months later. He had recovered from his wounds and was a general's aide at the division headquarters in Da Nang. He was in love with Muong. She was a poem; no, a song, and every day he sang her. Her mouth, her body, and the small hootch where he met her in the afternoons all gave off sweet tastes and odors that mingled in his senses until they were a musky, irreplaceable perfume. She was both evil and sweetness, and the mound of her teasing gentleness was an oasis. And yet they were surrounded by Da Nang's desert of decay: ancient packed-dirt walkways, odorous pools of stagnant water, vegetation that surged from the ground and quickly rotted as new growth replaced it. Da Nang was a city awash in chaos, waiting to die.

He was too young to comprehend the mysteries that Muong laid before him every time she made love to him amid the sweet perfume of her nation's sorrow. He was too naïve to know that Asia had seduced him, that after this fresh, intimate taste he would never be the same. Six months before, he had grown hard, hating the Vietnamese for their very misery and for his own fears. But once he started loving Muong, he came to love Vietnam.

In his mind he still walked narrow mud pathways between huts made of thatch and tin. The tropical sun had baked him brown. Now it drew a confluence of odors from the grass and the nearby ditch and the perfumed bodies of women who smiled warmly to him, asking him with their eyes to take them away from this hell, back to America. Incense and marijuana filled the dank, hot air. Old women chewed betel nut and watched him with opaque, watery eyes. He had come to trespass on one of their young, but secretly they wished for him also. He had come to be corrupted. He had come to fall in love, again and again.

He found Muong and embraced her. Sitting next to her, he sucked on a sweet ball that she placed on his tongue, and slowly his mind escaped from the fearful, heated hell that surrounded them. Then she took his hand and led him into the back room. The sunlight came in narrow shafts through the straw, painting her golden body as if she wore spots and stripes. Her breasts were high and small. Her smile showed him promises. He began loving her, and he was free. He was floating away from the very place they now lay, riding on her thin frame into a land where no one wished he were dead.

And then one day he was truly gone, wrenched from her arms back to the remote prison of Camp Lejeune, North Carolina. On the television he saw the demonstrations against the war, led by people his age who did not understand, who believed the world was three billion frightened little mice running from America, the alley cat of nations. He constantly thought of Muong. He did not know how to find her, but he was somehow desperate to talk to her. She had shown him too much. He could not shake loose from a gentle embrace that had ended years before.

When Saigon fell he was back on Okinawa. For some reason he was sure she was still alive, and that she was calling for him in the dark night as the tanks rolled by and young men were being marched off to concentration camps. During those nights he dreamed of a daring rescue, a secret landing on some beach in the South China Sea, then days of evasion until he reached Da Nang. He would sneak down muddy pathways and find her amid the odors and the decay, and bring her back with him. In his dream they always reached the sea, and he carried her into the waves, where they rolled laughing in the surf until they had cleansed each other of the sorrow and the guilt. But then he would awaken and would know that he was nothing but a self-torturing fool.

That summer he spent a week on Guam, searching through the massive tent cities of refugees for her face. He sent inquiries to other camps. But he never found her. The next year, he married. Two children followed. He loved his wife and children, from the bottom of his heart. And yet, when he cruised into the western Pacific, these old memories sprang out of his mind like genies.

Sweet Maria, sitting on the toilet with her Godiva chocolates and her rosary beads. Muong, leading him into a straw-thatched nirvana. He was growing old, but they were already old, or maybe even dead. And maybe that was it, anyway. The memories told him how far he had journeyed on these ships and in the jungle weeds. Somewhere in the odorous dank heat of a village now hidden behind a bamboo curtain, a woman who, incredibly, was now journeying through her fifth decade probably squatted in the packed dirt, sifting rice and chewing the numbing betel nut. A woman he once had loved. She was very likely toothless, although Fogarty could not fathom the slow destruction of her beauty. *My God*, he thought to himself. *Has that much happened?*

Anyway, it didn't matter. They were just that—memories, little licks of flame, while the dull ache he felt every time he thought of his wife and children making their way without him were like burning coals inside his gut.

Is my boy staring at my picture on his bedroom wall as I run laps and dream of my younger years?

He finished his thirtieth lap and began walking, his body dripping with sweat. A dozen of his young troops passed him as he walked, their own bodies tanned and glistening, their muscles young and sharply defined. Great troops. Well trained. Fogarty trained, their fitness and outer exuberance a mirror of his own. How had Napoleon put it? *There are no bad regiments, only bad colonels*.

"Hey, Colonel! Got your thirty in, huh, sir?"

"That means every marine in the MEU does thirty, Sergeant Atkins."

"No sweat, sir. Nothing else to do around here."

He walked past a row of H-46 Sea Knight helicopters, the standard troop carrier since his first days in the Marine Corps. In Vietnam the infantrymen had viewed H-46s as death traps because of the exposed hydraulic systems that were so vulnerable to ground fire. They had been improved, but still Bill Fogarty worried. They were old. And ground fire had improved, also. It seemed that every rifle squad in southern Asia and the Middle East carried Russian SAM missiles these days. Shoulder-fired SAMs worked. The American equivalent, the Stingers, had knocked down about 90 percent of its targets once the Afghan rebels started using them against the Russians. Did Mulcahy think about that as he stared at squiggly little lines on a map and dreamed of glory?

Bill Fogarty reached the hatch that took him inside the ship's superstructure. He walked aft, entering Officers Country. The ship's air conditioners washed over him in the dark, narrow passageways. He would take a shower, dress in his combat utility uniform, and then go check on the troops. Later in the afternoon he would inspect the gear of one of his rifle companies, taking a great deal of time with each infantryman, asking him questions, checking for the slightest indication of rust or dirt on their weapons, searching each face for signs of emotional stress.

Inspections kept them working, taught them attention to detail, kept them from becoming too bored or homesick on the long sea journeys. They also took Bill Fogarty's own mind off of things that hurt him deep inside, the kind of things he had never been able to share with other people. The things that were uncontrollable. The things he pushed away.

Like the uncertainty of the next few months. And his fear of what awaited him in a place he probably had never heard of. And a lingering image, a haunting movie in his brain, of helicopters struggling through a hazy wind the color of smog, their floors filling up with sand as the rotors struggled and churned toward some Mad Dog dream of destiny.

CHAPTER 3
WASHINGTON, D.C.

1

On the wall above the chamber of the House of Representatives, to the left of where the speaker now sat conducting the business of the House, was a quote from one of the Founding Fathers that had always caught Doc Rowland's eye. WE BUILD NO TEMPLE BUT THE CAPITOL. WE CONSULT NO ORACLE BUT THE CONSTITUTION. How lofty, how wonderful it must have been to have burnt with the purity of the Revolution! Before the days of multimillion-dollar election campaigns that brought politicians to their knees before the monied temple of the contributors. Before the time of computerized politics that caused them to await the wisdom of those oracles known as pollsters before they spoke.

Or maybe it all had been trash from the get-go, myths to feed the public. Rowland had never been accused of being a deep thinker, and he hadn't really thought about it that much.

The House had been called to order. The prayer had been

said to an almost empty chamber. A quorum had been called for, and as always his colleagues had appeared on the floor like ants going after a jelly roll, pouring into the chamber from the cloakrooms after having left committee hearings or lunches or meetings with constituents in their offices. It was grand circus to watch more than four hundred men and women, each of them possessed with the type of personality that could slap the back and shake the hand of a complete stranger, appear on the House floor and greet each other, to the amusement of the visitors in the gallery above and the folks at home who now could watch the proceedings on cable television.

Touch, pat, shake, smile. The human tools of American politics. Doc Rowland joined in the love feast. His wide face and startling blue eyes danced with merriment as he joked and laughed. He was lining up new allies for his latest crusade, the attempt to shut down the money-lusting Japanese firm Nakashitona, which had sold away America's security for a few billion or maybe trillion yen.

The speaker had conducted the early business of the House. Doc Rowland now moved with a dozen other members into the well just in front of the rostrum, below where the speaker sat. He was the senior member present. He raised a hand as he approached the microphone.

"Mr. Speaker!"

"The gentleman from Illinois."

"Mr. Speaker, I request permission to address the House for one minute, and to revise and extend my remarks."

"The gentleman from Illinois is recognized for one minute."

"Thank you, Mr. Speaker." Rowland stood before the microphone, holding the speech that Roy Dombrowski, his administrative assistant, had written that morning. The paper seemed almost lost in his wide, meaty hands. A childhood spent in farm work had permanently thickened Rowland's shoulders and broadened his chest. His face was spacious and open, the kind that automatically invoked trust.

His innocent blue eyes, coupled with a warm huskiness in his voice, had been his greatest political assets over the years. Even now he turned them on, for the C-Span cameras that covered his remarks.

"Mr. Speaker, as you know, I have had great concern from the outset over the decision of this administration to share precious technology related to the Iroquois antimissile system with certain industries in Japan. To my great and sad chagrin, the predictions that I and several other colleagues made have come to pass. Our technology, the backbone of our national defense, was passed on—actually, I'm being kind, it was *sold*—to certain North Korean businesses, who from all indications have already given precious data to the Soviets. We've had a hard time getting the administration to talk straight with us in this matter, Mr. Speaker, so we are unable to measure the actual damage to our national security as of yet. But it is clear that we have in fact been greatly damaged. Consequently, I have introduced legislation that will suspend Nakashitona Industries from all business in this country for a period of three years or until the matter is fully resolved, whichever is the longer period. I urge my colleagues to join me as cosponsors in this important legislation."

The speaker, mindful of the clock, cut him off. "The time of the gentleman has expired. The gentleman from Alabama is recognized for one minute."

Doc Rowland began walking toward the rear of the chamber, past the rows of wooden chairs that formed a semicircle around the rostrum. He heard Teddy Gilliland, one of the four more senior members he had usurped in order to become chairman of the Armed Services Committee four years before, call his name from the microphone in the well. Gilliland stood there, tall and slim and gray, now speaking in the slow, rolling tongue of the southern elite.

"Mr. Speaker, I wish to offer a tribute to a gentleman in my district who has been the backbone of Alabama high school football for almost a generation. But before I do, I'd just like to say that I hope Chairman Rowland will be careful on that bill. Nakashitona does a lot of valuable business in this country that is not related to defense work, and we don't want to throw out the baby with the bathwater on a matter that hasn't been proven all the way. . . ."

Bastards. Rowland waved lazily toward the rostrum, feigning good spirits as he reached the door that would take him into the cloakroom. They were after him, he knew that. He could say the sky was blue and one of them would remind the House that at night the sky turned black. But they shouldn't be playing games on this one. It was too important for that. In fact, this was one of the first issues in years that he cared about to the point of passion.

I owe the country on this one.

Doc Rowland rarely became sentimental about his work in the Congress. It was as if all the history and decorum that attended national politics turned on its head and became, after four or five terms in the Congress, a source of cynicism. Cynicism and irony, those were his emotional tools, and they seemed to fuel the Congress itself. Those monuments that permeated the nation's capital, and the lofty words that washed over the Congress every day, inundating its activities, became in a way artificial. They reminded Doc and the others that either the past was false, or the present was a disappointing mockery of what once was greatness.

Either their ancestors had lied, or they themselves were imposters when they spoke of traditions and ideals.

And so they became cynical, ironic, self-serving. The office, with its historical trappings and celebrations, became more important than the work. The work never seemed to go anywhere anymore, but the office bought them fame. They emerged from their little towns and little companies and little law practices to the Wonder World of Washington to become, for two or forty years, big. Small people, some of them; great people, others. But all of them emperors of a kingdom whose greatness, except for rare, fleeting moments, was more perception than reality.

You just couldn't get a goddamn thing done anymore.

He had tried to be different, and occasionally he had succeeded. But for the most part he had ended up like the others, bent on survival. He had cut his political teeth on the agony of Vietnam, polished his persona in the midst of Watergate, helped the Congress grab unprecedented power away from the executive branch and the states in the 1970s and early 1980s. Like so many others, he had at first reveled in the power, and then become paralyzed by its very enormity. The system was clogged up, so power became personal. Power became fame, not results. Except when an issue such as Nakashitona came along, he was burned out, bored with it.

Not that he would ever leave. Oh, no.

He loved summer in the capital. The heat could become unbearable, but it brought out things of beauty: flowers, trees, fresh young women whose loveliness burst raw through their light summer dresses. He walked outside on his way back to his office, watching college interns pass their lunch hour tossing Frisbees on the grass, waving to the occasional staffer who called out his name. He was sweating profusely by the time he entered the Rayburn Building. The guard at the entrance, a black man almost his age, smiled with empathy.

"It's a hot one, Mr. Chairman. Good day to stay inside."

"You're right about that."

On the elevator he saw a man in a blue polyester sport coat, a brown checked shirt, and a white polyester tie. Someone, probably the man's wife who now stood next to him in a lavender cotton dress, had sewn a little red cloth flower onto the tie, just below the knot. The man, who was in his mid-forties, was slightly bald and was wearing sideburns. He seemed inordinately pleased that Doc Rowland had noticed his tie. Rowland found himself wishing that he still had the man's naïveté.

"Doc? Mr. Chairman?" The man called softly to him, uncertain that he had actually recognized him.

There were people in Washington who thought Doc Rowland was dumb. They were the same people who believed that ideas rather than emotions were the forces that ruled the world, and that leader worship was an anachronism. Nor had they ever seen Doc Rowland work a crowd. If they had, they would have realized that the chairman was brilliant in a peculiarly American way: He was a people genius. And now Rowland proved it. He peered through this stranger's almost frightened eyes into his heart, and instantly grabbed his hand and slapped him on the shoulder.

"Yeah, that's right, that's right. How you doing, *cousin!*"

"I thought that was you!" The man's face had melted into a worshiping smile. Now he elbowed his wife, a plump, shy woman of about his age. "Honey, this is Doc Rowland. Remember I told you we ought to look him up! Doc, I ain't seen you since the Rotary in Mentonburg."

"Why, sure I remember! Last March it was."

"It's been a rough summer, Doc. All heat and no rain. But we're making it. Hey, I saw you on the TV the other day. Honey, we saw Doc on *Hello America!* not long ago, remember? Doc, you done a damn good job. You keep fighting for us, hear?"

"You know I'll do that." The elevator reached the third floor and Doc Rowland stepped out. "Tell them hello for me back there in Mentonburg, you hear? I'll be home soon. And we'll see what we can do about legislating a little more rain."

The elevator doors closed on the couple as they waved a warm farewell. Their leaving reminded Doc that he himself could never leave. They were dropping in on the capital for a few exciting days, and then would go back home to Mentonburg with fond memories and stories for their friends, including a tale of how good old Doc Rowland had recognized them on an elevator at the Capitol. But Mentonburg was their home. He could quit the Congress, yes, but he could never go back. It wasn't home anymore. Washington was home, no matter how hard he decried its insensitivities toward his people back in Illinois. At times he fantasized that he could again sit on the front porch of some white frame house out on a little farm or on the edge of a quiet city block, that he could take up where he left off and still be an emeritus citizen, but he knew it would be impossible.

And besides, he didn't want to. He knew too much, and he liked too much of what he knew. He remembered the very moment he had first comprehended that he would never go home. It was a crisp spring evening in 1969 when, almost frightened at his luck, he had put an arm around the shoulder of a young admiring woman as they drove up Constitution Avenue toward her Capitol Hill apartment. He had met her two hours before. She worked in another member's office. He had expected her to reject him, or at least slow him down. Instead, he felt her move her body against him in his car, and had marveled at the easiness of his good fortune. Driving in the car, her mouth now on his neck just below his ear and her breasts pressed into his side, he had said to himself, *I am somebody. I am a member of the United States Congress. I have baled hay in the hot summer fields and milked cows in the black lonely mornings of winter, dreaming as I stared out at pastures and lowing beasts that someday a woman like this would want me. I am alive, and I will kill before I let them take this away from me.*

And for more than twenty years he had feasted on fine women, and basked in the adulation of other men. He liked it. He needed it. It would be impossible to go back and again call the lush, rolling hillsides of Illinois home.

Pictures of those landscapes covered the walls of his reception area, along with recent photographs of Doc Rowland with famous people: President Everett Lodge, the defense minister of France, Miss Illinois of 1991. He waved to Mandy Reese, his receptionist. She was young, auburn-haired, and very pretty. She carried his past obsessions in the deep pools of her big brown eyes. She called after him as he walked toward his private office, her voice bright with the thrill of her third month in Washington.

"I watched your speech, Doc. You looked great!"

"You're a darling, Mandy, you're a darling. That's a pretty dress you got on today." He closed the door.

2

Roy Dombrowski, Doc Rowland's chief assistant and adviser, wore a small smile on his thin, bespectacled face as he hung up the telephone. He sat for another minute at his desk in the little nook he reserved for himself next to Rowland's inside door. The desk was small, no different from those of the other staff members, but the position said everything. Dombrowski often referred to himself as Doc's Semar, the clown servant so often present in the *wayang kulit* shadow plays of Java. Semar was a jester who in reality was a god come to life. His mission was to make a fool of himself before the gods, in order to deflect their anger and protect the little people from their excesses.

Dombrowski checked his watch, then knocked on Doc Rowland's door. Hearing no answer, he waited for a second as was his custom, and then walked inside Doc's private office. Rowland waved quickly to him as he entered. As usual, the chairman had quickly recovered from his bout with the blues. He sat back in the stuffed leather chair behind his desk. He was chewing the back end off of the cigar that was always present but never lit, Doc's way of supporting both the tobacco lobby and the antismoking campaign. He was talking on the telephone. The desk was piled with undone paperwork. Trinkets from his decades in Congress served as paperweights. They also comprised the decor of his inner office, covering the top of a half-dozen end tables.

Photographs and plaques dating all the way back to the 1960s completely blanketed a far wall, from just above the couch to the ceiling itself. Here was a young Doc Rowland

campaigning with Richard Nixon in Illinois in 1968, showing the aspiring President how to milk a cow. There was
an older Doc Rowland with Ronald Reagan in 1980, showing him how to drive a Gypsy Moth tractor. Over there was
Chairman Rowland just last year, in the cockpit of the new
Advanced Tactical Fighter.

Rowland gave off a dry, conspiratorial cackle as he whee-
dled and cajoled the person on the other end of the telephone
line. "You're right, goddamn it, you're absolutely right. I
know, I know. Jerry Clinkle wouldn't make a pimple on
the ass of a decent chairman, I know that. His brain wouldn't
fit inside a thimble, if you could figure out where to find
it. But he's got the committee, and you know how that goes.
No, I'm with you all the way, Steve. I know how bad you
all need reservoirs up there. It's been dry all over. What
are we talking, fifty million? Yeah, there's no sense in it.
I'll do whatever I can. I'll talk to Clinkle today, in fact.
Meantime, I need help on this Nakashitona thing. We got
to draw the line someplace, you know. I never seen such
a bunch of wobbly old ladies in my life like on this one.
No, I don't mind getting out front on it. Hell, if I was any
further our front I'd be on a one-man patrol in no-man's-
land! Okay. Just give me a statement, that's all. Give me
a little one-minute speech on the floor tomorrow, how's
that? Good, good."

Rowland hung up the phone, and swung the chair around
until he was facing Dombrowski. Behind him, the Capitol
Building loomed through a large window. It had taken Doc
Rowland twenty years to earn an office with that view, and
he cherished it. When he entertained people in his office,
he liked to think that the Capitol Building gave his leather
chair a special eminence, like a halo.

He chortled, nodding toward the telephone. "Lining up
a little help."

Dombrowski raised a hand in warning. "Be careful, Doc.
This one gives me gas pains."

"Calm down, Roy. They're beating down the door to get

on my bill. We'll have fifty cosponsors by three this afternoon. I venture we'll have a hundred by this time tomorrow."

"We could have problems in the District on this one."

"Are you kidding? Every time I go home I get asked about the Japanese. The home folks are *livid*, Roy, you know that."

"Yeah, Doc. Okay." Dombrowski eased himself onto the edge of Rowland's desk. "But you're way out front. The Japanese issues never hold. And you've got a few people around here who'd love to knock you down."

"We'll win, we'll win. It's going to be a fight, but I care about this one. And I want people to remember who took the first punch when it's all over." Rowland cackled again, appearing exuberant. "What you got?"

"Ron Holcomb is on his way over from the Senate side. He said he needs to see you on an urgent matter. He wouldn't tell me what it was. He said it was classified."

"Maybe he wants some advice on how to satisfy his wife."

"That's what I call down and dirty."

"Well, that's not what I've been hearing from her."

Rowland and Dombrowski laughed with intimate camaraderie. They shared many such secrets. Roy Dombrowski was the only person that Doc Rowland completely trusted, and it had taken almost eight years of working closely together before Doc had reached that point with Dombrowski.

"He'll be here any minute," said Dombrowski, standing again and heading for the door. "Do you want me to bring him in?"

"Frisk him first."

Dombrowski found himself laughing. "He doesn't have the balls to shoot you, Doc."

Rowland was laughing, too. "He doesn't have balls, period. That's what Janet says. In fact, we may have the first female secretary of defense on our hands, Roy!" Rowland toyed with his unlit cigar, looking for a moment as if he were mimicking Groucho Marx. "Do you know what the troops call him? Chicken Hawk. *Chicken Hawk*, because he didn't have the guts to serve when there was a war on, and now every time there's a crisis he wants to send them in."

"Be fair," answered Dombrowski. "We've got a four-star Joint Chiefs Chairman who has more staff time in Washington than Holcomb. And he doesn't want to send the troops in *anywhere*. The biggest military operation he's ever been personally involved in is a parade in front of the Pentagon."

"General Francis?" Doc Rowland snorted and shook his head. "He must have studied Dr. Spock at West Point. Hell, he'd argue against *spanking* the goddamn enemy. What a mess."

"Holcomb goes around Francis, anyway," said Dombrowski. "He and that admiral—Mulcahy. They have what I would call a symbiotic alliance."

"Sounds like weird sex," replied Rowland.

"Symbiosis. They use each other. Holcomb uses the military when the President needs a political diversion at home. Mulcahy needs a war before he retires, or he's not going to make the history books. And General Francis spends half his time leaking stories on both of them to his favorite reporters."

"Anyway, here we go again," said Rowland. "Drug wars, banana wars, oil wars, Lebanese civil wars, terrorism wars—Holcomb wants to send in the troops everywhere, and Francis talks like they're already shell-shocked after the slaughter at Verdun. So Holcomb gets them sent in, and before they can accomplish anything Francis gets them yanked out. And the country looks foolish. I think both of them need to be sent home."

"It's no better or worse than the Congress, Doc."

"For Christ sake, what kind of endorsement is that?" Rowland lifted his head and cackled, sprawled in his chair. "I have a fantasy, Roy. We lock the leadership of the

Congress and the Pentagon inside a big room, give each one of them a gun, and tell them only the last two people alive can come out. A day later we open up the door, and you know what? They're all alive, still sitting in the same spot, because we forgot to give each of them an aide to tell them who to shoot."

Dombrowski laughed with Rowland, too polite to tell the Chairman he fully agreed. "Anyway, I suppose you want to see Holcomb when he comes? He *is* the secretary of defense."

"Of course, of course! I want to tear him a new asshole on this Nakashitona thing! And then I'm going to talk to him about foreplay."

Dombrowski's buzzer rang on the phone at his desk. "That's probably Holcomb." He went to answer it, then stopped once more before he left the room. "He's a smart guy, Doc. Don't forget that. He knows how to work this town as well as anyone I've ever seen. He probably even knows you're seeing his wife."

"I doubt that. Anyway, what do you want me to do, apologize for making her happy? Hell, I'm probably saving the man's marriage."

Dombrowski laughed again. "Wow, what a guy. Anyway, be careful." He considered it as the buzzer rang again. "Skip the advice on foreplay."

3

One might have thought Doc Rowland and Ron Holcomb were long-lost friends, the way they shook hands and slapped each other on the back as they walked toward Rowland's conference table.

"Ron! Good of you to come by."

"Thanks for taking the time, Doc. I know you're busy."

"The hell you say. I always got time for you."

Roy Dombrowski and General Bear Lazaretti joined them

at the table, carefully silent, both prepared to take notes as
their principals negotiated. Rowland and Holcomb automatically sat across from one another. Finally, Doc Rowland
nibbled on his cigar and nodded toward the defense secretary.

"I'm glad you're here, because I wanted to get your views
on this Nakashitona thing. But you go ahead. We can come
back to that."

"Sure, Doc." Holcomb spurred General Lazaretti into
motion with a quick glance. In five seconds the general
handed him a sealed envelope. The outside was marked
with a diagonal red stripe. White letters proclaimed TOP
SECRET UNICORN. Ceremoniously, Holcomb unsealed the
envelope, and placed four grainy black-and-white photographs in front of Doc Rowland. Holcomb now grew officious.

"Mr. Chairman, I don't wish to insult your expertise,
but let me begin by saying that the Soviets are in deep
trouble, and that this is going to be a problem for us."

"We want them to be in trouble. Damn, Ron, we've been
trying to *get* them in trouble for my entire lifetime!"

"Not this kind of trouble." Holcomb folded his arms and
peered serenely at Doc Rowland, his very self-confidence
something of an insult. "They're in trouble with their own
people, and when that happens they make trouble overseas. They've more than doubled the MVD in the past two
years—"

Rowland cut him off. "What the hell is the MVD?"

"The internal police, Doc. On any given day there are
about fifty thousand of them out in local villages, cracking
heads and shooting demonstrators."

"Oh, yeah," said Rowland. "That MVD."

"For all practical purposes, they've lost their empire, and
they're in danger of losing the government itself. They've
outlawed strikes, and yet they know that a massive strike
can shut the nation down in one day. The coal strikes in
Vorkuta nearly shut the country down a couple years ago.

If it had spread to the railroads, you might have had a revolution. All this *perestroika* that the West has been so joyously celebrating has given them nothing except frustration at home. The economy is in a complete nosedive. It's bad, Mr. Chairman."

Holcomb now gestured toward the pictures. "These photographs were smuggled out of a village near Kredinka, in the northwest section of the Ukraine. I'll have to ask you to refrain from talking about them. If it became known we have them, our intelligence source would be compromised. To be frank, she would be killed."

"Yes, yes." Rowland picked up the photographs one at a time, squinting and frowning as if he were trying to solve a puzzle. "Looks like a bunch of dead people."

"That's what it is. Dead people."

"That's what you wanted to show me? A bunch of dead people?"

"Look at them." Holcomb peered intensely at Doc Rowland. "They've been executed. And they were emaciated when they were shot."

Rowland studied the photographs more carefully. The dozen or so carcasses indeed showed bullet wounds in the head, and every one of them was spindly and drawn, almost as if they had spent time in a concentration camp.

Holcomb took one of the photographs and pointed at the bodies. "We have reports of hard, confirmed cases of cannibalism in the areas surrounding Kiev and Kredinka. Children are dying of starvation, Doc, and families are *eating* their remains. Secretly, at night, after claiming to have buried them." He pointed again. "And the MVD are executing starving people for eating their young."

"You gotta be kidding me, Ron! We send them billions of dollars' worth of wheat every year. They've got to be doing this on purpose."

Holcomb became elusive. "I don't know that, although Stalin did the same thing to the kulaks sixty years ago— starved them and then shot them for trying to survive. The main point, though, is that it's going to get worse. The MVD can't keep a lid on this with everything else going on in the world. And starving people don't care whether they die from a bullet or from lack of food, Mr. Chairman.''

''So, what are they gonna do?''

''They could call on us to help, but we're powerless. How do we prove that's what's going on, and who wants to condone cannibalism? In any event, they're going to march on their leaders. And the Soviet government is then going to kill them by the thousands. And then millions will march. And words like *glasnost* and *perestroika* are going to fall into their graves with them. This isn't Romania or Lithuania. This is the center of the empire, the last circling of the wagons. The Soviets *will* keep killing their people.''

''Well, I knew that all along.''

''Not so fast, Doc.''

As the younger man leaned back in the chair and seized control of the meeting, Doc Rowland remarked to himself how deeply he disliked Ronald Holcomb, and how little he trusted him. Ron Holcomb never told a lie, at least not in the way he could be caught at it. But he was a master dissembler, capable of taking the truth and twisting it into so many directions that it became fantasy at the same time it was undeniable. That talent had been the defense secretary's ticket to advancement over the years, in every job he had held. He could never be forced to negotiate on anyone else's terms. He would never show Doc Rowland a phony photograph. But he was not beyond making a deliberately wild prediction. So what was real, and what was not? Rowland could not tell anymore.

''What are you telling me, Ron? Is this the view of the administration?''

''Subject to some interpretation, yes. The Soviet government is in big trouble with its own people. Some kind of crackdown is inevitable. And as you know they've been in trouble with their hard-liners. Their army leaders have become restless, as have many of their remaining allies such as Cuba. The Cubans just went into Ethiopia, at the request of the government there, which has been trying to put down what it calls an internal rebellion. I think that was a way for the Soviet leaders to placate their own army, as well as Castro.''

Holcomb was gathering the photographs as he spoke. Now he stopped, leaning forward and almost whispering to Doc Rowland. ''We believe the Soviets are now creating a larger incident in the Red Sea in order to shift the world's attention away from what they are going to have to do at home.''

''The Red Sea?''

''Ethiopia.'' Holcomb glanced at Lazaretti again, and in a few seconds a second envelope, and a second set of photographs, appeared. Holcomb now laid these in front of Rowland, and continued. ''Their naval and air forces have joined with the Cuban ground element, and are preparing to invade Eritrea. The French have picked up on this, and already have moved reinforcements into Djibouti. They've quietly asked for our help. They'd like to drive the Soviets out of Africa for good, and they claim that a Cuban defeat could topple Castro. I don't know. Quite frankly, I think the Soviets are happy to have the problem. They have a stake in Ethiopia, and they need the diversion from their failures at home. The world is going to focus on the Red Sea, and the Soviets are going to expel the media from the Ukraine, and crack heads.''

''Unbelievable. Unbelievable.'' Rowland felt his own adrenaline flowing as he imagined the battle that might take place in some far-off desert. ''You sure? The French and the Cubans and the Russians? Why the hell should anybody care about Eritrea? I'm not even sure where it is.''

''Actually, Doc, that's probably why it's happening there. The Soviets need a manhood issue for their hard-liners at home. If they pushed in any other place, world opinion would scream bloody murder. But no one gives a hang about Ethiopia. They've already been invited in by the Ethiopian government, which has been unable to defeat the Eritreans. And they can leave whenever they want.''

''So what are you thinking about doing?'' Rowland hesitated, not wishing to sound disloyal despite his personal reservations with Ron Holcomb. ''We're not going to fight there, are we?''

''Doc, I need something from you.'' Holcomb leaned back in his chair, knowing he had won. ''I need you to go a little softer on this Nakashitona thing. Just for a week or so. I'm on my way to Japan in a few days. I think we can iron it out. But we can't be working on two major crises at the same time. I think we can get some accommodations from the Japanese government without having a full-blown fight that could hurt both of our countries. They're our most important ally, Doc.''

Rowland struggled with that, still sucking on his unlit cigar. For one quick moment he had become distracted, thinking of Janet Holcomb's sturdy, muscular beauty, and the chance he would have to enjoy it while her husband was in Japan. Now he focused back in on the photographs in front of him.

''*Ally?* Come on, Ron. Anyway, the Japanese have nothing to do with this Red Sea thing.''

''They can shut us down in three days, Doc. Let's be honest. They put fifty billion a year directly into the financing of our national debt, just through their purchases of our Treasury bills! Can you imagine what the budget would look like without that money? Or what the stock market would do if they simply started selling off T-bills? A minor adjustment in their sales caused the stock market crash of 1987!''

Rowland was growing deeply frustrated, unable to keep up with Holcomb's twists and turns. ''What are you up to, Ron? We look at pictures of some dead people and you start talking about revolution in Russia. Then you shift to some goddamn dogfight in Ethiopia. And now your answer to all these problems is for me to back off on Nakashitona.''

Holcomb shrugged, giving off a helpless smile. "They connect. The whole world connects these days. Give me some breathing space on Nakashitona. We can't handle all of these at the same time. We're not strong enough anymore."

"Are we going to be involved in *Ethiopia*? Is that what you're telling me?"

Holcomb now smiled politely, gathering the second set of photographs and preparing to leave.

"I don't think so, Doc. But we do have the French request to consider. The President has authorized some intelligence sharing. And I've told Admiral Mulcahy out at Pac Fleet to go ahead with some coordination at the operational level."

Rowland stood, walking with Holcomb toward the door. "If the Soviets want an incident, why in hell should we give them one?"

"They're going to stir something up in Ethiopia, whether we like it or not. The question now becomes whether we let them succeed."

The two men shook hands again as Roy Dombrowski opened the door for the defense secretary.

"Please, Doc," said Ron Holcomb as he left the office. "Please. Just hang with us for a week or so on both of these. I'll keep you posted."

"You do that," answered Doc Rowland, feeling helpless to protest but not promising Chicken Hawk Holcomb a damn thing. "You keep me posted."

CHAPTER 4
THE SOUTH CHINA SEA

1

For three hours, Mad Dog Mulcahy had journeyed from stem to stern on the U.S.S. *Roosevelt*, leaving Admiral McCormick and Captain Shinn and a half-dozen other officers ragged, until they all had sweated through their khaki shirts and trousers. He went down below into the machinery spaces. He spoke to the chief petty officers in their mess, and to each squadron of pilots in their ready rooms. He dropped in unexpectedly on the enlisted living spaces, inspecting their bunks and showers for cleanliness. He walked through the mess halls and spoke to the cooks and the sailors on mess duty. He spent a half hour in the combat information center, peering into radar scopes and quizzing sailors about their expertise. Mulcahy was a dynamo, and as usual the sailors reacted well to him. He was merry and abrasive, forever talking to them, yelling at them, slapping their backs, shaking their hands, asking questions, praising them for their service.

Now he had climbed up to the bridge, high above the flight deck, and was peering out through the glass enclosure past the forward edge of the ship. The carrier rolled softly in the bright blue sea. There was power and beauty in the way the great gray flight deck gently rose and fell with the rolling waves as the ship cut a trough over waters where Mad Dog Mulcahy had spent much of the last forty years. A momentary exuberance overwhelmed him as he watched aircraft and machinery, and the sailors themselves, down on the flight deck. All this had passed him, and yet in a way he had preserved this moment for these young sailors through his own service. Yes, this was life at its very fullest. Living on the edge, ready to do battle, never mind the sycophantic tedium of Washington and even Hawaii.

He was going with them. They didn't know it yet.

"Are you ready, sir?" Rear Admiral McCormick held a microphone that activated the ship's 1-MC public address system. McCormick was still soaked with sweat from the rigor of Mulcahy's visit. His face was flushed, and Captain Shinn's ebony features were dripping with sweat.

Mad Dog liked to slap people on the back. He now slapped an unsurprised, somewhat weary Ward McCormick. "Damn right I'm ready."

McCormick nodded toward the ship's boatswain, who then took the microphone and held it in front of his boatswain's whistle, a long, thin tube that he carried around his neck on a white braided rope. He made the boatswain's whistle sing a plaintive, time-honored song, starting with a flat note and going higher to the edge of shrillness, then lower to the brink of sadness, the historic signal for all crew members to cease talking and listen.

"Now hear this. Now hear this. Stand by for a message from Admiral McCormick."

McCormick took the microphone. "Men of the *Roosevelt* battle group: As you know, Admiral Mulcahy, the Commander in Chief of the Pacific Fleet, flew out here this morning to wish us well on our deployment. Hundreds of you have been able to talk to him personally, and on behalf of the battle group, I wanted to thank him for spending some time with us. And the admiral wanted to say a few words to you also.''

Mad Dog took the microphone from McCormick and held it in his giant hand, an electric smile dominating his Daddy Warbucks face. The microphone had a narrow handle and a circular top, as if he were holding the top half of a telephone receiver. He squeezed the activator and gazed out to sea as he addressed the crew.

''Good afternoon *Roosevelt warriors*. I'm pleased to be on board.'' He wiped the sweat from his bald pate as he grinned wildly at McCormick, whose face visibly sagged as he dropped his little surprise. ''And I'm going to be staying with you for a few days.''

Mulcahy warmed to the microphone. ''I want you to think about a few things while you're out here at sea, working impossible hours and dreaming about getting laid. First, don't you ever forget that you're part of the greatest navy in the world! We can go anywhere, take on anybody, and win. Second, you should remember who this ship is named for. Teddy Roosevelt was a fighter! His spirit is alive on this ship, and we should all work to live up to the standards he set when he was assistant secretary of the navy, and then when he fought on San Juan Hill, and finally when he was President. And third, you guys stay sharp. You never know when you're going to see some action, particularly in the part of the world where we're heading. The goddamn Soviets are operating a carrier battle group out there, too. And for the first time in years, we've got Cuban soldiers crawling all over Ethiopia. It looks to me like they might be up to some mischief. So, work hard, be tough, and above all, be ready to do your jobs. That's all. Bravo Zulu and good luck.''

As they climbed down the interminable ladders from the superstructure, Admiral Ward McCormick eyed his superior rather warily. It was known throughout the Navy that Mad

Dog Mulcahy had both access and a direct, highly secure phone line to Defense Secretary Ronald Holcomb, and that they talked every day. McCormick could not hold it back. He politely queried Mulcahy. "Admiral, were you trying to tell us something up there?"

"I'm going to tell you a whole lot, McCormick. I'd like you to assemble your key officers in the war room. After lunch would be fine."

2

A small Huey helicopter idled on the forward deck spot of the *Saipan*. Its rotor blades snapped lazily, and its exhaust tubes shimmered, miragelike, from the heat of its engines. Corporal Mack Perkins, the crew chief, saluted Fogarty, now dressed in his jungle utility uniform, as he jogged toward the right rear door. Perkins seemed dingy and oily and tired, like the helicopter itself. His olive-drab flight suit was wet with sweat underneath the armpits and along his back. His hand dripped with sweat as he saluted. Fogarty peered beyond the visor on the corporal's flight helmet and could see that the twenty-year-old Perkins was growing a moustache. Fogarty returned the salute, and then patted the top of the young marine's flight helmet as he climbed aboard the helicopter.

"Working on one of those NFL moustaches, Corporal? Eleven hairs on each side of your face?"

Perkins shook his head, hiding his embarrassment with a tough-guy grin. As Fogarty buckled his seat belt and put on his own flight helmet, the corporal finished his preflight inspection of the helicopter, racing from point to point and finally climbing into the bird on the left side. He flashed a thumbs-up sign to the pilot, and in a few seconds the Huey lifted off the flight deck, immediately peeling away to the port side of the huge amphibious ship. The ship quickly disappeared behind them.

They made it look so easy. Fogarty loved them for it. It was not easy. It was deadly, even the simplest parts of it. A few years before, a helicopter pilot had left the Navy and miraculously made it into the National Football League, and when one sportswriter had asked him how playing football compared to flying helicopters, he had said, "When you've landed a helicopter onto the fantail of a frigate at night in a moderately rough sea, it kind of puts catching a football into perspective."

Because every now and then one of them didn't make it, even on the routine "milk runs" from ship to ship at sea. Like the young captain in the Persian Gulf four years before, with whom Fogarty had ridden on dozens of flights. The helicopter's gear box had locked in the sand-filled air, and as he fell from the sky into the hot, shark-infested water, the captain had deliberately put his own side of the helicopter into the sea first. The chopper sank before he could escape. Everyone else was rescued. The "mechanical failure" received two inches of coverage in the next day's news. The pilot's name was withheld pending notification of next of kin. And by noon the nation had forgotten him.

In twenty minutes the *Roosevelt* appeared to their front. The Huey came alongside the giant ship and idled at twenty-five knots, matching the carrier's forward movement. Captain Holmes, the pilot, talked through his voice mike to the air boss in the superstructure of the carrier, clearing their landing. Slowly the helicopter moved sideways, above the flight deck, at the same time maintaining its forward speed to match the movement of the ship. In a few seconds it appeared to be hovering motionless as it settled over its assigned spot on the flight deck. Finally the helicopter's skids bumped abruptly onto the deck and it was aboard.

Captain Holmes shut the engines down. Corporal Perkins opened the left door and quickly checked the Huey. Then he opened Fogarty's door. Fogarty spoke crisply into his own voice mike before he took off his flight helmet.

"Nice job. See you guys in about an hour."

There were no side boys, and no senior officers to greet him. But as he jogged toward the same doorway that Mad Dog Mulcahy had entered four hours before, the ship's 1-MC system announced Fogarty's arrival.

"*Commander, Fifty-first Marine Expeditionary Unit, arriving.*"

3

"Go ahead, Mosberg. Take the cover off it."

"Aye, aye, sir."

Captain David Mosberg, United States Navy, was standing in front of Mad Dog Mulcahy and the eleven senior commanders of the *Roosevelt* battle group. He held a pointer in one hand. To his right, on an easel, was a large map that he had taped onto plasterboard. The map was six feet long and four feet high. Mosberg had pasted it together in his stateroom, and then covered it with white paper, so that no one could view the classified information on it as he carried it from his stateroom along the ship's passageways to the war room where the officers now sat, awaiting his briefing. Mosberg had written "Top Secret Vortex" on the white paper covering with a Magic Marker.

Mosberg's face carried a flushed, perpetually apologetic grimace. He was slightly overweight, and his khaki shirt bulged over his belt. His gray hair was disheveled in the front, where he wore it too long and pulled it from left to right to cover a growing bald spot. He was the senior intelligence officer on Mulcahy's staff, and had made the trip with the admiral from Hawaii. Watching him begin his briefing, Bill Fogarty remembered that Mosberg was known as the smartest officer on Mulcahy's staff, and was also the admiral's most trusted analyst. Mulcahy had been so impressed with Mosberg's work that he had stolen him from a similar billet on the Joint Chiefs of Staff and brought him to Hawaii when the admiral had been selected by Defense

Secretary Ronald Holcomb to command the Pacific Fleet.

"Good afternoon, Admiral. Gentlemen. The following briefing is classified Top Secret Vortex."

Mosberg peeled back the paper covering. For thirty seconds no one spoke as the gathered officers studied locations and unit symbols. The markers on the map slowly meshed for them, so that it presented an overall military context, in the same sense that a painting might finally gel after an art lover absorbed its subtleties. The map showed military formations on land and at sea, from the eastern tip of the Horn of Africa, westward through the Arabian Sea and into the Red Sea. There were heavy ground concentrations in central Ethiopia, at neighboring Djibouti, and in the rebel province of Eritrea.

Mosberg slapped his pointer over Addis Ababa, the capital of Ethiopia. "About ten days ago, we started picking up a large increase in Soviet air traffic into Addis Ababa. As you know, they have to file international flight plans when they leave the USSR, and we've copied them. They've been running Condors, which are the largest military transports in the world, and Cocks, which are capable of carrying outsize cargo including main battle tanks, back and forth, day and night, from the southern Soviet Union. At the same time the Cubans have moved some heavy units up from Angola. It appears that they have also brought several shiploads of new troops and weapon systems in from Cuba itself. Our conclusion is that this is a major buildup."

Mosberg's pointer circled the sharp, mountainous areas just to the south of the Ethiopian capital. "The Pentagon ran an Elegant Observer satellite over the area on two separate orbits yesterday. The satellite picked up a large staging area right here, filled with trucks, supply dumps, and tents. We would estimate probably a hundred thousand Ethiopian soldiers are camped around the plantations of Mojo and Nagret, and along the banks of the Awash River. The roads are filled with T-sixty-four and T-seventy-two main battle tanks, and some of the best Soviet-made self-propelled artillery pieces as well. We count at least four batteries of SAM-six surface-to-air missile systems. These kinds of weapons are suitable for fast-moving, large-scale armored assault.''

Mosberg rested the pointer. ''We count about three dozen MIG Twenty-three Flogger aircraft on the runway at Addis Ababa, along with several squadrons of HIP and HIND helicopters.''

The intelligence officer now ran his pointer along the waterways of the Red Sea, and then out into the Gulf of Aden, which separated the Arabian Peninsula from the Horn of Africa. ''The Soviets keep minelayers and minesweepers inside the Red Sea at their anchorage in the Dahlak Archipelago, along with several small combatants. They also have four other amphibious ships—three Alligator-class LSTs and a large LPD, the *Ivan Rogov*—nested together off of Socotra, just outside the Gulf of Aden in the Arabian Sea. Farther out in the Indian Ocean, the aircraft carrier *Kiev* is cruising with a battle group that includes a modern Slava-class cruiser.

''This combination of assets gives the Soviets the capability, if they choose, to lay and sweep mines, to land naval infantry troops, to conduct shore bombardments, and to launch both fixed-wing aircraft and helicopters. It looks like the Cubans, who may be putting in a full division of troops, are sneaking their way along the border between Ethiopia and Djibouti. Our judgment is that they will soon gather in an assembly area next to the Eritrean border, ready to pounce on the Eritrean port of Assab. The Ethiopian units would then follow behind them, to occupy the towns that the Cubans conquer.''

Fogarty had quietly taken a seat in the third row, at the rear of the collected group of ship and squadron commanders. Now he leaned back in his chair, sipping on a cup of tepid yet overcooked coffee. He studied the body movements of the senior officers of the battle group as they listened to Mosberg. The men who commanded the aviation squadrons and the ships were highly screened professionals, the best in the world at what they did. If Mad Dog uttered the word, they would attack his chosen target instantly, without question. They had proven it time and again, sometimes at great cost—over North Vietnam, off the coast of Libya, along the ridges outside Beirut, against the Cubans in Grenada, against the Iranians in the Persian Gulf.

And yet, to this point they did not seem to recognize that Mosberg's briefing had an imminence to it. They twitched their feet nervously, and checked their watches, anxious to get back to other duties. They had been briefed on so many contingencies over the years that to them this seemed almost like another intellectual drill. No Americans were yet involved in the Ethiopian war, and no American political stakes seemed at risk. But Mad Dog had not come all the way from Hawaii simply because he liked riding on ships. In the notepad before him Fogarty wrote a single word, a measure of his disbelief: *Ethiopia?* He underlined the word, and then put a box around it.

Mosberg continued, slapping his pointer on the port of Djibouti, very near to the Eritrean town of Assab. "The French keep their largest overseas base right here in Djibouti, which used to be French Somaliland—about six thousand soldiers. They've been strengthening their garrison over the past week. Five combatant ships have come through the Suez Canal from the Med over that period, moving into the port of Djibouti. That includes the *Foudre*, an amphibious ship loaded with troops and supplies. French commercial aircraft have been flying other troops directly into the garrison, and military cargo planes have been carrying supplies to the Djibouti airstrip."

Mosberg now moved the pointer to the western edge of the Arabian Sea. "Finally, as you all know, the U.S.S. *Independence* battle group has been operating down here for several weeks, in support of Operation Shooting Star. When the *Roosevelt* battle group joins the *Independence* in the Arabian Sea, we'll have more naval power in one spot than in any time in years. We'll have two carrier battle groups, one of them with a battleship and both with Aegis cruisers and amphibious assault ships. That's a couple hundred combat aircraft, two reinforced battalions of marines with LCAC landing craft and their own helicopters, Tomahawk and Harpoon missiles, and the capability to use sixteen-inch guns for shore bombardment.''

Mulcahy nodded judiciously as he studied the latest developments on the map. He folded his arms over a growing belly, and pushed out his lower lip as if he were pouting. Then he stood, pulling his six-foot-three frame to its full height, and glared out at the gathered officers as he addressed them.

''What Captain Mosberg is saying, gentlemen, is that you may soon be leading your units against the Cubans.'' He immediately raised a hand, as if to fend off an inevitable question. ''I know what you may be thinking. I know you've been reading about the collapse of the Soviet Empire, and the end of the Brezhnev Doctrine. But the map doesn't lie! When the Eritreans finally kicked the Ethiopians out last year, the biggest losers were the Soviets. If they don't turn this thing around, they'll lose their only naval bases in the Red Sea, in the Dahlaks. If they can't operate inside the Red Sea, they can't threaten ships moving through the Suez Canal, or intimidate Yanbu', where the Saudi oil pipeline offloads. They'll lose face in Africa as a whole, especially since they switched from the Somalis to the Ethiopians back in 1977. And what are they going to do? The rebel armies in Tigray and Eritrea have gotten pretty good. And the Ethiopian Army couldn't fight its way out of a thick fog.''

Mulcahy paused, again raising a hand, this time letting it sweep over the entire map. ''And they see this as pretty low risk. The Sovs can engineer the crisis. The Cubans will be on Ethiopian soil until they're only thirty miles from Assab. They can jump across, take Assab, and link up with the Soviet Navy to establish a logistical base. After that, they can move along the coast and knock out Massawa and

Asmara in two or three days, destroying the Eritrean Army
and turning over the province to the Ethiopian soldiers following in their wake. And then in a week or so they can
all go home. It would be quick. They can justify it as a
direct response to the request of the Ethiopian government,
since no country has yet recognized Eritrea as a nation
separate from Ethiopia. And then it would be over.''

Mulcahy sat back down. He gave Mosberg a fatherly
nod. "Tell them about the French."

"Yes, sir." Mosberg pointed again to the French concentration at Djibouti. "The French, as you know, are
very—proprietary about their role in Africa. They are taking
this situation quite seriously. They appear ready to recognize
the province of Eritrea as a nation separate from Ethiopia.
They may shut down railroad traffic from Djibouti to Addis
Ababa, which would be a major blow to the Ethiopians,
since they rely on Djibouti's port, now that the Eritreans
have taken Massawa and Assab away from them. If the
French recognize Eritrea, they will defend that territory
against the Cubans. All this could happen by the time we
reach the Horn of Africa."

Admiral Mad Dog Mulcahy now laughed, revealing for
the first time his delight. "The French are independent
enough to get involved in this. It's outrageous, but it's
containable. It would be hard for the Soviets to expand the
incident beyond Ethiopia. They can't actually take it out on
NATO, since France isn't a member. They can't provoke
a border incident with France, because France doesn't have
a common border with any Eastern European country. What
are they going to do, attack the French in New Caledonia?
The big worry would be if the French got themselves caught
between the Cubans and the Soviets, and were outnumbered.
But I'm sure they've thought of that."

Bill Fogarty had scribbled a second note onto his pad.
Administration policy? Now he looked up and spoke guard-
edly to Mulcahy. "Admiral, has the President spoken pub-

licly about this? Is there a national policy, or a declaration of American interest?''

Mulcahy's eyes narrowed, as if Fogarty were insolent to so directly raise a question of policy in an operational briefing. "We are on the cutting edge, Colonel. You know that. The issue is not what they call 'ripe' yet in Washington.''

Then the admiral seemed to recover. He chuckled again, as if the question had not been asked. "I see Arneaux Humbert all over this. Don't forget, he was a foreign exchange student at the National War College when I was there. He served in Vietnam in 1953 as a very young man, just out of Saint-Cyr, and then was a company commander in Algeria. He's still bitter about what happened there. He's lucky he wasn't cashiered out when the generals revolted in 1960. He's a great soldier, and he is not afraid. He did a terrific job directing the Chad operations against Libya a few years ago, during the worst of it. He knows northern Africa, and considers it to be French turf. Lord knows how he ever made it to the top in France.'' Mad Dog smiled self-indulgently, his heavy jaw creased with wrinkles in what appeared to be rows of grins. "But I guess he'd say the same about me.''

"What is the scope of our involvement, sir? Will this be purely a naval operation, or will there be a follow-on insert of Army troops?'' It was Admiral Ward McCormick, the battle group commander, whose pale eyes now moved restlessly from Mulcahy to the map and back again.

Mulcahy declined to answer the question. Instead, he rose and tapped the map again, at the Dahlak Islands. "Our mission now is to listen to the French. And we watch two things. First, we keep an eye on the Soviet minelayers in the Dahlaks.''

"I don't understand that one, sir,'' interrupted Mc-Cormick. "They're loaded up, we can see that from the photos you brought. But it would be inconceivable to me that the Soviets would want to lay mines if they deploy their LSTs inside the Red Sea. They wouldn't want to screw up their own operations." McCormick pondered the map. "Now the mine *sweepers* I could understand. They're at the Dahlaks, too."

"No," said Mulcahy, reading the map as if his eyes were instead watching ship movements across an open sea. "They will lay mines to the north, to cut off traffic from the Suez Canal. That could isolate the Saudi oil pipeline at Yanbu', and more importantly it would bottle up our Sixth Fleet in the Mediterranean." His voice now became deep, and agitated, and he seemed to orate. "Our whole wonderful Sixth Fleet, just over the horizon as the crow flies, and yet a good month away if they have to sail through Gibraltar and around the Cape of Good Hope! And the ground would be over in a week or two, if the Cubans know what they're doing. After which, the Soviets would sweep up their own mines— you know, a classic gesture of humanity and goodwill after their guys win another one."

"Very good point, sir," said McCormick.

"I know." Mulcahy had expected the compliment. Now he pointed to the island of Socotra. "The second thing to watch is the Soviet fleet out in the open sea. They'll have to move before the ground units do. They can't be late. They have to be waiting for the Cuban armored column when it reaches the sea, and they have to control the sea at that point. So, we watch them in the Indian Ocean. We watch them in the Med. We watch them at Socotra. And when they move, we move."

"Sir, just what is it that we're going to do?"

Fogarty had asked the question. Mulcahy peered at him in response, and froze Fogarty's heart with his eyes. "When I decide, you'll know. And until I decide, I don't expect to have to report to my MEU commander. Do you have a problem, Colonel?"

"I'm not sure, sir." Fogarty had drawn up dozens of contingency plans during his years in Washington. He knew the intensity of analysis that accompanied every such plan, the debates and checks and counterchecks that were common inside the Joint Chiefs of Staff. Twelve sets of eyes now stared at him as he held Mulcahy's gaze. "First, if you were telling us to throw the bastards out of Havana, I'd be the first guy to lead the charge. But in terms of strategy, I'm a little fuzzy on what's going on here. Let me see if I have this right. The Ethiopians are a Communist regime. The Eritreans are—something, I'm not sure what. Whatever it is, they're damn sure not democratic. They used to be trained by the Cubans, until the Soviets switched from Somalia to Ethiopia in 1977. They've been fighting the Ethiopians for almost thirty years, so I guess that means they don't like the Soviets and the Cubans. But their biggest supporters lately have been Syria and Iraq."

Fogarty had felt himself growing ever more incredulous, as if the telling of these incongruities had enlarged them in his own mind. "Syria and Iraq, sir! So, what we're going to do is join with the Eritreans, who are promising us nothing, and the Syrians and the Iraqis, who hate us, and who by the way are fighting each other in Lebanon right now, in order to embarrass the Cubans and the Soviets? How is the President going to define our national interest?"

He had already gone too far, but he could not stop without saying it all. "With all due respect, sir, it seems like we'd be better off letting the Cubans and the Soviets embarrass themselves, then coming in and picking up the pieces later."

Mulcahy had not let go of Fogarty's eyes. "You left out the French."

"Yes, sir." He smiled lamely, attempting a joke. "They like that part of the world. Let them pick up the pieces."

A few titters filled the war room. Mulcahy paused for another moment, as if trying to decide what to do with this commander who bordered on insubordination. "You took an oath, Colonel? Do you remember it?"

"Yes, sir."

"To uphold and defend the Constitution, against all enemies, foreign and domestic."

"Yes, sir. I feel very strongly about it."

"*All* enemies, Colonel. You don't decide who the enemy is. The French are about to take a great risk. If they succeed, they will not only embarrass the Soviets and the Cubans, they will drive them out of Africa for good. They'll probably need our help. Fuck the Eritreans. Keep your eye on the bull's-eye. Now, are you on board or not?"

Fogarty stared back at the admiral. The large map filled with symbols was a brightly colored nimbus that shone like a halo around Mad Dog's angry face. Mad Dog and the map were a portentous sight. He touched the gold tooth that pressed against his sternum on the inside of his shirt, and imagined some Cuban soldier flecking out a crown from the jaw of one of his young corporals, and wearing it around his own neck as a trophy for the next twenty years.

And then his mind went back to a moment more than a year before, when he had accompanied Major General Frank Betti, the Marine Corps budget director, to a Pentagon briefing. Fogarty had sat in a chair next to the wall as General Betti joined budget directors of the other services at a long table filled also with Pentagon civilian staffers. His job was to shuffle through a thick notebook filled with statistics, as the general's "backup." As they discussed future needs for amphibious sealift, General Betti had begun to disagree with a young assistant secretary of defense on the likelihood of Third World conflicts in the near future. General Betti had begun, "Mr. Secretary, I disagree. I think—"

And the young man with the round lawyer's glasses and the pink shirt with its yellow power tie had cut the career infantryman off with a wave of the hand. "Well, that's the problem, General. You are not paid to think."

And neither am I, thought Fogarty as he finally answered the admiral. "Of course I'm on board, sir. I'm a professional, you know that. But if we fight an armored column of Cubans in the desert it's going to *cost* us. And I'd like to be able to tell my men that the price they're going to pay is worth it. That it's important to the country. Vital. Something to die for."

"You just said you'd fight in Cuba," answered Mulcahy. "Who the hell do you think you'd fight there? The Cubans, right? But the Congress wouldn't let us do that, anyway." The admiral's face lit up. "Well, let me tell you this, Colonel. It's straight from the mouth of the secretary of defense, just this morning. Castro's in big trouble at home. If we knock out the Cubans in Eritrea, he'll fall. Tell your men that, when you brief them on this operation."

Mulcahy laughed now, as if delighted with himself. "Congratulations, Colonel. It looks like we've finally got the bastards in a place where you can go kill them!"

CHAPTER 5
WASHINGTON, D.C.

1

The first time Ronald Holcomb saw the woman he would risk destroying his carefully planned life in order to love, she was walking across the lobby of the Commodore Hotel in Beirut, on her way for an evening swim in the hotel's pool.

He knew nothing about her. But she reminded him somehow of an elegant lioness as she descended a flight of steps into the lobby. She had square shoulders and a firm neck, and she held her head high as she moved into the lobby with a feline lightness, on the balls of her feet. She was wearing a light blue cotton shift that ended above her knees, showing strong, almost sturdy legs.

Her hair had first attracted him. It glistened under the ceiling lights as she walked, a dozen shades of blond, streaked by the sun and already wet from a shower. She had pulled it behind her face and ears, so that it fell onto her back. As she came closer he noticed full lips and a wide, smooth face. She stared straight ahead, watching no one, but he knew she was onstage, followed by the hungry eyes of dozens of men, mostly news reporters who were in Beirut alone, on temporary assignment. She clearly reveled in her audience, even as she ignored it.

It was September 1983. Holcomb had just turned thirty-nine, and was serving as the youngest undersecretary in the State Department. He was in Beirut after having traveled to Egypt, Israel, and Jordan, conferring on ways to resolve the seemingly endless Lebanese civil war. He had come to the hotel from the embassy, and had just finished dinner with a group of American journalists who were covering the multinational peacekeeping forces then stationed in the city. There had been a great deal of suspicion among the reporters, many of whom had also served in Indochina during the 1960s and 1970s. Several of them had badgered Holcomb to the point of insult during the dinner, predicting that the United States would soon increase its troop levels in Lebanon, as it had done in Vietnam in 1965.

Holcomb, who had recommended during White House meetings that the government triple the size of the Marine Corps contingent in Beirut, spent thirty minutes during dinner guaranteeing it wouldn't happen. Nor had he thought twice about the inconsistency of his recommending one policy in the White House and then a week later passionately defending the very policy he had argued against. One couldn't get too caught up in these things. He had lost at the White House, and so that was that. He was done believing that it should happen.

He was on his way out of the hotel when he noticed the blond woman. He stood near a pillar just across from the reception desk, watching her intently until she strode past him, walking toward the swimming pool. She passed within two feet of him, and gave him just the slightest smile, at the same time raising her eyebrows. He could have reached out and touched her, and he almost did just that. Her face gave off an intimacy, as if she were secretly telling him that the attention she was receiving was absurd, and that only he would understand.

Ronald Holcomb was married, with a ten-year-old son. His life had been a predictable, boring sequence of structured cages, from Andover to Harvard to Cambridge to Yale, and then into the cage of government service. He had married a law school classmate who had worked for Ralph Nader when Holcomb entered the foreign service, and who now was a lawyer for a public interest firm. Their relationship was best described as perfunctory. Sexual relations were an accident that occurred two or three times a year.

He had forgotten about the power of a woman's eyes. In fact, no woman had ever looked at him like that. And in eight months he would be forty. He couldn't stand the thought.

And so he rather blindly followed this feline creature as she crept onto the terrace. Without knowing what exactly he might even say to her, he sat in a lawn chair twenty feet from her and ordered a glass of Chablis. She quickly threw off the blue cotton shift, and dove into the pool. She was the only one in the pool. He sipped his wine and watched her swim three laps in a smooth, powerful crawl, then shift into a lazy breaststroke. Every now and then she glanced over at him, still smiling. It was almost surreal to watch her alone in the clear water of the Commodore's pool. A few miles away, people were killing each other and knocking down whole villages with terrifying abandon, for the crime of being born a Muslim or a Christian or a Palestinian or a Druze. Lebanon, once as beautiful and fresh as the woman who was swimming a few feet in front of him, was now devastated beyond hope. Its buildings were racked and destroyed. Its people were fleeing. Its very air was heavy in the lungs, filled with dust kicked up from artillery battles.

Holcomb was overcome with sadness as he sat on the almost empty terrace and watched the woman swim. She seemed free, removed from structure and even obligation. She was a newt, comfortable on land or in the water, a thing of beauty in a country that had turned to dung. At that moment, he longed to be like her, if only for a day. He wanted to be free of the responsibilities of government, and the pressures of cynical, arrogant reporters. He wanted to be happy, arrogant, unburdened. Not forever. Just for a while.

She climbed out of the water and began to walk toward him. She was sturdy and fresh and raw. She smiled at him again as she passed, and Holcomb surprised himself by calling to her.

"Can I buy you a glass of wine?"

"I'm all wet," she laughed, climbing back into her shift. "I'd freeze." Pulling the dress below her hips, she turned and faced him. "You're Holcomb, aren't you?"

He was taken aback, almost stunned. "How'd you know that?"

"I'm a reporter. I work for UP News. Do you think I'm on *vacation* in this miserable dump?" She held out her hand. "Janet Van Andel. And if you'll wait twenty minutes, you can buy me dinner."

She looked gorgeous when she again descended the steps into the lobby. She had pulled her hair back tightly into a bun, and now wore blue jeans and a white silk blouse. He bought her dinner at a small café three blocks away. Walking down the unlit streets past mounds of garbage and men carrying rifles as casually as if they were briefcases, Holcomb could not shake the fear that he might suddenly be taken hostage. At the other tables inside the café, dark men leaned over toward each other and spoke in whispers, constantly staring at him and Janet as they ate. He was nervous, out of his element. She was amused at his palpable fear, and then indulgent.

"Why don't you just put a sign with a bull's-eye on your back, Mr. Secretary? Look, nothing's going to happen to you here. They don't even know who you are." She watched them carefully. "Besides, they're Sunni Muslims, probably the only completely peaceful people in this city."

She touched his leg underneath the table, an act that made him jump, more from his knowledge that he was unavoidably attracted to her than from fear. "They're really looking at me," she said. "I normally come here with André. He's French but he's dark like them."

Holcomb had smiled then. "And how do we get rid of André?"

"It's pretty hard. We share the same room."

"Are you married?"

"No, but you are."

It occurred to him at that moment, as this beautiful seductive woman sipped a glass of wine and toyed with what looked like a shish kebab, that she could be setting him up for an embarrassing news story. He imagined reading the piece, and the explanations that would inevitably flow from it. Then he sat straighter in his chair, becoming suddenly officious.

"We are off the record, I assume."

He loved the way her eyes came alive when she laughed. She began poking fun at him and at the same time reassuring him. "We don't exist simply to *get* you, you know. As far as I'm concerned, this is personal. It has nothing to do with my job. For all I know, you're using me. Do you want to spill the beans to me about some government policy on background? Go ahead. I'll print it."

"Print this," said Ronald Holcomb, in the most uncontrolled moment of his adulthood. "Get rid of André, and come with me to Cyprus for the weekend."

The Beirut airport was still shut down, under constant attack by Druze artillery, so the next day they took a taxi through the devastated city and at its seaport caught a Russian-made hovercraft to Cyprus. Ever the bureaucrat, Holcomb wondered as the boat skimmed the calm blue waters of the Mediterranean whether he was breaking regulations by traveling on a Russian boat. In Larnaca they rented a suite at a hotel near the beach. That night they watched a fashion show in the courtyard of the hotel. The European and African models were lovely in their low-cut gowns and slit skirts and silk blouses. Afterward, Ron Holcomb made love to Janet Van Andel with a passion he had never before experienced. Evanescent visions of prancing models ran through his wine-soaked mind as he clutched her to him, and when he finally shuddered on top of her he felt as though he were escaping into a wild unknown, throwing away all the rigid boredom of a life to that point devoted only to his profession.

And he did not know it then, but he would keep throwing things away, even as he came to realize that Janet threw away nothing. She was a collector—of men, of experiences, of accolades.

Two nights later they returned to Beirut on an old steamer. The ship's captain was a squat, greasy man for whom the Beirut tragedy had become a bonanza. With the airport closed, the steamer made nightly runs from Larnaca to Beirut, carrying journalists and returning residents who had flown into Cyprus from Athens. The captain and his son kept their little restaurant open throughout the night, selling beer and sandwiches. They would take almost anything for a sandwich or a beer—a dollar, ten francs, a mark.

The boat trip was the greatest adventure of Ronald Holcomb's life. He and Janet masqueraded as a journalistic team. They sat through the night at a long table with a dozen others, smoking cigarettes and drinking beer and eating stale sandwiches. Janet was onstage, loving the attention she drew as the only woman. She and Holcomb shared beers and carried on a banter filled with double entendre about the American government's foolish policy in Beirut that entertained the others for a half hour. But the men never stopped watching Janet. And Holcomb realized that this would always be the case. Men never would stop watching her, and she would never stop enjoying their attention.

In the early morning, as the sky above the sea grew gray and then Lebanon's coastline appeared in the distance, they went into the small cabin he had paid for as part of their passage and made love. The sheets on the bed had not been changed for some time. The pillow smelled of tobacco and hair oil. But she pulled him into her as if she were the earth itself. And as she lay beneath him, lost in the sagging mattress like an angel on a puffy cloud, he thought to himself that this moment, with the boat shuddering and spewing oil, and the wrecked city coming into view through a small, filmy porthole, was as pure as gold.

They said good-bye on the landing. A contingent of French soldiers was offloading an LST fifty yards away. The soldiers had emplaced a machine-gun position very near the steamer, the gun pointing toward the devastated row of buildings that made up the "Green Line" between East and West Beirut. The soldiers manning the gun were just above Holcomb's head. He felt alive, palpable, afraid. It seemed to him that he was living a scene out of the movie *Casablanca*. He embraced Janet openly, knowing that he might now be recognized by someone in the cars that were gathering on the other side of the customs building.

"I leave tomorrow," he said. "Will I ever see you again?"

"I can come to Washington if you'd like."

"To live?"

"We can talk about that."

Within two months he had helped Janet Van Andel find a job as a public relations specialist at the Environmental Protection Agency. A month after that, he quietly separated from his wife. In early 1985, just before he was posted as ambassador to Bahrain, he and Janet married. When he was asked to become secretary of defense, he spoke a few words to President Ev Lodge and Janet was made an assistant secretary in the Department of Education.

She was bright, talented, and warm, and he could never stop loving her. But he could never pretend that he owned her body. He had not owned it when he met her, and he had never fully owned it since. Janet Holcomb was a woman who believed in what she called "physical friendships." He accepted it. There was no alternative. He did not have the ability to stop it. Nor could he risk the further embarrassment of a second divorce.

Even at this moment, as he and Janet shared the backseat of his limousine on their way to hosting an evening reception in honor of the Italian minister of defense, Ron Holcomb knew that his wife had been with another man within the past few hours. He had learned to see it in the softness that her eyes took on after an afternoon or evening of making love, and in the relaxation that invaded her body. She leaned back into the seat as they rode toward the Rothenberg House, her eyes lazily drifting from object to object as she stared outside the window. A small, secret smile sat comfortably on her face.

Yes, another man had been running his hands over her warm, tight skin, and burying himself inside her as if she were the earth. Another man. And Ronald Holcomb thought he knew who.

2

"Goddamn it, I *hate* the son of a bitch!"

Roy Dombrowski momentarily winced in the driver's seat as Doc Rowland yelled. Then he spoke with the patient tones of a counselor.

"Easy, Doc. Watch the old blood pressure. I can't have you stroke out right here on Constitution Avenue."

Rowland was holding a crumpled copy of *The Washington Post* in one hand, and twirling his cigar in his mouth with the other, as if it were the nipple on a baby bottle. The car made its way slowly in the evening rush hour traffic, passing the Washington Monument on their left, having passed the National Archives on their right as they made their way toward the Rothenberg House. And Doc Rowland alternately sulked and swore for several blocks as the car edged forward. Because he really did hate Ronald Holcomb.

There were many ways to hate in Washington. You could hate someone for his ideas, which had become rare, since ideas capable of rousing emotion seemed to have passed with the 1970s. You could hate him for his money, which also was infrequent in a town that deferred to rank and position, yet viewed money as mere fuel, gasoline for the engines of power. You could hate him for the way he did business, for having more influential friends than you did, or for having better luck. But the truest, deepest hate was reserved for the person who had zeroed in on your reputation, and knew how to marshal the media to attack it. Because power was more than position. It was credibility. The town even had a nickname for such media-dominated running gun battles: the Harvard Shootouts.

And Ronald Holcomb was a master warrior in such battles. He well understood the weapons: the anonymous leak to the press, the untraceable ''background'' story to a key reporter, the careful comments to an influential senator or editor that defamed and ridiculed, but always in the form of a Mandarin riddle, where the listener was forced to draw his own conclusion and the accuser could not be held accountable.

And now Rowland knew that Holcomb was doing it to him, with great effort and exuberance. A Ted Zingerle column in today's *Post* had claimed that Rowland was weak for reelection, and was facing an uprising on the Armed Services Committee itself. Such comments were like tossing bloody meat to the sharks, but were not as damaging as what followed:

> ''High-level Defense sources who asked to remain anonymous indicate that Rowland has repeatedly frustrated DOD leadership with his ''obsessive micromanagement.'' By that source's count, the Defense Department owes the House Armed Services Com-

mittee more than 900 reports, many of them regarding
"petty pet projects" of Chairman Rowland that have
little relevance to performance in the field. "Rowland
is an embarrassment when he is around our soldiers,"
the source commented. "His questions to them are
usually so patronizing and stupid that he leaves them
shaking their heads."

These sorts of attacks could not be countered without
throwing mud back on one's own face by dredging up the
nastiness all over again. *High-level source*, that odious term
for a coward. "*Obsessive micro-management . . . an embarrassment . . . patronizing . . . stupid.*" Rowland's blood
pressure had risen to the point that his ears now began to
hum. *Stupid!*

"The son of a bitch!"

"Calm down, Doc," answered Dombrowski.

It was vintage Holcomb: not factually inaccurate, no fingerprints, but a slam, perfectly placed. It worked the fine
line between truth and opinion, raising the question whether
Rowland was an expert or a meddler, and whether he truly
had credibility among his colleagues. If it took hold among
the piranha of the press, he would be a piece of bait for a
few weeks as other columnists and writers discussed his
"problems." At the same time, he would be managing the
Nakashitona legislation, which called for some special care
after his conversation with Holcomb about the dangers the
administration was facing in the Soviet Union and the Red
Sea. And now Holcomb had for some reason decided to
sandbag him in the press. *Alright*, he decided. *All bets are
off. I'm going full speed on Nakashitona.*

And yet he had to be seen with Holcomb. He could not
be portrayed publicly as hostile to the administration or the
Defense Department, even though he was criticizing both
for their handling of the Nakashitona matter. In fact, he had
to deal especially gently with Holcomb, since the defense
secretary had personally briefed him on the other crises

facing the government. And Holcomb would take the same
tack, working especially hard in public to show his support
of Rowland. Holcomb was a double-dealer, everyone knew
that, but the secretary had spent his whole professional life
mastering the bureaucracy and the people in it. A lot of
people owed him from past favors. Never mind believing
in something, Rowland often muttered to his friends. Holcomb could find the right people and move the issue and
get it done. Any issue. He was a man without ideology, a
modern gun for hire.

Roy Dombrowski drove up Eighteenth Street, and
stopped in front of the Rothenberg House. He gently patted
Rowland on the shoulder, smiling as if he were both father
and son. "Doc, don't get mad. Go in there and schmooze
the living hell out of Ron Holcomb."

"Don't worry. Don't worry. I know how to do this."

Rowland stood for a second by the curb, straightening
out the wrinkles in his suit. He put away his cigar, shook
his head at the mess his clothes had become in the sweltering
summer heat, and climbed the steps of the Rothenberg
House. A Marine guard in his dress blues came to attention
as Rowland reached the door, then sharply saluted him.
Rowland waved to the young marine, remembering again
his own days as a soldier in the Korean War. These young
troopers, he loved them. And then the Zingerle article
floated up from his subconscious again, like bile. *Patronizing. Stupid! I'll show him who's stupid.*

3

Ronald Holcomb watched Doc Rowland climb up the steep
steps, and carefully examined him as the congressman entered the ornate foyer of the Rothenberg House. He could
hardly keep from shaking his head with contempt. In Holcomb's eyes, the man who had stumbled into the hallway
was a political success, hidden inside the exterior of a human

catastrophe. Holcomb took in the damp, wrinkled suit, the too-bright tie, the heaviness that had accumulated on Rowland's frame over the years from too many evening receptions such as this one, and too little exercise. Rowland was still massively strong, like a football lineman. But he was puffing after having climbed twenty steps. His cheeks were flushed, and his sagging neck hung down a little bit over his collar.

Holcomb broke into a carefully controlled smile as he watched the chairman catch his breath inside the doorway. Rowland, he thought, was an all-American mess. He was beefy, tactless, intellectually defensive, and clearly agitated. Rowland did a visible double take when he first saw Holcomb, then nodded, forcing his own smile. They had to smile; people were watching. Besides, they dealt with each other almost every day. You couldn't carry on the daily business of government through continuing snarls, no matter whom you secretly hated.

This is the man my wife is sleeping with?

Rowland seemed a metaphor to Holcomb, a symbol. The chairman's obsessive self-importance, his lack of bodily discipline, and his celebration of authority over intellect were also, in Holcomb's view, the dominant characteristics of the Congress itself. But now Holcomb waved, feeling grand in the knowledge that Rowland would have read the Zingerle article, and sensing that the chairman would have guessed immediately that he was indeed the "official who spoke on condition of anonymity." It gave Holcomb a special sort of pleasure, knowing that Rowland knew, because he also knew that it wouldn't come up. Rowland had no way of proving it, or even alleging it. It was beautiful, staring into the face of the man you had just secretly savaged, knowing that only he and perhaps a few others shared your savage secret.

"Hello, Mr. Chairman! Good to see you tonight, sir. So glad you could make it."

"Hey, hey, Mr. Secretary. Yes, sir, it's a fine night and

I'm glad to be here. Yes, sir. Glad to be here. How you been?''

They shook hands, both beaming their best Washington smiles. As always, their eyes passed each other after one quick glance. Holcomb looked beyond Rowland, at a painting on the far wall. Rowland pretended interest in the next room, where a group of people now milled about, drinking wine and sampling hors d'oeuvres.

Holcomb picked up on Rowland's glance and gestured toward the room. "Please feel free to go ahead inside. You'll recognize most of the faces. And His Excellency the minister is in there with my wife." Holcomb paused then, staring with a calm intensity into Rowland's face. "You remember Janet?"

Rowland stared blandly back. "Sure, Janet. Sure I do. Well, that's good. Real fine. When are you meeting with the Japanese? We got a hot one on our hands, Mr. Secretary. A real barn-burner."

"Yes, we do," answered Holcomb. "I'm off to Japan day after tomorrow. I'll be meeting with Minister Tanashi the day after I arrive." Holcomb folded his arms, and rubbed one hand over his chin. "I appreciate your reticence over the past couple of days, Doc. Your Nakashitona bill has received a great deal of attention in Japan. I'm sure Tanashi is going to take me to the woodshed over it."

Thinking of the article in that day's *Post*, Rowland could not restrain himself. He put a meaty finger into the defense secretary's chest. "It's the Japanese who need to be taken to the woodshed, and I hope to hell that's why you're going over there. If you all did your job on this, there wouldn't be any need for me to introduce a bill. I've been careful, Ron. I'm as loyal as anybody you know when it comes to national security. But I'm getting sick of all the''—he paused, then threw the word at Holcomb as if it were a dagger—"*capons* in this town, running around like Chicken Little every time the Japanese cluck their tongues."

Rowland deliberately inspected Holcomb now, taking his

time as he did so. He started with the oiled, parted hair that had become quite gray over the past three years, then moved down beyond the gathered wrinkles of a narrow, quickly aging face, the cold blue eyes that remained averted, and the long, thin nose. He stopped at Holcomb's mouth. It always smiled, but it never grew warm. It betrayed the soft tenor of the voice, the handmade suits with their button-down shirts and power ties, the firm, tennis player's handshake. It made a mockery of the clever, thoughtful notes that inevitably followed up key meetings, handwritten and signed "Ron." Rowland suddenly decided that Holcomb's mouth belonged on a rat, up from the sewers of Brooklyn.

"Is Zara Boles in there?"

"Zara?" answered Holcomb, as if suddenly rediscovering Rowland. "Oh, yes, she's in there."

"Well, I figure I'll just go give her some hell about that *Post* article today. The Zingerle piece. I didn't know I could make the lady so mad."

"Zara is one of your most loyal friends, Mr. Chairman."

"Well, that's what I always thought. But you never can tell in this town, who your friends are, and who's out to get you. You know what I mean?"

Holcomb's face remained infuriatingly serene. "You know what Harry Truman said. If you want a loyal friend in Washington—"

"I know, I know. Get a dog. I know all about Truman." Rowland moved past Holcomb, deliberately bumping into him as he did so. "And I know all about dogs. Yes, sir, Mr. Secretary, a fine party. Appreciate you having me here tonight. Look forward to your toast. See you in a while."

4

The Rothenberg House was one of the several historic sites used periodically by the Department of Defense for receptions and dinners. The house, built in 1858 and once the home of a secretary of state in the Cleveland administration, was now an art gallery that specialized in Impressionist paintings from France, Britain, and the United States. Its proudest possession was one of Monet's famous Haystack paintings, depicting sunset in a farm pasture, heavy with the violets and pinks that characterized Monet's comparative works. The use of such facilities involved an unlikely, but happy symbiosis. The historic homes made it possible for Defense officials to entertain in a lush, traditional setting. The fee paid to the homes by the government helped them to stay in business.

Doc Rowland walked into the main living room as if he were a gunslinger entering an unfamiliar bar. The Monet hung over the fireplace, a large painting that at once dominated the room and soothed it with its haunting, moody colors. Rowland did not even glance at it. He did not care in the slightest about either the history of Rothenberg House or the artistic contributions on its walls. He cared about people, and particularly what the wrong people might try to do to him. He immediately swept the faces of the two dozen men and women who were talking animatedly in groups of three and four. He needed to find his friends, and he needed to fix the locations of his enemies. You either did that or you kept your mouth shut when you talked, except to say hello or to comment on how well the Redskins looked for the coming season.

Yes, there they were gathered, with their ribbons and their pearls, the top leaders of the Defense Department and their wives.

Blue-coated waiters passed through the groups, fetching drinks and offering appetizers. In a corner, two soldiers from the Army band played classical music on a violin and a cello. A haze of smoke sat like a cloud below the high, ancient ceiling. The air was stuffy but cool, and Rowland welcomed its moldy, smoke-filled ambience. It smelled ancient, and yet alive. People were talking too loud and their chatter filled the room, a sign that most of them were about two drinks ahead of Rowland. He perfunctorily grabbed a glass of wine from a passing waiter, so seasoned in this act after twenty-four years that he had no need even to shift his eyes to the tray.

Not bad, for a Holcomb gathering. Mentally, he marked the trouble spots around the room. He would follow those people as they drifted from conversation to conversation. Particularly Janet Holcomb. Doc Rowland's face was a window into his emotions, and he was devouring her so completely in private that he did not trust himself to talk with her in public anymore.

She was opposite him, on the far side of the room. Her blond hair glistened where it fell along deeply suntanned shoulders onto a bright red dress. A gold chain shone against her tan, and a ruby pendant dangled from it, between the rise of her small breasts. Catching that short glimpse of her, Rowland felt himself flush with the remembrance of the afternoon they had spent together. Then he consciously fought it back. She was fun, but that was it. *She is not like me*, he reminded himself. *She's like them. She even plays tennis*, he thought. They all did. Forget golf. How many deals were made on the edge of the tennis court in Washington?

Janet waved to him across the room, noticing that he was watching her. He waved briefly back. Then she surprised him by leaving the guest of honor, whom she had kept at her right hand, and walking directly over to him. She had turned the minister over to General Bear Lazaretti, who began escorting the dusky, rather muscular Italian around to meet other couples.

"Doc, how are you?" She formally pecked him on the cheek and then took his elbow, drawing him away from the crowd. As they stood next to a wall she lowered her voice. "I'm under orders to win you over tonight with my wit and charm, to disarm you and to pick your brain."

"Well, as I recall you did a good bit of that this afternoon,'' said Rowland. His startling blue eyes came alive. ''You better leave me alone before I embarrass both of us.''

''I'm sorry about the Zingerle piece.''

''I've been hit below the belt before,'' said Rowland. ''But it's awful nice of you to say that. Now. Why did you say that?''

''The honest truth?'' She continued to smile winningly. Her arm had not left his elbow. ''Because I think Ron knows about you and me. That's probably why he did it.''

''That's a hell of a reason. The son of a bitch.''

''Now, Doc.'' She patted him on the back. ''It's just Ron's little way of showing that he cares.''

''I think Dr. Freud ought to write a book about you guys' relationship. Sounds weird to me.''

''Are you complaining?'' She secretly nudged him. ''I'm not going to Japan, if you want to call me.''

''You sure, now?''

''Yes.'' Her face had remained completely controlled, so that anyone else in the room would have been certain that Doc Rowland was being patronized, even neutralized, by the wife of a man he despised. Her blond hair shone on her shoulders and he could smell the faint odor of an elegant French perfume.

''Then I'll call you day after tomorrow. We'll have dinner at L'Auberge.''

''I know a new place. Ethiopian food. Can you call me at my office?''

''*Ethiopian*? Was that a joke? Anyway, I'll do that. I'll do that.''

As Rowland walked away from her, he was so aroused that he felt dizzy, as if he might soon pass out from bliss. *I have died and gone to heaven*, he thought as he forced himself to concentrate on the business of the reception.

He needed to join a friendly circle, and now he considered his alternatives. Off to his right, Dr. Heinz Pfalzgraff and his wife Thelma, both bespectacled and pale, both wearing gray suits, were listening patiently to an apparently emotional diatribe being given by one of His Excellency the minister's assistants. Pfalzgraff puffed constantly on a briar pipe, one thick finger in the bowl, tamping it. He nodded from time to time, his bushy eyebrows giving his face an aging, Strangelovian wildness. His wife's eyes never stopped moving, from face to face, from painting to painting, from wall to wall, as if she were either analyzing or afraid.

Dr. Pfalzgraff was the undersecretary of defense for policy, one of a long line of defense experts who were foreign born and American educated. They seemed to have had a hold on national security issues from the time of Henry Kissinger. Rowland couldn't make any sense of that. To him it was a fad that had gone on too long. It was almost insulting to someone from middle Illinois, as if one had to be foreign in order to understand American defense issues. Pfalzgraff had come to the United States from Berlin in 1950 to study at Harvard, had met Thelma, who now was a prominent pediatrician and author, and had sought citizenship after their marriage. He had been a Harvard professor before coming into the administration.

Rowland considered Pfalzgraff to be in many ways brilliant, and in many ways completely stupid. He knew more about nuclear strategy and less about the American fighting man than anyone in the country, and yet in his present job he expounded with equal fervor on both. Just about the only contact he had with the man on the street was the twenty steps it took him to get from his Watergate apartment to his limousine, and from the limousine to the Pentagon's River Entrance. The rest of it, for more than forty years now, had been from the removed, egoistic fort of academia.

Rowland grimaced slightly, resisting the notion that he should join Pfalzgraff's audience and be lectured to. Pfalzgraff's world of Harvard students had provided him a didactic and sometimes dangerous attitude of intellectual infallibility. But Pfalzgraff was not a bad sort, and he was good at what he did know. Nuclear strategists were hard enough to come by. And so Rowland marked that corner off as friendly, although he moved away, toward the center of the room.

And there was Zara Boles, off to Rowland's left, worked up about something as usual. Zara had been a Missouri congresswoman for eight years, and had served with Rowland on the House Armed Services Committee. She had been a good friend, and Rowland had worked the system hard to help her become secretary of the navy three years before. She and he shared the same view of Ronald Holcomb. She was in many ways Rowland's most trusted source inside the Pentagon.

Now she had a small crowd assembled and was entertaining, pulling facts out of the air regarding history and current programs, taunting different people who offered rejoinders, cajoling others who were quiet, all the while joking. Zara talked with her hands, captivating people with the intensity of her face and the coaxing, preacherlike tone of her voice. And she was one of perhaps five people whom Doc Rowland liked and trusted enough to call a friend.

There she went again, her small hands slicing through the air, her blue eyes flashing. Watching Zara Boles reminded Rowland of other days and he felt nostalgic, as if he were her father or perhaps simply a proud tutor. He laughed, for the first time meaning it, and for the first time feeling at ease. Now she feigned exasperation in order to nail down a point. It was marvelous, marvelous. How he wished she were back on the Armed Services Committee!

"You know," said Rowland, moving into the group, "she talks with her hands like that because in Missouri you've got to move your hands all the time or the horseflies carry you away."

Zara flashed a girlish grin that made her look twenty years younger than her forty-eight years. She cradled his elbow in one arm, as if presenting him to the others. "But that's because we still have a few *farms* left in Missouri. You don't have any bugs left in southern Illinois because they can't suck the sweat out of an abandoned barn! How are you, Doc?"

"How am I? Don't you read the *Post*?"

Zara eyed the others in the group, who included General Roger Francis, the Chairman of the Joint Chiefs of Staff, and his wife Alicia; Evan Cartledge, the assistant secretary of defense for manpower and personnel, and his wife Carolyn; and Drake Phillips, the Pentagon's comptroller. "We were just talking about that."

"Well, I know who did it," railed Doc Rowland. "And I won't forget it."

"We know you won't, Doc," answered Zara, who then grew coy. "Of course, I don't know who you're talking about. But times will be tough the next time he has to testify in front of your committee."

"You can count on that." Rowland now bored in on General Francis. "Now, what I want to know is who the hell gave the secretary of defense a Distinguished Flying Cross? Not that I've got anything personal against the man, but what does a secretary of defense do to win a DFC, General?"

Francis bit his words off carefully, obviously embarrassed by the question. "Secretary Holcomb, as you know, is a helicopter pilot in the Army Reserves. It seems he landed a chopper in a bad rainstorm not long ago, during a drill weekend."

"Yeah, and then what?" Rowland eyed the general impatiently, as if waiting for more. "Did a war come in the wake of the rain? Did he go out and rescue wounded soldiers under fire? Did he land on top of San Juan Hill?"

They all chuckled at the reference to Holcomb's idol, Teddy Roosevelt. General Francis, who now seemed deeply embarrassed, shrugged helplessly. "Mr. Chairman, I'm sorry. I'd rather you raise the matter directly with Secretary Holcomb."

"General, with all due respect, you disappoint me," said Rowland. "How can a man be secretary of defense and fly in the Reserves? Is he going to fly his helicopter when a war comes, or run the Defense Department? This is nothing but a game. Why didn't he fly a helicopter in Vietnam? Then he could have tried for a real DFC.''

To press the matter further would be to put General Francis's loyalties at issue, so Rowland ended up shrugging also. ''Well, maybe I'll ask him for a report. Make that nine hundred and *one* reports you all owe me. And then that fellow Zingerle can write another column.''

After the others moved along to join different groups, Zara slapped her old friend and mentor on the stomach, as if she were angry at him. ''General Francis isn't that bad, Doc. He's one of the few who *doesn't* play those games. Why'd you do that?''

''I didn't do any more than Holcomb would do to me. I hate the son of a bitch.''

''Yeah, but you seem to like his wife.''

''What are you talking about, Zara?''

Ron Holcomb entered the room and stood facing the crowd, urging them toward the upstairs dining area. Zara took Doc Rowland by the elbow and moved him forward. ''I've known you a long time, Doc. You and she were getting pretty cozy over on the other side of the room.''

''Balderdash.''

Zara dismissed it, her eyes still knowing. ''Okay. Balderdash it is.''

Holcomb had positioned himself at the bottom of the stairs. Rowland and Zara began inching toward the stairs along with the others. She spoke softly to him as they walked.

''General Francis and I were talking about this Red Sea problem. He's worried because Holcomb has cut him out of the loop. It's getting out of hand.''

''How can Holcomb cut the Chairman of the Joint Chiefs of Staff out of the loop?''

''The President trusts him implicitly. He talks directly to

Mulcahy on the KY-fifty-nine radio, from his office. It's absolutely secure. Francis is worried that the two are pushing this crisis along, rather than reacting to it.''

"He's the highest-ranking military man in the country. Why doesn't he do something? Call Mulcahy? Tell the President? Face down Holcomb in his office, one on one?''

"What's he going to tell the President? I told you, Holcomb is golden with Ev Lodge. Anyway, he's listening, Doc. That's about all he can do.'' Zara smiled confidingly. "Anything the KY-fifty-nine can scramble, General Francis's people can unscramble. But it's too early to do more than that.''

"Well I'll tell you one thing,'' said Rowland, all the while smiling to others as they ascended the stairs. "I'm done keeping my mouth shut about Nakashitona. Your man's getting both barrels, starting tomorrow.''

"Be careful, Doc,'' said Zara Boles. "Ron Holcomb plays this town like a violin.''

5

The evening before Ronald Holcomb's departure for Japan, he and Janet entertained several guests in the President's box at the Kennedy Center, where *Cats* was making a record-setting return run. Among his guests was his old friend John Michaels, who had been secretary of defense a few years earlier. Holcomb and Michaels had served together on the National Security Council in the Nixon administration, and in the State Department during the early years of the Reagan administration. Michaels had introduced Holcomb to Ev Lodge at a private dinner ten years before, and had been instrumental in convincing the President to appoint Holcomb as defense secretary.

As the theater filled with joyous music and colorfully costumed actors, Holcomb and Michaels eased out of their seats, and moved into the sitting room behind the box.

Holcomb closed the door that led to the theater seats, went to the refrigerator and pulled out a bottle of champagne. The small green bottle had the President's seal on it. Holcomb popped the lid and poured two glasses, handing one to his old friend.

Michaels was profiting enormously from his years in government. He served full-time as president of the Jefferson Group, a leveraged-buyout firm financed by Japan's Sukihara Bank. Since Michaels had taken over the Jefferson Group, they had purchased, with Japanese money, a chemical plant in Ohio, a nationally based real estate group, three television stations, and Brainchild Industries, which provided computer services to the Department of Defense. In addition, he was making more than half a million dollars a year for sitting on the boards of eleven different corporations, running the gamut from defense contractors to food concerns to a British-owned hotel chain.

They sat across from each other at a small circular table. Inside the theater, the crowd applauded loudly. Holcomb, knowing the first act would end in a few minutes, leaned across the table and spoke without preamble.

"I've got problems with Doc Rowland on Nakashitona," said Holcomb. "I told him we needed some time and he slowed down for a day or two. But he's back at it again."

"Doesn't he understand the stakes?" Michaels shook his head as if Doc Rowland were a fool. "This isn't 1945. Hell, it isn't even *1985*! If his bill passes, the Japanese are going to take us to the mat. They've been financing our national debt for years. They'll stop buying Treasury bills. The stock market will go down to zero in three days. Everett Lodge would become Herbert Hoover in two weeks."

"You're preaching to the choir," answered Holcomb. "And I can't have Rowland off his leash if I'm going to make this thing go away."

"I know how to get to him," said Michaels, now flashing a comfortable grin. "Sukihara Bank is financing a buyout in his district."

"I heard that. Akasaka Industries," said Holcomb with a knowing look. He raised his glass as if making a toast. "Well, whatever you can do."

"For the good of the country," answered Michaels. Inside, the first act was winding up. Michaels sipped his champagne. "How's our old friend Mad Dog Mulcahy? I've got plans for him in the Jefferson Group when he retires, you know."

"He's on the way to the Red Sea."

"*What?*"

"Things are heating up out there," said Holcomb. "Mad Dog is on the *Roosevelt*, with the troops. You'll be reading about it in a few days."

Then he turned to greet wives and other friends who were now moving into the sitting room for the intermission.

CHAPTER 6
DJIBOUTI

1

The little S-3 aircraft dropped suddenly from the sky onto the narrow runway, and churned quickly to a halt. Outside, the landscape was desolate and gray, as hollow as the moon.

"Why in hell's name would anybody want to fight over *this*?" asked Bill Fogarty.

"You know what Sun Tzu said," answered Captain David Mosberg as he unbuckled his seat belt. " 'In the dead zone, fight.' Well, welcome to the dead zone."

"I thought he was talking about your crotch."

"What are you, a stand-up comic?" Mosberg was manacling a briefcase to his left wrist. "This isn't a very funny situation, you know."

"Well, no bullshit," said Fogarty. "The intelligence officer, who will make the assessment and then sit on the ship while I get my ass handed to me, has finally figured out that this isn't going to be funny."

"Why don't you stop whining, Fogarty? Nobody forced

you to command a MEU.'' Mosberg peered out of the window. "Anyway, clean up your mind, if that's possible. Here comes the jeep.''

Fogarty stood, preparing to exit the aircraft. "I wouldn't mind a few answers, you know. Your admiral is an asshole. How can you stand the guy?''

The crew chief had opened the S-3 aircraft's door only a few seconds before, but already Mosberg's face was flushed from the heat. He now gasped from the windblast as he stepped out of the plane. "Him? What about you? The admiral may be an asshole, but he's an admiral. You're an asshole, and you're only a colonel.''

Bill Fogarty followed Mosberg out of the aircraft, stepping onto what he was sure was the hottest piece of ground his feet had ever touched. He squinted, even behind dark sunglasses, at the arid wasteland that surrounded the Djibouti airport, as he searched for the jeep that Mosberg had already spied. An oven breeze devoid of comfort burned his lungs and sucked the moisture greedily from his face and arms, making him feel baked and broiled in his first minute on the ground. Finally the jeep zipped onto the runway. It halted next to them, and a huge soldier jumped easily out of the passenger side.

"You are Capitaine Mosberg and Colonel Fogarty? I am Sergent-Chef Planitzer. Come with me.''

Fogarty immediately recognized the man's uniform: The tall, deeply tanned sergeant was a member of the 13th Demibrigade of the French Foreign Legion, outposted on Djibouti. He wore khaki shorts, and a khaki shirt that hung loose on his muscled frame. The shirt was open along the sides, fixed by straps below the shoulders and at the waist. It appeared to have the texture of tissue paper. His desert boots were also khaki-colored and light, and were topped by tan socks that had been folded down over the boots themselves. A green beret, the hallmark of the Legion, angled jauntily over his left ear. He wore a khaki-colored web belt with shoulder suspenders. On the belt was a canteen of water, a first-aid pouch, and a bayonet with a tan handle.

Fogarty noted that Mosberg was holding back a shiver as they absorbed the wave of ferocity that emanated from this blue-eyed, cold-faced sergeant. Planitzer's head was shaved. His thick shoulders and tree-stump arms that hung from the open shirt gave him the build of a weight lifter. A large tattoo covered most of his left forearm, the continent of Africa pointing like a dagger from elbow to wrist, a naked woman and a leaping panther superimposed over it. The word "*Legion*" was written in large script at its base, inside a scroll.

"Over *here*."

The sergeant turned immediately away from them, and walked toward his sand-colored jeep. His accent was unmistakably German. They followed Sergeant Planitzer into the jeep, and Fogarty was further surprised to see a rugged Vietnamese man, also dressed in the minimal uniform that the Legion wore in the desert, as the driver. The Vietnamese soldier seemingly ignored them. He stared straight ahead through the windshield, his full lips pressed together. Shrapnel from some long-ago explosion had scooped out a divot of flesh from his cheek, and another on his right shoulder.

Mosberg elbowed Fogarty as they climbed into the rear seat, and almost whispered. "That driver reminds me of a pit bulldog, right after they chop its tail off."

Fogarty grunted. "Well, now that's an area where you qualify as an expert witness. Ask him if his name is Mad Dog."

"You better get your mind right or you'll ruin your career. The admiral doesn't like you."

"I don't give a rat's ass if he likes me or not. That's the problem with the Navy—you guys running around, sweating bullets over whether the admiral is going to let you kiss his ass." Fogarty peered out at the arid, salt-stained fields. "Anyway, what's he going to do, send me to *Djibouti*?"

Sergeant Planitzer was ignoring them. He reached over and nudged the Vietnamese man in the small of his back, a command. "*Quartier Gabode, Caporal Tranh.*"

The jeep lurched forward. Outside the airport it halted briefly at a roadblock manned by a tall, black Djiboutan, a member of the National Gendarmerie. He and the Vietnamese driver conversed in French, smiling at each other with the knowing, secret cynicism of soldiers. Fogarty grinned as he watched Mosberg clutch the locked and manacled briefcase to his stomach. The German and the Vietnamese Legionnaires were indeed ferocious, but not unlike many marines he had known. He could feel their intensity, and their almost palpable dislike of Mosberg's softness.

At the same time, despite the argumentative bantering that had now gone on for two days, Fogarty liked the brainy captain, and felt protective of him. He leaned toward Mosberg, an act of camaraderie, again almost whispering. "I wonder if these guys understand that you're carrying photographs that'll keep their sorry, arrogant asses alive."

"I wonder if they care about *being* alive?"

Planitzer raised his head sharply in the front seat, indicating that he had heard and was taking offense. Still, Mosberg continued in a soft near-whisper. "These are men who'll throw away their lives over a whore in a bar, Fogarty. Or a bad deal in a card game."

"The whore I'll fight for. I don't play cards."

"Come on, I mean it! Do they know what I'm carrying in this bag? Would it have the kind of value to them that might tempt them to drive to some spot out in the desert and cut my throat?"

Watching Mosberg's face, it appeared to Fogarty that the intelligence officer was imagining them doing just that—cutting through his jugular with a knife and then hacking off his arm at the wrist in order to undo the manacle. He now spoke louder, having decided to placate Planitzer without acknowledging that the sergeant was even listening.

"No way, Mosberg. They've already run to the end of the earth. That briefcase won't buy them anything. This is the best they'll ever do. The discipline and fraternity of the

Legion, a life whose only demands are from the Legion, and whose only loyalties are to it. They may hate you and me, and they may kill for a piece of ass. But they won't betray the Legion."

Planitzer turned slowly around in his seat and fixed Fogarty with a steely smile. "*Merci, mon Colonel.*"

The jeep drove along a stark, palm-lined square, past cafés and bars and hotels whose peeling Moorish architecture reminded Fogarty of the Buster Crabbe movies of his youth. Here and there off to the west, through the spaces in the buildings, he could see the royal blue waters of the Gulf of Tadjoura. Djibouti's deep-water port had historical importance to the French, who once had colonized the small country and named it French Somaliland. From Djibouti, naval forces might control the gateway to the Red Sea by interdicting shipping in the narrow straits called the Bab el Mandeb.

Fourteen years after the end of colonization, the French continued to protect Djibouti with a sizable full-time garrison—their largest base outside France itself. The permanent force of six thousand men included two infantry regiments, one of them the Legionnaire demibrigade, three squadrons of tanks, two light artillery batteries, antiaircraft units, a few ships, and two air force squadrons, one of Alouette helicopters and the other Mirage Interceptors. The French remained at the request of their former colony, which periodically was threatened from Ethiopia and Somalia alike. But the French were not reluctant to stay. The port was a key feature of the Horn of Africa. It was sometimes used for refueling by the United States Navy as well.

And now the permanent force was buttressed by units from France's Rapid Reaction Force. Fogarty could see the gray silhouettes of several recently arrived amphibious assault ships nestled in the harbor. They had come into the Red Sea through the Suez Canal, from their home port in Toulon. One of the ships was the *Foudre*, a new TCD landing ship capable of transporting a mechanized regiment, and also housing a thirty-bed hospital that could be rapidly expanded once a battle began. He knew that other troops had been flown into Djibouti from France by a combined fleet of commercial aircraft and C-160 transports. Six thousand more French soldiers were either bivouacked ashore or berthed on board the amphibious ships, comprising the main elements of a light armored division. The French units on Djibouti were backed by the aircraft carrier *Clemenceau* and two other combatants out in the Gulf of Aden.

Twenty combatant ships from the American Navy were slowly converging on the crucial straits as well. The *Independence* battle group had moved from the western Indian Ocean into the vicinity of Socotra, and the *Roosevelt* carrier battle group was now nearing the Arabian Sea. Fogarty and Mosberg had left it only twelve hours before.

Along the edges of the square, the bars and shops were busy, even in the unbearable heat. Small tables in the shade of the café terraces were filled with tough-looking French soldiers, Afar men swaddled in white, and European outcasts who sat lazily in their chairs and drank cold Kronenbourg beer imported from Alsace. Even in the middle of the day the terraces and the bars were dotted here and there with tall, beautiful African prostitutes, drawn from Somalia and Ethiopia and even Kenya by the lure of Legionnaire money. The Legionnaires were paid well, and they were known for throwing away their money. Several years before, one of their armored car units had driven off into the desert on an operation, bringing a mobile brothel filled with well-compensated ladies along with them.

The jeep approached an old fort, replete with turrets at its corners. Behind its white walls, Fogarty could see the tricolor flag of France, curling and snapping in the hot breeze. Another hard, tanned soldier waved them through the gate, his face holding the timeless intensity of a warrior on duty. They drove around the edges of a baked parade ground, now uncharacteristically made into a parking lot for jeeps, armored reconnaissance vehicles, and military trucks. Finally the jeep stopped in front of the headquarters building.

Sergeant Planitzer again jumped easily out of the jeep, and led them to the doorway of the headquarters. Inside, the huge soldier walked briskly past another guard without even acknowledging his presence, and then knocked on a closed door. When the door opened, Planitzer spoke quickly in his gutteral version of French, and then waved at Fogarty and Mosberg, pressing his hand against the captain's back as he ushered them quickly into the room. His assignment completed, Sergeant Planitzer gave the general a stiff salute and disappeared.

2

Général de Division Jean-François Avice stood behind a field desk in the starkly furnished room, scowling at first toward the door and then giving a small nod when he saw the two Americans. Off to one side next to a window, two other senior army officers sat at a makeshift conference table. They did not rise when Fogarty and Mosberg entered the room. All three men were smoking cigarettes. The air of the room was oppressive with smoke.

Fogarty noticed that General Avice wore the uniform of an airborne soldier rather than that of a Legionnaire. His shorts and uniform shirt were a dark khaki that was almost green. The epaulets on his short-sleeved shirt had three stars on each of his shoulders. His boots and socks were black, heavier than the sand-colored desert boots of the Legion.

The general was a squat little man with a wide, hairy face and a prominent nose. He had small brown eyes. His eyebrows were so bushy that they gave his face a pinched look as they shadowed his eyes and reached toward his close-cropped hair. Although he had shaved that morning, his jaws had a metallic sheen from the heaviness of his beard. He coolly stubbed out his cigarette in a metal ashtray as he inspected Fogarty and then Mosberg, using his thumb to smash the burning ashes. Then he came forward from behind his desk and greeted the Americans in French, even going so far as introducing the other two officers in his native tongue.

Fogarty glanced uneasily at Mosberg, speaking under his breath. "What's with all this Frog talk?"

"It's a game, dummy," answered Mosberg. "If you haven't figured that out, maybe you ought to go in the other room and lift weights with your buddy Planitzer."

"So what are you going to do?"

"Just shut up. You're embarrassing your country. Not to mention me."

Mosberg ignored Fogarty now. He stepped into the middle of the room, looking foolish with the case chained to his arm, his morose face with its receding hairline now deep red from the heat. Then he began to talk to the general and the others in fluent Russian, expressing his embarrassment at being unable to converse in French, but suggesting that perhaps they try Spanish. And suddenly they all began to laugh.

"*Da, da, da, horosho, speceba, gespeda,*" said General Avice, taking the point and then shifting to English. "So, Captain Mosberg, at least you are not English. We speak to the English only in French, or through interpreters." The general now gestured toward Fogarty. "And your friend, here, he is a very brave man. He calls us 'Frogs' to our face!"

"Don't give him too much credit, General. A lot of courage begins with stupidity."

Fogarty stepped forward and extended his hand. "Colonel Bill Fogarty, General."

"Fogarty?" Avice gave an impish smile as he shook hands. "Irish. It is no problem, Colonel. To be Irish in the modern world is an impossible burden."

"Yes, sir," answered Fogarty. "But that's why we took America away from the English."

"Ah, the Colonel is not only brave, he is funny."

"It isn't funny if you're English."

Mosberg shrugged at the French officers, who now were smiling so fondly that he expected them to break out the wine. "Why do the French and the British still hate each other so much? I've never been able to understand that."

General Avice laughed warmly, eyeing his fellow officers with conspiratorial delight. "Oh, we do not hate the English. We just cannot understand them!" Avice saw that Mosberg seemed confused. "You must think of it this way, Capitaine. We are a nation with more than three hundred different cheeses. In France, every day at lunch we rub our hands together and try to decide which one will be the best for that day. And the English? The English have one famous cheese—how do you say it, Stilton? And every day at lunch they argue over whether to cut it with a fork or a knife."

The general shrugged helplessly, making his point as the other two French officers laughed. "You see? For us it is the cheese that is important. For them, it is the argument. For us, life is pleasure, interrupted by debate. For them, pleasure is the debate itself. They love to argue about rules! And so we do not understand them." He shrugged again. "If you want to understand the English, ask a Belgian."

"If you want to understand the French," said Mosberg, "ask God."

"Ah, *oui*," laughed Avice. "Because God is French."

The group of men were now standing in a comfortable circle in the center of the small office, as if they were conversing at a cocktail party. Bill Fogarty had taken an immediate liking to the tough, witty Avice. Now he grinned and shrugged also. "Well, I thank God I'm an American. It's easier when you know you're hated by *everybody*."

General Avice and his officers laughed approvingly and elbowed each other, deciding that these Americans were indeed clever fellows.

It seemed rather odd for them to be joking about such ancient hostilities in the heat and dust of northern Africa, but at the same time it represented a part of the reason they all were there. Britain had once controlled a portion of Somalia, just to the east of Djibouti, as well as Aden, immediately across the narrow Bab el Mandeb. Aden was now a Communist state, the People's Democratic Republic of Yemen. Somalia had vacillated like a pendulum between East and West for years. The Italians had once held Ethiopia and a portion of Somalia, as well as Libya. The British had held the Sudan and Kenya. The French had been the masters of northern and western Africa. Old antagonisms lay just below the surface, just as surely in Africa as in the cemeteries of Europe.

Finally, as if an appropriate interval had passed, Avice nodded toward Mosberg's briefcase. "So, Capitaine, you have something for us."

Mosberg took out a key and unlocked the manacle on his wrist. Then he set the case down on the makeshift conference table, quickly working the combination on its lock. The general smilingly apologized for the table. "Sorry we are not so lavish out here, Capitaine. This is not like your *amiral*'s office. But then we do not have your defense budget."

"No, this is fine, General. You obviously haven't had to spend much time at sea if you think this is crowded."

"Ah yes. Admiral Mad Dog Mulcahy is coming west, to sail in harm's way with his battle group." General Avice was caustic, and yet impressed.

"Yes. Colonel Fogarty and I flew in from the *Roosevelt* battle group. They're still a few days out. But the admiral will be here. Don't worry about that."

"He and Arneaux Humbert, they are of the same school. They like to be up front, with the men. And in fact, they did study together, no?"

"At our National War College, as I recall. The admiral has a great deal of admiration for General Humbert, as you know."

"Humbert is a great military leader. France is very lucky

to have kept him, after the problems of the late nineteen fifties. He was a sympathizer in the revolt of the generals, you know. I studied under Humbert when I was a young man at Saint-Cyr. Tactics. He taught us the lessons of the Algerian campaign. And then when I was a student at the École Supérieure de Guerre, he was leading the fight in Chad. I volunteered to join his command there after I left the École. A brilliant leader. It is, how do you put it, ironic that our general and your admiral became friends so long ago, yes?''

"Yes. Or maybe fortunate.''

"Let's just stick with ironic,'' interrupted Fogarty.

"I should warn you,'' explained Mosberg. "Colonel Fogarty is yet to be convinced that his marines would serve any useful purpose in the Eritrean desert.''

"Then he shouldn't worry,'' said Avice. "We don't need your men, Colonel Fogarty. But we do appreciate your information.'' Avice tilted his head, studying Fogarty again. "Why are you here, if you don't like what we're doing?''

"Please, General.'' Fogarty fended off Avice's words with an upheld hand, conveying a sincere respect for the French officer. "I don't disapprove of what you're doing. To be honest, I don't even *know* what you're doing. I just don't see how my country fits into it. But anyway, Admiral Mulcahy wants me to take a look at your people. The admiral is very thorough.''

"Colonel Fogarty is the admiral's jaundiced eye,'' said Mosberg.

"We don't need your men,'' said Avice again. "And we don't need to be inspected. This is a—*little matter* of pride.'' And then he shrugged it off, focusing again on Mosberg's bag. "But we have nothing to hide from you. In our opinion you are here as an observer, and not an inspector, Colonel. Look around all you want. Now. Capitaine?''

Mosberg pulled out a zippered plastic pouch. A red stripe covered the outside of the pouch, marked TOP SECRET AMIDON in large white letters. The three French officers now sat across from the two Americans in their small metal chairs, staring intently forward, waiting.

Mosberg looked at the general again, feeling a bit hesitant as he unzipped the pouch. "I know I don't need to say this, General, but this is what we call back-channel communications in the Navy. It involves 'NO FORN' intelligence, meaning we're not supposed to share it with foreign nationals. If it got into the hands of the wrong people, it would enable the Soviets to determine just how good our aircraft photography units really are. I don't have the authority to give you these, but the admiral wanted me to talk to you through the pictures."

"Of course, of course." Avice took another cigarette from a light blue pack that Mosberg recognized as Gauloise, then tamped its unfiltered end against a knuckle before lighting it with a wooden match. He then inhaled the strong smoke deeply, waiting. One of the officers placed a large map of western Djibouti and eastern Ethiopia on the table in front of him, ready to copy the information from the photographs onto the map.

Mosberg took out a stack of black-and-white photographs, and then put both the pouch and his briefcase on the floor underneath him. "The Cubans have moved what looks like a heavy division to the head of their column, with some very good Soviet armor and artillery assets. This is new stuff. I know you have some intelligence on that already."

"Yes, but this will be helpful."

"The overall commander is General Abelardo Valdez, who also is the commander of the Cuban division. He is a good soldier, experienced in this part of the world. He was a hero in the Ogaden battles of 1977. But he has never commanded anything this large before. He's known as cautious in his preparations, but quite bold once a battle begins. He led a battalion deep into the Somali rear during the Ogaden fighting, taking a page out of Rommel's attacks in North Africa in 1942. At the same time, he's been trained in the Soviet Union. You can expect him to conduct a very

careful reconnaissance, and to use a heavy artillery bombardment before any attack.''

"Yes," said General Avice. "That will give us time."

"But not much. The main elements are within twenty
miles of Manda, which is just across from the Eritrean
border. Let me put this collage together for you." Mosberg
noticed one of the officers marking Manda on the map as
he assembled the photographs. "They're less than a hundred
miles from Assab right now. Our guess is that they'll move
their reconnaissance units forward within the next few days
and begin to probe the defenses at Assab."

"They are a long way from Addis Ababa," said General
Avice, waiting for Mosberg to put the photographs in order
so that they showed the road leading up to Manda, and the
Cuban forces there. "Maybe two hundred fifty kilometers?
And the rebels in Tigray Province are active, also. The
Cubans will be trapped if they cannot link up with the
Russian resupply at Assab."

"Yes, that's true," answered Mosberg, putting his finger
on a town almost midway between the Ethiopian capital and
Manda. "But they've put a good-sized base here at Dese.
Well-defended, no problem with Tigrayans. Helicopters and
supplies, a small hospital. And they're putting in some
infrastructure that can handle MIGs."

"I know Dese," answered Avice. "Even Dese is a long
way from their forward units."

The other two officers began to talk animatedly to each
other in French as they studied the photographs, which
showed with striking clarity the hulking guns and modern
tanks of the Cuban advance. They pointed to the 152-
millimeter artillery pieces, and to the SA-6 antiaircraft systems that formed a wide perimeter near Manda, facing outward in all directions.

General Avice dragged on his cigarette, chatting comfortably with his officers as he pointed here and there on
the photographs. He waved a hand at Mosberg and then
touched the SA-6s, as if to say there was no problem.

"These we know from Chad. The artillery, that is a surprise. And the tanks, they are very good, very fast tanks. Where is their reconnaissance?"

Mosberg pointed further along the road, toward Manda. "They have a battalion deployed ahead of them. It hasn't moved in the last twenty-four hours. We think Valdez is waiting for some of the Ethiopian straggler units to catch up with the column before he kicks off. The Ethiopians have had problems with their combat support units. They're short on trucks."

"The Ethiopians are terrible soldiers," said Avice. "They have no leaders. They run away. They leave their tanks and artillery for the Eritreans. The Cubans will do better to forget them."

"No," said Fogarty, speaking for the first time. "They need to leave the Ethiopians in the towns they conquer."

"Then they'll have no use for them!" Avice and his officers laughed heartily at the general's joke.

Mosberg traced an imaginary line across the photographs, on the other side of Manda. "In spite of the propaganda about this being an internal dispute, they're being very careful about the Eritrean boundary. They believe the provincial border will give them a sanctuary. Even though their supply lines are extended, it appears to us that they believe they can always retreat back across the border if things go wrong."

Avice and his officers continued to point at different elements of the reconnaissance battalion, talking rapidly to each other in French. The officer with the map was carefully marking positions and weapon systems, nodding in agreement with the general every few seconds.

Avice seemed inordinately pleased. He patted Mosberg on the shoulder, and pulled out another cigarette. "This man Valdez is a careful planner, and yet he has a very weak reconnaissance battalion! Motorcycles and BRDMs. *Motorcycles* in the desert! This isn't 1942. A couple of the BRDMs come with SAGGER missiles, but the range of the SAGGER is only three kilometers. He may have been a hero in the Ogaden, but we are not the Somali army, Captain Mosberg. You met Sergent-Chef Planitzer? A tough man, yes? There are many like him. My soldiers will run from nothing.''

General Avice patted Mosberg again, as if deciding that they had become great friends. He and his officers carried the beginnings of a breathless excitement in their faces and in the way they touched the photographs and marked their map. "And this general may be a brave man, but he has made a mistake. We will take the battle from him! His reconnaissance, look at this." Avice touched the photographs again, clucking his tongue. "Ah. We will be outgunned, but we will take away the general's eyes and ears. And then he will have to fight us deaf and blind.''

Avice looked at Fogarty again, with challenge in his small eyes. "Is that the way you see it, Colonel?"

"More or less. If I were fighting him I'd go after his reconnaissance elements right off the bat," said Fogarty, holding the little man's gaze. "With our rules of engagement, they'd have to fire the first shot, though. Particularly on the soil of a third''—he hesitated, thinking of the complicated sovereignty of Eritrea—"or maybe fourth nation. But I'd do it with close air support off the aircraft carrier, at least to start. We don't have the armored capability that you do. I guess you'd do it on the ground. I don't know. I haven't gotten a look at your units yet.''

"Then go see for yourself.'' The general's face crinkled into a merry smile. He patted Fogarty on one heavy shoulder. "You brought an extra set of uniforms, no?"

"Actually I did. The captain and I are supposed to spend the night here.''

"Oh, no, no!'' The general and his two staff officers watched Fogarty with a measure of ironic relief, as if they could finally let him in on the secret they had been hiding since he had arrived. "I have a message for you from the *amiral*. He wants you to observe us in the field. You are coming with us to Assab, Colonel!''

3

In the afternoon, Fogarty walked among the French soldiers as they returned from liberty and broke their bivouacs. Their mood was solemn as they took down their tents and carefully folded their shelter halves and sleeping mats and light, thin blankets. Few took notice of the American colonel as they filled their canteens and the "buffalo" tanks that would be pulled behind supply trucks with the last fresh water they would see for at least a day and perhaps two. They cleaned their weapons and drew fresh rations of ammunition and food. Those who had families wrote letters. By dusk they were milling about near their staging points, chattering and smoking, their faces filled with dread and a nervous excitement.

They formed in company units of 150 men and waited in the baked, salty dirt as the hot sun fell behind the mountains. The trucks came and the subdued soldiers climbed into the beds with their packs and helmets and rifles. They sat next to each other on benches, sweating in the heat, bent like old men, their packs heavy on their backs and their rifles between their knees. The Renault TRMs ground along sandy roads past the stark, somnolent square with its lazy palms and quiet bars and beautiful whores, leaving the town and moving in a snaking, dusty column to the port, where it brought them to the ships.

On the ships there were crew-served weapon systems that would land with them: tanks, armored personnel carriers, some mounted with HOT and Milan antitank missiles, towed 155-millimeter howitzers, a battery of Roland antiaircraft missiles, more jeeps, more trucks. And more men. The ships smelled of oil and stale food and the sailors of the crews joked sympathetically with the onloaded soldiers.

Fogarty boarded a creaking LST with General Avice's command group. Although he normally did not smoke, he accepted a cigarette from the feisty Frenchman and dragged deeply on it as the ship powered slowly out of port. The harsh tobacco smoke soiled the inside of his mouth, but somehow the pain inside his lungs calmed his fears.

"So, Colonel," said Avice. "You come with me in my command vehicle when we land. You will get a good look at my soldiers."

"You have good soldiers," answered Fogarty. "I've been with troops for more than half my life. I can tell a lot by the way an army breaks camp and makes a movement. These are well-disciplined, serious men."

"And they can fight," said Avice. "If we have to." The general paused. The two men stared at the white, baked earth and the patches of coral in the shallow waters that surrounded the port, then out to the rich, almost sterile beauty of the hot sea in the Gulf of Tadjoura. "And I think we will have to."

The flat plains of Yemen fell into the sea on the other side of the Bab el Mandeb. Across the strait there had been a sandstorm, and its leavings hung over the sea like a nasty yellow fog. The fog awakened the terror-filled dream that had haunted Fogarty since he had left Subic Bay. In the dream his assault helicopters were churning through the windblown sand. The blades were slowing down as it choked their gearboxes, and his boots were slowly being covered with sand that was blowing through the helicopter windows. They were two thousand feet above the desert, inside shuddering metal coffins. The enemy was below, laughing as the sand enveloped them. And they were going to die.

The ship began to tremble, and then they pulled out into the gulf, heading north. As it grew dark they passed the Musha Islands, small pocks in the open water where other ships had clashed with the coral and sunk years before.

By midnight they were landing in the salty marshes at Obock, protected from Cuban view by a string of mountains that surrounded the small port like a garland of pearls. The soldiers stumbled and cursed as they offloaded their equipment and found the narrow road that followed the coastline. Fogarty joined the general in his command vehicle as the French column filled the road. They bounced and jolted as the column moved forward. The air inside was stale, and smelled of fuel. He felt vaguely sick, and as lonely as he could ever remember. He was functionless, an ornament inside the cramped vehicle. Avice was ignoring him now, intense and serious as he took radio reports from his commanders.

They traveled all night, halting for two hours to consolidate the column at an old French fort at Ado Bouri, which was only five miles from the Eritrean border. Ado Bouri also looked out at the narrowest point of the Bab el Mandeb. As dawn came Fogarty sat on top of the halted command vehicle, staring out at a long, snaking column of tanks and personnel carriers and trucks. He fought back his weariness as he ate cold rations and sipped from a canteen and chain-smoked five more cigarettes. His green camouflage uniform was now filthy, stiff from sweat and salt water and the blowing dirt. He stank and his mouth was foul from tobacco and carrion. It had been one day, but he felt as though he had always been a useless, isolated observer, and as though the column had been on the move forever.

In the early morning light, Fogarty could see Perim Island less than ten miles away inside Bab el Mandeb. Perim was a Yemeni base. General Avice appeared at his side, taking a short cigarette break, and pointed out toward the island.

"We are being observed. The column will be reported. In a few hours, the Cubans will know."

And so it was time to make the fateful leap. They burst across the Eritrean border, making the twenty-five miles to Assab in time for lunch. They drove into the town past parched, square buildings with curved archways above the doors. Hyenas and vultures flitted nearby, unafraid of the column as they scavenged food that Eritrean soldiers had tossed into the streets. Odors from outdoor toilets greeted them on every block. Petroleum storage tanks hugged the small port down at the water's edge.

The Eritrean soldiers of the Assab garrison greeted them

at first with a caution that bordered on mistrust. But after watching the French soldiers quickly and expertly place their tanks and howitzers and antiaircraft systems into a defensive perimeter, the dark, thin Eritrean soldiers mingled among the Frenchmen, taking their cigarettes and talking with their hands to indicate likely avenues of attack and their own methods of defense. A few offered French soldiers a wad of *chat* in return for the cigarettes. *Chat,* a local weed, was chewed to take one's fears and pains away.

General Avice drove immediately to the Eritrean command post, in the center of the small town. He jumped out of his command vehicle and found Fikre Desta, the Eritrean commander. Desta was small and thin, about forty years old. He greeted Avice in Italian, and Avice answered in French. Finally Desta settled on English.

"I do not speak French," Desta said apologetically.

"English is okay." Avice gestured to Fogarty. "This is Colonel William Fogarty, an American soldier. English is his only language."

Desta smiled quickly, then retreated into the solemn dignity of a frown. "So long as you don't speak Amharic," he said, referring to the language of the Ethiopian rulers. "It will get your throat cut by my soldiers. But English is okay. I studied at American school. Peace Corps."

"Ah, *oui.*" Avice peered out toward the mountains that circled Assab in the distance. "Where are your defenses?"

"I have only one thousand men. Most of our army is in Massawa or Asmara. Or on the other side, near Sudan."

Desta joined Avice and Fogarty in the back of a jeep, and they toured the perimeter. The Eritreans had six Soviet T-55 tanks, captured from the Ethiopians two years before. The tanks were well emplaced, dug into parapets and covered with desert camouflage netting. Dozens of old 20-millimeter antiaircraft guns pointed upward toward the hot sun in the searing heat. Desta's soldiers worked on the tanks, cleaned the guns, and talked lazily with each other at their defensive positions.

"They will attack soon," mused Desta. "Yesterday the MIGs came for the first time. They were very bad. The pilots were afraid, and stayed too high. They missed us completely." Desta peered steadily at Avice. "But if the Russians come from the sea we are dead. We have nowhere to go. We are too far away from the mountains to run."

"No, no. We can beat them. We are in the sea also. What you see now are my lead elements. Now we can bring in the main body by ship. By tomorrow five thousand more will have landed at your port. They are on the way from Djibouti right now." He glaned quickly at Fogarty, as if daring him to voice his dissent. "And the Americans are nearby. Soon they will have two battle groups—more than twenty ships, two hundred combat aircraft."

"The Americans?" Desta seemed incredulous, as if not believing the little town he was defending was capable of summoning such vast attention from around the world.

Bill Fogarty had been studying the Eritrean defenses. Now he ran his fingers over a growing stubble on his cheeks and chin. Finally he understood why Admiral Mad Dog Mulcahy had sent him with the French to Assab. Yes, he decided, Mad Dog was a genius. The admiral had known that once Fogarty watched the French soldiers, and caught a glimpse of the battlefield, he would weaken. Because Mad Dog knew that fighting men drift naturally and immediately away from politics once a battle is joined. Politics became irrelevant when someone was trying to kill you. You thought of getting the job done, and you weighed the personal loyalties of those around you. And Bill Fogarty had grown to like the pugnacious little French general, and to respect the men he led.

The battlefield itself had assumed a sterility, devoid of the arguments that would soon thunder in Washington, Moscow, Havana, and Paris. And anyway, maybe Mad Dog was right. Maybe a defeat here could topple the Communist government in Cuba. *These guys can beat the Cuban sons of bitches,* he decided, surprising himself with the depth of his own feelings. His eyes caressed the nearby terrain. He was already imagining where he himself might use artillery and close air support, and how he would maneuver a mobile defense.

"Yes," said Fogarty, nodding to Desta. "It is possible."

Avice reached over and patted Desta on the shoulder. "We may not need the Americans. But we are not alone."

Avice halted his jeep at the western edge of the small city. "Do you have outposts toward the Cubans?"

"We have spies everywhere. And an outpost on that mountain."

Fogarty followed Desta's pointing finger and looked west, where the land rose steadily upward. He saw the distant peak, perhaps fifteen miles from Assab. Avice had pulled out a map, and was studying it. The mountain was along the route of the Cuban advance. It showed up on the map simply as "3209," denoting its height. Avice nodded energetically, convinced that he could destroy the Cuban advance party from there.

"It is a good choice. I will put a mechanized battalion and a battery of the HOT missiles on the mountain. The Cuban reconnaissance cannot attack the mountain. They are not strong enough. I have seen the pictures. If they attack, we destroy them. If they attempt to bypass us, we will cut them off and then destroy them. If the main body attacks, we will call the outpost back to join the defense of Assab."

He patted Desta on the shoulder again, this time comfortingly. "And if they attack, then our planes will come from the sea. And the Americans will come, too, if we need them. Hundreds of planes, maybe even the Marines. And we will destroy them here."

Avice smiled brightly, his face caked with dirt from the road, and heavy with the black stubble of an unshaved beard. His eyes were glowing with the challenge.

"It's okay," he told Desta. And then he turned to Fogarty. "You've met Colonel Michel Fourcade? A great soldier. I will send his battalion to the outpost. You can go with him."

CHAPTER 7
WASHINGTON, D.C.

Roy Dombrowski leaned over and jostled Doc Rowland, then turned the corner onto K Street. The town seemed to steam in the early morning heat. The sidewalks were empty, and there was little traffic. In an hour K Street would be packed with cars and the sidewalks would be filled. But just now Washington, like the rest of America, was waking up. And Americans were waking up to *Hello America!* Yours every morning on Channel 8, live from New York and elsewhere. And Americans watching *Hello America!* were going to be treated to a visit with Doc Rowland, chairman of the House Committee on Armed Services, "the guru of defense reform."

Just now, Rowland was slumped against the far window of the car. His shirt sleeves were rolled up. His coat had been thrown casually into the backseat. His tie was knotted loosely around his neck. He snored peacefully, his mouth open and his face pointing toward the ceiling. Dombrowski hit him again as he steered the car into the left lane of the one-way street and began to slow down.

"Come on, Doc. Hey. Reveille, Mr. Chairman. We're here."

Rowland sputtered, coughed once, and opened his eyes. "We here?" He rubbed his face with a thick hand that once had spent the predawn hours milking cows and tossing bales of hay. Of course, he would be quick to remind those who asked, back then a regular old average Illinois American could afford to own and operate a farm. But like the bright dawn that lit the eastern horizons of the great Midwest with fresh promise, Doc Rowland came alive. His pale blue eyes beamed as they surveyed the front entrance to Channel 8, the local NBS affiliate, pouring light and warmth onto his surroundings.

"What time is it, Roy?"

"Six forty-eight. You're on at ten after seven. I'll drop you off and go park. You okay, Doc?"

Doc Rowland suddenly cackled, as if laughing at himself, or remembering all the reasons that he should feel miserable. "I'm good. I'm good. I'm great. If I felt any better I'd have to take pills for it." He remembered his blood pressure medication. "In fact, I *am* taking pills for it."

Rowland rubbed his face again, and its loose flesh moved around with his hand. The bags underneath his eyes were pronounced in the early morning, but the eyes themselves were as always ageless, blue and startling. Doc Rowland could sleep anywhere, and wake up singing. And he had indeed spent a lot of nights in a lot of strange places. Over the past two decades he had slept in almost every neighborhood in the Washington metropolitan area, almost always with a friend, more often than not a friend who was very attractive indeed. And he had always awakened with a smile and a fond farewell, with old Roy there to pull him out of the mire if things got too sticky.

But he'd stopped all that, or at least slowed down on it. And when it came to business, his mind could focus in immediately, with the piercing precision of a laser beam. Dombrowski halted the car in front of the entrance to the

NBS Building. Doc straightened his tie and grabbed his coat from the backseat, then called to his administrative assistant as he closed the car door.

"Be waiting right here three minutes after I'm done, Roy. You know I got that House leadership breakfast this morning."

Rowland turned and walked toward the building. He waved grandly to the guard inside the door, who recognized him immediately and let him in.

"Morning, Mr. Chairman!"

"Hey, how you doing, how you doing? You still working morning shift? When they going to give a good man an even break, that's what I want to know? Where do they want me?"

"You can go right back to Makeup, sir. Straight down the hall."

"I know where it is. Mary back there?"

"Yeah, she's back there somewhere."

Mary Thornton was sitting with the makeup attendant in the small powder room, sipping coffee from a Styrofoam cup. She gave Doc Rowland an easy smile, filled with secrets. They had met ten years before, when she was an assistant producer on *Face the Press* and Rowland was a new subcommittee chairman. She had been in her early thirties, and at the time was recently divorced. Doc Rowland, in the middle of a second unhappy marriage, had taken to her like a duck going after a june bug. She remembered him fondly, understanding as she had the limits of his ability to become involved, and needing as she did just then some affection devoid of commitment. And good old Doc Rowland had helped Mary Thornton make it through more than a few lonely nights. Dr. Feel Good, yes sir. The Ugly Duck. These days, happily remarried, she still found it in her heart to steer him toward interviews on some very good subjects. And old silver tongue never let her down.

"Hey, there, Mr. Chairman."

"Mary girl, I got up in the middle of the night just to

come see you for a few minutes. Now, what do you think of that?''

"Same old Doc. Always up, in the middle of the night.''

"Well, you always seem pretty ready yourself, sister.'' The woman applying his makeup chuckled along with them, having no hint of the innuendo in their conversation. In a few moments he was swabbed and powdered, dabbed and brushed, ready for the camera. Mary led him down a narrow hallway.

"We're in Studio A this morning. You'll have four minutes, which isn't bad for a network show, you know. Carlene Mathis will do the interview. She'll be asking you about the Nakashitona legislation, principally. She may want your view on the Red Sea crisis, too.''

"The Red Sea crisis?''

"You're slipping, Doc. It's the top of the news this morning. The whole place looks like it's ready to blow up. The French recognized Eritrea as a separate nation, and moved combat troops into a port town called Assab. The Soviets say this is an interference in the internal affairs of Ethiopia, and are protesting what they call harassment of their ships off of the coast.'' She squinched her nose, as if learning a whole new vocabulary. "Some place called the Dahlak Archipelago. They're hinting that they'll bomb the Eritrean capital if the 'harassment' continues. We're moving *two* carrier battle groups into the Arabian Sea, and President Lodge has hinted he may send forces inside the Red Sea if the Soviets become active.'' Finally she shrugged. "I don't know. But you'd better come up with something pretty quick.''

The smart son of a bitch, thought Rowland as he focused his mind, preparing to go on the air. *He's done it. He's taken the pressure off of his Nakashitona problem at the moment he's leaving to meet with the Japanese.* "All this happened overnight? It doesn't pay to go to sleep in this town. And who the hell cares about Eritrea, anyway?''

She laughed, shaking her head at his irreverence. "Well,

you'd better start caring, Doc, and quick, too. We're on the air in less than four minutes."

They entered the studio. Rowland quickly scanned the news stories in the *Post* and the *Times*, and then began focusing his mind on what might be asked about the Red Sea and especially the Nakashitona matter. His Subcommittee on Investigations, which he chaired in addition to the full committee, had held hearings the day before. There was no doubt that a major compromise of American technology had occurred, and it was clear that members of Nakashitona Industries had sold the essential elements of the Iroquois air defense system through North Korea to the Soviet Union. In the hearings he had reminded witnesses that when the United States had shared the technology with Japan three years before, he had led the protest, predicting just such a compromise. The hearings had been covered by all the television networks the evening before, and he was the pivotal person in each story.

His antennae were going giddy. Nakashitona had all the ingredients of a major scandal. It could end up with heads rolling inside the administration, particularly Ronald Holcomb's. But the President himself was still denying that the evidence pointed toward Nakashitona. Ev Lodge was simply afraid of the Japanese. Rowland was furious, and most of the congressional leadership shared that anger.

But now, with a clarity that caused him again to both curse and admire the defense secretary, he understood why Ron Holcomb had pleaded with him to go easy on Nakashitona. The Red Sea was going to be a press magnet while Holcomb made a deal with the Japanese to fix things with Nakashitona.

The hell he will, vowed Rowland as he waved to the camera crew inside the studio. "Thanks for the tip, Mary. I didn't see that. I just woke up, in fact."

"On the prowl, Doc?"

He winked as they sat him in the chair and fixed a small microphone onto his tie. "To the best of my recollection,

I slept alone last night. But I don't remember for sure. And anyway, I'm in love.''

"Love, is it? Anybody I know?"

"I damn well doubt it. But someday you might."

The sound man put an earpiece in Doc's right ear. He faced two cameras. Between them was a monitor that showed him what was actually on the air. He saw a news flash from the previous day's subcommittee hearings. He saw himself pointing the gavel from the chairman's seat, ranting angrily as Whip Stowbridge, the hapless deputy secretary of defense, sat uncomfortably in the witness chair. The sound level increased in Doc's earpiece, and he could finally hear his own voice.

"Mr. Secretary, I cannot for the life of me understand why you are quibbling about whether it was Nakashitona that leaked these secrets to the Soviets! Even the Japanese media says so! Now, the American people are furious about this loss of technology! We've been having a hard enough time keeping up with the Japanese economically, and now we're losing military secrets to the Soviets through the Japanese? It's time to draw the line, Mr. Secretary. We don't need any of this cheap stonewalling. We need the help and guidance of the administration in order to act in the best interests of our country!"

A short news flash followed, mentioning the administration's continuing refusal to point the finger at Nakashitona Industries despite clear evidence of its culpability. The announcer intoned that hearings in the matter would continue, and that many in the Congress had grown severely critical of the President's reluctance to cooperate.

A commercial came on the monitor. In New York, Carlene Mathis began talking to him. "Mr. Chairman? Good morning, sir. Can you hear me all right?"

"I hear you fine, Carlene. How are you?"

"I'm very good, thanks. That was quite a job in the hearing yesterday. Seems like we're in for another real mess, doesn't it? Why can't the Defense Department ever do anything right? Listen, we're on in about twenty seconds.''

"That's fine, that's fine."

The commercial ended. Doc Rowland sat straight in his chair as Carlene Mathis appeared on the monitor, recapping Rowland's part in the news and introducing him. He made certain to face one camera, and to hold his gaze steady. Nothing made a politician appear more shifty to a viewer than to watch his eyes dart from camera to monitor to camera. On the television sets at home it gave an interviewee a furtive look, as if he were glancing uneasily from side to side, afraid of the truth.

She began addressing him. He forced himself to smile comfortably. "Good morning, Mr. Chairman. Thanks for being with us."

"Good morning, Carlene. Good morning."

"Let's get right to the heart of things, Chairman Rowland. In the hearings yesterday a number of allegations were made directly against the President, and especially against Defense Secretary Holcomb, for his having pushed the sale of the Iroquois technology to the Japanese three years ago in the first place, and then for their lack of cooperation in determining the role of Nakashitona Industries in this technology leak. These were highly unusual, and personal attacks. You have in the past accused the Defense Department of 'obscene neglect,' I believe that is how you put it, in the management of the Iroquois defense system, and yesterday you issued some very strong language regarding the failure of the administration to come forward with a damage assessment and a clear course of action. My question is this: Do you believe the Defense Department has reached the point under Secretary Holcomb where a credible assessment of this problem is impossible, due to a conflict of interest that we might not even be aware of?"

There was nothing to gain by either going after Holcomb or defending him. Doc went right into his planned statement, his vernacular immediately improving and his face the very vision of power and sobriety. "Well, Carlene, I think we have to remember that this Nakashitona thing is a most serious matter. We're talking about the one true edge we've had on the Soviets for the past several decades, since they passed us in sheer numbers of weapons systems, both conventional and nuclear. And that edge is the technological brilliance of our people. Now, the record will show that I strongly opposed sharing the Iroquois technology with the Japanese. I even held hearings on it, after the leaks from Toshiba a few years ago that greatly aided the Soviet submarine program. Toshiba sold sensitive materials to the Soviets and what happened? Nothing. The Congress voted sanctions, and Toshiba's profits went up fifty percent in the first year of sanctions. What has happened with Nakashitona is exactly what I and some of my colleagues were predicting. From everything we can tell, the Soviets now have the Iroquois technology. This is a unique system, as you know. It can track more than twenty tactical missiles at the same time, and automatically destroy them. The Soviets can adapt their missile systems at sea and on the land once they learn how to go against Iroquois. It's unclear how much of the technology they've been able to rob, but it's possible that they can now also build their own similar system. All this, courtesy of Nakashitona.''

"Do you see motive in this on the part of the Japanese, Mr. Chairman?''

"How's that?'' He watched her pretty face on the monitor as she asked him again.

"Motive. The Japanese accused the United States of racism and economic blackmail after the Congress voted sanctions against Toshiba four years ago. Is there something to the Nakashitona situation that is not on the surface—a government involvement, perhaps?''

His heart raced. Did she know something that he did not? He forced a chuckle. "No, Carlene. At least from what I've been seeing, I would say that the Japanese motive is sheer greed. The Japanese have been buying and selling the world, and their companies don't understand or even care about the stakes in selling technology to people who might want to turn it right back around and use it against them. You know what they say where I come from. A dollar is more beautiful to a businessman than a lovely woman. Except these days I guess they've all got a yen for the yen.''

She smiled sweetly. ''I see. How about our own government? You stated that the Defense Department may be withholding information from the Congress about the extent of the damage that has been done to our national security. What possible motive would there be in that?''

''Well, that's what I can't figure out. They say they're still evaluating the matter. I appreciate the need to do that, because whatever comes out of this will have serious international repercussions. And of course the whole administration has to deal with the implications, not just the Defense Department, so they all have to come to an administration position. But I think they know a lot more than they're telling, and I don't like that.''

''Many commentators are laying this problem directly at the President's feet. Is the administration holding back because they're afraid of possible Japanese retaliation?''

Rowland immediately ducked, as was his habit. One never accepted an interviewer's conclusions, and never concluded for an interviewer. ''Well, Carlene, I guess there are those who might make that inference. Personally, I'm still looking at it.''

''Thank you, Mr. Chairman. One last question, if I might. I'm sure you've been following the events in the Red Sea over the past twenty-four hours. The Cubans, who were asked by the Ethiopian government to help restore order in that country, seem ready to do battle with the French. The French now insist that the province of Eritrea is a separate nation. The Soviets are threatening the Eritrean rebels, claiming that their anchorage in the Dahlak Archipelago has been repeatedly sabotaged. Large numbers of American and French ships appear to be on their way to the region, and soon may be inside the Red Sea. This is a highly volatile situation. Are we going to be getting involved, and more importantly, *should* the United States be playing such a high-risk game in the Red Sea of all places?''

Rowland could feel the unrelenting power of this issue, and its attraction to the media. In another day, it would overwhelm the American news machine. He decided to duck again. In a day or so he would have a feel for where it was going, and be able to position himself with a formal pronouncement. ''Carlene, I haven't seen the classified briefings on the matter yet. Of course, I've asked to be briefed on it first thing this morning. I'm very concerned, as are most government leaders, but without more information, it would be wrong for me to speculate on the matter either way.''

She smiled demurely, ending the interview. ''Thank you, Mr. Chairman. We appreciate you being with us this morning.''

''Why, you're very welcome, Carlene.''

On his way out of the studio, Mary Thornton nudged him with an elbow. ''What do you really think about this Red Sea thing? I mean, we've had so many improvements in our relations with the Soviets, and then all of a sudden here we are, on the edge of a *war*! I don't get it.''

It occurred to Doc Rowland that Mary, whose position with the network allowed her to talk with a wide variety of prominent people, could be helpful in spreading a little bile around town. The makeup lady handed him a Wetwipe as they passed her room. He quickly rubbed his forehead and underneath his eyes, removing the powder and blush. Then he handed the used Wetwipe back to the woman and continued walking with Mary.

''Thanks, honey. Well, here we've got Ron Holcomb on his way to Japan, kissing the ass of the same people who are refusing to apologize for stealing our military secrets. People are calling the President a coward for not standing up to the Japanese, so here he goes, throwing troops into some ridiculous snotsquirt battle to show he's tough. Now, where's our real problem? In the Red Sea, or with the Japanese? And you can bet that the President and Holcomb aren't going to fight *that* battle.''

"*Fight* the Japanese?"

"Stand up to them. You know what I mean.''

Doc Rowland patted Mary Thornton on the back as they reached the front door. Outside, Roy Dombrowski was waiting in the car, having already fetched it. The guard nodded to Rowland from his chair behind the desk in front of the door, and Rowland leaned over and shook his hand, winking at him and grinning. *Touch, pat, shake hands, wink, grin, wave.* Those were as much his duties as holding hearings and going on television shows.

"You take care of my friend Mary, hear?''

The guard seemed genuinely to appreciate the recognition. He smiled at his good friend Doc Rowland, chairman of the Armed Services Committee, who by now was almost his cousin. "We always take good care of Mary. See you next time, Mr. Chairman.''

"Yeah, yeah. I guess so, unless they decide to give a poor man a break and take you off that early morning shift, huh?''

"Right on!''

Doc Rowland beamed, pulling out a cigar from an inside pocket and holding it in one beefy hand.

"But you know, I don't have anything personal against Ron Holcomb. I never particularly cared for the man, but that's because he's a secretive, slimy elitist.''

"Yeah, you're right, Doc,'' said Mary Thornton, grinning, as they reached his car. "That doesn't sound personal at all.''

Inside the car, Roy Dombrowski handed him the *Post.* His administrative assistant smiled sheepishly as he drove off into traffic that had become quite busy over the past half hour.

"Sorry about the Eritrean story, Doc. I thought you were up on it.''

"Ah, don't worry about it, Roy. I think I handled it okay."

"No, you handled it perfectly." Dombrowski adjusted his sunglasses, now turning down Twenty-third Street and heading toward Constitution Avenue. "Put it back on the Pentagon until we can figure out what's going on, and then stick it through Ron Holcomb like a lance. It's going to get bigger." Dombrowski pointed to an article on the bottom of the front page, keeping his eyes on the road. "Another thing, for the Leadership breakfast. I didn't get a chance to brief you on this on the way in, but Manny Mulqueen died last night. Heart attack, from out of nowhere—boom."

"Well, what do you know," said Rowland, staring at a picture of the man who, until the moment of his death, had been the chairman of the House Committee on Administration. "Sorry to see that. Manny was a dear, dear friend." He studied the story for two or three quiet moments, and then peered at Dombrowski from the corner of one eye. His funereal pall had grown into a mischievous grin. "Great career move, though. Old Manny's been trying to make the front page of the *Post* for ten years!"

CHAPTER 8
THE HORN OF AFRICA

1

In the far reaches of the Indian Ocean, where the Arabian Sea began to blend into the Gulf of Aden, two white helicopters powered their way westward, seemingly alone in the empty vastness of the clear blue sky. They had been flying in that direction for almost an hour, and were seventy miles beyond the nearest American ship. Far to their north was the Arabian subcontinent. Far to their south, Somalia's coastline jutted out into the sea, making the famous Horn of Africa. And to their front, Admiral Mad Dog Mulcahy searched for Russian ships.

The LAMPS III helicopter shuddered along at 130 knots, two thousand feet above the sea. Mulcahy sat in a jump seat between the pilot and the copilot. He peered feverishly ahead through the darkened visor that fell down in front of his helmet. And finally he keyed the intercom, holding the voice mike against his lips as he talked.

"In front of us. At about two o'clock."

The pilot held his aerial map against one knee. He checked the map, carefully comparing the helicopter's position with several landmarks on the Somali coast to the south, and a few small islands that were extensions of the island of Socotra, behind them as they entered the Gulf of Aden. Then he peered forward in the direction that Mulcahy had indicated. "Roger, sir. I've got it. That's got to be the Russkies out there."

"Let's go take a look."

"Aye, aye, sir."

The helicopter turned smoothly, trembling even more as it began dropping altitude and shifting course toward the Soviet ships. Mulcahy could see three of them, and then four, traveling in a close column, their hulls low and sleek as they cut through the gulf toward the west. They were twenty miles away in the open sea, heading for the Bab el Mandeb.

A few minutes later, Captain David Mosberg came over the intercom. He was sitting in one of the helicopter's rear seats, peering out a side window, and had caught the hull number on the largest ship. "The big one is the *Nicolaev*, all right. She's packed to the gills. Looks like two Alligator LSTs sailing with her, and a Krivak frigate as escort."

Mad Dog growled back. "Well, let's go pay the assholes a little visit."

"How close do you want to go, sir?"

Mad Dog glared briefly at the pilot. "Hell, man, this is international waters. Let's yank their chain. Pull up next to the *Nicolaev* and hover."

The sea was as calm as glass. The sky was cloudless, faintly hazed just above the water with sand from a recent Yemeni sandstorm. A few miles away, they could begin to pick up objects on the front helicopter deck of the *Nicolaev*, one of the newer Soviet amphibious assault ships. The five-hundred-foot ship was loaded with trucks, armored vehicles, and supplies. The *Nicolaev* had a bow ramp and stern doors for amphibious offloading. In addition, inside its hold, the

Nicolaev carried at least two Lebed air cushion vehicles, capable of offloading forty tons of cargo at a time, or two tanks, from the *Nicolaev*'s hull in the open sea. The Alligator LSTs were capable of providing heavy shore bombardment, and could carry up to seventeen hundred tons of cargo apiece.

Mosberg came over the intercom again. "They're on a supply run from Socotra. They'll pass through the Bab el Mandeb in four or five hours. They must know the French have Assab, now. I can't figure this out. Maybe they think the Cubans are going to knock the French out of Assab. Either that or they're heading for the Dahlaks."

"It's a power play," answered Mad Dog. "They can put that stuff ashore at a dozen places along the Eritrean coastline if they want to. They're telling the French they're not afraid of them, and they're telling us they'll do what they damn well please inside the Red Sea."

"Ahhh!" Mosberg suddenly held his face. "My eyes!"

The helicopter's windshield had seemingly erupted with a blinding light, as if the sun had reflected off a huge mirror on the ship below. And as they began to approach the *Nicolaev* on its port side, a heavily accented voice cut into their radio frequency, filling their headsets. *"American helicopter, you are entering the airspace of a Soviet warship. This is your last warning. I say again, this is your last warning."*

The pilot immediately veered away from the Soviet column. "That light looked like a laser, sir!"

"Are you all right?"

"Yes, sir. But we'll be in deep *kim chi* if they bounce that laser off of me and my copilot! Besides, that was a final warning. They could blow us away in a heartbeat, and claim they thought we were in an attack pattern."

"The assholes! We're in international waters!" Mad Dog looked behind them as the helicopter turned away, heading back toward the American battle group. "They've run their IL-thirty-eights right up to the fantail of our carriers! A hundred yards abeam, deck level, and those things are as big as a P-three!''

Mad Dog flipped a finger at the Russians as the helicopter powered back toward the aircraft carrier. ''All right, if that's the way they want to play, we'll tail the bastards. I want the *Dahlgren* to join their column.''

In twenty minutes the helicopter landed on the huge flight deck of the *Roosevelt*, which had just steamed into the Arabian Sea and had added its battle group to the U.S.S. *Independence*'s ships. And fifteen minutes after that, the guided missile destroyer *Dahlgren* broke away from the battle group and headed into the sunset, sailing for the Bab el Mandeb, under orders to tail the Soviet column inside the Red Sea as part of a ''freedom of navigation'' exercise.

2

Seven hundred miles west of Mad Dog Mulcahy, camped among the network of small streams that fed the Ethiopian cotton plantations of Dubti, Major General Abelardo Enrique Valdez was ready to move. In fact, he had been ready to move for several days. And now he was fighting back a growing fury within himself, a temptation to tell his higher command that through their incompetent and cowardly hesitation they had turned a quick and relatively simple operation into a very dangerous one, whose success could no longer be predicted.

Valdez sat forlornly inside the heat and dust of his mobile command post, a BRDM-2 armored vehicle loaded on the inside with communications equipment. A small cigar burned between the thumb and first finger of his right hand. With his left hand he pressed the handset of a ciphered radio against an ear. Valdez was a strict enforcer of radio silence during troop movements, but spoke several times a day on the ciphered system to his lead reconnaissance units. He was now listening to a report from Colonel Emilio Rosales, the commander of his reconnaissance battalion, forty kilometers to his front.

The reconnaissance battalion had been reconnoitering to the front toward Eritrea, and on its eastern flank near the Djiboutan border. It was now passing through the remote towns of Serdo and Deda, paralleling the Djiboutan border as it approached the small villages of Lofefle and Manda.

Manda would be the jump-off point for the invasion of Eritrea. Once the main elements of the division caught up with them, the reconnaissance battalion would move forward, probing the Eritrean defenses at Assab, yet another hundred kilometers to the front. Colonel Rosales and his men were the eyes of the division. Based on their probe of the Eritrean defenses, General Valdez would quickly prepare an assault plan, heavy with massed artillery and armor. And then the attack would begin.

Valdez had wanted to take Assab quickly and ruthlessly, with his own troops. At the port, they were to link up with Soviet supply ships, and hopefully also capture the Assab oil storage facilities intact. Then he had planned to shift the operational rear area two hundred miles forward, from Dese to Assab, and continue the advance.

Only the Cuban units had the tactical skills to quickly defeat the Eritreans at Assab, many of whom had been trained by the Cubans before the Soviet flip-flop in 1977. And yet, Valdez knew he could not afford large casualties at Assab, because his troops would also be necessary to spearhead the advance on Asmara and Massawa. The Ethiopian rabble that followed in his wake would be more useful later, as occupation forces in Massawa and Asmara, or in a campaign of messy, costly street fighting, if the Eritreans chose to stay in the cities and fight. But that was not likely. Once Assab fell, the battle would have been over. The former guerillas defending Massawa and Asmara would have seen the tanks and artillery of the Cuban advance, and would have quickly fled to the far mountains west of Asmara, near the border of Sudan.

But now, all that was nothing more than a fading dream. The French were in Assab. His superiors had held him up for too long.

Valdez had set his division headquarters at Dubti because the streams of the cotton plantations provided them water. He was traveling with the main body of the division, well forward along the route of advance. Tanks, trucks, armored personnel carriers, and self-propelled artillery pieces covered the horizon as if they were natural to the desert, a sort of African tumbleweed. Whenever Valdez walked along the road behind his mobile command post, he could see the long, sleek tubes of his 2S3 section, the enormous 152-millimeter self-propelled artillery pieces at rest on both flanks of the road, pointing north, their tubes muzzled with a sleeve to keep the dust out during the advance. The 2S3s were new, having been flown in directly from the Soviet Union. His men had learned to drive and fire them in Cuba, using computerized simulators. Farther forward, dozens of 2S1 howitzers lurked in the desert sand, painted yellow and black like the others to blend in with the sand and dirt, their 122-millimeter guns also masked from the dust. And in all directions there were T-64 and T-72 tanks, many of them just flown in from the Soviet Union as well.

No Cuban general had ever commanded such a powerful force in combat. For that, Abelardo Valdez had at first felt deeply honored. Now he felt used, sure that he would end up a scapegoat if the operation failed.

Behind the Cuban division, the main body of the assaulting Ethiopian Army was now stretched out for almost sixty miles. Ethiopian supporting elements straggled even farther back than that, all the way to the waters of the Gewane reservoir, a hundred miles to the Cuban rear. The Ethiopian leaders were in no hurry to fight. Their best Ethiopian soldiers had been executed a year before by government leaders who suspected them of disloyalty. The generals who remained were either relatives of the political leaders or politicians. Valdez had no use for his supposed allies.

The Ethiopian column moved slowly, like a thousand caterpillars. A good portion of it was still on foot, awaiting the dispatch of more trucks that were being sent from other parts of Ethiopia and had not yet arrived. At night the Ethiopians and many Cuban units had to move off the road in order to camp on the Awash River, which paralleled the road to the west.

Water, that was the dilemma. And momentum. Every day the helicopters brought them water for cooking and drinking, but his men could not bathe, and Valdez worried about a time when the helicopters might fail mechanically or be pulled away and the water canisters would not come. And every day the high command, from back in the safety of Addis Ababa, worked him as if he were a yo-yo. At times they urged Valdez forward, at other times they were warning him to be wary of attacks from across the Djiboutan border. He was already growing weary of their interference. What did they want, these bastards?

But at least he could control his own ground forces. He would use them boldly, and at the same time carefully. That was the mark of a great general, he thought again, congratulating himself on his own sagacity. You used an army well if you remembered the hunting pattern of the panther: to prowl quietly, to stalk your target carefully, to gather yourself soundlessly, digging in your haunches and focusing on your target. And then, when the moment came, to leap forward onto your prey with all the ferocity and power you could muster, and to completely destroy him before he could regain the power it took to fight you off.

"We have no movement," reported Colonel Rosales as Valdez listened on the radio. "The border is absolutely quiet."

Valdez remained cautious. The reconnaissance battalion's lead elements were moving by motorcycle on the dusty, bouncy roads. The motorcycles each had a sidecar with a machine gun, and behind them were armored BRDM-2 reconnaissance vehicles, also with machine guns. But that was little solace when they now were facing the French, instead of Eritrean guerillas.

"Alright, alright. Proceed," commanded Valdez. He handed the phone to Sergeant Reuben Alarcon, his personal radio operator, and dragged heavily on his cigar.

Outside the command vehicle, he peered across the vast wasteland he had been ordered to traverse. He was amazed and proud at the power of his division, but he was also secretly overcome by anger. Abelardo Valdez felt he was a victim of his own success.

He had led a battalion during the Ogaden border war in 1977, and had become famous for a spectacular armor attack deep in the Somali rear area, leaving them in such disarray that they fled the Ogaden altogether. He was awarded the coveted Hero of the Republic of Cuba Medal, as well as the Ernesto Che Guevara Order, First Class, both of which he treasured beyond words, and loved to wear on his dress uniform. But after the battle, he had also been ordered to remain in Ethiopia for an additional year beyond his normal tour. And now he had been sent back as commander of the largest assault force the Cuban Army had ever assembled.

If you failed, they brought you home. If you succeeded, they separated you from your family and the beauty of your homeland, and asked for more. And the more you succeeded, the longer you stayed away from home.

But Abelardo Valdez was a good soldier, and proud of his membership in the Cuban Communist party. He had studied at the Gomez Revolutionary Armed Forces Academy, and had received specialized training in armored warfare in the Soviet Union. He would never have complained about his assignment; he merely resented his fate, in the manner of all good, if covert, Catholics. It was simply not right to be here in the middle of a desert that he detested, while so many changes were taking place at home.

Not only in his country, and in the region, but especially with his son. Antonio was a wonderful boxer, a vision of power and grace, the most beautiful part of the general's life. Valdez was sure Antonio would win the middleweight gold medal in the Pan American Games, and might also win at the Olympics in Barcelona. But the boy had been showing dangerous anticommunist tendencies, and needed personal supervision. Just before Valdez departed, he had actually caught Antonio singing "El Hombre Es Loco," a popular song, when Fidel Castro had begun to speak on the radio.

Not that Valdez believed his presence in Ethiopia involved the soundest logic by the Supreme Leader. But public utterances of disloyalty might incarcerate his son, and certainly could end his athletic career.

He visualized Antonio's quick, catlike movements and the power and variety of his punches as he himself stood on the desolate road, surveying the wasteland around him. He was his son's most ardent fan. He came to all of his fights and sat at ringside, basking in the adrenaline that flowed like magic between them. To see all that ended, to see a young man's life destroyed because of a brash, quick tongue, was almost more than he could bear. He felt helpless. He wanted to finish this operation, and return home. What did Africa have to do with Cuba, anyway?

He stood on the road, his chest heaving and his throat gagging from the heat. Dust and scrub were all around him. He was inching carefully toward a town that he would soon destroy, while in his heart he dreamed only of the life that was passing him by in Cuba. Life was a cruel joke. Valdez spat contemptuously into the Ethiopian dust, a dry, salty powder that he felt he would never fully wash away. The dust had already sucked off three years of his life, and now this.

But there was a glimmer of hope. If only he could begin the battle, it would not last long. Or perhaps he would become ill. No, he dismissed that. He had an iron constitution. Three years of African service and never so much as a day of dysentery. Well, maybe he would be wounded.

He began to bargain with God. A foot he would give, to

return home, so long as Antonio also might make it to the Olympics. *A foot, God, for my son's Gold Medal.* Or perhaps a leg. Below the knee. No more. Nothing in the head; that would be like death, even if he survived. Or in the stomach or the chest. A body wound in the fly-bitten heat of the desert would probably kill him before he could receive medical treatment.

But a leg, yes. Below the knee.

And then he could hear God or maybe Fidel saying, *Stay, Abelardo, and win the battle of Ethiopia. You will receive another Hero of the Republic Medal, another Che Guevara Order, First Class. No, they will name a medal in your honor. Your son will receive a medal and you will receive a medal and you will both be heroes to your country, linked together in history, forever remembered for your victories.*

Ah, but what did it matter. It was out of his hands.

Overhead as he stood on the road he saw a thin vapor trail high in the cloudless sky, miles and miles away, off to the east over Djibouti. A jet aircraft had come from the north, and was curving back to the southeast, away from Ethiopia, toward the Gulf of Aden.

There had been one yesterday as well.

Abelardo Valdez knew in his heart what that meant, although in his head he worked hard to deny its implications. He tossed his cigar into the dirt and stared intently for a full minute into the eastern sky, at the vanishing gossamer of white.

Cabrones. They could follow you anywhere on earth.

First there were the French, and now this. For all his careful tactics as he advanced on Assab, for all his insistence on radio silence, he knew he was being watched.

By *Yanqui* reconnaissance aircraft.

And I will be blamed, he thought again and again as he paced along the perimeter, watching his soldiers droop like unwatered plants in the scorching heat, and the powerful guns and speedy tanks take on layer after layer of sand, as if they were sinking into the desert itself. *They give me a*

*hundred thousand Ethiopian soldiers, and then they can't
find enough trucks. They tell me to invade Eritrea and then
they hold me up at the border, on the edge of victory, as
the enemy builds up its defenses.*

His huge army sat sweating and uneasy, drinking up their
water and eating their rations, with a supply trail that
stretched back more than two hundred miles, while Assab
with its seaport that would feed and supply them was only
a day's attack in front of where they sat. It did not make
sense.

And he did not trust this town. Its drab streets were
cluttered with debris, lined with homes made of mud, wood,
and lava blocks that soon fell away into an endless desert
scarred by lava floes and salt pits. Dubti seemed to be
inhabited only by goats and camels and a handful of Danakil
tribesmen. They were lean, handsome people who tattooed
the faces of their women and carried daggers or rifles. They
drifted in and out of the small marketplace on foot, or riding
mules or camels. They stank unbearably, as if they had
never bathed. And they seemed to hate Valdez and his
soldiers, most likely because in the searing heat there was
little water, not enough to share with these foreign soldiers.

Valdez had never seen more than a dozen townspeople
at one time, although there were supposed to be two hundred
inhabitants. The Danakils were known for castrating their
enemies, and Valdez's soldiers were not sleeping well at
night. One of his soldiers had been killed by a crocodile a
week before, on the lush, muddy banks of the Awash River.
Since then they feared and hated everything in this miserable, baked desert: the people, the herds of baboons that
watched them along the roadways and near the narrow
streams, the smells, the sand, the salt.

It was time to get moving.

Valdez was an ardent student of history, and a romantic
as well. He was imagining himself as Field Marshal Heinz
Guderian in 1940, having punched a hole through France,
only to be halted by the German high command at the peak

of his advance, and then forced to sit a few miles away and watch as the enemy evacuated from Dunkirk.

France. He spat again, watching his spittle roll into a tiny ball as it hit the dust. He took out a cigarette and lit it. The French had beaten him to Assab, and now the high command could not decide whether to fight them, to bypass them, or to call off the operation. And so he sat impotently in the desert, wishing for a hot, soapy bath, a soft, giggling woman, and a glass of cold water.

He was not afraid to fight the French, although he worried that his division would lost too many men and weapons in the battle for Assab, and then be hurt as they raced toward Asmara and Massawa. The French would not have the troops to fight in those cities, he knew that. But he could not continue the attack to Asmara and Massawa without a logistical base along the sea. His supply lines were already dangerously long, and he would be two hundred miles from the two cities after he turned the corner at Assab.

And so he sensed that the battle should be fought at Assab. The French could fight, but they were light on armor and artillery. They did not have the firepower of his division. And a defeat at Assab would be a spectacular blow to both the French and the Eritreans. He daydreamed in the heat of the desert, licking salt off his lips and spitting yet again after he dragged on his cigarette. The salt blew in the wind with the sand, and then stayed when the sand fell away. It was in everything; his eyes, his hair, the wrinkles on his hands.

In his daydream Valdez imagined the surrendering garrison of French soldiers being loaded onto waiting Soviet ships and then taken back to Djibouti, stripped of their weapons and their pride, their release a condition for French withdrawal. It would be a glorious scene, one that would be played in the international press, filling his family and his friends back in Cuba with joy. And it might mark the end of the campaign, with an international agreement returning Eritrea to Ethiopian control.

The Soviets and the Americans would stay out of it, he knew that. They would only operate on the fringes, and mostly at sea. The Soviets would supply his forces and the Americans would peripherally aid the French. And so the key would be to contain the battlefield, to isolate the French forces from any chance of reinforcements. And then to defeat them quickly.

Valdez went back inside his command vehicle, and studied the large area map he kept taped on a wall. The French had no more troops in the region. They could reinforce only from the Mediterranean. He decided that the answer was for the Soviets to surreptitiously mine the waters south of the Suez Canal. It had been discussed earlier and approved, although only if the ground war went poorly. The ground war was indeed going poorly. It had not yet begun, and the French controlled Assab, an unexpected development.

Mining the waters south of Suez would keep the French and much of the American Navy bottled up inside the Mediterranean, and create fear and chaos for international commerce. It would isolate the battlefield, and at the same time make the capitalist nations all around the world scream like wounded pigs for a quick solution. And then Valdez could send Emilio Rosales forward with his reconnaissance units, drawing the French into a fight. And once their defenses were exposed he could defeat them with a massive tank and artillery attack, backed up by Cuban air strikes out of Dese and Mekele, where he had moved his MIGs forward from Addis Ababa. A week, that was all he needed after he took Assab. Maybe ten days.

Valdez picked up the handset to his ciphered radio, calling the high command in Addis Ababa. They were being stupid by waiting this long to make up their minds. His men were growing tired and cynical and even afraid as they sat waiting on the edge of their greatest victory. It was time to move.

Let's get this over with, or call it off. We are turning into rocks out here.

3

Night came quickly in the Dahlak Archipelago, just off the coastline from Massawa. The sun shimmered across the water and then disappeared behind mountains far to the west, on the mainland of Eritrea. And soon the stars hung round and bright, like lanterns in the cloudless equatorial sky.

As darkness fell, the *Pripyat*, an Alesha-class Soviet mine-layer, moved out of the Dahlak anchorage and slowly made its way through shoals and small islets, heading north. The two hundred sailors of the *Pripyat* had rested during the day. They were now busy on the bridge and in the diesel rooms, or preparing the four 57-millimeter guns for possible action. Or they were aft, working on the ship's four mine tracks.

When they reached the northern Red Sea, beyond Port Sudan on the western coast and Yanbu', in Saudi Arabia, on the east, the sailors on the *Pripyat*'s mine tracks would systematically lay more than two hundred highly sophisticated acoustic mines, the likes of which had never before been used in naval warfare. The journey would take a night, another day, then part of another night, with time left over to lay the belt of mines under the cover of darkness. The *Pripyat* would then steam southeast for another day, back to the waters outside of Yanbu', from whose port the oil pipelines of Iraq and Saudi Arabia fed large tankers from around the world. Outside Yanbu', again under cover of darkness, the *Pripyat* would feed another hundred mines into the sea, making a deadly belt around the port.

The *Pripyat* steamed steadily north until it cleared the Dahlak Archipelago, and then cut to the northeast, making eighteen knots. All night the minelayer was alone on the calm waters of the Red Sea. The only light was from the stars. The only sounds were the familiar vibrations and tremblings of the ship itself.

And then just after dawn, the sailors on the bridge heard an eerie scream to their front, coming at them just above the water. They stood wide-eyed as an American EA-6B Prowler aircraft skimmed the surface of the sea, perhaps a hundred feet above them and just off their starboard side, roaring past them at more than four hundred miles an hour. The EA-6B was from the *Roosevelt*, and had been making a routine surveillance sweep of the Dahlak anchorage when it picked them up. It brought back photographs so clear that Admiral Mad Dog Mulcahy could read the fear that had been on the sailors' faces as they watched the aircraft from the bridge of the minelayer.

Mad Dog sat on the couch of his flag cabin on the *Roosevelt*. He positively gloated as he shared the photographs with Captain David Mosberg. "What did I tell you? *Huh?* I've been calling these bastards' shots every step of the way! It's the *Pripyat*. They're going to try and seal off the Suez Canal, and then claim they don't know who laid the mines."

Mosberg nodded his agreement, giving Mulcahy a rather surprised grin. "I've got to hand it to you, Admiral. I never thought they'd do that."

"Of course they would, Mosberg. They'll do it, and then they'll deny it. Hell, we could take pictures of them doing it, and they'd claim we falsified the pictures. In fact, they'd love it. They'd say it's all a CIA plot to discredit the Soviets because they've complained about French aggression and called for an international settlement to the Ethiopian crisis. That's the way they do business." Mulcahy guffawed. "You're the intelligence officer, Mosberg. You should know that."

"I track enemy movements, sir. You're the one who is an expert on their intentions."

"Stop kissing my ass, Mosberg." But Mad Dog Mulcahy wasn't serious. He loved to have his ass kissed. "All right, here's what we do. We up the stakes. We're going to send the *Dahlgren* up toward the Suez, like a bat out of hell. Flank speed. She's got to beat the *Pripyat* up there."

Mad Dog gave Mosberg a wild, gap-toothed grin, his Daddy Warbucks eyes aglow. "Do you think the Soviets have the balls to lock up an American combatant inside a minefield in international waters?"

Mosberg considered it for a moment, trying to read Mulcahy's eyes. He spoke hesitantly. "I'd say, if they're going to deny they laid the mines, then they wouldn't have any qualms about locking up the *Dahlgren* in the process."

"You're absolutely right, Mosberg!" Mad Dog seemed strangely exultant as he paced around his cabin. Mosberg could not understand the admiral's happiness over the prospect of having a warship marooned in the northern Red Sea.

Finally, Mad Dog rejoined Mosberg on the couch. "Next question. Do you think those assholes back in Washington have the guts to stop the Soviets from laying those mines, Mosberg? Hell, no. Their idea of bravado is to go make a speech at the United Nations after it happens. In the meantime, the Soviets will have isolated the French fleet in the Mediterranean, and we'll be ordered to stay out of the fight while the Cubans wear down the French at Assab."

Mad Dog pounded the photograph into the coffee table. "And if the French get their asses kicked by the Cubans, it will be an international humiliation! Worse yet, we'll have to sit out here with all this firepower and watch, after I told General Avice we'd help. What a goddamn disaster. I'm so ashamed of my country." He sat back in the couch, his eyes on fire and his lips tightened into a determined scowl. "I'm not going to let that happen."

Mosberg had been attempting to follow Mulcahy's logic, but he felt lost. "Sir, I'm not quite sure how we're going to stop that by sacrificing the *Dahlgren*."

"Don't be a dufus. We're not sacrificing anything. The *Dahlgren* is going to be our ante into the pot, Mosberg. In for a dime, in for a dollar, do you know what I mean?"

"To be honest, I don't, sir."

"Well, stop thinking like an intelligence puke for a minute, and follow my train of thought. If the Soviets lay mines out there in the Red Sea and then deny having done it, we've got a problem, right? Commerce is disrupted, people back in Washington scream, eventually a few minesweepers show up—especially Soviet minesweepers doing the Lord's work, you know how that goes—and the problem goes away. No matter that the French just got their asses handed to them, and Eritrea just fell.''

Mad Dog Mulcahy grinned triumphantly. ''But if the mines lock up an American warship in international waters, one that has been conducting a goddamn *freedom of navigation* drill, then America is *pissed off*. They're going to want to do something about it. And you know who's going to help us? The French.''

Mosberg began to comprehend Mad Dog's genius. ''They have a minesweeper in Djibouti.''

''Exactly.''

''They can come through the Mandeb and get the *Dahlgren* out.''

''That's right. And at the same time, we'll be able to send warships into the Red Sea. In fact, we'll *have* to, to emphasize our right to navigate in international waters. The milquetoast marauders back in Washington will wet their pants, but they won't be able to stop us. And our warships in the Red Sea might just make a port call in Assab, if we can be smart about it. Which will give the Cubans goddamn *gas pains*. And if our ships take a few rounds from some Cuban machine gun, we'll damn well retaliate. And America will *love* it.''

Captain Mosberg looked at Mad Dog Mulcahy with un-adulterated awe, as if he were John Paul Jones himself. ''Admiral, you're a dangerous man.''

''You're goddamn right I am,'' answered Mulcahy. ''But these are dangerous times, Mosberg.'' The admiral jumped up from the couch and again began pacing furiously around the small stateroom. ''Now, get me Admiral McCormick up here. We've got to be quick about this.''

Five minutes later Admiral Ward McCormick, the commander of the *Roosevelt* battle group, reported to Mulcahy's cabin. And within a half hour, the *Dahlgren* was headed due north, breaking off from its desultory accompaniment of the Soviet supply column near the Dahlak Archipelago and heading at flank speed, thirty-three knots, toward the Suez.

4

At the port town of Assab, just inside the narrow Bab el Mandeb, General Jean-François Avice had quickly built a fortress of artillery, infantry, and armored troops that were continually resupplied at the very facilities that General Abelardo Valdez had hoped would provide his own rear base. And the intelligence photographs provided to the French on a daily, if covert, basis by Admiral Mad Dog Mulcahy clearly indicated that the Cubans would soon cross over the Eritrean line from Manda, in an initial move on Assab.

The morning after the French took Assab, Bill Fogarty had joined Lieutenant Colonel Michel Fourcade as he moved his mechanized infantry battalion twenty miles to the south, and emplaced them on the southern slopes of a hill that was simply called "3209" on their maps. The narrow road had cut through huge, moonlike scabs of lava, dead forests of rocks, whole lakes of salt that reminded him of snow. The wind was filled with salt and dust. This was not a place for an amphibious assault, thought Fogarty as the battalion inched its way toward the outpost. The sand would eat the engines out of helicopters. The heat would suck the moisture from his men. Water would be more important than bullets. If his men were to fight here in the desert, it would have to be over with quickly.

Fogarty liked the French colonel. In his youth, Fourcade had been one of France's best middle-distance runners. He was still muscular and hard at forty-three. During his African tours of duty, as Fourcade jokingly put it, he leaned out like a jackal. He had an agile grace, and an easy rapport with his soldiers. As they drove, his knowing eyes darted across the landscape above a long, pointed nose and thin, grimacing lips. Fourcade knew what he was looking for, and he knew how to fight.

The outpost looked directly down at the road that led to Manda, some forty miles away. Soldiers from the small Eritrean platoon that Fourcade's men had joined on the mountain had actually been in Manda, and even in General Valdez's headquarters at Dubti, many times during the past few days. They had drifted among the Cubans, riding on the backs of stinking camels, dressed as Afars. The Cuban soldiers had been so repulsed by their stench that they had avoided the swaddled Eritrean scouts, urging them to leave the small towns. And so they had, moving east or west rather than north toward Assab, then later making their way back to the outpost along gulleys and small streams, across the lava floes and the thick scabs of salt.

So Fourcade's men and their Eritrean compatriots knew that the Cuban soldiers were miserable, stricken with ennui, and afraid of all the creatures of the desert. And they knew that the photos were correct, that General Abelardo Valdez's reconnaissance battalion was readying to make its move toward them. And most important, they had confirmed that the reconnaissance battalion was too weak, that the days of motorcycle scouts and armored reconnaissance vehicles without artillery capability were over, at least in modern armies.

Fourcade's own battalion was strong, and mobile. France had emphasized armored maneuverability for almost forty years, and he had proudly shown Fogarty his array of reconnaissance vehicles. They were heavily armed, and fast. His AMX-10 *canons roulants* vehicles were actually light artillery pieces that carried thirty-eight rounds of ammunition for each of their 105-millimeter guns, and yet could travel fifty miles an hour. The guns on the AMX-10 were highly modern, with laser range-finders and a low-light television system that made them night-capable. Also on the outpost with him were Panhard and Sagaie EBR vehicles, which fired 90-millimeter cannon and could travel seventy miles an hour, several Renault VCAC HOT Mephistos, each of which carried four HOT antitank missiles on a retractable launcher, and dozens of AMX-10P infantry fighting vehicles, each armed with a 20-millimeter cannon. Each AMX-10 carried a squad of infantry soldiers at speeds up to fifty miles an hour.

It was late afternoon. The sun would fall quickly, and in a half hour it would be dark and cool. Fogarty sat on a boulder, sipping water from a canteen and chatting with Fourcade. From the French position on the forward slopes of hill 3209, they could see for almost twenty miles across the empty desert, down the road that led to Manda.

Fourcade lit a cigarette and pointed toward Manda. "I think they're coming tonight," he said. "Your aerial photos from this morning show them on the border. They will use that road."

"They've got no choice," agreed Fogarty. "Unless they want to go back to Addis Ababa."

"No," said Fourcade. "They'll come. And we know all about them, thanks to the photos. We'll destroy them, and after that I think the main body will call off its attack." The colonel slapped Fogarty on the shoulder, a gesture of camaraderie. "As my general likes to say, we'll take away their eyes and ears. And we will break up their assault, too. You'll see, Colonel. We know all about them. They know very little about us. Ah! It's over."

"I wouldn't be so cocky if I were you," warned Fogarty.

"Why not? We're ready. And besides, the national symbol of my country is the cock, Colonel. As your women are fond of pointing out."

Fogarty measured his counterpart, a grin creasing his face. "You're a piece of work, Fourcade. I wouldn't let you within ten feet of my wife."

"Yes? But could you keep your wife ten feet away from *me*?"

"She'd take one look at your skinny Frog body and puke." They both laughed, and then Fogarty sighed. "Nothing like talking about it, huh? Out here in the desert, surrounded by goddamn hyenas. Hey, Fourcade. You ever had a hyena? Female, of course. I mean, I wouldn't want to accuse you of being perverted or anything."

The French colonel's eyes had slowly narrowed as Fogarty spoke. Now his small head jerked away from Fogarty, looking south.

"Listen," said Fourcade.

Fogarty followed Fourcade's eyes. The desert was empty, but in his ears Fogarty felt the vibrations of distant motors, even though he could not yet hear them.

"They're coming," said the French colonel. And then he quickly ran to his command vehicle, where he grasped the radio handset and began speaking rapidly in French.

And now, from miles away, Fogarty could hear the noises. The Cubans were indeed on the move. He could make out the soft whines of distant motors far to his front. All around him, the French soldiers had sprung into motion, running toward their vehicles and calling to each other in hoarse whispers, as if the Cubans might hear them from ten miles away. The quiet air of the desert around them was now broken only by the occasional cry of a hyena, or the hushed conversation of Fourcade's soldiers as they reported from their positions on the night scopes or inside the vehicles.

The noises at first were soft and intermittent, like the occasional snores of someone sleeping far away. But as the black sky closed over the desert like the ceiling in a small room, the sounds seemed to echo off the sky and the rocks, and then again inside the chambers of each soldier's personal nightmare. The sounds grew more frequent, and in moments all of Fourcade's soldiers were in their vehicles, on alert.

Fourcade tapped Fogarty on the shoulder, beckoning him. "Colonel, you come with me."

Fogarty followed Fourcade into his command vehicle. The French commander was speaking rapidly into his radio handset. Fogarty recognized the names of two of his officers, Hernu and DuBois. Outside, vehicles were churning into new positions, and in a moment Fourcade's vehicle moved forward as well, moving down the slope of the hill.

"I'm leaving Hernu for rear security," explained Fourcade as the vehicle slowly made its way down the slopes of the hill. "And for maneuver if we are heavily engaged. The others will form an ambush closer to the road."

At the bottom of the hill, Fogarty climbed out of the vehicle and saw that, with the help of Eritrean guides, Fourcade had placed most of his battalion into a wide ambush formation. After a half hour of maneuvering and incessant radio chatter, the French battalion was in position and quiet again. The soldiers were feverishly working their night scopes, with their weapons ready to fire. Fourcade placed his heavy weapon systems forward with a clear field of fire, and kept the infantry fighting vehicles in an arc behind them, ready to react. The wide and lethal ambush formation still commanded the heights above the road, less than a mile from its center.

For almost an hour they waited, sweating and queasy. The soldiers peered through the night scopes on their weapons, and after a short time picked up the Cuban column. They followed the Cuban advance, working their laser range-finders, ready to fire at any moment and achieve a first-round hit. Fourcade monitored the scopes, whispering hoarsely into his radio handset as he assigned targets to the gunners on his larger vehicles.

The Cuban column approached them, keeping to the road, and moved slowly past them, its main body of perhaps two dozen vehicles on the road, with flank security on both sides. Fogarty watched, almost gasping from the tension, as Fourcade let the lead elements pass. The French commander wanted their rear vehicles in his kill zone, so that he could seal the whole battalion off from behind, preventing their escape. And so his soldiers held their fire. The BRDM vehicle on the Cuban left flank passed less than a quarter of a mile from Fourcade's forward guns, bouncing slowly over rocks and washboard gulleys in the dark, its 12.7-millimeter machine gun pointing straight ahead and its crew buttoned up tight inside the vehicle. The Cubans were oblivious to the French presence.

Then, inexplicably, the Cuban column stopped. On the command vehicle screen Fogarty could see soldiers disembark from several vehicles, and begin to converse, as if they were arguing. Perhaps they had reached a checkpoint. Perhaps they had become lost. Perhaps they sensed the nearness of the French. It was not clear. But Fourcade seized the moment, speaking calmly into his radio handset.

"Open fire. I say again, fire, fire, fire!"

The side of the hill seemed to explode like a volcano as the French vehicles opened fire. Artillery blasted the Cubans at short range, the double explosions of discharge and impact echoing off of the nearby mountain. Fourcade had carefully targeted the lead vehicles and those at the rear, as well as the Cuban command vehicle and those carrying the SAG-GER antitank missiles. A dozen BRDMs were immediately blasted apart from direct hits. A hit on the command vehicle killed Colonel Emilio Rosales, the battalion commander who was the favorite subordinate of General Abelardo Valdez, and destroyed most of the Cubans' communications equipment. The artillery fired again. Heavy machine guns cut through the column, their tracers leaving low, steady trails of red as they dropped screaming men and perforated the armor of other vehicles. HOT missiles flashed and boomed, the two Cuban BRDMs equipped with SAGGER missiles disintegrating as missiles hit them broadside.

The Cubans had been completely surprised. They had no clear view of the French, and they had little cover to protect their vehicles. There was almost no return fire. With Colonel

Rosales dead and the radios knocked out, the surviving Cubans had no commander, and no way to contact the main body back at Manda. A few vehicles surged forward and then off into the desert, attempting to escape the killing zone, but were also hit.

"Now," said Fourcade into the radio handset. "Assault. Sweep the killing zone."

In a few seconds, the infantry fighting vehicles churned into action. Fogarty had exited the command vehicle. He stood on a boulder and watched the AMX 10-P vehicles move quickly in a line behind the main guns, pouring down from the hillside and heading south to cut off the road to any Cuban retreat. The heavy guns on the hill continued to rake the Cuban column, freezing the Cuban vehicles in the killing zone.

Having cut off the Cuban retreat, the infantry fighting vehicles stopped for a moment and dismounted their troops, then advanced in a wide assault line toward the Cubans, their center vehicle on the road itself. The French vehicles were sweeping forward into the killing zone, their 20-millimeter machine guns blasting the vehicles and men in front of them.

The firing on the hill stopped. French infantrymen who had dismounted from the AMX 10-Ps walked forward in an assault line between the vehicles as they moved toward the wreckage of the Cuban column. A dozen gasoline fires reached up into the night from the carcasses of the Cuban BRDMs. Ammunition "cooked off" inside many of the vehicles, causing French soldiers to startle here and there, hitting the ground or firing their weapons toward the sounds. A half-dozen artillery flares went off in front of the advancing French, behind the Cuban column, lighting the desert like a football stadium. Every now and then a Cuban soldier moved, and a cacophony of small arms and light machine gun fire greeted him.

As the French soldiers neared, Cuban men began screaming from near the vehicles. Fogarty and the others could hear the screams. Some wished to surrender. Others were crying for water or medical help. The French soldiers shot some of them in the confusion of the night, and loaded others onto their personnel carriers, taking them prisoner. When the vehicles returned to the main position, they counted only forty-seven Cubans who had survived the perfectly executed ambush.

"Now," said Fourcade, who had never once lost his calm, clipped manner, "it is time to go home."

"Alright," said Fogarty as the command vehicle bounced along the rocky terrain on its way to the road. "That's what we call your basic perfectly executed military-type ambush."

"We were lucky," answered the French colonel, his dark eyes now bright from lack of sleep. "They fell into our laps. If they come again, the next time will be a hard fight."

They were still twenty miles from Assab. Fourcade ordered his soldiers to make one final sweep of the littered battlefield, and then he formed them in a column on the road. The remainder of his battalion motored down from the forward edges of hill 3209, and as dawn crept over the far mountains to the east, the vehicles raced back to join the main defensive lines at Assab.

The Cubans had lost their eyes and ears. But soon the jets would come.

And in the early morning the MIGs appeared, strafing a dead battlefield twenty miles away from the French defenses. The MIGs made several passes over the charred vehicles, dropping their bombs harmlessly against the side of the mountain from where the French had attacked, and then departed, heading back to the safety of Dese and Mekele.

An hour later, the vultures were again circling overhead, picking out human morsels for lunch. Families of hyenas were inching their way down from the mountains toward the battlefield, chattering and crying to each other, ready to scavenge as well. A dozen Danakils riding camels appeared from the lava floes and salt pits farther west, dismounting

and searching the littered roadway for souvenirs. The tribesmen stripped dead Cubans of their rifles and ammunition
as the vultures and hyenas waited to pick their bones. The
bodies were everywhere along the road, arms and legs and
heads blown off or mutilated by the explosions that had
killed them, the skin itself swelling and blistering in the
scorching heat. The baked earth of the desert was scarred
and broken here and there from the bombs and the artillery.
Smoke still curled and smoldered, emanating in little wisps
from the ashes and twisted metal of the wrecked Cuban
battalion.

But the MIGs had deliberately attacked a graveyard, not
yet wishing to confront the Roland antiaircraft batteries and
heavy guns that still waited for them at Assab.

CHAPTER 9

1

Over the Western Pacific

Along both sides of the white Boeing 747's fuselage were
the words UNITED STATES OF AMERICA. The huge aircraft
droned westward over the vast expanse of the Pacific, flying
at forty thousand feet. Inside were two flight crews, a
kitchen staff, a communications detachment, and five passengers. In the cold darkness of his private cabin in the tail
section of the plane, Ronald Holcomb was trying to sleep.
He shivered even though he was lying underneath three
blankets. He had come back to his cabin to rest, but had
spent the last three hours sky-high on adrenaline, his mind
racing with an energy that kept his eyes wide open in the
dark.

But he finally had it figured out. He knew whom to talk
to. He knew what to ask for. And he knew what he would
be willing to give up.

It would be useless to argue directly with Hideo Tanashi about the Nakashitona problem. The Japanese foreign minister was a politician, of the same ilk and with about the same tendency toward demagoguery as Doc Rowland. He had held his post for less than a year, and in his twenty years as a member of the Japanese Diet he had made only one brief visit to Washington. Tanashi was an America-basher, and a racist who believed in eventual Japanese world dominance, through economic rather than military means. He had gained a wide following inside Japan for his public utterances that Japanese technology had replaced American and Soviet militarism as the key to world power. Tanashi was looking for a loud, public confrontation, and the next day's meeting was likely to give him what he wanted.

By contrast, Makoto Harada, the vice minister of foreign affairs, was a friend. Holcomb had known Harada for seventeen years, since Harada had been political counselor at the Japanese embassy in Washington. Harada had spent more than a decade, off and on, in the United States. He had studied at the University of Michigan and at Tufts. His family had a diplomatic heritage that went back four generations. He understood the pressures Holcomb was facing at home. And, to be truthful, he had more ability to get things done than did Tanashi.

In Japan the vice ministers of each government agency held the true power. These were men—not unlike Ronald Holcomb—who had prevailed in an intense academic competition while still in their teens, and had then excelled in a series of tough government assignments until they reached the top. They stayed in the background, but they also knew how to unravel the complicated issues, and how to reach a compromise. Holcomb had asked for a private dinner with Harada on his arrival in Tokyo. If things worked out, the two men could formulate the structure of a compromise on the Nakashitona crisis before the formal meetings of the next day.

Holcomb had been stirring in his bed for several minutes,

thinking to get up. And now the door to his cabin resounded with three knocks.

"Yes?"

It was General Bear Lazaretti. "We're about an hour out, sir."

"Right, Bear. I'm awake. Thank you very much."

He shaved in the cabin's private bathroom, carefully working the razor around the seams that age had begun to bring to his neck and chin. Then he dressed. He wore a dark gray woolen suit, a white shirt, and a red silk tie. Fastening the tie, he could not help but admire himself in the mirror. He looked a lot better than he felt. But that had been the case more often than not over the past three years.

The bright light hit him like a jolt when he opened up the door and entered the main compartment of the aircraft. Toward the front, Ed Stooksberry, his bodyguard, and Sherman Novotny, his press assistant, were lazily playing a game of cards. Nearer to him, Lazaretti was waiting with a pile of briefing papers, as was Hank Eichelberger, his assistant secretary of defense for security programs. The four had been his constant traveling companions. He felt comfortable with all of them, and trusted Bear Lazaretti and Hank Eichelberger with many of his private strategies.

Holcomb sat across from those two, nodding at the same time to Stooksberry and Novotny, who interrupted their card game to wave to him. A light lunch sat on the counter between them, prepared by Ricky Tamuvalo, the Filipino mess specialist who accompanied Holcomb on his trips.

He ceremoniously checked the wine bottle, then sipped from a lead crystal glass. "A Sonoma Valley chardonnay. Ricky did very well for us this trip. What time is it?"

General Lazaretti started in, his thin face intent on a sheaf of notes. "Sir, it's fourteen hundred in Tokyo. I don't know, that means about one in the morning in Washington. We'll land at Atsugi, take a car into the Okura Hotel. General Jim Furst will meet us in Atsugi and give you an update on local defense issues."

His military aide paused for a moment, hesitating. "Minister Tanashi wanted to have dinner tonight. No agenda, just an informal, social meeting. I sent your regrets, indicating you'd be too tired, but the embassy says he's offended. It's become a pecking-order thing. He may find a way to bring it up tomorrow."

Holcomb waved a hand in the air. "No issue is too small for him to be offended, is it? Don't worry about it. I don't want to talk to him until I know what he's up to."

"Yes, sir." Lazaretti peered toward the front of the aircraft, and received a thumbs-up from the communications officer, who sat in a cubicle, in front of a small radio. "Sir, we have the KY-fifty-nine hookup to CINCPAC when you're ready."

"Good. I'll take it right now."

"Yes, sir." Lazaretti rose from his chair, making a circle in the air with one finger, indicating that the communications officer should put the call through to the Indian Ocean.

Holcomb followed Lazaretti up the aisle, containing an amused grin as he watched the addled movements of his military aide. Bear Lazaretti was intelligent and yet somehow naïve. The silver-haired former fighter pilot, who remained strikingly handsome at forty-nine, had commanded a wing in Germany before coming back for his fourth tour in the Pentagon. He was working on the Joint staff when Holcomb selected him as his military assistant.

Holcomb liked to say privately that Lazaretti had a penchant for playing politics with a small *p*. The general was unable to comprehend the duplicity and multiple agendas at the Cabinet level and in the Congress. He lacked the shrewdness of a Mad Dog Mulcahy, who seemed to know immediately the issue behind the issue, the secret agenda that was being explored while the visible problem was being confronted. Lazaretti's blood raced when talking about which officers should be selected for various commands, or which service should control close air support missions on the battlefield. Holcomb knew that on such issues his military aide put a special, conniving spin, particularly when they affected the Air Force. But on larger policy matters, Lazaretti was absolutely lost.

And that was all right. On one level, Lazaretti's loyalty could be bought cheap—a three-star assignment to one of his friends, an occasional concurrence with one of the less innocuous recommendations in his incessant stream of memoranda. On the other, his political myopia was helpful to Holcomb's professional privacy. Even at this moment, Lazaretti didn't have a clue as to the real reason Holcomb wanted to speak with Mad Dog Mulcahy on the secure telephone.

Hank Eichelberger, who had remained in his seat, was just the opposite, at least with respect to shrewdness. Just now the former CIA agent sat studying a sheaf of intelligence reports, a small sneer on his face. He was tall, thin, and bald. With his dark, angry eyes and his large, hooked nose, he had the face of a hawk. Holcomb heard Eichelberger curse as he marked up one of the reports, and commented to himself at the incongruity of the assistant secretary's gruff appearance and high, piping voice. Eichelberger was a cynic who considered the dark side of every issue, and who indeed had lived the dark side of many of them. He was a counterweight to Bear Lazaretti, and Holcomb often encouraged them to debate, secretly delighting in playing the judge to their adversarial views of human nature and international affairs.

They reached the communications station, and General Lazaretti took the radio handset from the communications officer. "Captain Crane, thanks."

"You're welcome, sir."

The young Air Force captain immediately left the compartment and entered the crew spaces toward the front of the plane, closing the door behind him. Then the general put the handset to his ear and keyed it, waiting for Admiral Mulcahy to pick up on the other end. The KY-59 was a completely secure system, which could communicate anywhere in the world using satellite technology. Holcomb's conversation would be as private as a bedroom whisper.

"Yes, sir, Admiral," said Lazaretti. "One moment for the secretary." Lazaretti handed Holcomb the receiver and also walked away, returning to his seat, where he would be out of earshot.

"Thanks, Bear." Holcomb waited for a moment, watching the general depart, then spoke into the receiver. He felt a thrill that he did not deny as he began to speak to Mulcahy. In all of history, the power that came with this kind of conversation had been accorded only to a handful of men. Ronald Holcomb knew that if he sneezed just now, half of the *Roosevelt* battle group would catch a cold.

"Mad Dog, how do you read me? Over."

Mulcahy's voice came back immediately, ingratiating and yet energetic, sounding as if he were talking into an empty barrel. "I've got you fine, Mr. Secretary. It's so good to hear your voice, sir!"

Holcomb half smiled. Mulcahy could be a sycophantic jerk, despite all of his bravado. "Yes, you too! How is it going out there?"

"We're all-systems go. Fidel got a bloody nose in the desert the other night. I guess you heard about that. I've got a Marine colonel on the ground out there, observing."

"I heard that. And the bastards laid their mines, didn't they? The President personally denounced them today, and of course the Soviets denied doing it."

"Yes, sir, I know. The Suez Canal is completely shut down. I hear the United Nations wants to pass a resolution, but they don't know who to blame! Our ship—the *Dahlgren*—is locked inside the minefield just south of the Canal. Don't worry about that. She's bait. We can get her out if we have to. And the Saudi pipeline is out of business. Yanbu' is surrounded by about two hundred mines, in a perfect belt. They did a good job."

"The French are committed to freeing up our ship?"

"That's a roger, sir. The Frogs are sending a minesweep up toward the *Dahlgren* today."

"I'll make sure the President personally thanks them, and commits to helping them, at least at sea."

"Good, sir. I'm sending a couple ships into the Red Sea tomorrow. The air group is ready to go at any time. We'll be all over these bastards in a day or two."

"Roger that. Good. Listen, I've got a deal cooking with the Japanese. I want you to get ready to do something."

"I'm standing by, Mr. Secretary. Ready to copy."

"Don't copy this, Mad Dog. Just do it. Bring half of the minesweepers we have in Bahrain into the Red Sea. Get them moving today."

"Roger that. Good idea, sir."

"And start thinking about liberating Yanbu'."

"Yanbu'? *Saudi Arabia?*"

"The pipeline. Right."

Holcomb detected a moment of hesitation on the other end, as if he had caught the admiral off guard. But Mulcahy quickly recovered. "Oh. When you say 'liberate,' you don't mean the port. You mean clear a sea-lane for the ships."

"Exactly. International waters. That minefield has at least four Japanese tankers trapped inside Yanbu'. They're loaded up, ready to come home. I want to—talk to the Japanese about that tonight."

Another pause. "Roger that, sir. I get it. Smart idea."

"Good, good. I'll talk to you soon."

"Aye, aye, sir. And don't worry about us. We'll do Yanbu' out of our hip pocket, and still take out the Cubans!"

"I've never worried about you, Mad Dog. Out."

Walking back to his seat, Holcomb felt his nervousness surround him like a straitjacket. He wasn't worried about Mad Dog. He was worried about the Japanese. And he was beginning to worry about whether Everett Lodge would thank him or fire him if he knew the lengths to which his defense secretary was going to keep the President out of trouble.

He took his seat across from Lazaretti and Eichelberger. The plane had begun its descent. Holcomb watched the massive urban sprawl of the Kanto Plain appear beneath him. In the distance he could see the snowcapped Mount Fuji rising from a yellow haze, so beautiful and serenely powerful that he had no trouble understanding why generations of Japanese viewed the mountain as godlike. The extent of the urban buildup was incredible: Japan had a population half that of the United States compressed into an area about the size of California, only 10 percent of which was habitable.

Holcomb grew conscious of his powerlessness as he peered out of the window. It sat heavily in his stomach, making his face ashen and drawing it into a frown. He spoke absently. ''Did you know that when MacArthur left Japan after Truman relieved him in 1951, more than two million Japanese lined the roads from Tokyo to Atsugi to wave good-bye to him? We're sort of—reversing his route this afternoon. All the dignitaries of the Japanese government, and Tokyo's entire military garrison, stood at attention at Atsugi when his plane took off. It was almost as if he were the emperor himself. He made Japan's postwar resurgence possible, you know. Not that they would ever admit it today. But think of where Japan would be if George Patton had become Supreme Commander of their occupation! He wanted to hang the emperor as a war criminal, and personally ride his famous white horse down Pennsylvania Avenue.''

Ronald Holcomb marveled at the urban morass below him. ''I wonder what MacArthur would think of it now? I wonder what advice he'd give us.''

''I can answer that.'' Eichelberger eyed Holcomb narrowly, as if measuring him along the seams of his character, looking for tatters and flaws. Holcomb remarked to himself that the former Company man's face held a stare that MacArthur himself might have reserved for some weak-kneed State Department pretender. ''He'd tell you to chill out, Mr. Secretary. In Asia, the man who shows no fear is king.''

No Japanese dignitaries awaited them at Atsugi. And an hour later they reversed General MacArthur's historic route. It was raining. The road itself was devoid of pedestrians, packed instead with thirty thousand cars. And not one of them was American, except the three in Holcomb's party and two Corvettes that the driver said belonged to members of the Yakuza, Japan's mafia.

''*Ya-sans* no good,'' said the Japanese driver, smiling; he then moved his hand straight down in front of his eyes, indicating a flat face. ''They are mostly Korean, anyway.''

2

Tokyo, Japan

''You have a problem, Ronald,'' said Makoto Harada. ''Maybe even more of a problem than you think.''

''*We* have a problem,'' answered Ron Holcomb somewhat hopefully, sipping from a thimble-sized sake glass and feeling the warm rice wine roll easily down his throat.

''What you mean, 'we,' white man?'' And then the Japanese vice minister of foreign affairs laughed kindly at his own little joke, which he had learned years before by watching American television. Finally he shrugged, an invitation. ''Well, let's work on it.''

Makoto Harada's high forehead and thin, elongated face reminded Ron Holcomb of the samurai and emperors in the celebrated Japanese artworks from centuries before. Even now, watching Harada as he sat on a cushion across the low dinner table dressed in a gray business suit, Holcomb had no trouble imagining him in a flowing kimono, with his hair pulled back and tied behind his head in the old style, wielding a two-handed sword. Harada was tall for a Japanese, and lanky. His hands were thin, almost feminine, and as he talked he sometimes moved his long fingers languorously in front of his acne-scarred face, as if he were directing an orchestra.

But he spoke perfect English, flavored with the nasal lilt of the British upper classes. On the eve of World War II, Harada's father had been posted to the Japanese embassy in Britain, and Harada himself had spent three years in a British boarding school. Holcomb often thought that Harada affected the accent, as a reminder to arrogant, caustic Americans of his doubly genteel heritage. His ability to speak English fluently set him apart from the generations of politicians who had gone before him. Harada, decided Holcomb, represented the new Japan: cosmopolitan, assertive, and yet still anchored in the traditions and discipline of the most ordered society on earth.

"You know that if the American economy fails, the rest of the world will go down with it."

"The American economy isn't going to fail, Ronald. Although in the eyes of many Japanese, the Americans have failed their economy. It's a tricky question when you see it from this side of the Pacific." A geisha crept soundlessly into their private room, her head lowered, and knelt at the end of the table. Harada gestured toward her tray. "You like sushi very much, as I recall?"

"Yes, thanks."

Holcomb allowed the geisha to place two pieces of fresh, raw tuna onto his plate. He knew he was being entertained in one of the most exclusive restaurants in Tokyo, but in contrast to the open lavishness of top American restaurants, in Japan this meant simple elegance and absolute privacy. He and Harada sat alone in a small, simply furnished dining room surrounded by sliding paper walls. Four smiling geisha dressed in exquisite silk kimonos had met them as they entered the restaurant from the street, taking their shoes and fitting them with black leather slippers. Other than their hostesses, they had seen no one as they were led to their dining room. And except for the periodic interruptions, when one of the women would enter the room, offering small portions of food or refilling a glass, they were alone.

"So, your family is well?"

"Very well, thanks. Janet sends her best."

Holcomb knew better than to directly confront Harada. The verbal fights that were such a common form of discussion in the United States were interpreted by the Japanese as deeply embarrassing. Their Confucian upbringing taught them that one argued only when all other avenues had failed. Even with his Western exposure and his palpable love of American niceties, the vice minister would retreat behind a veneer of politeness if challenged, and then immediately report to his superiors that the American defense secretary had arrived in Japan in an angry mood. And Holcomb would be left without a clue.

"Then tell me, Makoto. How does our relationship look to—certain people—on this side of the Pacific? What are they saying about the Nakashitona problem? Because on my side of the Pacific, our people are deeply angry that this corporation sold off American technology to *North Korea*, that ended up in the hands of the *Soviets*."

Harada toyed with his food, then put down his chopsticks and took a deep, preparatory breath. Holcomb knew that his longtime acquaintance wanted to speak directly, and indeed had probably been given permission to do so. "From this side, Ronald, it is difficult for our people to understand how the Americans can even claim that it's your technology. You couldn't build the Iroquois system without the computer chips that are made right here in Japan! Your factories can't even produce a one-megabit semiconductor, at least not the kind the Iroquois needs! It's too complicated for Americans. We are accused of being imitators, but your technology is now a full generation behind ours. So . . ."

Harada stopped talking for a moment. He waved a hand in front of his face and shook his head apologetically. "This is getting crazy. But most Japanese feel that Nakashitona was selling its own technology. And that your country is angry because it needs a new enemy. That we are being scapegoated, Ronald. By a nation of racists.''

''That's unfortunate. We're not talking about the computer chips, Makoto. We're talking about the codes for the Iroquois system itself. Japan didn't develop those, and you couldn't begin to.''

''*You're* not talking about computer chips. *We* are. You couldn't fly your F-sixteens and F-eighteens without them. You couldn't shoot a tank, or guide your missiles! Just see how far American weapon systems could go without our semiconductors.'' Harada paused, eyeing Holcomb as he sipped from his own sake cup. ''Or how far the Soviets could go if they did have our semiconductors.''

Holcomb stared quietly at Harada. ''Is that a threat?''

''No, no. The government has no position. I'm only giving you a flavor for the mood in my country, Ronald. These are the things people are saying. You're going to face it directly tomorrow. Japan is feeling—very independent. There is a great frustration here. We've been propping you up, at the same time you've taken us for granted. You can't deny it. We've been financing your national debt when you should be doing it yourselves. We've recapitalized your industries. We make a great deal of the crucial technology for your weapon systems.''

''You've gotten a good return on your investments.''

''That's true. And we have no fantasy about putting America under. We have a good many businesses of our own in your country now, and we benefit when you are strong. But that doesn't mean we have any further obligation to prop you up. There are a lot of areas here in Asia with good investment potential. Singapore. Thailand. Malaysia. The Philippines. China. Even Siberia . . .''

The dread that had tightened around Holcomb as the plane began its descent five hours before was now palpable. It seemed to squeeze his chest, so great was Holcomb's fear that a Japanese-Soviet rapprochement would occur at a time when he would be at least partly to blame. ''You've never gotten along with the Russians. Not in your entire history.''

"That's true. We don't trust the Russians. Most Japanese won't say this to an American, but Japan will never forgive the Russians for staying neutral in Asia during World War Two, even hinting that they would help negotiate a settlement, and then declaring war on us only *one day* after you dropped the atomic bomb! But you don't trust them either. And you seem rather keen to negotiate with them just now.''

The vice minister grew coy. "We've had feelers from them recently. They're interested in exploring the return of the Kurile Islands and signing a final peace treaty from World War Two.'' He chose his next words carefully, as if he were writing a diplomatic pronouncement. "There are many in our government who see great benefits in stronger ties with the Soviet Union, both for the stability of east Asia and for the economic interests of Japan. Sort of like when Nixon made peace with China.''

"Will I be told that tomorrow?''

"No, not as a warning. Only as an observation. But it would be unfortunate if you pushed too hard tomorrow, Ronald. Minister Tanashi is—deeply upset. And he is very smart. Someday he will be prime minister. The country is angry. He reads its moods very well.''

"We've protected your interests all over the world. You can't survive without your sea-lanes. In the Persian Gulf, when you were getting more than half the oil that passed through the Strait of Hormuz, it was the American Navy that kept your oil tankers moving—''

"Yes, and we are thankful for that! But remember, we had no quarrel with Iran. In fact we retained—excellent relations with them the whole time. Also, that wasn't the Soviets.''

"In the Red Sea right now, it *is* the Soviets. They've mined the port of Yanbu'. You have four tankers marooned there right now, filled with oil.''

"*Was* it the Soviets? Many Japanese doubt it.'' Harada seemed to catch himself. "And anyway, our people are asking where the American Navy is, now that there is indeed a crisis.''

"We're on the way," answered Ronald Holcomb. "I ordered our minesweepers to steam from the Persian Gulf this morning."

"That will be very helpful," said Makoto Harada, pointing to his sake glass as the geisha again entered their dining room. "May I ask you to mention that tomorrow? Minister Tanashi will be happy to hear that when you meet." He sipped his sake. "And there is progress on the Japan-bashing legislation in your Congress? We do not understand this man Doc Rowland."

"We're working on that," said Holcomb, now breathing a bit more easily. "I've got somebody working on that right now."

3

Washington, D.C.

From his earliest childhood, summer's glories had been overwhelmingly sensual to Congressman Doc Rowland. When the dark earth of southern Illinois unfroze from winter, it grew musky and alive. The corn fields filled with an exuberance of green stalks that soon would provide fodder to the world. Patches of soybeans and vegetable gardens brimmed to overflowing at the edges of his little town. Cattle grazed in the pastures after a winter of eating dry hay inside the barnyards, their young, unsteady calves sucking greedily at their teats. Powerful, rutting bulls demonstrated clearly to every farm boy the wonders of creation. The cocky love cries of domineering roosters echoed in the henhouses and the barnyards. And behind the barn, or underneath the shady oak and walnut trees that grew in thickets next to the muddy, newt-filled streams of distant pastures, young couples shook off the confines of winter and tested their own creative urges.

He had brought this unspoken view of summer's meta-morphic power with him to Washington. In summer, Doc Rowland ran hot and happily wild, surrounded as he was with those other evidences of the joys of pollination and procreation who flocked to Capitol Hill in their bright, pretty dresses, their skin golden with the suntans of beaches and nearby swimming pools. But there had never been a summer like this one, for Janet Holcomb seemed to be exploding all over him with the sap of newfound love.

They had known each other for years, but had become lovers suddenly and completely. Rowland had stopped her in the hallway of the Rayburn Building just after she had accompanied the secretary of education for his testimony before the House Appropriations Sub-committee on Education. He invited her to the Members Dining Room for lunch, and before the afternoon was out she had agreed to come home with him. The morning after they first made love she had awakened him in his McLean town house at six o'clock with a telephone call, and had been on his doorstep within a half hour, falling into his arms and out of her clothes, then devouring him for an hour on his rumpled king-size bed before they both set off for work.

For the past two months he had seen her several times a week, in the morning at his home or during lunch in small, remote restaurants that he had discovered over the years, or in the evenings at other restaurants, from which they would hurriedly depart for the glorious oasis of his town house. He had even dared to meet her at the Kennedy Center two nights before, where they had watched a play and had drinks at the outdoor bar on the center's roof before heading back across the river to McLean. At first he had told himself that he was fighting Ron Holcomb on the battlefield of her body. But that was no longer true. He was reeling under the power of her unleashed attraction.

Once, he had asked her the whereabouts of her husband, and she had made it clear to him that Ron Holcomb neither knew nor cared about what she did, so long as it did not embarrass him. She had also told him that he should not pursue the inner workings of her marriage, and after that he had dropped it. And so Doc Rowland, perhaps for the first time in his fifty-six years, had fallen over the cliff without looking down to see if there was a river below. He was hopelessly attracted to this young, bright blonde who seemed also to be lost inside the kindness of his wit and the delight of his irreverence.

He had not looked seriously at another woman for six weeks. For him that was a record. *I only want to be in love. Is there something wrong with that?*

And tonight, by God, like some ageless Egyptian pharaoh he was dressed and oiled, prepared for the journey into the glorious afterworld. His insides were embalmed in a bottle of the finest French Chevalier-Montrachet wine, vintage 1980, and sated with a roasted salmon fresh from Alaska. He was royally swaddled in a new summer seersucker suit, and underneath he wore a pair of bright red Jockey shorts, just for the fun of it. He chuckled with anticipation as he followed Janet Holcomb toward the front door of her square brick colonial home, with two large pillars announcing the front porch. Rowland assessed both the house and the neighborhood as he followed her. Two million dollars for that house, he decided, maybe even more. Ron Holcomb didn't buy that on his government salary, he thought. Even with both their salaries. Somebody's got a rich daddy.

She wore a yellow silk dress that fit her loosely, with a wide black belt that accentuated the flare of her hips. Her hair fell away from her face and down her shoulders, revealing exquisite Mabe pearl earrings. Her smooth cheeks were tanned. She smiled and exuded an energetic sensuality, like the cover girl on some *Sports Illustrated* swimsuit issue. Janet Holcomb seemed just in from a swim or a jog, her muscles toned, her body tanned by the sun, and her face emanating an almost innocent freshness.

"Come on in."

She unlocked the door and immediately proceeded to a

digital box on a nearby wall, punching in a series of code numbers to turn off the burglar alarm system. Then she walked toward the back of the house, casually turning on light switches as she passed them. Doc Rowland followed her, peering into side rooms and up the curved stairway at first, still leery of being a lion in a tiger's den, a fox among the wolves.

"You sure your son's not around?"

She was in the kitchen, pulling out a bottle of wine from a cabinet. "You mean Ron's boy? He's off in Maine, on Outward Bound. Relax, Doc. He won't be back for a couple weeks. I think you'll be out of here by then."

"Maybe not, maybe not." Doc Rowland chuckled, taking off his coat and sitting at a barstool next to her kitchen counter. "But I guess Ron"—he paused for a moment, hating the thought of calling Holcomb by his first name—"will be calling you or something?"

She smiled sweetly as she poured two glasses of a *qualitats mit predikat* Moselle wine, revealing straight white teeth that once had worn braces. "Don't hold your breath. And he won't be back for three or maybe four days, unless his meetings with the Japanese break up early. In which case the command center will call me on that special white phone in our bedroom closet and tell me that my husband is inbound. Isn't it nice how the Pentagon takes care of those little things for me? Here." She handed him a glass of wine, and raised her own. "Thanks for dinner. That was a great place."

He raised his own glass, having now loosened his tie. His face was brimming with happiness. "Dr. Feel Good, at your service, ma'am."

"Are you really a doctor," Janet Holcomb asked, "or are you just a Ph.D. who likes the title?"

And Doc Rowland found himself laughing hilariously. "You been around this town too long, honey. Let me tell you: I'm a doctor of *life*! Hell, before I came to Congress I was a farmer, a soldier, an artificial inseminator, a milk distributor, and finally started up my own business installing furnaces. I—''

"Now, wait a minute." She had raised a hand, stopping him, and was coughing, pretending to have choked on her wine. She sat next to him on another barstool, leaning forward on the kitchen counter, her face now less than a foot from his own. "An artificial inseminator? Of what?''

"Cows, cows! What did you think, people? That's why they started calling me Doc!" He gave off his famous cackle, finally relaxing on this foreign terrain, the kitchen of his most hated enemy's home. "After all that experience I could probably do it to people, but I'll tell you, it would take all the fun out of making love, just to think about it.''

"Then don't think about it," Janet Holcomb interrupted, her smile growing mischievous.

Doc saw that she was fascinated. It amazed him, just as it always did, that the most mundane and forgettable experiences of his youth should provoke such interest in the intellectual, sophisticated environment of his later adulthood. If he had discovered a new law of physics and won a Nobel Prize she would have been polite, but faintly bored. But sticking a rod up a cow's ass, that was different, it was exciting, it was—beyond the scope of their comprehension. And so he indulged her.

"Here's the way it works. You show up at the Browns' farm on Wednesday afternoon and you've got a metal canister of bull sperm you keep frozen with dry ice in the back of your pickup. You holler to Mrs. Brown when she comes out the door, 'Hey, Miz Brown, you got the heifer all tied up in your barn yet?' And she points the way. And you reach into your canister and pull out a vial of sperm from some prize Holstein or Guernsey bull—she gets her pick, you see, the farm wife not the heifer—and you load it up inside a long glass tube.''

Janet was laughing now, shaking her head. Her warm blue eyes were unbelieving and her smooth face was lit with the earthiness of it, and with admiration for Doc's ability to spin a yarn. He continued, leaning a little closer to her, one arm on her shoulder for just a moment. "So you get yourself a bucket and fill it with water. Then you take your tube and the bucket and walk into the dark corner of the barn. And there's Bessy, muling and lowing, swaying her head side to side as she fights the rope that's got her tied to the stall. Now, you've got to sneak up behind her. And here's the toughest part. You jam your fist right up her, her . . ." Rowland made a fist, holding it just in front of Janet Holcomb's face. Somehow he knew that she had become aroused, or maybe merely more aroused. "Her ass. No, that's right! Anybody in the Congress tells me I'm exaggerating when I tell them I know what it's like to be up to my elbows in cow dung is a liar!"

"God, Doc. That's what I love about you. You're always so full of happy shit."

And now Rowland laughed. "Hell, you're worse than I am, Janet! You scratch that New England chrome, get behind that Mercedes, there's a John Deere tractor and a barnyard, sure enough!"

"Well, who do you think settled New England, lawyers?"

"To tell the truth? Yeah. Lawyers, professors, and bankers. But I know that's not fair. Somebody had to feed them until they built the railroads out to Illinois."

She punched his shoulder softly, her voice now lowered as she sipped from her wineglass. "So, anyway, what happened to old Betsy?"

"Bessy, honey. Bessy. Yeah, you sweet-talk old Bessy now, working your hand inside, patting her rump with the other one, and she starts to settle down. You start feeling around with that hand until you get to where you can feel her—her female parts. Then you massage them, and relax them." Janet Holcomb's hand was on his thigh, massaging him, relaxing him. "And then you get that glass tube and slide it inside her, her vagina, and when you can—" She leaned forward and kissed him. Her lips were soft, yielding, and she gave him just the end of her tongue. He set down his wineglass and held her face in his hands, brushing back her soft hair and kissing her for a long time. It felt so good that it hurt. It came from too deep inside her, and his response was being pulled out of a place inside of him that he had thought was dead, or at least retired.

Finally she pulled away from him, and he looked at her half-closed eyes. "You don't want to hear how Bessy gets it?"

"Yeah, Doc. How does Bessy get it?"

"Let's see. Where was I?" She kissed him again, for a long time. His hands found her breasts and then he and she were standing, and his hands moved down her muscular back, finally pressing her hips into him. He was aroused, and yet confused. There was too much power coming out of her and entwining him, too much emotion. This wasn't the sort of playing he had become used to. It was serious, and he was afraid.

"I never asked. But why me, Janet?"

"Because you're safe." She pulled away from him. "Now, didn't you say you had to make a phone call?"

"Oh, damn." He pulled a card out of his pocket. Roy Dombrowski had called him during dinner and told him that Warner Haas, back in Illinois, needed to talk to him as soon as he could make the call. "Mind if I use this phone?"

"Go ahead."

He dialed the number, shaking off the wine and concentrating on Warner Haas, and what he might want so badly that Doc Rowland should call him at home on a weekday evening. Haas was one of Rowland's largest financial supporters. He was a developer in Euphoria, a town that had once boasted the largest tractor factory in the United States. In recent years, Euphoria had gone through a severe recession. The factory, Gypsy Moth Industries, had fallen victim to Japanese infiltration of the farm machinery market. Employment had dropped from almost eight thousand workers to less than a thousand in the space of only nine years.

Euphoria, once a thriving town of forty thousand, had actually dropped in population during those years, driving down the real estate market and closing many service industries.

The Japanese had undermined the farm machinery market through a technique known as dumping, whereby they "priced down" their exports, charging much less in the United States than in Japan for the same products while the Japanese government protected the home market from foreign competition. The idea was to drive out the overseas competition with extremely low prices while maintaining an income base at home that preserved the industry. It was the same technique that had worked with calculators and televisions and motorcycles and pianos and video cassette recorders, and it had worked with Gypsy Moth. The company had gone moribund, amid accusations of worker inefficiency and outlandish labor costs.

Haas had railed for years against such Japanese business practices, and had leaned heavily on Doc Rowland to assist in opposing unfair-trade laws. Rowland had consistently spoken in favor of protectionist trade legislation that would require "equal treatment" among trading nations. But he had never been able to fully assuage Haas and the other leading businessmen in his district, and apparently had failed yet again, despite his strong showing on *Hello America!* and the harsh legislation he had introduced to punish Nakashitona Industries.

For the first time in ten years, Doc Rowland was facing a strong challenger in the next election, and Rowland needed Haas if he wished to be reelected. And a phone call from Haas usually meant that some arcane promise had come due, fully known and understood only by this man whom Rowland viewed alternately as his greatest supporter and his most persistent tormentor.

"Hello."

"Warner, how you doing, cousin? How's the weather back there?"

"Good to hear from you, Doc."

Haas seemed hesitant, almost preoccupied. That usually boded ill. Doc Rowland braced himself for an unusual request, and at that moment hated Warner Haas, hated being in the Congress, and dreamed again of the freedom he might gain if he could only give up Washington and inseminate cows again, or maybe retire to the South Sea Islands. Anything but being a slave to the man who paid his political bills. Money, thought Rowland again. Money, money, money, the source of fear, the root of sin, the grist of greed. And Warner Haas had it.

"What's up, Warner?"

"Doc, we need to talk for several minutes. Are you able to do that right now, or should I call you back a little later?"

"No, no. I'm fine. I'm fine. Go ahead, Warner. What's on your mind?"

"You might be a little surprised at what's on my mind, Doc. That's why I need a few minutes to talk."

"So talk, man. I'm all ears, as they say."

"Let me say, first, that I thought you did a pretty good job on *Hello America!* the other day."

A *pretty good* job? What was this? Rowland bit hard into his tongue to keep from replying. Haas continued.

"There were a few comments in the business community out here about your little joke. You know, when you said that a businessman loves a dollar more than a pretty girl and all. But we know the pressures you're under up there in Washington, Doc, and we've been behind you all the way. And Lord knows there's been more pretty girls than dollars back here over the past few years." Haas paused, as if waiting for a reply, then continued. "By golly, look. Nobody's been a stronger supporter of the need for fair trade than I have. The damn Japanese have pretty near ruined us out here. I don't need to tell you that."

"Well, I don't know how much stronger I can be on the thing, Warner. For God's sake, I'm out here on point as it is. I've got a bill in that's going to shut Nakashitona down cold. My staff has been telling me to be a little more careful. But it hurts me when I go home and see what's happened. This one's from the heart, Warner. And of course the national security part of it is pretty severe. We're dealing with people who have no conscience. That's my reading of it.''

"We think you ought to listen to your staff, Doc.''

Rowland's eyebrows gathered. He sat forward in Ron Holcomb's breakfast chair, querulous. "What does that mean?''

"Just be careful, that's all. Doc, you know we're all very patriotic out here, and none of us would condone what this company did when it sold off that stuff, whatever it was—''

"Technology, Warner! The Iroquois antimissile radar system! The most sophisticated antimissile technology our military has, that's what it was!''

"Right. Well, that's a damn disgrace. Although there's a lot of people out here—not me, you know that, Doc— but some others, who think that it isn't such a big thing anymore, with the world changing like it has. Particularly now when we've got a chance to straighten some things out, to bring the community back on track. So let's not throw the baby out with the bathwater, if you know what I mean.''

Where the hell did you pick that up, on C-Span watching Teddy Gilliland after my speech the other day? "No, I'm afraid I don't know what you mean, Warner. What the hell do you mean?''

Warner Haas's voice was tentative, almost apologetic, and yet at the same time deeply defensive. "We tried this one way and it didn't work. It's time to try it another way. We were visited a couple weeks ago by a Japanese consortium. They're interested in buying out Gypsy Moth and refurbishing the factory. Akasaka Industries. They make riding lawn mowers and small tractors. They're going to put in a whole new industrial park. They want to screen the workers, and even take some of them back to Japan for retraining. They're promising to get rid of the union, too. They tell us they'll have five thousand people working in the factory within fifteen months.''

Haas became urgent, almost ferocious. ''Now they're saying if your bill passes, the bank that's financing them is pulling out. *They're going somewhere else!* Look, they've got the capital to pull this off. No one else does. I didn't create this problem, Doc. I didn't devalue the goddamn dollar. I didn't vote for a string of budgets that busted the bank. I didn't hedge on protective legislation that might have kept them from dumping underpriced goods on our market. *And goddamn it, I've never even bought a Japanese car!* But here we are, Doc. This is reality.''

''So what are you asking me to do, Warner?''

''Nothing, Doc. Nothing. Just go easy. That's all we're asking. We're out here, trying to make America grow, and for now we're going to have to be doing it with Japanese dollars.''

''The Japanese dollar isn't a dollar, Warner, it's a *yen*. And you're putting Americans to work in Japanese factories! Our people will become wage slaves! Where do you think the profit from that factory is going to go? And who the hell put the American factories out of work in the first place? Do you remember that, Warner?''

''Yeah, I remember, but that doesn't even matter anymore, Doc. Believe me. You can sit up there in Washington and holler all you want, but it's history. Job are jobs. Money is money. Growth is growth. The entire chamber of commerce is on board. We want Japanese investment in Euphoria. It's the only way out of this goddamn sinkhole we've fallen into, no matter how it happened. If you've got a problem with one Japanese company, you go ahead and fix that problem. But if you wipe us out, we're going to remember. We're all good Americans. We don't like breaches of national security, selling off our, whatever it was.''

''*Technology*, Warner!''

''Right. Technology. We'll back you on that. Although

like I said, we'll probably be *giving* it to the Russians in a few years, if things keep going the way they have been. But anyway, don't solve a problem and create five new ones. And for sure, don't create a problem that's going to hurt your hometown friends. Don't get me wrong. We just want to grow again, that's all I'm saying.''

"I hear what you're saying, Warner. I hear you.''

Doc Rowland hung up. He shook his head in wonderment, addressing Janet Holcomb, who was watching him with an amused smile. "He doesn't want to grow again, he wants to grab a bundle of money again. He wants to roll in the clover with some goddamn Japanese yen! Well, I'll be a son of a bitch! How do you like that? I try to solve a real problem, and they threaten to cut my heart out!''

She walked up and cupped a hand gently over Rowland's groin, then spoke softly. "No, not your heart. He's got you by the balls, Doc. Give it up.''

"You sound like your husband.''

"I told you not to mention Ron.''

"Okay, okay.'' He kissed her gently on the forehead, putting Warner Haas out of his mind for a while.

Her warm face brightened. "Come with me.''

She took him by the hand and walked into the living room. In the backyard, patio lights illuminated a small swimming pool. She pushed a button on the wall and a pair of lush floor to ceiling drapes mechanically closed. She turned a dial and the entire room darkened, so that the greatest glow was from a small track light that filtered through a stand of bamboo in one corner. She pressed another button and a hidden stereo began playing Tchaikovsky. The low, somber cellos and high, exultant violins of that great composer's music did battle in the richly furnished room. She stood by the couch, next to a finely carved Malaysian wood sculpture, and dropped her dress onto the floor, her own body more of a work of art to him than any piece of wood. And he was lost, lost, in the elegance of her flesh. The bra came off. She lifted one leg at a time out of her panty hose. And then she stepped out of that pile of silk and nylon and walked toward him, lifting her knees as if she were indeed just walking out of the sea.

"I swear you look like a goddess."

She kissed him and when he touched her now she moaned. She pulled away and slowly undressed him as the cellos and the violins did battle on the stereo. She began laughing softly when she saw his red undershorts, and he chuckled too, feeling at once corny and gallant.

"Just for you."

"That's sweet. You like me, Doc?"

"You bet."

"Betsy was never like this, huh?"

He laughed merrily, stroking her face and feeling the warm strength of her thighs. "Bessy, honey. No, old Bessy was never much for the glass tube. Now. *Betsy*—"

She put a hand over his mouth and looked at him with eyes that had become commanding. "Shut up. I don't want to hear about Betsy."

CHAPTER 10

1

Ethiopia

Clumps of bedraggled Cuban soldiers had watched for fifteen minutes as two large Soviet-made HIP helicopters worked their way toward Manda from the western mountains, out of a sky so richly blue that the only stain was a pastel haze on the horizon, which came from windblown sand. Now one of the HIPs hovered over the landing zone that General Abelardo Valdez's men had cleared on the outskirts of Manda, its roaring rotors driving salt and sand into their clothes and faces and equipment with a stinging power that raised welts on exposed skin. The soldiers on the ground turned their faces down and away from the helicopter, keeping their hands over their eyes and trusting fate that the HIP would not throw a blade, or lose power from a gearbox destroyed by sand, and then crash, sending steel their way instead of dirty wind. It slowly settled into the

zone, the long camouflage-colored fuselage with its bul-
bous, windowed nose and wheels hanging underneath like
curled paws reminding Valdez of a huge praying mantis.
And then the pilots pulled back the throttle, idling the rotors
while a steady stream of sick, wasting soldiers were carried
aboard by their comrades.

Valdez shook his head steadily as he watched from his
command post a hundred yards away from the landing zone,
smoking a cigarette and cursing the indecisive fools who
had been dangling his division like a lobster over a cook
pot for more than two weeks. The sick soldiers were now
inside, and the helicopter powered up its engines, causing
other soldiers around the landing zone again to cover their
faces with their hands and lean away.

Characteristically, Valdez spat into the dirt, scowling as
he watched the helicopter lift off. It turned a tight circle
just above the ground, raising a wake of dust behind it. In
a few minutes it would join its escort gunship, which had
been orbiting around Manda, and head back toward the
distant mountains. In an hour the helicopters would land at
Dese, the capital of the province of Welo. Dese was the
forward base of Valdez's helicopter elements. It was halfway between Addis Ababa and Manda, more than a hundred
miles behind Valdez to the west and south.

A sudden wave of rotor wash engulfed Valdez as the HIP
passed overhead, throwing dirt and salt down the back of
his collar and up into his nostrils. Then the helicopter was
gone. Twenty more soldiers had departed with it, debilitated
from the heat and the foul water. His men had functioned
well in the relatively lush heat of Angola, raised as they
were in the tropical richness of Cuba itself. But the northern
reaches of the Ethiopian desert were draining them, sucking
the moisture from their bodies and fouling their insides.
They were weak from the heat, short-tempered by their lack
of movement, and sometimes disoriented.

Danakil tribesmen had killed three of his men at an outpost four nights before, stripping their weapons and dis-

appearing into the desert. A rumor had started among his soldiers that the men had been castrated, but it was not true. They were dead, though, and that was enough. Dead without revenge. Valdez did not have the inclination to chase stinking tribesmen through the desert when he was supposed to be fighting Eritrean soldiers and maybe Frenchmen, in a historic campaign to liberate the cities of Eritrea.

By now he was supposed to be at Assab, linked up with Soviet ships that could bring food, care for heat casualties, and supply ammunition and fresh water. Instead, he was trucking in water from Dubti, seventy miles behind the forward elements of his division, where the Awash River broke apart in irrigation channels that fed small cotton plantations. The Awash water was muddy, odorous, fit only for animals and Danakils. His men were getting sick from it. And from fear.

He had made Dubti the rear headquarters for the Ethiopian follow-on units, and had brought a small helicopter detachment up from Addis Ababa and stationed it there as well. He had also established two air bases closer to Eritrea, one at Dese, and one at Mekele, the capital of Tigray Province. Both Dese and Mekele were protected by the mountains, and had runways in excess of six thousand feet, so Valdez had brought most of his helicopters and MIG fighters forward from Addis Ababa to shorten the tactical radius his aircraft would fly. From Dese the MIGs could support his move toward the sea, and the helicopters could provide gunship support. In addition, the helicopters could evacuate serious casualties to the hospital at Dese, and could carry others farther back to Addis Ababa. From Mekele they could support the attack on Edd, and the eventual conquest of Asmara. Mekele was like the top of an isosceles triangle, with legs less than one hundred miles long extending toward the sea, one to Edd and one to Asmara.

Valdez had decided to bypass Assab. He would allow the French their odious little vanities, give them that small corner of Eritrea, and meet the Soviet fleet at Edd, eighty miles closer to Asmara. It was a gamble. Edd was due north of Manda, twice as far for him to push his armored units over rough terrain, and his trucks over narrow little unpaved roads. His map showed a protected anchorage but no port, so the Soviet mother ships might have to shuttle supplies and water to him from offshore rather than unloading directly onto a pier.

But he was convinced that the French could not fight him at Edd, or on the road as he raced for the small port. They were dug in at Assab, and were ready for him there. After the loss of Colonel Emilio Rosales and virtually all of his reconnaissance battalion, Valdez had no doubt the French would give him a bloody and aggressive battle, no matter how hard he pummeled them with his heavy artillery and tanks. But the French could not defend all of Eritrea, and they would not attack the Soviets at sea.

So he would move on Edd, with the same quick ruthlessness he had envisioned for Assab. He would push a company of self-propelled artillery and a detachment of tanks into a blocking position between Edd and Assab, ready to cut off any French attempt to stop the column as his lead elements headed for Edd. There he would at last link up with the Soviets. And after that he would replenish his water supply, give his men a bath, and set up a rear base at Edd, defended principally by Ethiopian units. And then the movement toward Asmara would begin.

Ah, Rosales. Valdez walked along a row of tents. Inside the tents his soldiers hid from the heat, cleaning weapons and writing letters. He waved to them, cheering them and asking questions to keep them alert, and a fresh wave of guilt overwhelmed him. He had personally picked Rosales. He knew the young man like a son. Rosales had been a smart soldier, and a brave one. Valdez felt as though he had killed the young colonel himself.

Only twenty-seven soldiers of the reconnaissance battalion had made their way back to Manda after the French ambush. They had hidden in gullies of salt and lava, and in the shadows of overturned vehicles as the French soldiers swept through the killing zone of the ambush. They had fearfully called to one another after the French had departed, and then searched the battlefield in the dark until they had found two partially damaged BRDM reconnaissance vehicles that were still operable. As the sun broke over the desert, Valdez had met the returning soldiers on the outskirts of Manda. Several of them were riding on top of the crippled vehicles. The survivors were shocked, catatonic, and their fear infected the men who helped them out of the vehicles. Their uniforms were ripped and soiled. They bled from shrapnel and from the desert, and flies clung to their wounds like huge black scabs. Their eyes were knowing and yet opaque, forever changed.

After he listened to their account of the ambush, Valdez had returned to his command vehicle and secretly wept tears of anger and shame. Then he had vowed revenge. He had not spent thirty years fighting for revolutionary change in the world, only to go home in shame. They would take Asmara. And when he returned to Cuba he would give these devastated soldiers the front car in Havana's grandest victory parade. He would speak warmly of Rosales in his own speech, and would recommend the young colonel for the Hero of the Republic of Cuba Medal.

Asmara would fall quickly, Valdez was sure of it. The Soviet Navy would begin bombarding the port city of Massawa any day now, a prelude for his dash toward Edd. Once the Soviets began attacking the Eritreans directly, morale among the Eritreans would crumble. Massawa could be blown to shreds from the sea. The rebels would begin preparing their retreat from Massawa and Asmara even before the Cuban division began its attack. And the rebels would flee from Asmara to their enclaves in the northern mountains rather than fighting the Cubans, leaving tanks and artillery pieces behind. Then the Ethiopian soldiers who followed in Valdez's wake would fill the streets like an army of ants, controlling the cities of Eritrea once again, and rooting the

Eritreans out of the mountains in the coming months.

But most important, once Asmara was taken he could go home. Valdez wished to feel his arms around his wife, and to see his son fight in international competition, even more than he wished for a victory parade in Havana.

"Two days," Valdez said to his soldiers again and again as he moved among their tents and tanks. "In two days we break for the sea." His feet burned from the heat of the sand and his stomach roiled from bad water. He felt light-headed as he walked. His mouth could no longer taste the cigarettes he constantly smoked. His khaki uniform was stiff from sweat and salt, and his eyes were now sinking inside a burned, unshaven face.

He encouraged his men, and yet his reassuring smile was fed not by his battle plan but by the memory of a beach near Havana where he had first made love to his wife, and of the thought of watching young Antonio glide gracefully inside a boxing ring. He spoke warmly of conquering Asmara because he dreamed of his first hot, soapy bath and of the dark, full-breasted whore who would scrub him, in the best room of the best hotel of Asmara. And most of all he dreamed of leaving the salt and sand of this hell called Ethiopia, and of going home.

And yet his smile infected his men's spirits. His optimism was almost a palliative to their nightly fear of the Danakil tribesmen, and the memory of the battered reconnaissance vehicles that had limped back to Manda with the numb, defeated remnant of Colonel Emilio Rosales's battalion.

The helicopters had now disappeared over the mountains. A small convoy of trucks carrying water and rations up from Dubti was spewing white dust a few miles to the south, leaving a cloud on the desert floor that Valdez and his soldiers watched almost languidly in the afternoon heat. Tomorrow when the sun cooled down, the soldiers would break camp and load their vehicles and prepare for the hundred-mile journey to Edd. It would take no more than ten hours for the armored units to make a proper tactical move if things went well.

And in a few days, if they fought hard and well, they would be in Asmara.

2

Assab

"I hate vultures," said Bill Fogarty to Michel Fourcade as they sat together in front of the whitewashed facade of General Avice's command building. Three huge vultures had gathered in the street just down from them, and were ignoring them as they pecked through a mound of garbage as casually as pigeons in Central Park. "I hate vultures worse than I hate rats. And I hate the *shit* out of rats."

"Well, I'm sorry you do not like your accommodations," said the French colonel. "The next time you travel with us, I'll ask that we fight where there are peacocks."

"Peacocks. Every time you talk about a bird, it's got to be a cock. I'll tell you, Fourcade, you've got a fixation." The Frenchman shrugged blandly, demurring with a smile. Fogarty stood, throwing a piece of lava at the birds, who did not so much as lift a wing at his threat. "Once when I was in Vietnam I woke up with a rat on my chest. It was like the devil sitting on me! I froze, man. I waited for five minutes before the damn thing hopped off of me. Well, this morning I look up and one of those vultures was on my window ledge, giving me the same look. I had to pinch myself to make sure I hadn't died and gone to hell."

"You are in hell, Fogarty, you just haven't died yet. Although sometimes I notice you smell like the dead. Maybe you want an angel in your window, so that you think you've gone to heaven? Anyway, the *amiral* is letting you go back to the ship soon. Then it will be better. Think of us out here—screwing *female* hyenas, no?"

Both men laughed. Fogarty's comment just before the battle on hill 3209 had become a running joke.

"Yeah," said Fogarty. "We rot on the ships, and you guys have all the fun."

"You may be back," said Fourcade.

"No," answered Fogarty. "I think you guys have put the Cubans in a box."

"So, you had your little taste of Africa, and now you can go home."

"I didn't even want a taste, Fourcade. I don't know why you Frogs give one small damn about this place."

"Because we like hyenas. Why? Would you rather have the Cubans and the Russians out here?" Fourcade stood up, dusting the seat of his trousers. "Anyway, in an hour the convoy will be here. And I can read about our battle in last week's *Le Monde*. And maybe there will be a letter from my wife."

They began walking toward Fourcade's battalion, which now was in reserve in an inner perimeter near the port itself. Around them, the French fortress bristled with activity. Jeeps drove along the baked roads, and helicopters churned overhead. Below them in the small harbor, three ships from the previous day's convoy were easing into the sea, on their way back to Djibouti. The journeys were indeed as regular as a mail run. Every day the French ships steamed from Djibouti to the small Eritrean port, carrying troops and weapons and supplies, further bulking up the town against a Cuban attack. The shuttle run took no more than 120 miles. The ships would leave Djibouti in the morning, cutting through the calm, pristine waters of the Gulf of Tadjoura, around the coast and through the Bab el Mandeb. In the narrow strait of the Bab el Mandeb, the French sailors watched carefully for signs of activity from the fortified Yemeni island of Perim only 10 miles off the Djibouti coast, and then steamed around a collection of small islands and coral reefs, into the protected coves of Assab harbor.

Once the convoys docked, soldiers from the Assab defenses unloaded the supplies from the ships, working through the afternoon and well into the early night. The next morning the ships reversed their course and steamed back to Djibouti. The French were dug in at Assab. The destruction of the Cuban reconnaissance battalion, and the indecision of the enemy's higher command, had given the French time, and they had used it to become almost undefeatable.

They had just finished a morning meeting with General François Avice, who had told them that the minesweeper *Andromède* was entering the Red Sea with the morning convoy. Avice spoke every day on his secure radio to his own high command in Paris, to his ships that were patrolling inside the Red Sea, and to Admiral Mad Dog Mulcahy, out with the American battle group in the Gulf of Aden. Two dozen French and American warships were concentrated in or near the southern Red Sea, keeping watch on the Soviet amphibious task force that was now nestled into an anchorage off of the Dahlak Archipelago, awaiting further orders. Avice had told them that the Soviets had mined the northern reaches of the Red Sea, and that it was either a diversion that would allow the Cubans to save face as they retreated back to Addis Ababa, or an attempt to isolate the French from their home bases in the Mediterranean so that the Cubans and their Ethiopian counterparts could sustain a determined attack.

Avice's superiors in Paris were optimistic that the Americans would soon recognize Eritrea, as a gesture of mutual support now that the *Andromède* was going to rescue the American destroyer *Dahlgren* from the Soviet minefield. Avice seemed to believe it would not happen. Fogarty, piecing together the chain of recent events and remembering his time in Washington, knew that either it would happen quickly—a finesse of Congress and the media—or not at all.

Avice's Eritrean counterpart, Fikre Desta, was constantly at the French general's side. Every day the French general would walk or ride along the perimeter of his defenses with Desta, as a show of solidarity to both French and Eritrean troops. Avice and Desta passed Fogarty and Fourcade as they walked. They saluted the general, who returned their salutes and then patted the thin, dark warrior on the back, as if he also were sharing their respect.

"Your general seems to like Desta a lot."

"He's a good fighter, Desta."

"Yeah," muttered Fogarty. "But for who? He was trained by the Cubans before the Soviets threw off the Somalis and started supporting the Ethiopians. I don't trust the guy."

"Maybe you would like someone loyal to Mengistu?"

Mengistu was the Ethiopian Communist ruler. Fogarty shook his head hopelessly. "Desta's a Communist, pure and simple."

"He doesn't like you, either, Fogarty."

"I guess he knows I haven't gotten caught up in the magic of fighting so that one Communist regime can kick the hell out of another one. Even if it does mean that through some magical formula Castro's going to fall through the cracks in the process. Who the hell's going to replace Castro? Probably another Communist."

"Ah, Fogarty. You Americans are so simple-minded about these things. Good and bad, what does it matter? Diplomacy is not like going to church." Fourcade sighed with finality. "You don't belong in Africa."

"You guys are great fighters, Fourcade. I'd be proud to stand beside you in battle. I mean that. But if I were you, I wouldn't exactly be bragging about France's success in foreign wars. What does your country get out of all this?"

"I think it's good you're going back to your ship," said Fourcade as they neared the fighting vehicles of his battalion. "Because out here, it will only get more complicated."

Later that afternoon, the small daily convoy from Djibouti cleared Perim Island, moving slower than usual with the

Andromède at its tail end. In a few miles the column would
begin to turn toward the islands that formed a cove around
Assab, while the *Andromède* and the destroyer *Primauget*
would continue steaming north, toward the Saudı port of
Yanbu', and the U.S.S. *Dahlgren*, which was still marooned
on the other side of the Soviet minefield. The sailors were
relaxed in the calm waters and the hot sun. The convoys
had become routine.

Perim Island was the crucial choke point for the convoys.
The island, as well as much of the opposite coast across the
Bab el Mandeb, belonged to the People's Democratic Republic of Yemen, an ally of the Soviet Union. Once the
convoy made it inside the narrow strait, though, the far
coast belonged to the Yemen Arab Republic, a neutral nation
allied to Saudi Arabia. But the sailors knew they were
watched from Perim, and that there were radar, artillery,
and antiaircraft installations on the island.

The French convoy finally cleared Perim Island once
again and its sailors immediately relaxed, preparing to dock
at Assab. They paid no attention to the uninhabited coastline
of the neutral Yemen Arab Republic inside the strait. Instead, they became consumed with their preparations to
enter the shoals that surrounded Assab, with rigging the ship
for its harbor call, and with unlashing the cargo that would
be unloaded in the blistering heat. None of them noticed
the tiny flash or the trail of narrow smoke that emanated
from the barren, salty marshes along the supposedly friendly
coast. Nor did their radars detect the missile until it was
too late.

The flash was a Soviet-made STYX antiship missile,
much more powerful than the fabled French Exocet that had
done such damage in the Falkland Islands and the Persian
Gulf. The missile skimmed the surface of the placid water,
covering the twenty miles from the Yemeni coast to the
peacefully steaming convoy in less than five minutes.

It erupted with a screaming suddenness, hitting the small,
160-foot minesweeper *Andromède* amidships, just above the

waterline. The fuel-enhanced explosion of the missile nearly blew the minesweeper into two separate pieces. A fire erupted in the engine spaces as the ship's diesel fuel ignited immediately, and then spread throughout the stern of the ship. The *Andromède* listed quickly onto her port side. Flames engulfed her, and she sank within fifteen minutes.

A dozen sailors had been thrown into the sea by the blast of the missile. A few others had been on the bridge, and were able to scurry down ladders and jump clear of the ship before it sank. The rest of the sailors, more than thirty of them, died from the blast, or in the fire that followed it, or were trapped inside the ship and drowned.

The supply ships of the convoy moved quickly into the port of Assab when the *Andromède* was attacked, while the *Primauget* and the amphibious landing ship *Foudre* remained in the *Andromède's* vicinity for several hours. Helicopters from the *Foudre* circled the wreckage, picking up stunned survivors from the hot sea and treating them in its hospital. The helicopters then returned to the burning sea, searching hopelessly through the flames for others.

The *Primauget* conducted a futile bombardment of the Yemeni coast, but it was too late. Its 100-millimeter guns now peppered empty salt marshes. The STYX, like the Silkworm missiles favored by Iran, required only a few hours to emplace a launch site, and once the missile was fired the sites could quickly be abandoned. And besides, the STYX had been fired from the coastline of the Yemen Arab Republic. The Communist soldiers of the missile's crew had violated foreign territory to launch the STYX, and the French destroyer was retaliating by shooting onto the mainland of a friend.

CHAPTER 11

1

Washington, D.C.

"Well, looky here, Mr. Secretary," said Billy Parks. "We got an escort."

Parks's aged, ebony face had lit up with interest as Ronald Holcomb's limousine turned from Massachusetts Avenue onto the Rock Creek Parkway. Another car had hurried through the light behind them, and now was pulling up alongside the limo in the choked early morning traffic. Holcomb, who kept a regular work schedule when in town, was apparently being electronically ambushed.

Parks smiled grimly, nodding toward the other car. "Yes, sir, some of our favorite friends."

The red-white-and-blue license plates on the dented, cream-colored Chevrolet indicated that it was a diplomatic staff car. Next to Parks in the front seat, security agent Ed Stooksberry read the plates carefully, verifying Billy Parks's observation.

"SFC zero-one-one. FC, that's them. Yes, sir. The Russkies are out early this morning. Look at that car. It's still wet from the dew. They either been out all night and picked us up as a target of opportunity, or another car's been trailing us, too, and vectored them in from the other direction."

The man and woman in the car's front seat were both in their forties, dressed neatly as if commuting in from the suburbs to work. They stared straight ahead, unspeaking, seemingly ignoring the limousine next to them. Parks and Stooksberry ignored them also, but finally Stooksberry spoke softly to Holcomb.

"Don't use the car phone. They'll be listening."

"Well, let's give them something to bring back to the embassy," answered Holcomb, feeling gallant. "I'll put a call in to Pete Swearingen, and tell him the President is leaning toward supporting his proposal to lay mines around Vladivostok as a response to what they've done in the Red Sea."

"Just think, sir," laughed Stooksberry. "We could start World War Three right here on the car phone."

"We'll save that for another day," said Holcomb. "Report this when we get to the Pentagon."

"Yes, sir." Stooksberry continued nonchalantly, accustomed to such situations. "I imagine we've got a chase car on them, anyway. We keep *them* under surveillance all the time. You know, if we took all the spooks and the chase cars off the road, morning rush hour would be a snap."

Parks suddenly tipped his Greek fisherman's cap and waved to the driver of the other car, who still ignored them. Holcomb, in the backseat, returned to his reading. The cold war may have warmed up, but the intelligence services never lacked for work. There was always a reason to mistrust, to be afraid of the future, and thus to spy.

The nearness of this sort of activity had strained his credulity at first, but after three years he was used to it. America was so saturated with spy novels and movies that it was hard to accept the reality of such intrigue. But here it was, every day: electronic surveillance so sophisticated that they could pull out your telephone conversations from the very air, if you muttered a key word of importance to them that activated their systems. Other devices that could pick up and translate the vibrations your voice made against a windowpane. And every moment on the phone, at work or at home, you had to assume you were being wiretapped, either by friends who were afraid you might leak classified information, or by enemies who prayed you would.

It was so subtle that Holcomb never fully believed it, even when it was happening. Like so many others, he had become numb to reality, simply because every aspect of this life was so intense. Reality's nastiness became lessened through its own mundanity. But there it was, one lane away.

And the Soviets were working their intelligence systems especially hard just now, trying to anticipate what Everett Lodge might do next, after the destruction of the French minesweeper just off of Assab.

Holcomb had watched the morning news accounts of the previous day's meeting at the United Nations, where the United States and France had jointly protested the Soviet mining of Red Sea waters, and accused the Soviet Union of fostering unrest in the region. The news showed the Soviet delegate, Anton Ludnik, denouncing "the French invasion of Eritrea," and warning the Americans against recognizing the "rebel province." Ludnik had also angrily continued to deny any Soviet involvement in the mining activities, and claimed that the mines had been laid as part of "an irresponsible disinformation campaign, a plot by the American CIA to discredit the Soviet Union." Ludnik then repeated Soviet Foreign Minister Turbochev's earlier call for an international settlement of the Eritrean question.

The news then showed the delegate from the People's Democratic Republic of Yemen as he addressed the UN General Assembly. The screen was filled with Ambassador Mahmoud Salim, his voice pitched in rage as he waved a fist in the air. Salim's hot eyes flashed at the French and United States delegates as he delivered his government's official statement regarding the sinking of the *Andromède*, and the loss of life of more than thirty French sailors.

"The People's Democratic Republic of Yemen declares its solidarity with its brother countries Cuba, Socialist Ethiopia, and the Soviet Union, as well as all progressive societies around the world. It condemns the imperialist invasion of Socialist Ethiopia by France and the United States, and will join them in all actions necessary to rid the Red Sea of the military aggression by those countries. The right of the Ethiopian people to remain united under one government remains supreme, and the support by the imperialist nations of France and the United States for the lawless rebels in Eritrea must stop immediately. Until the Ethiopian question is resolved under a multinational tribunal headed by the Soviet Union, the People's Democratic Republic of Yemen considers itself aligned with Socialist Ethiopia, and in a state of hostilities."

And so the Red Sea region was at war. And although the United States had not officially recognized Eritrea, two aircraft carrier battle groups were poised to join the hostilities. Not to mention the three American minesweepers that had entered the Red Sea the previous night, under heavy protection from destroyers and carrier aircraft.

The Soviet staff car escorted them all the way to the Pentagon, its occupants never once looking toward them. Finally, Billy Parks pulled up to the Mall entrance, and Holcomb walked briskly into the Pentagon. It was five minutes to seven. He was hosting a quick breakfast meeting with Secretary of State Richard Fumaro and CIA director Adam Noel, and then would hold his first staff meeting since his return from Japan the day before.

2

Nothing of major significance would occur during staff call, Holcomb would make sure of that. When things got tough, Holcomb, Hank Eichelberger, and a few others closed the circle, worrying about leaks to the press and to their political enemies as they analyzed their options. The issues headed for the back rooms and the two- or three-man meetings. And Ronald Holcomb would continue what many, including Navy Secretary Zara Boles, had publicly commented was his most fundamental mistake: closing the door with people such as herself relegated to the corridors, wondering why they were not trusted, and what, exactly, was going on.

But Holcomb did not view it as a mistake. He was as mistrustful of his own staff as he was of the Soviets themselves. Many of his key staff members were not "his," anyway. They had been forced on him by the White House in order to repay favors done during the presidential campaign. Consequently, a good percentage of his staff actually owed their ultimate allegiance to other political figures. Some wrong little tidbit uttered by Holcomb while he privately struggled with options might come back to haunt him if it were relayed to an adversary, either through an article in the media, or a carefully positioned speech.

Holcomb knew that because of his secrecy, several of his key assistants were on the verge of rebellion, which only fueled further leaks to the media. But the leakers were fighting on his turf, so they would never win. Holcomb was the master leaker of the entire Lodge administration, and in Washington that was an invaluable talent. Covert relations with a multitude of reporters largely insulated him from press criticism, because he had become a protected "anonymous source." At the same time, it allowed him to use these same contacts to attack his enemies.

Besides Fumaro, Noel, and the President, only Hank Eichelberger knew the full measure of bad news that had come out of Holcomb's meetings with the Japanese. The hard-bitten assistant secretary had argued strongly against offering American minesweepers as escorts for the Japanese tankers trapped at Yanbu', and had seemed disgusted when the idea received the unanimous support of the others. Instead, he had recommended that the government demand a formal, public request from the Japanese to emphasize their dependence on the American military. Eichelberger had lost, thought Holcomb, but he was a pro. And there would be no leaks. Eichelberger literally hated the media, whom he blamed for the fall of South Vietnam and a litany of other disasters. So, at least for the moment, internal security was complete. And there was no public rift inside the administration over sending American warships into a sophisticated minefield to free Japanese tankers.

As he walked along the Eisenhower Corridor, Holcomb could see several of his immediate staff approaching his office, the under secretaries and assistant secretaries of defense who met daily with him and his deputy secretary Whip Stowbridge. They were carrying notebooks and walking with staff assistants, checking out last-minute details in case Holcomb might ask about some latest budget matter or arms proposal or weapons evaluation. Most of them were in their late forties or their fifties, and most were gray of hair and pale of skin. They wore simple suits and careful, conservative ties, traditional cuts from Joseph A. Bank or Brooks Brothers that were never either in or out of style. They waved to each other, as they did every morning, in a familiar manner that nonetheless was impersonal. He had always found it curious that people at this level by necessity trusted each other with so many secrets, of the kind on which governments might rise or fall, and yet shared almost no personal feelings, never allowed themselves an intimacy that might be called true friendship. Even the secrets were removed, objective, passionless.

He waved to them as he passed through his outer office. They were now gathering in groups of two and three, discussing the morning headlines, arranging meetings to coordinate positions on key issues, comparing assessments of the problems in NATO or on Capitol Hill. Sid Rose walked into the room behind him and Holcomb could hear the whole crowd brighten. Rose was charismatic, with the presence of an actor or perhaps a comic. He was an exceptional dresser in a room full of gray wool suits and rep ties. He never stopped talking or moving. Rose was the perfect link to the Congress, thought Holcomb again, moving into his inner office and closing the door. He was a brilliant lawyer, a master of the legislative process, a wheedler, a deal maker. And he knew where the bodies in the Congress were buried, as well as how to dig them up when a favor came due.

Yes, as always, he would give the staff a show, and yet tell them nothing.

"Ready, sir?" Bear Lazaretti peeked through the door.

"Right, Bear. Bring them in."

His personal office was a room as large as a whole floor of a town house. There were two separate sitting areas, one just inside the door through which his staff now entered, and one on the far side of the room, near a second door that went into an adjacent conference room. Deputy Secretary Whip Stowbridge had just entered through that far door, from his office on the other side of the conference room. Along the walls were sculptures, rifles, and swords, ornaments that reminded one of America's military legacy. On the walls were photographs of generals who had gone on to better things: George Washington, Ulysses Grant, Dwight Eisenhower. In the center of the room was a large wooden desk stacked with papers and military memorabilia, and behind the desk was a phone bank with hundreds of direct lines to military and civilian leaders throughout the world.

Holcomb went immediately to a blue easy chair at the corner of the room just inside and to the left of the doorway. Sherm Novotny, his assistant secretary for public affairs, sat next to him on a cloth-covered couch. The blue easy chair was Holcomb's throne, from which the defense secretary held his staff meetings.

"*Good morning, sir. Good morning, sir. Good morning, sir.*"

As the members of the staff sought their chairs, Holcomb noted a subtle change in the personalities of the fifteen key assistants. They each greeted him with a nod or word or a wave, and then assumed a variety of different roles, much like a king's court. It seemed timeless to him: They were minor dukes and princes, mirroring the manner of their relations with the king. The more confident showed a bit of swagger in his presence. Those who had made a career as facilitators demonstrated their suavity, moving with smiles and whispers to their seats, touching the shoulders of other staffers or ostentatiously pointing to passages in briefing papers to make their abilities visible to him. Others, more unsure of their position with Holcomb, quietly and anxiously took seats in the back row, as if to hide from his questions. A few, including Whip Stowbridge, Zara Boles, and Hank Eichelberger, walked with a nonchalance that indicated they were almost oblivious to the others. Those few were the ones whose instincts told them that they, too, might someday own the throne. Or maybe they already did, in the manipulative manner of aspiring Bismarcks.

But Sid Rose was the court jester, and it was his show. Even Ronald Holcomb smiled expectantly as he began the meeting, knowing he would soon be entertained.

"A few quick matters. First, as all of you know, there is a great deal of tension within the government right now, both with respect to our problems with the Japanese and regarding events in the Red Sea. The meetings in Japan were—constructive, but not conclusive. The Red Sea crisis varies from minute to minute. At the same time, it appears that the Soviets have moved troops into the Ukraine and are actively using them, apparently to prevent a civil war. I would remind all of you that this is not a time for public speculation by officials of this department regarding any of this. We are working directly with the White House on the problems, and there are enough people in the Congress and the media who are willing to second-guess what we're doing without their being fed by leaks from inside the Pentagon."

Holcomb paused for a moment, looking around the room as he allowed his warning to sink in. Many nodded dutifully, acknowledging him and even taking careful notes. He noticed Navy Secretary Zara Boles bristling, though, and heard her clear her throat before she spoke.

"May I make a recommendation? Don't you think it would be more helpful to the government's position if you arranged some briefing for us on just what the government position actually *is*? That is, if we have a government position."

Right, thought Holcomb, feeling his own face tighten as he suppressed his anger. *And then you can pick up the phone and call your friend Doc Rowland.* "At the right time, Zara, we'll do that."

"We're asked a lot of questions by the media. It would be helpful to know how to respond."

He froze her with a cool stare. "If you don't know, the proper response is 'No comment.' Let me do the talking, Zara. Or the White House." *And the leaking*, he laughed secretly to himself. Then he nodded toward Sid Rose, announcing the beginning of the show.

"Sid. How did things go in my absence?"

And Rose came alive from his chair just to the right of Deputy Secretary Whip Stowbridge, throwing a perfectly manicured set of fingers into the air as the rest of the staff set down their pens and eased into their seats. "How did things go? Damn, Ron, you decide to go off to Japan right when the government is ready to fall apart! First of all, I'm working my ass off. Here it is August, and we don't even have an authorization bill yet. I've been begging. I've been pleading. I've been offering plane rides to London. I've guaranteed the Blue Angels in two hundred congressional districts next year. I've been lying to the mothers in the Congress about how ugly their kids are. But what have we got? No bill in the House or the Senate either one."

Rose's eyes were round and his face was becoming flushed as he continued. "The House members are going to tear each other's hearts out if this goes on much longer. Look at Doc Rowland, for God's sake. I mean, he just pounds the *shit* out of you in front of national TV on this Nakashitona thing. And he's been a friend! This Japanese thing worries me! He's always carried the buckets, always voted with us! He's not even returning my phone calls anymore. But he likes you, Ron, no matter what he says on *Hello America!*''

"Oh, yes," said Ronald Holcomb. "Doc and I have always gotten along quite well."

"I know that. He had to come out against you on Nakashitona. Listen, you've got some blistered asses over there on that one. It isn't helping the authorization bill. I mean, Doc Rowland's committee is a revolt waiting to happen after he cut the throats of those four guys who outranked him to get the chairmanship three years ago. Every time he's tried to bring up the authorization bill he gets knocked down by his own people. They're in full stall, trying to embarrass him. Especially Teddy Gilliland. They're still so pissed off about how he got the chairmanship that they forget the country needs to be run. He's like the guy whose head was held under water: You don't even see the bubbles anymore. They'd love to do a number on him. But even his own goddamn *committee* is supporting him on Nakashitona! And they never miss a chance to remind me that the administration went ahead with the technology transfer in spite of their warnings."

Holcomb blinked slowly, nodding his head, indicating that it was time to change the subject. "I'll have better news on Nakashitona in a week or so. What else, Sid?"

"You'd better," answered Rose. "We lost our opening with Sad Joe Barksdale. When he saw that Doc Rowland wasn't slowing down on Nakashitona, he pulled the authorization bill off of the Senate calendar. We're dead in the water, Ron! People over there are starting to eat their young. They're giving up on the Leadership. Ed Stratford is getting suicidal. He isn't even talking to Barksdale anymore. He says he's done everything he can to shake the bill loose. And he's stopped drinking, so I think he's telling the truth. And he owes us, after the helicopter I sent into the shopping center last year to bring him back for the TPX vote. That little gig got the phony bastard reelected. The people of Vermont thought he was a god, being pulled back to work his magic by Gabriel and a chariot full of angels. Get—''

"Sid, slow down," interjected Holcomb, barely retaining his anger at his "good friend" Doc Rowland. "What else?"

"What else? Oh, jeez, I hate to tell you. Let's see." Sid Rose consulted the yellow legal pad that he kept on his lap. "Oh, yeah, this is good. Kip Lincoln wants part of the 45th Infantry Division to be stationed in Alaska. He's *hot* on it! Poor choice of words, but he's been a friend, too."

Holcomb held one hand into the air, shaking his head. "I don't see the purpose in that. We can rotate soldiers through for cold-weather training."

"Ron! The purpose—the *purpose*—is to put dollars into Alaska, and to get Kip Lincoln reelected! But I'm with you, I'm with you. Listen, I told him, 'Kip, it's not like Ron's a goddamn county water commissioner, passing on projects to your cousin Guido.' But it didn't help. Maybe they don't have water projects in Alaska. Or maybe they do and he has a cousin Guido who's on the take. Anyway, he stopped returning my calls. But have breakfast with him. He's had it with me. Hell, the only thing he and Doc Rowland have in common is that they both won't talk to me." Rose leaned forward, pleading. "Aw, Ron. Give him a breakfast."

Holcomb checked his watch. "Just for you, Sid, I'll have lunch with him this week. Do you think you can arrange that?"

Rose grinned triumphantly, way ahead of him. "He's holding today for you."

Holcomb chuckled, his etched face knowing and ironic. "I was afraid so. Anything else?"

"Are you kidding? Martin Jucinski wants us to turn over the National Guard armories in Brooklyn so he can use them as shelters for the homeless. He says the National Guard is a ripoff, that we aren't going to war anyway, and that we're losing the war against homelessness. He's introducing a bill on it today. His district just went seventy percent black with redistricting, he's got a black activist already campaigning against him, and he's getting beat up in the polls.''

Rose grinned with unconcealed admiration for the New York congressman. "He'll win, though. He knows how to work that district. Last week he got endorsed by thirty black ministers representing six thousand families. Three others were found dead in an alley on Third Avenue. That was a joke, Ron. Actually they won't find the bodies until next December, after they've voted.''

"How about the Senate, Sid?''

"You mean you don't want to hear about the march the Animal Rights League held against you for shooting dogs and cats for wound research, or the bill that's going to be passed this week prohibiting us from testing the ATAK antiaircraft system in Maryland?''

"Well, I'll pass on the protests. I've gotten more letters on dogs and cats than I have on nuclear missiles. What's this with ATAK?''

"Bruce Vokakis. He's got a bill that will prohibit live firing at the Aberdeen Proving Ground, pending an environmental impact statement.''

Holcomb scoffed, sitting back in his chair. "That's a stall! Pure grandstanding. Vokakis has opposed every defense issue for the last ten years. I'd call him a pacifist, but that would be too kind.''

Rose was aglow, his arms flailing as he warmed to the expectant chuckles of the rest of the staff. "He's an evil, evil man, Ron. *But he's got two hundred thirty-one cosponsors*! Nobody's going to vote against an environmental impact statement. What the hell is a statement when endangered tree canaries are being threatened?''

The entire staff had been laughing and groaning along with Rose throughout the exchange, and hardly a note had been taken. Now Sid Rose was finished. Holcomb went quickly around the room, receiving updates from the other staffers on matters under their jurisdiction. As the staff meeting drew to a close, Major General Bear Lazaretti made a final point.

"Sir, General Francis would like to brief you on some operational matters."

Holcomb checked his watch. He had no desire to talk operational matters with the Joint Chiefs Chairman until after he had called Mad Dog Mulcahy, whom he was now consulting several times a day. And he had other calls to make as well. "Well, I now have lunch with my good friend Kip Lincoln. I'm at the White House this afternoon, talking about the Japan trip with Felix Crowell and some others at the National Security Council." He nodded again to Stowbridge, indicating that his deputy should take the briefing by the Chairman of the Joint Chiefs of Staff. "Whip, meet with the general, would you? And I'd like an update from you before I leave for lunch." Holcomb hedged, making sure. "Unless it's urgent, that is."

"Oh, no, sir," said Bear Lazaretti. "It's not an urgent matter, and I can get you a summary if need be."

"Alright, Whip can take the briefing." Holcomb stood up, indicating that the meeting was over. "Anything else? Thank you all very much."

Zara Boles stayed behind, not bothering to hide her unease. When the others had gone, she spoke quietly to the defense secretary. "I just want you to know that if you can't trust me with the logic of our Red Sea operation, I'm going to have to start responding to the questions I'm getting by asking a few of my own. That's not a threat, Ron, but I've been in this town as long as you have, and I have my own credibility to protect."

He looked at the former congresswoman for a long moment, and then nodded, feigning his agreement. "Yeah, Zara, you're right. I'm sorry to put you on a limb. Give me another day or so, and I'll bring you in for a detailed briefing."

Once he was alone, Holcomb picked up his private line and called his good friend and predecessor John Michaels. They had not talked since the evening at the Kennedy Center. Michaels was ebullient as he assured Ronald Holcomb that Doc Rowland had indeed gotten the message regarding his attacks on Nakashitona Industries.

"We've got old Doc boxed in," laughed Michaels. "In a few days he's going to be *begging* you to rescue him from his own goddamn legislation!"

3

Illinois

Doc Rowland could hardly believe his eyes: The Onnetka High School parking lot was nearly full. He peered through the dim evening light at rows of trucks, wagons, and cars as he walked toward the school's main entrance. Suddenly his heart raced.

"They all here to listen to me?" He guffawed. "Must have been that new suit I wore on *Hello America!*"

Roy Dombrowski quietly coached him as they walked. "Remember, Doc, this is going to be a split audience in here. You need to be careful tonight. Real careful. There'll be the usual home stuff. And they're going to ask you about whether the President has been holding back information to your committee on Nakashitona. Some of them are going to want to know about what's going on in the Red Sea, particularly since we've got that ship trapped up there. But the big thing's going to be Japan, because it means their jobs."

"I know, Roy, I know."

Dombrowski seemed unnaturally worried. "Focus in, Doc! Half the people will be pulling for you to bash the Japanese, especially since you took the lead on Nakashitona. The other half are going to be scared. Akasaka is the first glimmer of hope they've had in five years. Hugh Alcott is running against you on this issue, all by itself! He's playing to both sides, telling them that on the one hand your position on Nakashitona isn't backed up by the Defense Department, particularly since the cold war has come to a stall, and that on the other it's going to hurt their bank accounts.''

Dombrowski hesitated, searching for the right mix of seriousness and sarcasm as he peered carefully at his boss's face. "He's saying you're just a xenophobic racist. Even though it's a year away, I don't need to remind you that this will be the closest race you've ever had, Doc. Hugh Alcott has been waiting for years to run against you on the right issues.''

"I know all that.'' Rowland cheerfully elbowed his frowning administrative assistant. "Dammit, Roy, relax! This isn't Washington! These are *my people*, you hear?'' They walked past a large poster just outside the entrance that proclaimed TOWN MEETING TONIGHT, EIGHT O'CLOCK. CONGRESSMAN DOC ROWLAND.

Dombrowski persisted. "You're going to have to separate national defense questions from the economy. Play up Alcott's inexperience. Show him as unable to understand the complexities of national issues. He's been a state legislator for ten years. He wouldn't know an M-one tank from an M-sixteen rifle.''

"Careful Roy, careful. That's what they said about me twenty years ago, and I used it to my advantage.''

Dombrowski looked down at Rowland, smiling whimsically as they reached the stairs leading into the gymnasium. "How's that, Doc?''

"Hell, man! When you sound like you know too much about the problem, they think you're the problem!''

Doc's fat face assumed a cheery farm boy's glow as he heard the chatter and the shouts of the crowd inside the gym. He straightened out his patterned polyester sport coat and waved at a man who had noticed him. Then he patted Roy Dombrowski on the shoulder, muttering into his assistant's ear as they walked through the door. "These people don't want to hear a lot of numbers and definitions. They want somebody who fights for 'em. They got assholes talking down to 'em every day."

"*Hey, Doc!*"

"Well, hey, cousin!"

A score of people waved to Doc from different places in the crowd as he entered the gymnasium, and his charisma went into high gear as quickly as if Roy Dombrowski had flipped a power switch. Doc waved and chuckled, pointed and hollered, seizing the spotlight like a world heavyweight champion entering the ring for a fight. Many in the audience now cheered and clapped, and its collective mood brightened.

They did love Doc. He was the embodiment of all their secret fantasies, the living proof of the American Dream. He was Just Like Them. He had come off of the farm. He had been born into cow pies and chicken shit and hard winters and baking summer droughts and he had never really left them, never taken on the airs of that city far to the east that they both loved and feared. They saw him frequently on the television, read about him in the newspapers, and he had remained a home boy, always true, always true.

The stands had been pulled out, as if for a basketball game. They had filled one entire side of the gymnasium, sitting there in their Levi's and bermuda shorts, their halter tops and baseball caps. Doc walked up to a microphone that had been placed at center court, needing no one to introduce him. On the wall above them, a recent banner boasted ON-NETKA PIONEER POWER—STATE CHAMPS 1990. With one short question, he jumped again into their midst, like a minnow set free from the frightening confinement of a fisherman's bucket, back into his native cove.

"I'm so proud of those kids. Are the Pioneers going to do it again this year, or what?" And they all cheered brightly.

He spoke nonchalantly, without notes, one hand in a

trouser pocket and the other occasionally waving into the air, as if he were leaning on a fence post, chatting with a few hundred of his closest friends. "I haven't been out here in Onnetka for a few months, and I just wanted to stop by and pay my respects. To thank you good people for all the support you've given me over the years, and to give you a little update on the things we've been working on for you in Washington."

Rowland gestured toward Roy Dombrowski, who was standing underneath the net at one end of the basketball court. "You all know Roy, my administrative assistant. Born right in the state, up in Adenton, served in Vietnam, got his master's degree from the University of Chicago. If you've got any problems with veterans claims, or Social Security, or damn it, anything that's not being addressed by that bloated bureaucracy that's supposed to be taking care of you, tell Roy about it tonight and we'll get right on it when we get back to Washington. I mean it. You know that. Give your name and your problem to Roy." Dombrowski gave them a small wave, smiling shyly.

"Now." Doc Rowland paused dramatically, slowly surveying the crowd from one end of the bleachers to the other. "Before I came in here a few minutes ago, somebody told me to be careful about what I said. Told me that I needed to worry about how I talked to my own people. Told me that I was facing a tight race next year, that people needed to understand the difference between my announced opponent and myself. And I said, 'I been talking straight to people for my whole life. The day I got to mouse around and try to sound like a New York lawyer, by God I'll just go find another line of work!' "

They were smiling approvingly, clapping politely, sharing his cynical view of politicians. No matter that Doc Rowland was one of the smoothest politicians in the country; after more than two decades in the Congress, he could still run against Washington. No matter that he was growing weary of his job, even as he clung to its amenities; he was a world-class fighter, and he valued his reputation as a champion.

He continued. "So let me speak straight. I've spent just about my whole adult life working to solve problems. That's what it amounts to, really. All of you know about life. Every time you solve one problem, another one sneaks up from behind you and grabs you by the throat or stabs you in the back. In the Congress, I've used the same kind of logic to fix problems that my daddy taught me out on our farm, twenty miles down the road from this school. I've brought some of Onnetka into the Congress, and I like to think that Congress needed some of Onnetka to help find its way. You know who I am, and what I stand for. I don't need to sell you a bill of goods, and I couldn't if I wanted to. You know how I'll vote because you've got twenty-four years of votes to look at and think about. No surprises."

He shrugged and then gave off his little boy grin. "So, I don't need to give you a long speech about what I'll keep on doing. We're going to keep this country *strong*! We're going to look after our farmers and our workers! We're going to make sure nobody takes benefits away from our retired people. We're going to give our young soldiers and airmen and sailors and marines the very best of everything that they need to keep protecting us. Even now, as we sit in comfort here in Illinois, hoping our Pioneers are going to take the state championship and making sure our kids have enough dessert to eat, those young people are out all over the world, working day and night, defending us. That's what Doc Rowland stands for. Now, what do you want to talk about tonight?"

A dozen hands immediately went up, but one elderly woman stood and walked to the front of the stands. She was bent and wide-hipped, and as she walked she absently held one hand against her blue polyester slacks, on the side of a hip. Without asking Doc she took the microphone from him, pushed plastic glasses rims up her nose, and spoke to the crowd in a scratchy drawl. "Long as I live I will never forget how Doc helped me when my husband was sick and then passed away. Called me up from Washington when he heard Omar was on the edge of death. Got me my VA death benefit. Got me my Social Security. I don't know what more you people want. Politics is never figured out all the way. We can talk politics all day long, and Lord knows we seem to, particularly in the winter. But this is a man who cares about people.''

The crowd applauded politely as the woman walked slowly back to her place in the stands. Doc Rowland nodded his appreciation, a devilish gleam in his eye.

"Thanks, Mom." They all laughed. "Seriously, Mrs. Adkins, I'll never forget your Omar, because I used to bale hay for him when I was a boy and I never met a fairer man with money. So it was an honor to help him out when he met his final reward. You and others like you make my job worth doing.''

As the crowd again applauded, Rowland pointed toward a gaunt man in a baseball cap, sitting in the back. "Yes, sir.''

The man stood in the stands. He was about forty. His eyes seemed hollow below the bill of his baseball cap. He was tall, and underneath his plaid working shirt Doc could tell his narrow frame held tight muscles and a flat belly. His voice carried without a microphone. He was a farmer, Doc thought expertly, listening to the rolling drawl of the southern Illinois region, carried over by its early settlers from Kentucky and Virginia. "Doc, Jamie McKnight, from over at Grayville. Proud of the way you've stood up on national defense. I'm chapter commander of the VFW over there, and on the state executive committee. We follow the issues pretty close. I'd like your comment. The *Chicago Tribune* had an article today on the Russians moving into the Red Sea. We stood by in the early 1970s while they moved in and took control of Angola, and when they helped starve millions in Ethiopia a few years later. All we keep hearing from Washington is peaches and cream, and yet here they are moving ships into the Red Sea. What are they up to, and what are we going to do about it?''

Doc quietly congratulated himself on picking the man. It was not luck, it was instinct. He needed to answer a national defense question so that he could set the stage for the inevitable questions regarding Nakashitona, Akasaka, and the Japanese in general. If it had been a Japanese question, he would have had to start with a long preamble on defense, anyway. "I know you all stay close on the defense issues, and let me tell you I appreciate your support. You boys who have been overseas and had to suffer through our foreign commitments understand why all this is so important."

Doc again surveyed the crowd in a moment of dramatic silence. "Lord knows we all want peace and good relations with the Soviets. Just as much as we want crime to end. But you don't end crime by telling your police force to stop preventing it, and you don't keep the Russians in the box by bringing all the troops home. They're still on the move, don't kid yourselves!'' He planted an important seed for later. "They're doing everything they can to steal our technology. Yes, that's right. Using spies and foreign corporations.''

He gestured toward his questioner. "And Jamie, here, has made a key point. Right now, they're picking a fight in the Red Sea, so they can move their navy in. 'So why should we bother?,' some people ask. 'Where is Ethiopia, anyway, and who cares?' Let me just say two things about that. First, I'm not the kind of man who can walk by a pond where someone is drowning and just shrug and say, 'That's okay, it isn't my kid out there flailing in the water.' We aren't made that way out here. We learn to depend on each other and to help each other, and we know that's the way our country should act as well. So long as our neighbor pulls his own fair share and isn't taking advantage of our goodwill. And second, there's a lot more at stake than Ethiopia.''

Rowland paused for a moment, walking in front of them

as he waited for his statement to sink in. "Did you ever look on a map and see where the Suez Canal is? Or where the Saudi Arabian oil pipeline comes out? Did you read the other articles in the paper, about how the French just lost a minesweeper to a foreign attack because they've been protecting the little province of Eritrea, whose freedom fighters have liberated their people from the ugly rule of the murderous Ethiopian Communists? That French minesweeper was on its way to help an American ship, marooned in a Soviet minefield! We can't back away from this kind of aggression! Let me say to you folks, that the minute we lose our ability to protect our allies and assert our national interest on the open seas, that *very minute*, even though a shot has never been fired, we have lost our freedom."

The applause was so loud that Doc Rowland nodded over to Roy Dombrowski, an indication that he wanted to put out a press release on the matter when he got back.

"Yes, sir. Right over here."

The man was wearing a suit. A real estate agent, thought Doc. Or an insurance salesman. He was in his early fifties. His face was pale and lined. And most important, he seemed scared. Not frightened of speaking, or even of the question he was going to ask. Scared of life like a man who had once been burglarized and now was being asked to unlock his front door every night when he went to bed.

"Ted Ragland, Doc. From over in Euphoria. I'm one of the people working with Akasaka to bring in the new plant facilities over there." A few people spontaneously applauded. The man seemed encouraged. His voice grew louder. "Look, the Japanese are saying that if you push this, Nakatona—"

"Nakashitona," corrected Doc Rowland, knowing the question already.

"Right. I never can say those foreign words right. Anyway, that if you push it too hard, their bankers are going somewhere else. They'll be forced to cancel the deal! He told me that, Doc. He's one of the negotiators from Aka-saka. Look, we're all behind you, but we need this plant. They're saying you're making the Nasah—oh hell, whatever you call it. Naka*shito*na. That you're making more out of it than you should, because of other reasons. That's what Hugh Alcott is saying, too. You need to be sure of what you're doing on this, Doc. Principles are fine, but I got two kids in college, and this place has been bust for five years.''

Again, they applauded. Doc's antennae were going giddy now, telling him that Roy Dombrowski had been correct, that this was indeed a very big cow pie, bigger than he had imagined. He began to respond. ''These are two separate matters, Ted. Two separate matters. One's government, the other is business. One's defense, the other's economics. We've got a Japanese company that's been caught *red-handed*, if you'll excuse the pun, selling off technology that cost us billions to develop, that can be used against us. On the other hand, we've got a company that wants to build a plant over in Euphoria. Now, if the Japanese *link* these two problems, I'd say that's blackmail. If the Japanese say they'll pull out their investments if we don't back down on a matter of national security, why, that's worse than black-mail. That's economic warfare. We can't let that happen.''

''They say you don't have proof, Doc. That even the Defense Department isn't going as far as you are in this bill you've introduced. Look, we all bashed the Japanese. We tried to tell the government what was going to happen. I don't like what's happened, but it happened. And it was government policy that ruined us once. Just don't let gov-ernment policy ruin us again.''

Ragland sat down. The entire crowd applauded. For the first time in his career, Doc Rowland had lost control over a home crowd. He stumbled, looking for words. Finally he nodded toward Ted Ragland. ''We've had hearings, Ted. The Defense Department testified on my bill, and the admin-istration muzzled them! We can't put up with that. All of you know I wouldn't hurt folks back home, just to make a point. But you need to back me if the facts are there. You need to, for the long-term good of the country.''

The gym was silent. Ragland stood back up. ''Don't you think it's about time somebody else suffered for the long-term good of the country?''

And again the entire crowd applauded.

CHAPTER 12
THE HORN OF AFRICA

Ronald Holcomb did not realize it as he placed his call to John Michaels, but he had missed a very important "operational briefing" after his Pentagon staff call.

In the Gulf of Aden, aboard the aircraft carrier U.S.S. *Roosevelt*, Admiral Mad Dog Mulcahy received the end result of that briefing, in the form of a message on the ship's encrypted radio, to be followed by written orders. In what seemed to be a routine communication, Mad Dog was being recalled to Hawaii, for "consultations." The message was signed by Admiral Jefferson Davis Smith, Commander in Chief of all forces in the Pacific, known as CINCPAC. It was endorsed by General Roger Francis, Chairman of the Joint Chiefs of Staff, and concurred in by Deputy Secretary of Defense Whip Stowbridge.

Reading the message, Mulcahy knew immediately that Smith and Francis were carefully asserting their operational jurisdiction over him, in a way that would not legally contradict the way Defense Secretary Holcomb was using him. His two seniors had attempted to bridle him for years, and now, with a serious crisis in the air, they feared his combative inclinations, and the power of his personality. They wanted him physically out of the region, so they could control the operation. In other words, they were rather politely relieving Mulcahy of command.

He threw the message into the trash bin of his stateroom, surprising Captain David Mosberg with his sudden, bellowing anger. " 'Consult,' my hind ass. Goddamn noncombatant staff officers, the hell with them! I'm not going to let them screw this up, just when we're about to pull it off!''

He would obey the orders, but he was not going to go quietly. Nor would he depart on the next S-3 that skipped out from the *Roosevelt* battle group toward Diego Garcia. Because he had made promises to General Avice, and he was going to keep them. *And besides*, he reasoned, *Holcomb hasn't said a word to me. Who the hell do they work for, anyway?*

But now it had to happen fast.

Two hours later his small Marine Corps Huey helicopter made its way westward from the Gulf of Aden, flying toward the narrow Bab el Mandeb. The Huey chugged along at 100 knots, a thousand feet above the sea. Behind it, another Huey followed close, in chase. Not far away, an AH-1T Sea Cobra gunship ushered the two helicopters through the sky like a patient sheepdog nudging two lost lambs. The Cobra was armed with 20-millimeter machine guns, 5-inch rockets, Sidewinder air-to-air missiles, and a TOW missile system capable of destroying tanks and other armored vehicles.

After flying over the port of Djibouti, the Huey crossed the Gulf of Tadjoura, and then went inland to avoid a possible missile attack from Perim Island or from Yemen on the other side of the Bab el Mandeb. As the little helicopter neared the Bab el Mandeb, a flight of F/A-18 Hornet aircraft from the *Roosevelt* screeched through the strait at almost 600 miles an hour, keeping a tight orbit that intimidated any possible activity from Perim Island or Yemen. The

Hornets carried an array of armaments, including HARM antiradiation missiles and SPARROW III air-to-air missiles. A second flight of F-18s followed in a few minutes. The second flight was loaded with iron bombs and laser-guided ordnance, to be used if necessary against a fortified ground target. The Hornets made loops in the Red Sea and the Gulf of Aden, coming back again and again through the Bab el Mandeb.

The Huey flew low, close to the peaks of the dry mountains along the Djibouti-Ethiopian border, and headed up toward Assab. From inside, Mad Dog Mulcahy could see herds of hyenas scatter among the mountain rocks as if the Huey were running along in their very midst, chasing them. The mountains disappeared and soon in the flat, dry plains of the Danakil Desert he could see tanks and guns and soldiers, brown from camouflage and dust, and after that the small town of Assab, nestled against the sea. He was coming in from behind, having avoided the kind of surprise that took out the *Andromède* a few days before.

What a trophy for the bastards, he thought, his blood racing madly, if they bagged themselves a four-star admiral.

French and Eritrean soldiers watched the Huey fly over them. Their bodies were baked dark and thin by the sun. Their hands were on their hips. Their uplifted faces held the calm contempt of those who know they are at the very edge of danger.

A red smoke grenade popped in a clearing just outside the city. A yellow one popped fifty yards away, and then a green one popped on the far side of the yellow grenade. In moments, the three helicopters neatly fish-hooked and settled into the three landing zones, shutting down their engines as French soldiers inside the landing zones directed them with hand signals.

General Jean-François Avice waited near Mulcahy's helicopter, standing in front of a dirty jeep. His boots were covered with dust but his uniform was freshly laundered, and his pinched face shone like steel from a recent shave.

Colonel Bill Fogarty stood at the general's left, also in a laundered uniform, sporting a recent haircut.

The general was in good spirits. His small brown eyes twinkled as he and Fogarty saluted Mulcahy, who now approached alongside Captain David Mosberg.

"Mon Amiral, it is good of you to visit." Avice shook Mosberg's hand. "Capitaine, you have not worn your handcuffs today."

Mosberg laughed sheepishly, remembering his arrival in Djibouti with his briefcase chained to his arm. "There are no whores in Assab, General. I feel safer here. Especially since Colonel Fogarty seems to have survived."

"Yes, yes. Colonel Fogarty has taken full control. He even chased the hyenas out of town." Avice elbowed Fogarty playfully. "No temptations for the Capitaine, eh?" Now he gestured magnanimously to Mulcahy. "This is not your chauffeured limousine, Amiral, but it is better than a camel, no?"

"It's better than an hour in a goddamn Huey, too," growled Mulcahy. "I feel like I've had my kidneys rearranged." He slapped Avice on the back, then gave Fogarty a look that told him his return to the *Saipan* was going to be a pit stop, on his way back into the desert. "Colonel? You ready to go?"

"Whatever you say, sir," said Fogarty, conscious of Avice as he and Mosberg headed for a second jeep. As Mulcahy and Avice climbed into the lead vehicle, Fogarty called to them in schoolboy French. "*L'audace, toujours l'audace.*"

"We'll talk about that!" Mulcahy yelled as the lead jeep pulled away.

"I'll bet we will," muttered Fogarty.

Assab had become a fort. Its outskirts were ringed with tanks, artillery, and antiaircraft batteries, protected by soldiers in fighting holes and sandbag bunkers. An inner circle of armored personnel carriers and infantry units spanned the edges of the town. In the town itself, soldiers and other

armored units were strategically placed in reserve, where
they could maneuver toward the front lines at the right place
to counter the spearhead of an attack. Everywhere soldiers
were digging trenches and filling sandbags to make bunkers
and abutments. Puma and Alouette helicopters flitted overhead or sat inside revetments. Huge rubber fuel bags lay
near them, sitting in gutters that had been scooped out of
the salty earth by small bulldozers. And supplies from another French convoy were being unloaded at the docks where
Assab joined the sea.

As they drove through the streets of Assab, Fogarty turned
to Mosberg, smiling mischievously. "I haven't seen you
since you delivered me into exile. I bet you thought I'd be
dead by now, you sorry son of a bitch."

"I had my hopes, Fogarty," the intelligence officer
teased. "How are the French?"

"They're perverted as hell, but they're good fighters."
Fogarty's eyebrows raised, as if he were telling a ghost
story. "They fuck hyenas in the desert, Mosberg. It's really
weird." He saw that Mosberg was suppressing a laugh.
"Anyway, they don't need us to knock off the Cubans."

"That's what you think."

"Oh, I see. You're not going to be satisfied until I *am*
dead, are you?"

"Talk to the admiral about it. I'm just an intelligence
puke."

"Don't shift the blame, Mosberg. I'll haunt you from
hell."

Finally the driver stopped at a house-sized building made
of stone. Climbing out of the vehicle, they walked underneath a high, curving doorway, built in the Moorish style.
Avice had put his headquarters in the town's only hotel.

"Come inside." Avice smiled to Mulcahy. "Welcome
to my little flat."

The hotel bustled with activity as French soldiers moved
in and out. One room had become a communications center.
Underneath a huge map of the region, which was heavily

marked with grease pencils of varying colors, a half-dozen radios crackled as Avice's operations officers talked with units on the perimeter and others out at sea. Another room nearby held a dozen more radios, for communication with higher headquarters, including the operations center in Paris and the *Clemenceau* battle group out in the Gulf of Aden. A helicopter passed over the top of the hotel building, shaking the furniture and drowning out their voices for a moment.

Avice flung an arm sideways, gesturing toward a closed door, and they followed him inside. Mosberg recognized Sergent-Chef Planitzer, who stood almost casually outside the door in his khaki desert uniform of green beret and shorts and an open-sided shirt, a submachine gun hanging lightly from one thick shoulder. Mosberg nodded to the soldier as he walked past him.

"Sergeant Planitzer, how are you?"

The huge, muscled Legionnaire showed no expression. He scratched the daggerlike tattoo of Africa that covered one forearm. He took his time responding, coolly surveying Mosberg, and then Mad Dog Mulcahy, as if both were mere pretenders.

"*Bon jour, mon Capitaine. Mon Amiral.*" Looking at Fogarty, the sergeant displayed overt respect. He came to attention, his heels thudding. "*Mon Colonel.*"

"The guy likes you," said Mosberg as they entered the room.

"No," answered Fogarty. "He doesn't have 'like' in his vocabulary. But he respects the shit out of me, Mosberg. I taught him how to call in American close air support."

Inside the room, Mulcahy took a chair, and was flanked immediately by Mosberg and Fogarty. His khaki uniform was now wrinkled, and soaked with sweat. He nodded almost deferentially to Avice. "Your men look good, General. Surprisingly rested, and clean, for the time they've been here."

"We are not strangers to Africa, mon Amiral. We have

been here for a very long time. Algeria. Chad. Djibouti. Kolwezi. And the sea feeds us like a mother.'' Avice shrugged nonchalantly. "The *Foudre*, she is a wonderful ship. Like another town coming here with us. We use her laundry. Our soldiers can see the doctor in her hospital. She gives us food. General Valdez, he is roasting in the desert like a skewered pig.''

The French general paused, as if waiting for Mulcahy to begin the meeting. Finally he continued. "So, mon Amiral, it is good of you to visit with us. We could have spoken on the radio, but I think you wanted to come ashore for a while? This is a long way to come for coffee.''

"We had to retrieve our Marine commander,'' began Mulcahy. Then he grinned, as if confessing. "I don't know how secure our communications are. And I didn't want anybody to be listening, anyway. Even my own people.''

Mad Dog surveyed Avice, instinctively liking the small, sarcastic Frenchman. "I want to help you. I want to win this, whether my goddamn government wants to or not.''

He let his words sink in. "Mind you, I have no evidence that they *don't* want to win. But they've ordered me back to Hawaii, and that isn't a terribly good sign. And my government has a long record of getting cold feet once they start something like this. The politicians are great until the first shot is fired. And then they wet their pants.'' Mulcahy snorted. "Think about it. When was the last time the United States has stuck it out when we've had a long-term commitment?''

"So, Lord Nelson is recalled to London, just before the Battle of Trafalgar. My country should have been so lucky two hundred years ago.'' Avice was only mildly taunting Mulcahy. "I am sorry you are leaving, mon Amiral. You have been very helpful. But in France we will understand.'' His small eyes twinkled. "Remember, our generals revolted against De Gaulle. You know Humbert, yes?''

"There'll be no revolt, General.'' Mad Dog seemed inordinately conscious of Fogarty's presence. But he loosened up now, pulling on his huge nose as he watched Avice. And then he chuckled. "A little insubordination, maybe. But no revolt."

Mad Dog nodded toward Mosberg, who dutifully opened up his briefcase and placed a stack of fresh aerial photographs on the small table between Mulcahy and Avice.

"General, my instincts are pretty good. I feel in my gut that this whole thing is going to blow up in the next few days. And I think I know what's going to happen." Mulcahy continued to talk as Mosberg moved the small table away and spread the photographs onto the floor. "The Cubans are hot, tired, and demoralized. They're getting sick out there."

"*Oui*. We have been watching them." Avice smiled warmly. "My Eritrean scouts, they are very tough. They visit the Cubans every day, dressed as Danakils. A few nights ago my scouts caught three Cuban soldiers asleep. They slit their throats in the dark."

Mosberg lay a large map of Ethiopia next to the photographs, arranging them so that Mulcahy could illuminate several locations on the map with the photographs. And then Mad Dog pointed to the cities of Dese and Mekele, in the mountain provinces behind Eritrea. "The Cubans have moved their air support up from Addis Ababa, closer to Eritrea. This is a major buildup, accompanied by large stocks of bombs and ammunition." Mulcahy's finger ran along several points in one photograph. "This is Dese. Trucks loaded with bombs and missiles, new revetments on the airstrips. Right here."

Avice carefully scrutinized the photographs, now quite serious as he pulled out a cigarette and lit it. Mulcahy continued. "That means they're not pulling back, in spite of the hammering you guys gave them a few days ago. But I don't think they have anything to gain by attacking you. They need to reach the sea. I think they're going to bypass you and try to link up with the Soviet fleet closer to Massawa."

Mulcahy picked up a photograph of the Soviet anchorage at Dahlak. "The Soviet ships are ready to roll. They've got the *Nicolaev* anchored at Dahlak, as well as two Alligator LSTs. All three ships are packed to the gills. They've also got a frigate in there"—Mulcahy pointed—"right here. A Krivak-class, the *Ladny*. The LSTs can put out a pretty good shore bombardment, and so can the frigate. We think they're going to lay down a heavy barrage on Massawa pretty soon, supposedly in retaliation for the 'attacks' on ships at Dahlak a couple days ago. That will shake the Eritreans up, make them nervous. And then the ships are going to steam south. Where they stop is where the Cubans will be heading."

Mulcahy dropped another photograph onto the floor. "Look at this. I got it maybe two hours ago." It was an aerial shot of the Cuban perimeter at Manda. Mad Dog carefully pointed to one section of the Cuban lines, manned by tanks and self-propelled artillery units. "The tents are gone. The lead elements of the Cuban division have packed their trash." He handed the photograph to General Avice. "These guys aren't taking down their tents because they want to get a better suntan, General. My bet is that the Cubans will move out soon—I'd say as early as tonight, or tomorrow morning."

General Avice studied the photographs and the map, his eyes going back and forth for several minutes, deep in thought. He finished a cigarette, mashing it out as always with a callused thumb, and then lit another.

"I have been thinking about this already, mon Amiral. You are right, we are too strong here for General Valdez, and he has grown weak in the desert. There are only three places for him to meet the Russians, unless he becomes desperate. Bera'isale"—Avice pointed to a place fifty miles north of Assab—"a good cove for ships, but close enough to us that he would expose his flank to our attack. Edd"—he pointed to a place thirty miles farther up the coastline—"farther from us than Bera'isale, but almost as close to him, since he is coming from inland. Or Karmu, just to the north of Edd.''

Avice squinched up his face and shook his head, as if to dismiss the thought of any other alternatives. ''Beyond that he is channeled toward the sea by the mountains. He will have to pass Edd and Karmu, anyway. And closer to Massawa the reefs are bad. It would be hard for the Russian ships.'' Avice shrugged. ''If he goes farther than Karmu, he may as well try for Massawa. And he does not have the fuel or the water to do that.''

Mad Dog leaned forward, holding Avice like a prisoner inside the fire of his wide eyes. ''Can you beat him to Edd?''

''Mon Amiral!'' Avice considered Mulcahy shrewdly, as if this were the final betting in a very large poker game. ''You would have us leave our defenses, and put us in between the Cubans and the Russians? The fox does poorly when he is between the hunter and the hounds.'' Avice thought about it some more. ''And how would you help?''

''We brought three minesweepers through the Bab el Mandeb two days ago, so they can escort the oil tankers out of Yanbu'. They're moving out of Yanbu' tonight or tomorrow. As long as they're in the Red Sea, we're going to keep combatants in here with them. I've got an Aegis-class cruiser in here right now, and two destroyers.'' Mulcahy's eyes glanced almost hesitantly at Fogarty, daring him, and then burrowed into Avice. ''I'll bring the *Saipan* in tonight.''

''The *Saipan*.'' Avice dragged on his cigarette, his own eyes narrowing. ''That is your amphibious assault ship.''

''That's right.'' Mulcahy again looked at Fogarty, and then surveyed his French counterpart. ''Listen, this may cost me my career, but there's not much after CINCPAC Fleet, anyway. Why have a job if you're not going to do the right thing when the time comes?'' He took a deep breath. ''If you beat the Cubans to Edd, I'll land the Marines.''

"Then after you leave for Hawaii, they will pull the Marines back?"

"No, they don't have the balls to do that. They don't have the balls to put them in, and they don't have the balls to take them out. That's been the problem for thirty years. Nobody in Washington can make a decision until it's too late. They make speeches and they yell at each other while the world turns to shit. So fuck 'em. Just *fuck* 'em."

"I have your word?"

"You have my word. The Marines will land, and they will fight."

"*Colonel?*"

The room grew silent as six sets of eyes waited expectantly for Fogarty to respond. He thought of Michel Fourcade, who had fought so gallantly on hill 3209. He thought of the dead North Vietnamese soldier whose tooth he still kept around his neck. He thought of his Marines abroad the *Saipan*, Fogarty-trained and led, who would now fight no matter how he responded, but perhaps with a less capable leader directing their battle. Loyalties, he fretted. They kill common sense. They drown the intellect.

Mad Dog leaned over and almost whispered, in a voice intense with conviction. "*We will topple the Castro government, Colonel.*"

At that moment Fogarty hated Mad Dog Mulcahy, but he could not dismiss the admiral's rank and position. Fleetingly, he convinced himself that if it came to it, he could attack Mad Dog later, in a congressional hearing perhaps, or in a magazine article. But those were unfamiliar, distant arenas. He was being given an order to face an enemy on a real battlefield, and he did not know how to say no.

"If those are my orders, sir, I'll fight. And if we fight, we'll win."

Avice pondered it for another minute. "Alright, mon Amiral. I will send Colonel Fourcade's reconnaissance battalion to Edd tonight. He will beat General Valdez to Edd.

But Amiral, do not forget your promise.'' General Avice appeared vaguely troubled. ''Colonel Fourcade has only a battalion. It is your career, but these are the lives of my men.''

CHAPTER 13
WASHINGTON, D.C.

1

In the Cabinet room of the White House, President Everett Lodge had asked his key national security advisers to remain behind after the weekly Cabinet meeting. The only missing member was Vice President Lowell Jackson, a former governor of Texas, who was at that moment suffering acute gastroenteritis in his bedroom at the American embassy in Mali, where President Lodge had sent him on a goodwill visit.

The six other men sat in leather chairs around the wide mahogany conference table that Richard Nixon had donated to the Cabinet room in 1970. The President, gangly and familiar, his face baggy and his hair dyed charcoal-gray, occupied a center chair that was, by tradition, two inches higher than the others. Secretary of State Richard Fumaro sat just to the President's right. At seventy-one he was the oldest and most experienced Cabinet officer. The back of Fumaro's chair sported four brass plaques, like chevrons on

SOMETHING TO DIE FOR

a high school letter sweater, denoting other Cabinet positions he had held. Secretary of Defense Ronald Holcomb sat on the left side of the President, running a nervous hand through rapidly graying hair. He was the youngest man present. CIA Director Adam Noel, an international businessman and longtime financial supporter of Everett Lodge before joining the Cabinet, sat just across from the President. Plump and intense, Noel was shuffling a ream of classified briefing papers as he prepared for the discussion. National Security Adviser Felix Crowell, on loan to the Cabinet from his position as a professor at the Harvard University School of Government, adjusted heavy glasses and studied his own pile of notes from his seat to Noel's right. And Eric Hewlett, the President's chief of staff, sat to Noel's left. Hewlett, a balding, chain-smoking Californian who once produced highly successful television documentaries, had been the President's campaign manager and political adviser for more than a decade.

Hewlett lit a cigarette and checked his watch, staring out through the windows that opened to the Rose Garden. He was searching for the President's helicopter, which would soon arrive to take Everett Lodge to Andrews Air Force Base. Lodge was scheduled to deliver a major foreign policy address in Chicago that evening, before the grand banquet at the Veterans of Foreign Wars national convention.

"We've got about twenty-five minutes, Mr. President. And you have a full house in the Roosevelt Room for the afternoon stand-ups."

"Right, Eric. Let's get with it." Lodge leaned back in his chair, smiling as he nodded to his National Security Adviser. "Felix?"

Crowell gathered himself, glancing up from his notes at the portrait of former President Dwight Eisenhower, who smiled watchfully at the group from above a nearby fireplace. The national security adviser's eyes then caressed the busts of George Washington and Benjamin Franklin, which flanked the fireplace, hollow reminders of great struggles that formed a nation. Finally Crowell cleared his throat, and spoke.

"We need your guidance in the face of three widely divergent but connected international crises. The Japanese are stonewalling the government on Nakashitona Industries' technology leak to the Soviets. They are literally daring the Congress to pass Doc Rowland's legislation invoking sanctions against the corporation—"

"Absolutely no movement from Tanashi," interrupted Ronald Holcomb, confirming this comment. "A very disappointing meeting. He seems to actually *want* the legislation. In my opinion he thinks it will set the Japanese people into motion, perhaps to the point that they'll make him prime minister."

"Do you think that will happen?" The President had turned immediately to Holcomb, a measure of his trust in the defense secretary's judgement. Crowell looked on, not concealing his irritation at having had his briefing knocked off the rails in its first ten seconds.

"I don't know. But I will predict that if Rowland's legislation passes, the Dow Jones Industrials will drop at least five hundred points within two days. Because the Japanese will start selling off Treasury notes by the bundle, just to show us who's got the greater power in the relationship. They showed us they could move our stock markets with T-bill sales in the October 1987 crash. But they can do a lot more now."

"And they won't budge on the Nakashitona apology? It seems like such a simple thing."

"Not to them, sir. And particularly the idea of reparations, which they regard as having to pay twice for their own technology." Holcomb gave a small smile, offering up his little treasure. "But we have two pressure points. Nakashitona has hired some very good people to work the Hill. They've retained the law firm of Murdock and Fein, and they're also represented by Bettinger Associates."

"You can't top that," quipped Hewlett. "They may as

well drop a nuke over there,'' Murdock and Fein had, as senior partners, three former Cabinet officials, Bettinger Associates was directed by a former secretary of state. The President nodded his agreement, and Holcomb continued.

"The other pressure point is Rowland. We've got him on the ropes. I have him waiting in the Roosevelt Room right now, for a two-minute stand-up with you. He wants to talk. I think he's ready to make a deal."

"Good, good. We'll talk to him."

Holcomb nodded apologetically to Crowell. "Sorry for interrupting, Felix."

"Quite alright." Crowell adjusted his glasses, continuing his briefing. "The second issue regards the domestic difficulties of the Soviets. They appear ready to send in troops to suppress what they are calling a civil war in the Ukraine, in order to stop a rash of violence among local citizens who are rioting in protest over food rationing."

"Food *rationing*? Get serious, Felix. If they wanted to solve the food problem they'd be trucking in bread instead of soldiers!"

This time it was CIA Director Noel Adams who interrupted. "The protests over *starvation* conditions have allowed the Soviets to covertly send in MVD and KGB agents to incite the locals to violence. Now they're using the bloodshed they provoked as an excuse to deploy their army. They're not going to suppress a civil war. They're going to kick all the reporters out of the area, and then kill off a few thousand key political dissidents who've been preparing a campaign to secede from the Soviet Union. This is the worst crisis they've faced so far—it makes Lithuania look like a warm-up. We've got *hard* intelligence to that effect."

Crowell demurred as the President watched the argument. "The point for our consideration is that they're sending in troops to maintain internal order. And the issue for us is what position we're going to take in the international community. Do we announce our support, do we simply say it's an internal problem, or do we condemn it?"

"No," said Secretary of State Fumaro, carefully measuring his words. "The key question is whether we allow them the free ride in the world media by not revealing that they've set the whole thing up themselves, in order to kill their own people."

"Out of the question," answered the CIA director. "We'll reveal our intelligence sources, and they'll be killed along with the leaders of the secession movement. And there's no press there. No one would believe it, anyway."

"Prepare a list of economic sanctions we can impose on short order. We can talk about this again. What else?" The President had not lost interest, but he was growing restless. Across the table, Chief of Staff Eric Hewlett checked his watch again, and searched the lawn for the helicopter.

"The third issue is the Red Sea. The region is at war, with the impression around the world that we and the Soviets are on the verge of confrontation, atop two pillars of battling enemies: the Eritreans and the French on one side, the Ethiopians, Yemenis, and Cubans on the other."

"Well that clearly is not a problem," interjected Holcomb, again frustrating the national security adviser. "In fact, Mr. President, it will only work to our advantage. The Soviets are not going to risk a direct military confrontation with us, and we can manage the crisis without confronting them. But the perception"—he emphasized the word again as Everett Lodge's eyebrows rose admiringly at his logic—"the *perception* will be that you've faced down the Soviets. And *that* will add strength to your presidency at a time when we lack the ability to deal with the other two issues, sir!"

"We've made it clear at the UN that we condemn the Soviet actions so far." The President's eyes had lit up. "Maybe I could even slip a sentence or two into my VFW speech tonight." He hesitated. "How are the polls?"

"Actually you're seven points up," answered Eric Hewlett. "You've got a sixty-three percent approval rating in the Harris and a sixty-five in the Gallup, Mr. President.

And the confidence factor is solid for the first time in your presidency.''

Ronald Holcomb continued, noting the immediate look of satisfaction on the President's face. "The public is strongly behind you, sir. They view your decision to send the minesweepers inside the Red Sea as an act of courage. And there's more than an eighty-percent approval rating of your decision to keep the navy close by, in case the Soviets attack the French."

Again the President seemed pleased, despite the knowledge of everyone in the room that Ronald Holcomb had made those decisions himself, and then carefully maneuvered the President into taking credit. It was not that Everett Lodge lacked political courage, as it had so often been intimated in the press. He simply had a tendency to get bogged down in thoroughness. He reveled in research, consulted the polls, made dozens of phone calls to friends around the world when under pressure, putting off decisions as he reassured himself that he was taking the precisely correct action. And so Ronald Holcomb and a few others had begun making decisions for him early in the presidency and had never stopped.

"So your recommendation is to leave the other two problems alone, and let the Red Sea run its course?"

"More or less," answered Holcomb, unwilling to be held accountable in such a precise manner. "We can't push the Japanese any further on Nakashitona without bringing an enormous backlash. We can't tell the Soviets how to handle an internal dispute. But we *can* affect events in the Red Sea, and that shows your strength as President. By escorting the Japanese tankers out of Yanbu', we can create some goodwill with the Japanese people, which will help us on Nakashitona. By declining to get directly involved on the issue of repression in the Ukrainian 'civil war' we can at least look at economic pressure, and preserve the gains we've made in Eastern Europe."

Secretary of State Richard Fumaro had retreated into silence, drumming his fingers against the edge of the table. Finally he ceased his drumming, and placed both small hands palm down on top of the table. "Mr. President, I've spent a hell of a lot of hours sitting here at this table, my hair growing white and my belly going soft as I've served you and two of your predecessors. And I think I know bullshit when I hear it." Fumaro looked almost contemptuously at Holcomb. "Ron, you're a bright guy, but let me be honest. You're a little slick. What you're recommending is that we duck two raging bulls in order to step on a *titmouse*."

Holcomb grew defensive. "These are big problems, Richard. My recommendation is that we begin to solve them at the point where we can have the most effect."

"No, it isn't." Fumaro sat upright in his chair. He was a small man who had indeed grown white-haired and heavy over the years, but his craggy face now burned with indignation. "Your recommendation is that we dance around the big problems in order to keep the goddamn *polls* up! To *hell* with the polls! Our job is to guide this nation! Now, look. First of all, if we don't stand up to the Soviets when they kill off dissidents in the Ukraine, how are the dissidents in Eastern Europe going to know we'll back them if things turn around? Or I guess you're saying that we won't, and that this business in the Ukraine is a signal from the Soviets to Eastern Europe, too?"

The others remained silent, almost embarrassed as Fumaro continued. "And secondly, we're on the verge of losing control over more than simply our economy. We devalued the dollar to keep foreign investments coming in. We sold off our factories. Twenty percent of our so-called *domestic* automobile production is actually Japanese cars and trucks. Japanese real estate investment is now more than twenty billion dollars a year. A half-million Americans now work directly for Japanese factories alone, in their own hometowns. And most dangerously, we've financed our national debt on foreign capital—the Japanese put in sixty billion dollars a year, directly into our debt!''

"Richard," interrupted the President, now leaning back in his chair to avoid the vitriol that was flowing from the man on his right to the one on his left. "We've done quite well with this economic arrangement you seem so worried about. Jobs are at an all-time high. Unemployment has been low for several years. New factories are sprouting up all over the country. Even if they're foreign-owned, don't forget that they are hiring American workers.''

"Yes, sir," said Fumaro. "We protect the Japanese— and a lot of other countries—with our military. And they need our markets, at least for now. But it's a small step from being a market to becoming a colony, no matter how big the colony happens to be. If you don't believe that, consider what Ron just said. If we don't back off on holding one of their corporations accountable for selling off military secrets, they're going to crash our stock market! And our response is to worry about the *Congress*?''

Fumaro continued, his once-strong voice now hinting of an old man's warble. "We're on our way to becoming the world's recreational center, a nation not to be taken seriously. Where are we still the undisputed leader? Music. Movies. Fast food. Drugs.'' He waved a hand in the air, as if dismissing all of them. "I can just see the billboards fifty years from now as you come over the bridge and stop at the tollbooths outside Manhattan: A smiling, beautiful naked woman, and the sign saying AMERICAN ASS IS OUR MOST IMPORTANT PRODUCT.''

The room was silent for a moment. Then the President eased the tension with his fabled good humor. "That's what I like about you, Richard. You have a way of sugar-coating your opinions so they don't upset anyone.'' And then the others laughed. "We just need a little time, Richard,'' continued the President. "A few weeks to sort the issue out.''

For the first time, Everett Lodge turned in his chair and focused in on Fumaro, now giving off the warm, commanding smile that had made him an effective negotiator for years in the Senate. "We need to slow down the carnies and the snake oil salesmen over on Capitol Hill, before they decide to pass another one of their famous joint resolutions that win them applause when they go home and speak to the Rotary Club, but don't solve any problems. We need to keep Doc Rowland on his leash for a while."

Fumaro shook his head knowingly, clearly disgusted. "On his leash for a while? Ron's already pounded him back into the Stone Age."

The President had risen from his chair, pretending he had not heard. Instead, he pointed at Holcomb as he reached the door. "In the meantime, keep up the pressure in the Red Sea, Ronald. It does seem to be our only clear strong point right now."

2

Doc Rowland seemed to lean into Roy Dombrowski as the two men stood among the crowd in the Roosevelt Room, as if he were seeking reassurance from his longtime aide. He nervously twiddled an unlit cigar, putting it into his mouth and then into his coat pocket and then pulling it out again. He looked fruitlessly through the crowd for a familiar face to greet, or for a hand to shake. The next ten minutes were going to be among the most important of his life. And, no matter how many times he had been in the White House, he could never cease being overwhelmed by the awesome power it represented, and the historic events that had taken place inside the building.

The people surrounding Rowland and Dombrowski in the Roosevelt Room were part of a tradition that was almost as old as the White House itself. They had journeyed from distant points around the country to be favored with thirty ceremonial seconds with the President. The room, named for Theodore Roosevelt, was the morning meeting place for the White House staff, and for others from the government who came to confer with the President's closest advisers. It also was the collecting point for presidential visitors, and decades ago had been nicknamed "the morgue," for its function of keeping the President's callers "on ice."

Teddy Roosevelt dominated the room's decor. Above the mantel of the fireplace was a bronze bust of the former President, and near it, encased in glass, was the gold medallion presented to him when he won the Nobel Peace Prize in 1906. The furniture was made of dark, heavy mahogany, in the style of Queen Anne and Chippendale. A long rectangular table took up most of the middle of the room. Over the fireplace itself was a century-old painting commemorating the signing of the Declaration of Independence. On the far wall across from it, another large and equally old painting showed the Yosemite Valley in the 1860s.

In a few short minutes the visitors would be ushered one at a time, or in their small groups, across the hallway into the Oval Office, to have their photographs taken and to say a few words personally to the President. Next to Rowland and Dombrowski as they stood near the doorway were six white-haired survivors of the Bataan Death March, waiting to present the President with a petition regarding the importance of the bases in the Philippines. On the other side of the veterans was a nubile, dark-eyed beauty queen wearing a gorgeous peach-colored dress and a red sash with the words MISS TEXAS OIL AND GAS on it, standing with three paunchy, doting oil industry patrons who could not keep their eyes off of the young woman. Across the table, three unsmiling native Alaskans dressed in Eskimo clothing were holding a huge, freshly caught salmon inside an open rectangular box. Whispering quietly before the shrine of Roosevelt's gold medallion were five well-dressed, fiftyish New England women carrying some sort of proclamation, along with the model of an eighteenth-century sailing vessel.

It might have been 1791, instead of 1991. The People were in from the far reaches of America, bearing gifts that illuminated the nation's diversity, and waiting for their moment with the man they had elected as their leader, the symbol of their living and their dreams. And none of them appeared either to recognize or be interested in Doc Rowland, "the guru of defense reform." In this place he was indeed a minor potentate, a vassal himself, up to pay homage to the king.

Finally Rowland saw the President in the corridor outside the room. Lodge was following Eric Hewlett out of a door that led from the Cabinet Room into the darkened hallway.

Others saw him, too. "There he is," whispered one of the Alaskans, clutching the odorous salmon to his Eskimo suit. And twenty people now peered into the corridor, hoping for a glimpse.

Rowland had known Lodge for twenty years, since the two men were fellow legislators. They had never been close, but they knew each other's methods, and in a sense they had shared twenty years of the same disasters, from the common vantage point of the nation's capital. Lodge was canny and yet naïve, an odd but somehow effective combination. The son of a longtime congressman, he had split his youth between the chaotic turbulence of Washington and the austere loneliness of Montana, growing to adulthood affected by the paradox of the two communities.

Looking into the President's face at that moment and seeing the creases on his forehead and along his cheeks, lines of worry and of thought that had become etched like historical inscriptions into Lodge's face over the past two decades, Rowland felt an uncommon warmth come over him. It was almost as if they had spent their youth together, remembering battles fought on the House and Senate floors. And now Everett Lodge was going to help him figure out a tough one.

"Doc!" The President saw him and broke away from his normal pathway to the Oval Office just across the corridor, ambling up to him and grabbing his hand, literally pulling him out of the room and into the hallway. "Get in here, Mr. Chairman! Good to see you, sir!"

Lodge waved magnanimously to the others who were waiting for their half minute with him, and gestured toward Rowland, one hand now behind the congressman's back.

"Folks, I appreciate you all coming today, and I want you to know that this is the chairman of the House Armed Services Committee, Doc Rowland! He's a great American, a great man! We're going to have a little visit, and I'll be with you all in just a few minutes."

The waiting guests smiled deferentially and nodded, captivated by the President's personal style. Old Everett Lodge could even out-cousin Doc Rowland, and for that moment Rowland admitted he had a political superior.

A brotherly smile now relaxed the lines on Rowland's own face. "You know, Ev," he said as he followed the President into the Oval Office, "I can remember when you were a reasonably young man."

Lodge laughed, now placing an arm on Rowland's shoulder. "Hell, Doc, don't give me that. I can even remember the name of your first *wife*! How're you doing, good buddy?"

"Well, I'll answer that in about three minutes, Mr. President. Or maybe two."

They were alone now, approaching the chairs that flanked the Oval Office fireplace. Rowland stared for a moment past the President's desk, which had first been given to Rutherford B. Hayes in 1880 by Queen Victoria, and his eyes finally rested on the beauty of the Rose Garden. It was a grand view from the three large windows behind the desk, a view that few in the country had been privileged to enjoy. For a fleeting second he envied his old colleague that view. And then he admitted to himself that his greatest desire was to get his business done, and get the hell away from the heat that was corroding Ev Lodge's face every day, aging him before his time.

"All right, Mr. President, I won't waste any more of

your time. I've got this Nakashitona bill ready to come up on the House floor tomorrow. It's going to pass. I've had thousands of letters of support. A majority of the House has cosponsored it. And now I'm hearing it's going to cause a catastrophe. I hear *you* don't want the bill. I've got Michaels and Bettinger and half a dozen other million-dollar big shots trying to kill it on the Hill. For Christ's sake, they're even working my district, scaring the hell out of little people who are afraid for the future. Quite frankly, I don't know what to do."

Rowland paused for a moment, as if giving the President the opportunity to get him off the hook. Lodge remained silent, waiting for him to finish. Finally he shrugged.

"So I figured I'd come on over here and ask you what the hell *you* want to do. And how you figure you're going to solve this Nakashitona problem."

The President smiled enigmatically, peering at Doc Rowland with the satisfied look of a cat toying with a dying mouse. "You know, there was a moment at the beginning of the Civil War when Ulysses Grant and Robert E. Lee shook hands on the banks of the Potomac, one going north into Washington and the other heading for Richmond. They were friends, but they fought for different causes."

"Aw, the hell there was, Ev! Goddamn it, you forget I'm from Illinois. Grant wasn't even in the Army when the war broke out. He was back home, working in his dad's store."

Lodge remained coy, never losing his grin. "Well, whatever. You get the point. Doc, you got a lot of mileage out of beating up on me with that bill. Now what do you want me to do?"

"Well, I've got an idea."

"I figured you did."

"Well, I do." Rowland pulled out his cigar and fiddled with it. Outside, the President's helicopter was settling into the White House lawn. Eric Hewlett stuck his head inside the Oval Office doorway.

"Mr President. Sir, five minutes."

"Right, Eric."

"Okay," said Doc Rowland. "Look. I've got so many cosponsors on the bill that I've brought it up under suspension-of-the-rules. I did it at first because I didn't want any Christmas tree amendments. You know, people are so mad at the Japanese that they'd be putting all kinds of sanctions in—hell, we'd end up with a no-trade bill! Under suspension, you can't have any amendments."

"I know what suspension is," answered the President, his eyes narrowing slightly as he attempted to read Doc Rowland.

"Yeah, I know, Ev. So you also know that you need a two-thirds vote under suspension, instead of a simple majority."

"Yes?"

Rowland smiled hopefully, daring to nudge the President with an elbow. "Well, mount a campaign against my bill. Your party is filled with free traders. Get them to oppose the bill on the floor. All they need is one hundred forty-six votes to kill it."

"And then you will have made your point, and at the same time I'll have room to work with the Japanese."

"That's right. That's right."

The President persisted, as if wiggling a knife inside Doc Rowland's belly. "And after we're done you can continue to beat me up on the thing, blaming the problems we're having with the Japanese on the administration and the free traders."

"Oh, no. You have my word. You pull this off, I'll back off." Rowland dropped his own trump card. "But I don't like Holcomb, you understand? You dump Holcomb, or send him off to be an ambassador somewhere, and I'll zip my mouth on Nakashitona."

The three Alaskans were now standing at the doorway of the Oval Office. They were smiling with anticipation as they held the salmon, which weighed at least sixty pounds and had begun to smell, in their collective arms. Everett Lodge greeted his waiting guests with a warm, winning wave. Then he slapped Doc Rowland on the back as he ushered him toward the doorway, not promising Rowland any more than Rowland had promised Chicken Hawk Holcomb ten days before.

"Okay, Doc. I'll look into it. You see what you can do. And I'll see what I can do."

CHAPTER 14
THE RED SEA

1

Colonel Bill Fogarty jogged slowly, interminably along the hot, sticky flight deck of the *Saipan*. It was an obstacle course. His shoulders almost brushed the fuselages of dull green helicopters parked on the flight deck. He stepped over thick black fuel hoses, and dodged pieces of equipment. The odd odors of a combatant ship at sea embraced him— old oil, fresh paint, the wet exhaust from the mess hall and the laundry, all mixed in with the sweat and ennui of lonely men. Nothing on earth smelled like a navy ship, and that aroma filled him with a quarter century of memories.

He was shirtless. His tanned body rippled with muscles, and now was dripping with rivulets of sweat. In a strange way, he was thankful to be back on the *Saipan*. Its dull routines were comforting, as if he had escaped the scorching prison of Assab and made it back to his home. Because the routines never changed, even in the royal blue waters of the Red Sea, whose ancient reaches had now gone volatile from mines on one end, missile attacks on the other, and a bur-geoning war on the landmass in between. You lifted weights and ran. You wrote letters home. You inspected the troops and made them clean their weapons again and again. You ate lousy food. You watched movies at night. And you waited like a pawn for some bigger hand to move you.

Fogarty gazed with amusement at a peculiarly American phenomenon taking place along the edges of the flight deck as he ran. Dozens of his young troops sat in clusters of three and four, almost oblivious to the equatorial sun, listening to their tape recorders and snapping photographs. Every-thing seemed to be favored by their eager cameras: the sea, other ships in their column, the aircraft that darted overhead every now and then, the small, arid islands they occasionally passed.

The rifle-toting tourists, he thought to himself again, thinking of an antiwar slogan from the Vietnam War. *Join the military. Travel to exotic places. Meet interesting peo-ple. And kill them.* In another day they might be dead, but just now they wanted to take pictures and listen to the "sounds."

Music from the tape players cut into the still air. As Fogarty jogged along the flight deck, he heard a mix of music—new songs, old songs, rock and country and soul, all providing his marines an emotional umbilical cord back to home. One cluster of young men sat shirtless in the heat, their bodies tanned, their heads shaved, scratching bulldog tattoos and bouncing to the beat of "Bad Moon Rising," an oldie-but-goodie sung by Creedence Clearwater Revival.

Fogarty's brain played tricks on him as he ran past them and heard the song. For a few moments he himself was very young again, commanding a rifle platoon of thirty men in the dirt and bake of Vietnam, instead of a Marine Expe-ditionary Unit of more than two thousand on the edges of the Horn of Africa. And far down inside a place he had all but forgotten, he was afraid.

"Hope you got your things together. Hope you are quite prepared to die . . ."

A dozen CH-46E Sea Knight helicopters sat at their stations on the flight deck. In the hangar deck below were four huge CH-53E Sea Stallion heavy-lift helicopters, six AV-8B Harrier jets, four Huey "slicks," and four Cobra gunships. Other ships in the battle group that had entered the Red Sea the night before also carried helicopters and Harriers, most notably the *Fort McHenry*, a six-hundred foot dock-landing ship that was visible off the *Saipan*'s starboard bow. And the two American aircraft carriers that now cruised the Gulf of Aden, one of them just outside the Bab el Mandeb, were home to more than 150 combat aircraft. The French carrier *Clemenceau*, which had moved near Djibouti, boasted another 40.

As always, the '46s on the flight deck brought back memories of hot, contested landing zones and torrential monsoons, of jungle rot and medevacs, all playing more tricks on Fogarty's emotions. The large assault helicopters reminded him of his youth, just as surely as Creedence Clearwater Revival did. Crew chiefs and mechanics climbed in and out of the '46s, their sweating hands and faces streaked also with oil and grease, lovingly touching the helicopters here and there, checking gauges and making final preparations. The Sea Knights were old. They had been a part of the Marine Corps for as long as Fogarty himself. The V-22 Osprey tilt rotor aircraft that would be their replacement had not yet made it to the fleet. But the '46s would do the job. More slowly, to be sure—two dozen combat-loaded marines at a time, at about 140 knots. More carefully, more vulnerably. And the larger, newer CH-53Es would lessen their burden by taking the heavy artillery and the cargo ashore, sixteen tons at a time.

It would work. If the landing zones were uncontested.

He finished his run, and then walked along the cool dark passageways of Officers Country to his stateroom. Inside he took a long shower, savoring it, and drank several glasses of the pure distilled water made by the ship's boilers, re-plenishing his system from his run. From that moment forth the water would become a luxury, a life-giver. Soon it would reach the rare, elevated level of a precious memory, a com-modity to be dreamed about and wished for. There would be no water at Edd. He feared that fact more than he did Cuban guns.

He started a letter to his mother, and then began to worry. She had been ill, and in the passel of letters he had received upon returning to the *Saipan* was one from his sister, hinting that his mother might be dying. Any mention of combat might kill her. So he threw it away, vowing he would write her a long note when they pulled him and his marines back out of Edd. He wrote a short one to his wife Linda, again not mentioning what was about to happen, but instead writ-ing of the islands he had seen and of the heat, and lamenting rather moonfully that he probably would not be in California in time for Thanksgiving or Christmas again this year. He ended lamely, almost admitting his dread by asking her to please tell the kids how proud he was of them, and how much he loved them.

He even started one to the President, an angry note that ended, "*Just remember I died in a place called Edd.*" But it seemed melodramatic and tasteless, so he threw it into the trash bin also. And then he was ready.

He dressed slowly, as if he were a gunslinger preparing for a shootout in an old western movie. His jungle boots were brightly polished, and as he laced them their shine caused him to remember how over the months another pair had become scuffed and bleached by rice paddy water, until the black boots became rough and beautifully blond, the great distinction that had set him apart from the "rear pogues" and marked him as a "bush marine." But that had been more than twenty years ago. And he had lost his carefully nurtured boots in a hospital after he was wounded, when busy corpsmen had cut through the laces and thrown them into the trash, on top of dozens of other boots, mingled in with piles of torn uniforms that were soaked with blood.

The wages of my profession, thought Fogarty. *Blood-soaked uniforms tossed into the trash, to be buried like the quick.* He snorted unhappily as he inspected himself in the mirror prior to leaving his stateroom. *And so we all return to the first love of our youth. This is the world. Have faith.*

His company and squadron commanders were waiting for him in a ready room near the flight deck. As he entered they all came to attention, sodas and coffee cups held carefully in one hand.

"Carry on, gentlemen."

They returned to their seats, all the while watching him. He strode toward a large aerial map of the southern Red Sea region. The map had a clear plastic covering, and was marked on land and sea with unit designators that showed French, Cuban, Ethiopian, Soviet, and American positions. He read the faces of his younger commanders with one slow scan of the room as he stood before the map. He both liked and dreaded what he saw. In their faces was himself, reflected once. They were trusting, they were good, and they knew how to fight. But some of them were probably going to die.

He began by putting them all at ease. "Well, it's nice to see all your shining faces after my little vacation on the mainland. I can report to you that the good news is the Frogs are good fighters. And the bad news is that liberty in Eritrea sucks."

They laughed appreciatively. Then Fogarty picked up a long pointer and slapped the map at its most crucial point. "This is Edd. I doubt any of you have ever heard of it before, but in a few days I suspect it'll be world famous. And in any event, our job is to take it, and hold it against all comers, until we're relieved."

They said nothing. All of them had known that already. Fogarty then went into a traditional mission brief, beginning with the military situation and covering all elements of execution, administrative considerations, logistics, and communication responsibilities.

"Let me review the situation. An attacking force of about one hundred thousand Ethiopian soldiers, led by a reinforced Cuban division, left Addis Ababa almost a month ago, with a mission of reconquering the major cities of Eritrea and allowing the Ethiopian Army to regain control of the province. The Cubans were going to quickly take Assab"—he slapped the pointer onto a portion of the map covered with grease marks indicating a large French presence—"where they would set up a rear supply point fed by the Soviet Navy, and then continue up the coast and retake the port city of Massawa and the capital city of Asmara." Each time he spoke, Fogarty's pointer indicated the locations on the map. "As we all know, the French surprised everybody by moving over from Djibouti, and beating the Cubans to Assab. The Cubans began an attack on Assab, and their reconnaissance battalion was destroyed by French mechanized infantry forces in the vicinity of hill thirty-two oh nine, up here."

He made a pronouncement as if he were a judge. "Gentlemen, I was present at the execution, and I am pleased to report to you that the Frogs are not without *cojones*."

His commanders laughed quietly. Fogarty held the pointer in both hands, one on each end of it, and paced in front of his commanders. "The Cubans have been stuck in the desert, waiting for further orders because of the changing political situation. In the meantime, they've moved their tactical air and helicopter support up to Dese, right here, and to Mekele, over here. And from all indications, they are getting ready to move out right now, bypassing Assab and heading for Edd, where the Soviet Navy is supposed to link up with them. Last night, a French mech infantry battalion left Assab and headed for Edd. I know the commander. He's the same guy who waxed the Cubans up on hill thirty-two oh nine, and he's good. The Cubans are coming at them with tanks and heavy artillery. The Soviets may try to sandwich them from the sea with LSTs and at least one combatant ship. The Sovs did bombard the shit out of Massawa last night, and were taking on more ammo off the *Nicolaev*, just off the Dahlaks, a few hours ago.''

Fogarty grinned wryly, sharing a cynical joke without telling it. ''Our operational commanders''—he fought back the temptation to speak disloyally of Mad Dog Mulcahy in front of his subordinates—''have guaranteed to the French that we will join them at Edd, which should keep the Soviets out of it, so long as we don't reinforce the French while they're in contact with the Soviets. Actually, we don't expect the Soviets to engage the French, any more than they did at Assab, unless they beat the French to Edd.'' He raised his eyebrows. ''Of course, if the Soviets beat the French to Edd, the Frogs are in a shit sandwich, and I doubt we'll be able to help.''

He turned back to the map, and tapped it with his pointer at a place farther north, in the Red Sea itself. ''Meanwhile, the navy is escorting the first tanker convoy out of Yanbu'. Right now they're about a hundred miles north of Edd. But there's a chance the convoy will be nearby while we're conducting air operations. Tell your pilots to be watching for it.''

Fogarty stared solemnly at his ground commanders. ''I've marked your defensive sectors in Edd on the map. We've got a French-speaking marine coming in with me on the third helicopter, to coordinate any problems with the French. He'll be available on the command frequency if you need a translator. The Frogs will be securing the landing zones for us, so don't shoot at the guys in the funny uniforms who are popping smoke for you in the LZs. Take all the ammo your men can hump, take a lot of water, and make them go easy on drinking it. We'll secure Edd, then start running LCACs from the *Fort McHenry* as soon as the beachhead is secure.'' The LCAC, an air-cushioned landing craft that operated from the bowels of the dock-landing ship *Fort McHenry*, could move seventy tons of cargo at forty knots, and would quickly build up the marines' defenses.

Fogarty traced a line across Eritrea on the map, thirty miles away from Edd. "I don't expect the Cubans to be any closer than right about here by the time we get to Edd. This area is filled with lava floes, and it's going to be pretty tough for them to move through it. If they've got any sense at all, when they find out we're waiting for them at Edd, they'll withdraw from Eritrea. But if they had any sense they'd have withdrawn when the French cleaned their clocks outside of Assab, so don't hold your breath. Obviously, if the Cubans decide to fight, we'll have to hammer them hard, and quick. We can't get caught for a long time at Edd. We're too small and there's no water. We'll rely very heavily on close air support to take out their armor before they get to Edd. We've got fighter and attack aircraft standing by to launch from the *Independence* and the *Roosevelt*, as well as French aircraft from the *Clemenceau*."

He smiled slowly, taking on the tough nonchalance that they all respected. "This is a nasty place, guys. Don't fuck it up. Use your ammo and your water carefully." And then he checked his watch. "We've got three hours. I'll be in all your company areas between now and then if you have questions. Form up on the flight deck two hours from now. Locked and cocked, and ready to fight. Talk to your men, pump them up. They've got to be mentally ready for what they're going to see out there."

He smiled coolly. "If you're looking for a reason to give them, tell them that Admiral Mulcahy personally passed on the guarantee of the secretary of defense that if we smash the Cubans up here, there will be a revolution back home. We're toppling communism in Cuba at the same time we're helping the French. So let's go kill some Cubans."

As he walked out of the ready room, Fogarty could hear his younger officers calling to each other, a guttural sound borrowed decades before from the Turks. "*Uhruh. Uhruh.*"

Uhruh was Turkish for "kill."

2

Edd

Against the desolate coastline of Eritrea, eighty miles north of the main French positions at Assab, Colonel Michel Fourcade rode slowly from point to point along the defensive perimeter his men had formed around the tiny town of Edd. He peered out at a dusty, cluttered village made of salt and lava and mud. There was indeed a usable, protected harbor, where a dozen old wooden fishing boats were now beached. The men of Edd spent much of their time in the narrow boats, catching shark and mackerel. A mile away, down the flat beach from the harbor, the land curved out into the sea, making a cove. At the outermost point of the cove, on the other side of a thousand sea gulls that now swirled and dove above the water or walked the beach, was a small, square mosque. Its white rock foundation and onion roof were as majestic alongside the squalor of Edd as the Taj Mahal might seem at Agra.

Inside the village, bare-chested women with eyes rolling in fear had greeted the French arrival by clearing the streets of children and even the goats, retreating into homes made of salt blocks and chunks of lava. As the French moved into defensive positions, lean, dark men whose black hair appeared to be rubbed in butter silently patrolled outside the rows of homes, their fierce eyes offering neither warmth nor hostility to the French soldiers. Teka'a Mahmud, an Eritrean soldier on loan to Fourcade, had calmed the villagers' fears, but had not reduced their reserve.

Fourcade's battalion had made the journey to Edd in the early hours just before dawn. They had traveled along a narrow scar of a road, over patches of scoria and basalt and lava, maintaining radio silence and keeping the headlights of their vehicles off, lest ships in the nearby sea pick up their movement and alert the Cubans. Fourcade almost pitied the Cubans, who now were certain to be wending their way slowly across the Danakil wasteland. In another hour, the heat would become unbearable. The Cubans would be forced either to keep moving, punishing their vehicles and their soldiers, or to wait out the middle of the day in a halted, undefendable column, risking their water supplies.

But that gave him time. He had won the race, and now he could prepare a solid defensive position. His infantrymen had dismounted from their fighting vehicles, and were busily clearing a half-dozen landing zones for the American helicopters that were scheduled to come within a few hours. His junior commanders were now choosing the right pieces of terrain on which to place his supporting arms, including the AMX-10 *canons roulants* vehicles with their 105-millimeter artillery pieces, the Panhard EBRs with their 90-millimeter cannons, and the VAB HOT Mephistos with their 132-millimeter antitank rockets.

Those had been good weapons to use in the night ambush of a weak Cuban reconnaissance battalion, but they were not a terribly powerful arsenal with which to fight an armored division. Michel Fourcade pondered that as he halted his command vehicle near the sea, jumping to the ground with his agile, athletic grace.

He put his field glasses to his eyes, and looked out into the sea for signs of the American marines. Inside the vehicle, his radio operators had been talking to General Avice's command center at Assab. As soon as the marines were inbound, Fourcade would switch one radio over to their command frequency, and coordinate their assault landing.

He searched slowly. There was nothing. He continued to scan from right to left, until two bumps appeared on the calm waters of the sea as he searched the far horizon. But they were coming from the north, and Fourcade knew the marines would be coming from the east. His heart went cold.

Perhaps it is the American convoy on its way down from

Yanbu', he thought, knowing it was not. Soon the bumps became ships. The ships took on the unmistakable silhouettes of Soviet Alligator-class LSTs, their high prows angling back into low, sleek hulls, the smokestacks and superstructures built entirely in the stern. Fourcade knew that the LSTs usually moved at fifteen knots. Calculating, he figured that they were less than an hour away, and perhaps only thirty minutes out.

For a moment, Fourcade felt as though he were falling through the air, so quickly did his heart race. And then he felt like throwing up. He raced back to his command vehicle, and grabbed his radio operator by the shoulders.

"Caporal Reboul, get me my commanders!"

Thirty seconds went by, and then a minute. Finally his commanders were on the radio net. Fourcade spoke calmly, but his hand was trembling as he held the handset next to his mouth. "We have two Russian ships approaching from the north, approximately five miles out. Cease all activity at the landing zones, and place your men in defensive positions toward the beach. Capitaine DuBois, move the VABs to my location immediately. Lieutenant Hernu, turn the AMXs around. Keep range and distance with the laser rangefinders, and be prepared to fire the one oh fives at my command."

Fourcade gave the handset back to Reboul, noticing that the sandy-haired young corporal had gone ashen. The young man's coffee-colored eyes were pleading with Fourcade as if he were a priest administering the last rites. Fourcade slapped Reboul hard on the shoulder, shaking him out of it.

"Get me General Avice. Hurry!"

Reboul was speaking quickly, his voice filled with dread as he broke into the command net, interrupting less urgent traffic. Fourcade could hear his vehicles churning in all directions as they moved into new positions. Nearby, the VABs carrying the HOT missile launchers screeched and halted, seeking terrain features to provide them cover. A haze of dust rose from the ground fifty meters away as one vehicle parked behind a scab of lava.

Fourcade had no doubt that the Soviet ships were able to pick up on his movement. And finally General Avice was on the other end of the secure radio communication.

"What is it?"

"Mon Général, it is Fourcade. We have a little problem here. The Russians are coming toward us in two *bolshoy desantny korabls*. Alligator class."

Avice was silent for a moment. "Of course. They are trying not to repeat the lesson of Assab. They are meaning to secure the port for the Cubans before we beat them to it." The general seemed almost pleased. "But they took too long bombarding Massawa. They are too late."

Wonderful, thought Fourcade, watching the ships move ever closer. He could see the forward deckhouse on the nearest LST, which seemed headed right toward him, just on the other side of the ancient mosque. Rocket launchers were mounted on the deckhouse, for the purpose of shore bombardment. Fourcade felt naked, standing next to his command vehicle and clutching his radio handset.

Avice continued, speaking with a calm that was infectious. "Be careful, Michel. If there are no naval infantry, they won't try to engage you. They may be there simply to keep our ships away. Don't fire at them unless they start to offload soldiers."

"They see me, mon Général. We had to realign our defenses and point the heavy guns toward the sea. There is dust everywhere, and very little concealment. We are easy targets."

"If they see you, they should turn away. Do you see the big ship?"

"No, the *Nicolaev* is not with them."

"Then they are no threat. At most they will have a company or two of naval infantry. If they don't land soldiers, the Americans will be with you soon. If they try to land soldiers, drive them away and the Americans will come later. We have the destroyer from the *Clemenceau* battle group here with the morning convoy. The *Primauget*. I'll send her up to Edd immediately.''

Avice paused. Fourcade continued to grasp the handset, watching the Soviet landing ships slowly traversing the peninsula that marked the cove's entrance. He tried to imagine the general's face just then. He knew Avice would be smiling, his small eyes bright from the tension.

"Anything else, Michel?"

"No, that is all." Fourcade hesitated, then could not hold it back. "Yes, there is. Mon Général, these are Russians."

"Let the politicians argue over that, Michel. They are soldiers and sailors, that's all. And you are a better soldier. So, don't worry. Take care of your men."

The two ships rounded the cove, now near enough that the French soldiers could read the numbers on the hulls. They steamed slowly in the placid waters, coming ever closer, and Michel Fourcade felt paralyzed as he watched them approach. He reasoned that their draft was probably shallow enough for them to offload directly onto the beach inside the small harbor. They would inch toward the beach and drop their bow ramps, rather than debarking landing craft or aircushioned vehicles from the stern while offshore. So there would be no magical moment for Fourcade to make the distinction between ships that were steaming past him, and ships that were landing infantry soldiers. If he waited to see if the bow ramps would fall, making a runway from the inside of the ship to the beach, he would have waited too long.

General Avice's instructions did not apply. Michel Fourcade was on his own.

The ships turned toward the beach, a half mile out, their high bows now directly confronting Fourcade. If they dropped the bow ramps his whole world would be changed. He would have to defeat them soundly, and that would cost him soldiers. It also would bring on a major international incident, and would probably keep the American marines from being able to join him on the beach. For a moment

Fourcade silently cursed the Americans. This had been their idea, and now they would leave him alone to die.

He picked up his command frequency handset, his eyes never leaving the two ships, and called for the commander of his 105-millimeter artillery vehicles. "Hernu!"

Lieutenant Hernu's voice was steady and low. His father had fought for four years in Vietnam, and then in Algeria. His great-grandfather had died in the mud at Verdun. "Yes, mon Colonel."

"Fire one round between the two ships. DuBois!"

The commander of the HOT Mephisto vehicles, whose antitank missiles were deadly against armor targets, answered immediately, as if he had anticipated the call.

"DuBois here."

"There are big guns just under the bridge, and rocket launchers on the forward deck. Be prepared to return fire immediately."

Within fifteen seconds the 105-millimeter artillery gun erupted, and a shell burst in the sea, having passed between the two approaching vessels and landed just behind them. There were great swells in the water as the LSTs immediately reversed their engines, and they backed quickly through white foam and churning water.

Then suddenly the ship on their right let go with a burst of 57-millimeter shells from the twin guns mounted just under the bridge. The shells pumped in a slow rhythm, giving off little bursts of smoke, and the ground along the beach and near the French positions erupted with their explosions.

Captain DuBois did not wait for further orders from Colonel Fourcade. Within seconds two HOT rockets roared off of their platforms on his vehicles, one impacting on the forward deckhouse, causing a huge explosion that destroyed the rocket launcher, and the other hitting the gun mount of the 57-millimeter guns just below the gun tubes. The HOT was designed to penetrate 32 inches of armor. The gun platforms on the ship were easy targets, and the ship was now on fire.

Through his field glasses Fourcade could see Soviet sailors running on the main deck of the ship, and climbing down from the bridge. The other LST had held its fire, and was moving quickly out of range. Fourcade thought for a moment about destroying its rocket launchers as well. He knew that once the ship was more than two miles out to sea, it would be too far for his rockets to reach it. He waited, watching the ship's movements, and then grasped his handset and called an end to it.

"Cease fire. Be prepared to resume firing on both ships if they shoot again."

The Soviet ships did not shoot again. The fires on the first ship continued but they had not spread, and the ship was steaming slowly away. Its forward deckhouse and the gun mount smoldered with dark, curling flames, and occasionally flashed from secondary explosions of ammunition caused by the heat. Sailors were still running madly along the decks and ladders. The second ship was now out of range. Curiously, it headed east toward the American marines, rather than north toward the Dahlaks.

Fourcade breathed slowly, feeling momentarily drained as his adrenaline level returned to normal. He looked down and realized that he had been gripping his radio handset so tightly that his knuckles were white. He put the handset back to his ear, and congratulated his commanders.

"Very good. Very good job. But be ready. Those are the Russians. Be ready."

He patted his radio operator gently now, as if he were the young man's father. "You feel better, Caporal Reboul? Get me General Avice."

Avice had been waiting. He immediately came on the net. "So, they have gone away?"

"Yes, mon Général, but we had to take them under fire. They were approaching the beach. They were going to lower their bow ramps. I decided not to wait. I fired a warning shot and they began shooting at us. We destroyed the gun mounts and rocket launchers on one of the ships. They were still on fire when it left. The other one is moving east, toward you. Be careful of that one."

"Excellent, Michel. Do you have casualties?"

"We are checking now."

"Let me know. The Americans have a hospital on the *Saipan*. We can medevac our casualties on their helicopters when they land. Also, the *Primauget* should reach you in less than an hour. She has a Lynx helicopter, and can take the men on board if"—Avice seemed to pause—"if something were to happen to the Americans."

Fourcade grew hesitant. His eyes did not leave the sea as he talked with Avice. "I don't think this is over, mon Général. If something is going to happen to the Americans, then perhaps I should return to Assab. I can't fight the Cubans on the ground and the Russians at sea with my little battalion."

"You're not alone, Michel. Don't worry. The Americans will come, I promise. But they might not come to Edd. We'll have to see. They are watching the Russians and the Cubans. I am talking to them all the time."

None of his vehicles were damaged by the wild firing of the Soviet guns, but two soldiers were dead. They had taken cover in a crater made of lava, and a 57-millimeter shell had impacted between them. Six others were wounded. For fifteen minutes it was quiet as Fourcade's men nursed the wounded soldiers. In the village the goats coughed and whinnied and the children cried. And then Avice called him again on the radio. The general's voice was crisp, authoritarian. Again Fourcade could imagine Avice's face as he listened on the handset. The general would be somber now, his lips pressed tight into a determined frown.

"Keep some units to your rear, watching the sea. Point the rest of your battalion toward Assab, straddling the road. The Cubans have turned away from you. They are moving between us, toward the sea. The Russian ships are steaming there also. The Americans are coming, but they are going to take Bera'isale."

CHAPTER 15
WASHINGTON, D.C.

1

At around eight-thirty every morning, the dimly lit hallways of the congressional office buildings came out of their shadowy silence and burst into life. Janitors turned the hall lights on. Staff members began to arrive, retrieving stacks of newspapers and packets of mail from office doorways and stepping inside. Office lights went on, one by one, until the hallways were bright. Telephones began to ring. Smells of fresh coffee and tobacco and new perfumes mingled together in the morning air. The sound of printing machines gave the offices a trembling, sibilant backdrop as they churned out propaganda to be mailed, tax-free, to constituents.

And by nine o'clock, as if the curtain had gone up on a New York play, the whole catastrophe of Congress was in full swing. Constituents and lobbyists prowled the halls. Members of Congress dashed off of elevators and into offices or meeting rooms. Key staff assistants in shirtsleeves scurried alongside their members or sauntered down the corridors with heads down and hands in pockets, beset with the problems of the universe.

But at eight o'clock, the office spaces held the dark, echoing emptiness of a morgue. It was so still that Mandy Reese, Doc Rowland's receptionist, could hear the mail cart work its way along the corridor with an eerie clarity as she sat alone at her desk. The bundles of mail plopping in front of the closed doors of the offices down the hall, and the mail cart's creaking wheels, were the only sounds other than the noise her fingers were making as they typed on her word processor.

The creaking wheels grew closer, and soon a bright though somehow clownish face leaned forward into the office, bidding her good morning.

"Hey, Mandy! We've got to stop meeting like this."

She sighed wearily, though secretly enjoying the attention. "Good morning, Ogre."

Ogre Gwalcek was a graduate student in political science at George Washington University. Like many area college students, Ogre worked part-time on the Hill, although unlike most, he worked in the congressional mail room. He stood awkwardly in the doorway, almost in a trance as he studied Mandy Reese's tweed skirt and corduroy blazer. He let his eyes linger dreamily on her auburn hair as it danced along her shoulders when she moved her head. At her feet was an elegant leather briefcase, the old kind with straps over the top. He knew it had been her father's, and had teased her that her hands were too small to go all the way around the handle. Her answer, a typical rebuke to this mere mailman, had been that her brain was big enough, even if her hands were not.

She sat staring back at him, her eyebrows raised. "I said good morning, Ogre."

"Yeah, I know you did." Ogre reached into the mail cart and began unloading several bundles of newspapers, packages, and envelopes, placing them on the floor just inside the door. "Your man is getting more mail than anybody in the Congress right now, did you know that?''

"*Know* it?'' She seemed tired, and even exasperated. "That's why I've been showing up early here for the last two weeks. I spend half my time just logging it in. And the phone rings all day long!''

Ogre's long, angular face was lit with delight as he leaned against the doorway. He stared upward with merry eyes, invoking the gods. "Just keep those cards and letters coming, folks!'' Then he nodded to her, as if offering a deal. "If you need a job after your man gets beat, look me up. I've got connections.''

She laughed warmly at that, obviously deciding that it was safe to flirt with him. He could feel her eyes moving carefully over him, taking in his worn blue jeans and the frayed turtleneck sweater his father had thrown out years before. He knew his hair was shabbily cut, and that his fingernails were still black from having repaired his old Ford truck over the weekend. But he also sensed that, in this world of coats and ties and capons who submerged their personalities in order to please their bosses, he was at least different, and thus perhaps interesting.

"Well, that's thoughtful, Ogre. But you know we're going to win in a landslide. Doc hasn't dropped below seventy percent of the vote in twenty years. And besides, the election is a year away.''

"Keep telling yourself that. This Nakashitona thing is hot nationwide, but it isn't as popular back home as you guys would like to pretend. I hit all the offices, you know. And who the hell pays any attention to the mailman? Everybody talks in front of me as if I were some kind of brainless robot—congressmen, legislative aides, committee staffers. But I've been listening, and your man's in trouble. Not only that, but you're in a borderline district in the presidential campaign. The President could come in next year and campaign for your opponent if Rowland pushes the administration too hard on the Japanese thing. So, you just remember''—he dared to walk to her desk, and even tap her shoulder—"I can fix you up. Yeah. Probably get you a promotion."

"Uh huh. Doing what? Dancing topless in your favorite bar?"

"Who needs a bar?" They both laughed. He liked the music in her voice. He wanted badly to touch her again, this time with an embrace. She wasn't taking him seriously, he knew that, but at least she was laughing with him.

"That bill is up today."

"And it's going to pass. We've got more than two hundred thirty cosponsors, Ogre!"

"Yeah, but Rowland doesn't *want* it to pass! Can't you see that?"

Mandy Reese struggled with his assertion, and then dismissed it. She frowned, not yet cynical enough about Capitol Hill to comprehend. "No, if he didn't want it to pass, he could bury it. He's the chairman of the committee. He doesn't even have to let the bill get to the House floor."

"Normally. But not on this one." Ogre's arms were folded now, and she gazed at him with some irritation, but also with the beginning of a new respect. "Rowland's got thousands of letters coming in, congratulating him on getting tough with the Japanese. This country is going *bananas* over what the Japanese have done to us. At the same time, they've got us where they want us economically. No one wants to get hurt. It's the American way, don't you see? Doc's a hero, as long as nobody gets burned! And the first people to get burned are in his own district—the Akasaka deal! I read the papers. Sukihara Bank is threatening to pull out of the Akasaka project in Euphoria if the legislation passes. Your opponent, what's his name, is making mincemeat of Doc on the issue. Why the hell do you think he's already announced for the seat, a year before the election?"

"Alcott."

"Yeah."

"He's a jerk."

"They always are. Opponents are like ex-husbands. None

of them are ever worth a damn." Ogre rubbed the back of his head with one hand, then shrugged casually. "So what can Doc do? Back off on the bill, and look like jelly for the rest of his congressional career, a man who caved in to the Japanese on an issue of principle? Hell, no. He's got to go forward with the bill, and hope it dies somewhere. That way he's made his point, and at the same time nobody gets hurt."

"Ogre, you're just a poli-sci whizbang, that's all. That sort of logic belongs in a classroom. Look, Doc could have watered the bill down if he was worried. The average American wouldn't know the difference."

Ogre had inched his way forward, and was now sitting on her desk. In the hallway, a few people began walking by, the first arrivals in other offices. Ogre was in love. He wanted to keep talking to her at any cost, on any excuse, but especially to capture her mind with his brilliance. That was the way you won women on Capitol Hill: Forget muscles or movie star eyes, have a mind and a future. "He gets a majority of Congress to sponsor his bill. And then we find out that the situation is even *worse* than we'd imagined, with all the revelations in the hearings. So, how can he water it down?" Ogre chuckled, as if the situation were worthy of comedy. "He only had one option, and he played it. He went to Chairman Caldwell, over on the Rules Committee, and got the bill put on the calendar under the suspension of rules."

"But that doesn't fit, Ogre. You suspend the rules when you have a sure thing. When you suspend the rules on a bill, you need a two-thirds majority, and you can't amend it."

"That's exactly the point, Mandy. He's gambling that the sanctions against Nakashitona are so severe that one third of the House will go against him when they find out there won't be any amendments to adjust the bill. Then he wins both ways! He's been tough on the Japanese, and at the same time the free traders in the Congress will vote against the suspension. Hey, I mean, completely suspending a multibillion-dollar company from doing business in this country for three years is serious stuff, no matter what they did. It could kick off a trade war, and protectionism around the world like we haven't seen in a hundred years. There's plenty of room to argue against that without looking like you're being soft on the Japanese.''

She was watching Ogre with sincere respect, unsure whether to believe him or not, but captivated by his logic. ''You're pretty smart, Ogre.''

''He met with the President yesterday. I'll bet he tried to cut a deal.''

She stared at Ogre for a moment longer, having just lost her political innocence. ''I'm not sure I agree with you, but that's not bad thinking.''

''For a mailman.'' He rose from her desk, returning to his mail cart. ''See, you need to understand that I'm not really a mail clerk, Mandy. This is sort of like Superman, you know, and you're Lois Lane. After I get my graduate degree, I'm going back to Pennsylvania and step into the phone booth and I'm going to run for the Congress. I'll be back here in a big way, no fooling. Play your cards right, Mandy, and when I'm President I'll put you in my Cabinet.'' Wonder of wonders, she was genuinely laughing, none of this Capitol Hill patented smile routine. ''In the meantime, I'd be happy to buy you a beer after work.''

''All right. If you'll stop dressing like a bum.''

''Hey, hey!'' He walked out of the door, his long arms flailing as if he had just scored a touchdown, and stuck his head back inside before he began pushing his cart toward the next office. ''For you, I'll wear a tuxedo to work. I'll call you at five o'clock?''

''Okay, Ogre, call me at five. Although I doubt I'll be out of here before six, with all this mail.'' She waved good-bye to him and picked up the latest mountain of mail from all over the country, mail that was making Doc Rowland a hero, on an issue that only a few people knew he wished would go away.

Mandy decided that she liked Ogre Gwalcek, and that he was indeed going places. Behind those worn blue jeans and the tattered sweater was a budding genius. It amazed her, this place. You never knew. On Capitol Hill, even the mail clerks had the potential to be President some day.

2

"I really like that necklace, Magnolia."

It was eleven o'clock that morning, and Doc Rowland sat in a barber's chair at the House hair salon. His hair was wet, having been shampooed and conditioned and combed straight back, awaiting the magic touch of Sweet Magnolia's expert scissors. He saw himself in the mirror, grinning and devilish and aging, but he did not mind the wrinkles or the gray. He had young cat's eyes that glowed back and lit the room around him.

Her name was really Maggie. But she was from Atlanta, and it seemed that every southern girl secretly dreamed of Tara. And so Doc had decided, joking with her, that Maggie was not a name fit for mansions and waiting servants. It sounded more like a maid's name itself. But Magnolia? He smiled, watching the way her round young face had, as always, warmed to his compliment. Magnolia, for all its silliness, conjured up visions of perfume and hoop skirts and gallant young men in gray.

"No, I really do. That's a beautiful necklace."

"Why, thank you, Mr. Chairman." He was conscious of her breasts against his shoulder as she cut his hair, and her curled blond hair brushing his cheek. The necklace was eighteen-carat gold, with six black star sapphires mounted in a circle around a diamond, on a pendant shaped like a bursting star. Doc Rowland had never seen anything like it. And tomorrow was Janet's birthday. He knew the necklace would look beautiful around her long, tanned neck, the pendant glimmering near her small breasts in the summer sunlight. And then Ron Holcomb would have to ask her where it came from. And perhaps she might even tell him.

"Where'd you get that necklace?"

"You really like it?" Magnolia girl seemed deeply pleased. "I got it when I was on vacation in San Francisco last summer. Down near the waterfront, in Ghirardelli Square." She snipped away at his hair, making conversation to pass the time. "We have to get you looking good for the cameras today, Mr. Chairman. I like your tie, and that dark suit. I'm going to leave your hair a little fuller on top. It'll lean out your face, and make you really handsome. Yes, sir."

"You are a darling." She snipped some more, blew-dry the top, fidgeted along the sides with a brush. He watched her in the mirror as she worked intently, and then finally made up his mind. "I want that necklace, Magnolia."

"*This* one?" She smiled but her eyes were afraid of him. She seemed alternately humored and perplexed, as if she were dreading the possibility of having heard him correctly.

"Yeah, honey. The one you're wearing. I haven't got time to go to San Francisco."

"Well, Mr. Chairman, neither do I, not for another six months, anyway. And this is"—she struggled for a description—"personal! I've been wearing it for two months. Look, I can order you one if you'd like. It would be here in thirty days or so."

"I haven't got thirty days. I need it today. It's important to me, Magnolia girl. Real important. I'll pay you. How much do you want?"

And now she seemed almost angry, as if she were on the verge of being raped, as if she were a peasant girl in the town square, responding against her wishes to the implied power contained in the languidly pointing finger of the local earl. "Mr. Chairman, I don't want to sell it, to tell you the truth. I paid three hundred and twenty dollars for it."

"I'll give you three hundred and eighty. But I want it right now. What do you say?"

"You can't give it to anybody, Mr. Chairman. At least I wouldn't! It's used. It—it needs to be polished."

"That's okay, honey. Don't you worry. All that can be fixed."

His hair was done. Magnolia wiped his forehead and neck with a towel and removed the cape from around his neck. She held the cape in one hand and stared at him for a moment, as if attempting to balance the weight of his office against the value of her necklace, or maybe her pride. And then she slowly walked into a side room, emerging a few minutes later carrying it in both hands. Her round blue plantation-girl eyes were heavy with sadness, and she pouted a bit as she walked toward him. She looked confused, and a little bit afraid.

"Mr. Chairman, I'm not sure about this. I mean, I feel a little taken advantage of, to tell you the truth."

He had already written out the check. "Honey, you know how much I appreciate it. This is actually a tribute to you. You got great taste, Magnolia! Great taste. Now, here. You order yourself another one, and spend the extra money on some perfume or something. That's not such a bad deal, is it?"

"Well, no, I guess it isn't." And besides, it was done. She worked up a pleasant smile, forgiving him or perhaps herself. "Your hair looks good, Mr. Chairman. Break a leg on that bill today. I'll be watching for you on the evening news!"

"Right, honey. You're a darling to say that."

For five minutes after he left the hair salon, Doc Rowland felt on top of the world. He was wearing a new charcoal-gray wool suit, a white shirt, and one of those yellow Washington power ties he had made fun of for the last five years. He had the kind of haircut that made him look almost presidential. He was carrying inside a plain white plastic bag the perfect birthday gift for a woman he was sure he loved, and who he thought loved him, a gift literally stripped from the body of another woman who had unwittingly modeled the product for him. He had become the hero of half of America for his stand against the money-hungry Japanese businessmen who would sell national security away for a profit.

Now, that was living.

And that little girl had no right to get so carried away about her necklace. After all, he reasoned, I gave her a sixty-dollar profit. And she can order a new one. Janet is going to look gorgeous with this around her neck.

And then he began to grow queasy, thinking of how close he was playing the odds on his Nakashitona bill. Because Ogre Gwalcek was right. Doc Rowland didn't want that bill, and he hadn't heard a word from the President about his idea to kill it. Half of America had made him a hero, but the other half wanted to work for the Japanese. Including half of the people in his own district.

And those weren't winner's odds.

3

Terrence Romulus, the speaker of the House, pointed over to his right, where Doc Rowland was standing at the counsel table, a sheaf of papers before him and Roy Dombrowski sitting erect and somewhat nervously at his side.

"The gentleman from Illinois."

Doc Rowland took a deep breath, and took a roll on the roulette wheel. "Mr. Speaker, I move to suspend the rules and pass the bill HR Seventeen fifty-three."

The House floor bustled with people talking in small groups, slapping backs and telling jokes, lining up support for efforts big and small. The speaker almost yawned. "The clerk will report the title of the bill."

Below the speaker of the House on the rostrum, the clerk of the House read rapidly, his voice tinny, almost lost in the largeness of the room and the competing backdrop of private conversations. "HR Seventeen fifty-three, the Nakashitona Sanctions Act of 1991."

"Is a second demanded?"

Evan Yates, the ranking minority member of the House Armed Services Committee, stood across the aisle from Rowland, rubbing his moustache as he peered at the notes in front of him on the minority counsel table. "Mr. Speaker, I demand a second."

"The gentleman from Illinois is recognized for twenty minutes, and the gentleman from California is recognized for twenty minutes. The chair recognizes the gentleman from Illinois."

With the passing of that small, seemingly inconsequential moment, Doc Rowland already knew that he was in serious trouble, that his gamble would likely fail. His decision to move the bill through the Rules Committee to the House floor had not been popular within the President's party. As late as that morning, there were indications that he would be opposed on the floor by the free-traders, led by Peter Gabriel, a powerful member of the Ways and Means Committee. A "Dear Colleague" letter from Gabriel to every member of Congress had indicated that he might also demand a "second" during the debate, and speak strongly in opposition to the bill. That would have given Gabriel control of the opposing arguments, and would have brought the free-traders out in force.

Doc Rowland knew that with one phone call from the President, Gabriel would have done just that. Gabriel by himself could deliver 150 votes and kill the bill, on the grounds that it was the wrong solution to the problem, one that could result in an international trade war, and possibly a worldwide recession. But that was a highly sophisticated argument, one that would have been dangerous to make. The free-traders would have run the risk of appearing both pro-Japanese and antidefense, at a time when the Nakashitona revelations had stirred the anger of many Americans.

And so the President had not come through, and Gabriel had not shown. And Evan Yates, who supported the bill for his own manipulative reasons, now controlled half of the debate as the ranking minority member of the committee. Apparently, the President and Gabriel had decided that the bill could be killed or diluted later on, without opening them up to criticism by Doc Rowland on some television show after he "lost" the bill on the floor. Which did not make Doc Rowland a terribly popular colleague at that moment.

Now Doc Rowland had no choice but to pass his bill. And he knew that they were going to support him with every bit of venom and malice they could muster.

"Mr. Speaker, I am the original sponsor of HR Seventeen fifty-three. It is my bill. It is the committee bill. It reaches the floor today with two hundred forty-three cosponsors, which means that a majority of this body not only supports the language of the bill, but feels strongly enough about it to join me in emphatically recommending it to the full House. This is a simple bill. It has only one provision. It states that Nakashitona Industries of Japan, and all of its wholly owned subsidiaries, will be suspended from doing business in this country for three years, or for so long as it takes them to fully account for their leak of U.S. technology to North Korea or other countries precluded from access to such technology. The bill would be effective immediately upon becoming law."

Doc Rowland paused for a moment, taking another deep breath. He knew that what he was about to say, which had been carefully crafted by Roy Dombrowski the night before, would end up on the evening news. He felt vaguely like an imposter in his dark wool suit and his power tie, with his new haircut that had shortened his sideburns and lengthened the top. He was no longer an aging farm boy, playing the margins of the issues as the cameras rolled. He was out front, all alone, beyond the recommendations of his staff and his colleagues and even his strongest backers at home.

He felt lonely, and afraid. And so he had no choice but to speak with strength and conviction.

"I know a lot of my colleagues, people whom I respect, think I've gone too far in this legislation. To them I say, if you have a better solution to this terrible problem, then bring it to the floor of the Congress today, right now, and offer it! I know a lot of people, including economic commentators and some members of this body, believe that it's harmful to the world economy to take drastic steps against a foreign corporation, that we are inviting trade wars and a wave of protectionism. To them I say, if an American corporation were ever to violate the secrets of a foreign ally, we should *all* support that ally if it decides to ban that corporation from doing business in that country as a result! I know a lot of other people, people who are well-intentioned, and who need jobs and places to work, are worried that this legislation will cause Japanese businesses to pull out of planned development in this country."

Doc Rowland's bright blue eyes narrowed as he paused, letting this point sink home. "And Mr. Speaker, a lot of people in my own district, including some of my longest political friends, hold that view. But to them I say, rather sadly, have we sunk this low? *Have we sunk this low?* That we should be obliged to turn our backs on blatant leaks that compromise our national security, simply because we are afraid that other Japanese companies won't let us be their servants? I do not believe so, Mr. Speaker. And unless somebody has a better recommendation, I believe this bill should pass. I reserve the balance of my time."

The speaker of the House nodded, pointing to Evan Yates. "The gentleman from California."

"Great job, Doc," said Roy Dombrowski as Doc sat down. "That's exactly where we need to be."

Yates twirled one edge of his moustache, giving Doc Rowland a seemingly sincere smile as he began to speak. "Mr. Speaker, I rise in support of HR Seventeen fifty-three. As I mentioned to the chairman during our committee markup on this bill, I'm not convinced that the Japanese are the real culprits in this matter. In fact I'm of the firm belief that the Department of Defense, through its shoddy management of the Iroquois program, ended up tempting a small number of individuals inside Nakashitona Industries to the point that they decided to make some extra money. As a result, it does seem something of an injustice to damn the array, as we say in the law, for the excesses of a very few people. But quite frankly, I know how strongly the chairman feels about this bill, and at this time I don't see any other alternative.''

Yates pounded yet another nail into the coffin. ''My colleagues should contemplate that the chairman has actually left us no alternative, at least until the Senate acts on the matter. By bringing the measure up under suspension-of-the-rules, there can be no amendments that might cure the overkill, and thus no debate on alternatives. He has given us only two choices: either support this bill, or let Nakashitona go scot-free, at least for this session of the Congress. Given those two rather draconian choices, I would urge my colleagues to vote for the bill.''

Other members lined up and spoke, until the tepid endorsement became a litany. Teddy Gilliland, as always hoping to unseat the man who usurped his right to the chairmanship of the committee four years before, spoke eloquently in his slow, measured oratorical style, urging his colleagues to ''get behind the chairman on this bill. It's his bill and even though we might make it a little bit more reasonable when we sit down with the Senate, this isn't the time to go back on the chairman. I can sympathize with those among you who are worried that the bill might cause problems in your districts, but''—a slight pause, and a smiling double entendre—''don't forget it's causing the chairman problems in his district, too. And he's sticking to the bill, no matter what.''

Peg Groelsch of Wisconsin spoke passionately, a small fist in front of her face as she decried the ''mammoth damage to our national security programs. Normally I don't agree with the chairman on his view of national defense, and of course we might want to shape the language of this legislation in conference. But this is the way the chairman believes the issue should be solved. And for the moment, he should be supported.''

Even Peter Gabriel managed to support the bill. The Ways and Means Committee powerhouse walked slowly to the microphone, looking more like a frumpy college professor than a congressman, and frowned as he grudgingly spoke in favor. ''Mr. Speaker, as you know I believe this bill could potentially harm us more than it could help solve the problems it purports to address. As I've said before, I don't think the best way to solve a national security problem is to invoke a massive trade sanction that could trigger a protectionist war at the exact moment in our history where we need more international economic cooperation. However, the chairman of the Armed Services Committee has put a lot of his colleagues into an unwelcome box, if I may be frank. The way this legislation is now designed, to vote against it would appear to be a vote in favor of the severe damage that Nakashitona Industries allowed to occur. I can't in good conscience vote that way, although my conscience also causes me to hold my nose when I vote for the chairman's bill. But there you have it. And I hope we can fix this mistake in conference.''

The bells rang. The cloakrooms and the closed circuit television announced a recorded vote on HR 1753, the Nakashitona Sanctions Act of 1991. The members of the House held their noses, slipped their voting cards into the slot, and pushed the buttons. And Doc Rowland won by a vote of 413 to 11. It was the greatest victory of his entire political career. And yet he knew it had cost him dearly, in terms of angry colleagues and lost credibility.

And it brought a telephone call from Warner Haas back in Euphoria. Haas told Roy Dombrowski that he didn't really need to talk to Doc, but to pass on to him that Haas and a few other key financial backers had just contributed a thousand dollars apiece to Doc's opponent. Hugh Alcott's early campaign was burgeoning, and his campaign literature would soon be filled with damaging quotes from Doc Rowland's colleagues, made on the House floor during debate over the Nakashitona bill.

CHAPTER 16

1

Bera'isale

Out on the Red Sea, just off the coast from a tiny town called Bera'isale, the U.S.S. *Saipan* had entered Condition One, and was preparing to go to war. On the flight deck of the *Saipan* the CH-46 helicopters began to come alive, their huge twin horizontal blades moving slowly at first, snapping at the air like angry bullwhips, and then moving so quickly and ferociously that they had become an almost invisible pair of shadowed lines. The air churned all around them and the noise of their engines and the rotor blades gave the green monsters a trembling power that was palpable.

Steady streams of burdened men ran toward the rear of the twelve helicopters, led across the busy flight deck by yellow-shirted sailors. The infantrymen ran up the rear ramps of the helicopters and sat along nylon bench-seats, leaning forward into the dark, narrow aisles, their M-16 rifles between their knees. The packs on their backs were heavy with rations and water and ammunition. Extra canteens of water had been stuffed in the leg pockets of their camouflage trousers. More ammunition was strapped in green cloth bandoleers and slung across their chests, already carefully loaded inside magazines. Mortarmen followed. Other marines carrying Dragon antitank missile launchers boarded the helicopters.

Below, on the hangar decks, marines armed with .50-caliber machine guns and TOW antitank missiles had loaded their equipment into CH-53 heavy-lift helicopters. Crewmen from the *Saipan* were already moving the CH-53s onto the ship's external elevators, ready to raise them to the flight deck once the CH-46s had launched. The TOWs were similar in size and capability to the HOT missiles used by the French soldiers of Colonel Fourcade's battalion.

Colonel Bill Fogarty jogged easily from the *Saipan*'s island at the edge of the flight deck, his helmet tightly strapped, and climbed up the ramp of the third CH-46, located near the bow of the ship. His two radiomen followed him, their PRC-77s strapped to a pack board that also carried a pack and the same rations as the infantrymen. Inside, he took a seat near the rear of the helicopter, and then gave a thumbs-up to the crew chief, who spoke to the pilot on his intercom mike. The first wave was loaded up. Fogarty was ready to go.

Welcome to the CH-46. Sit on the bench. Put your weapon between your legs. If the helicopter starts to fall, put your head down there, too. And kiss your ass good-bye.

The helicopters lifted off one at a time, beginning with those at the bow of the ship, and turned immediately toward the shore, twenty miles away. Fogarty fretted as he watched the sky fill up with the CH-46s. He was going into Bera'isale cold, and that disturbed him. But there was no alternative. The Cubans had indeed turned in the desert, and were breaking toward the sea. There had been no time to deploy SEAL teams or reconnaissance units to secure the little town and to clear landing zones for the helicopters. His only consolation was that the Cubans also had acted spontaneously, and would very likely have no forward units in the town.

They passed over three small desert islands. In minutes he saw the bright reefs that surrounded Bera'isale, and the narrow wooden fishing boats inside the harbor. A flight of F-18 Hornets streaked along the coastline, moving from left to right over his landing zone. Another flight followed, moving low and relatively slow. The Hornets were loaded with laser-guided munitions and iron bombs, prepared to attack Bera'isale. Lower, and much slower, four AH-1 Cobra attack helicopters made a similar run over the village itself. But there were no targets in the open wasteland. In the cockpit of the helicopter, the copilot turned back to him, smiling tightly but with confidence, and gave him another thumbs-up. The landing zone appeared secure.

The CH-46s assumed a wide formation, several hundred meters apart, in an echelon that approached the coastline at an angle. They were under orders to land along the narrow road next to the town, which was the only area Fogarty could be sure was clear enough of debris and obstacles to accommodate the CH-46s. The unpaved road curved in an arc around the tiny town, bending away from the sea and then back toward it.

The lead CH-46 dropped altitude, and the others followed. Twelve helicopters landed sequentially, only seconds apart, at hundred-meter intervals along the road. Infantrymen raced down their rear ramps through swirling clouds of dirt and debris and sought cover in the burning desert, their very landing already forming a hasty perimeter around the outskirts of the town.

And then the CH-46s powered off. Their rotor wash covered the marines with a second coat of dust and salt and sand as the helicopters lifted out of the landing zones and headed back toward the sea. The *Saipan*'s CH-53s were already inbound, and would land within ten minutes, carrying more weapons, more ammunition, more troops. The

CH-46s would onload another two rifle companies when they returned to the *Saipan*, and would drop them off within a half hour. Two fully loaded LCAC air-cushioned landing craft were already in the water aft of the *Fort McHenry*, and at Fogarty's command would race to the small port carrying light amphibious vehicles, tanks, and more supplies.

In an hour or two, Fogarty would have more than a thousand marines on the beach, as well as five tanks, eight jeep-mounted TOW missile launchers, fourteen light amphibious assault vehicles, thirty-two Dragon antitank missile launching teams, eight 155-millimeter howitzers, plus an array of lighter mortars, machine guns, and smaller weapons. He also would have a squadron of AV-8B Harrier jets under his command, which were capable of dropping laser-guided munitions, iron bombs, and antipersonnel cluster bombs.

And if it came to it, he had 150 of the most capable combat aircraft in the world to back him up, from the aircraft carriers *Roosevelt* and *Independence*.

Bera'isale was only one hundred meters from the road. Fogarty spat salt and sand from his mouth, in a manner that General Abelardo Valdez might have appreciated, and began walking into the town with his command element. The town was eerily still, as if abandoned. The CH-53s were already in sight. His advance support teams were now working busily in the town, clearing landing zones for the big helicopters bringing supplies, and checking the beaches for the best places to offload the LCACs. The heat was worse than at Djibouti and Assab, as intense as anything he had ever felt. When he walked over shards of lava, the bottom of Fogarty's boots burned as if he were stepping on a lit charcoal grill.

Corporal Pinky Garst, one of Fogarty's radio operators, joked with him in a languid Mississippi drawl. "Colonel. Hey, sir. This what you mean when you talk about Nebraska? You know, small farms, plenty of wide open spaces?''

''Hell, no,'' replied Fogarty, trudging toward the harbor area. ''We don't have any beaches in Nebraska, Garst. And to tell the truth, we don't have any small farms there anymore, either.''

''Anyway, sir. It ain't this *hot* in Nebraska.''

''You think this is hot? Talk to me in an hour.''

But he knew the Cubans were feeling the desert heat more than he. They had been stuck in its parching misery for weeks, and had been on the move from Manda, through the worst part of the desert, for at least ten hours. Fogarty checked his map as he walked, putting his finger on the last position report he had made on the Cuban advance. They were probably about thirty miles away. From the terrain, he judged that they would be required to break away from the road that would have taken them to Edd, and instead to make their way across the desert floor, coming at him from the southwest at an angle to his left, where the desert broke for a few miles between two large lava floes.

If they were going to attack, he needed to hit them with close air support as far away from Bera'isale as possible, before they were able to take advantage of their superior tanks and artillery. But he had to be able to fight them on the ground as well. He needed to bring the LCACs in immediately, and to keep them shuttling to and from the *Fort McHenry* until his tanks and vehicles and ammunition were fully ashore. He needed to position the TOW teams that were now landing on the lead CH-53s, to place them on key pieces of high terrain that would give them a good angle on advancing Cuban tanks. He needed to swing the F-18 Hornets into a visual reconnaissance flight in front of him right away, so that he could get a feel for just how far away the Cubans were, and whether they were really going to fight.

Fogarty checked his watch: It was three in the afternoon. There was plenty of time left for the Cubans to attack before nightfall. He needed to do a lot of things. And he needed to do them very, very quickly.

Garst was staring in amazement at the vastness of the empty, burning desert, perhaps contemplating his first moments on the soil of the continent that had spawned many of his ancestors centuries before. Fogarty elbowed his radio operator.

"Garst, I know you've been on that ship for a long time. But don't get involved with any of these local women. They're jealous as hell."

Garst laughed comfortably, pushing his helmet to the back of his head as he surveyed the nearby village. "That's okay, Colonel. There's plenty of me for all of them."

2

Washington, D.C.

At the Pentagon a short time later, the hot line from the Chairman of the Joint Chiefs of Staff rang insistently next to Ronald Holcomb's desk. Holcomb had been following the transit of the convoy out of Yanbu' minute by minute throughout the morning. He had also talked with Admiral Mad Dog Mulcahy little more than an hour before. And he knew immediately the subject of General Roger Francis's call.

Holcomb checked his watch as he picked up the telephone receiver. It was not quite eleven o'clock in the morning. He answered with his best clipped, official tone.

"Holcomb."

"Mr. Secretary, we have a serious problem in the Red Sea. I think you need to get into the command center immediately."

"What's going on, Roger?"

"We were a day late on our man Mulcahy. Let me give it to you quick, sir. The French have attacked a Soviet ship that was coming ashore in Eritrea. It isn't sunk, but it's seriously damaged. We don't know what the Soviets are going to do in retaliation. The Cubans have turned in the desert, and are bearing down on a town called Bera'isale.'' Francis paused for a moment. ''And our man just landed a reinforced battalion of marines at Bera'isale.''

Holcomb felt immediately nauseated, completely betrayed. Mad Dog hadn't told him about the French engagement with the Soviets! He never would have allowed Mulcahy to land the marines if he had known the French and Soviets had exchanged fire. The realization that the Soviets might become involved exploded over him in an avalanche of paralyzing fear, sending his mind reeling. Ronald Holcomb's first thoughts were of tomorrow's headlines, and the lead stories on the news that night. *Blunder in the Desert*. He scrambled desperately to imagine how he would position himself in the media if the battle widened beyond control.

Instinctively, Holcomb postured. ''You've got to be kidding, Roger!'' His eyes flitted about the room, staring at reminders of past military glories as he searched for time. ''Who gave the authority for the marines to land? Who ordered this?''

''Mulcahy appears to have done it on his own, sir.''

That was almost true. Mulcahy had informed Holcomb an hour before of his decision, but he hadn't mentioned the Soviets! Still, Holcomb knew he shared part of the blame. He could have told the admiral to desist, or asked him directly about what was happening at Edd. He imagined the congressional hearings that might spin off the debacle, and postured again. ''I thought you were recalling Mulcahy back to Hawaii for consultations!''

''The message traffic went out yesterday, sir, with written orders to follow. He was ordered back to Hawaii. But let's just say he decided to take his time en route.''

Holcomb was fully adrenalized now. His ears hummed as his blood pressure rose dangerously, and in less than a second he tossed away all loyalty to the man who had been his favorite admiral. "This is a disaster, Roger. Relieve him, and pull those marines out of Eritrea until we can sort the matter out."

Francis's voice sounded hopeless and angry. "We can relieve Admiral Mulcahy, Mr. Secretary, but it's going to be a lot harder to get the marines out. They're on the ground, and they're rapidly reinforcing their position with LCACs and helilift. It takes a lot longer to undo that than it does to do it. And we estimate they could be in contact with the Cubans within the next hour or so. If they pull out, it's not only risky, but we'll look like fools in the eyes of the world. It'll look like they ran from the Cubans. That would be devastating for our relations in the international community, particularly Latin America. And a lot of marines might be killed in the bargain."

"The Cubans are that close?" Holcomb thought about it for another moment, his mind now working furiously. "Where's the convoy?"

"The one escorting the tankers out of Yanbu'? I haven't heard, sir. I suppose it's proceeding normally. I'll have a full report for you when you reach the command center."

"Alright." Holcomb now knew that he had to sacrifice Mad Dog, or go down with him. And that was no choice at all. *The manipulative bastard!* "And call Davis Smith out at CINCPAC. Tell him Mulcahy's relieved, and that I'm directing you to run the rest of the Eritrean operation. Personally."

"Yes, sir."

"And General, I don't need to tell you this, but we'd better beat the Cubans—decisively. Or both our heads will roll."

The general hesitated for a moment on the other end of the line. "It's going to be bloody, sir. You'd better be thinking about that."

3

The Gulf of Aden

For as long as he lived, Mad Dog Mulcahy would never be able to shake the glad mendacity in Admiral Jefferson Davis Smith's voice as the Commander in Chief, Pacific, relieved him of all operational authority in the Red Sea.

Jeff Davis Smith, his immediate superior, had been so intimidated by Mulcahy's intimate relationship with Ronald Holcomb that he had scarcely protested Mulcahy's continuing insubordination over a period of two years. The man who commanded all military forces in the Pacific had not so much as whimpered when, more than a year before, Mulcahy had literally ripped his hot-line telephone connection to Smith out of his office wall up on Makalapa Heights, leaving the cord dangling loose and bare-wired on the carpeted floor as a symbol to staff and visitors alike of his defiance. The same Jeff Davis Smith that Mulcahy loved to publicly label a ''boy scout'' to the media and government visitors, as a measure his scorn for Smith's straight-arrow ways, was now joyously dressing down Mulcahy from five thousand miles away.

Smith had not even bothered to use a secure radio channel to do so. The senior admiral's instructions played over the command frequency on the *Roosevelt*, and were heard by hundreds of the crew.

''I'm relaying the orders of the secretary of defense. You no longer have any operational authority in the Red Sea. I say again, you have no operational authority in this emergency. You are ordered to return to my headquarters immediately, for further instructions.''

That sort of directness meant big trouble. As Mulcahy felt the stares of Admiral Ward McCormick and others in the *Roosevelt*'s war room, he wondered just how far he had fallen from Ron Holcomb's good graces. He knew the defense secretary would be outraged that he was not personally told of the French-Soviet encounter at Edd, but he had planned to claim it slipped his mind in the "fog of war," since it did not involve American troops, which was the purpose of his radio call to Holcomb in the first place. He was going to claim that it was only a fleeting encounter anyway, a mistake, irrelevant to the remainder of the operation.

But he also knew that if he had indeed mentioned it, Holcomb would have gotten cold feet in the best tradition of his compatriots in Washington, and backed out of the operation at the last minute. And the French would have been left stranded on the beach at Edd, just as General Avice had predicted. Politicians were politicians, but among warriors a promise was a promise. So he had taken the risk of silence, to ensure the landing of the marines. *Okay*, he decided. *And now maybe I'll pay. But I don't think so. We're going to kick the Cubans' asses, and the rest will be forgotten.*

"Roger, roger," he answered Jeff Davis Smith in his best laconic drawl. "I was on my way back, anyway."

Fifteen minutes later Mulcahy's S-3 shot off the forward left catapult of the *Roosevelt*, heading for Diego Garcia. He would return to Hawaii. But he was damned if he would report to Jeff Davis Smith's headquarters, to be chided like a recalcitrant schoolboy. In his view, Jeff Davis Smith wouldn't make a pimple on the ass of a true warrior, and he was not about to listen to that armchair admiral preach to him about protocol. He was taking a gamble, but he was giving America a *win*! Surely Holcomb would back him on that much of it, once it was over.

4

McLean, Virginia

"Get in here!"

Doc Rowland cackled merrily, opening the glass door of his stand-up shower and pulling Janet Holcomb inside.

"Do you want your back washed, Doc?"

"Hell, no."

She giggled delightedly and fell into his arms, kissing him and pressing her tight athletic body against his. A steady stream of warm water washed over them. She was wearing the necklace, and nothing else. Her body was deeply tanned, making the bands of whiteness around her breasts and hips alluring, as if he were staring into the darkness and her most private secrets were gleaming back to him, moon-bright and entrancing.

Doc Rowland held her wet face in his hands and then kissed her again as the water cascaded from his face and hair onto her own. The water made rivulets down her neck and between her breasts. It settled into the hollows underneath her eyes, and the valleys where her neck met her shoulders. It made his fingers slide when he ran them from her face down her neck and over her chest and shoulders. His sliding fingers drew a soft moan from her pursed, enjoying lips. Her eyes were now closed, and her chin was high. She smiled dreamily, running her own hands over his hips and thighs. Her pink nipples had grown small and hard. And when he touched her between her legs she was wet inside, from a sweeter, warmer flow.

She put her arms around his neck and leaned back into the tiles, her eyes now half open and smoky, and she sought him with her body. "I want you right now. Right now."

And he obliged her, taking one leg behind the knee and holding it in the crook of his elbow as he leaned into her, pushing her against the tiles. She was all wetness and muscle and music and the water washed them, giving her mouth and body a constant freshness. Within a minute she was moaning and shuddering, her eyelids pressed together with the intensity of her orgasm and her head moving slowly, side to side. "Oh, God. Oh . . . oh . . . oh."

Doc Rowland joined her, shuddering with joy. Then he went onto his knees in the shower, washing her feet and legs and body, kissing every part of her, worshiping this miracle that had so surprisingly drifted into his life. She was not Ron Holcomb's wife and he was not a fifty-six-year-old journeyman, putting yet another touch of scarlet oil onto a very large sexual canvas, a lifetime mural filled with feminine delights. No, this was fresh and new and beautiful, and only between them. It had never happened before, in the entire history of the universe. Or at least it had never happened to him, and that was the same thing.

He turned off the water and stepped outside, throwing her a large, heavy towel and wrapping his massive body inside another one. Then he walked into his bedroom and lay on his king-sized bed, sated and happy. In a moment she sauntered into the room, smiling and erect, the towel tucked over her breasts as if it were a sarong. Her straight blond hair was pulled back, still wet and dripping. She stood beside the bed, enjoying his devouring eyes.

"Happy, Doc?"

"If I was any happier I'd be a brainless goon. Come here."

"I've got to get going. Look at me! I've got to dry my hair." She touched the pendant below her neck. "It's really beautiful. I love it. Thanks so much, Doc."

"I love *you*. In case you haven't figured that out yet." His comment hung between them like a ripe, swollen fruit that she did not yet dare to pick. And so he left it alone again. "What do you have to do, anyway, Janet? Why don't you just stay here? I'm done for today. In fact, I need a break after the vote on my bill this morning. We'll just waste the afternoon, and then go get some dinner."

"No. I'd love to, but I've really got to go. I've got work to do at the office, and then Ron's having a dinner party for me tonight at Germaine's." She hesitated for a moment, and then said it. "Doc, you probably shouldn't even tell me that. I mean, I really care for you, too, but it won't get us anywhere."

"Would you ever consider marrying me? Not that I have a very good track record." He chuckled, examining her face for clues. "Like they say, real doctors bury their mistakes, and Doc Rowland married his. But that could change."

"No," she answered, reaching down and running her thin fingers through his hair. "That would probably be the biggest mistake of all. Doc, I'm thirty-six, an assistant secretary of education, married to a rather well known man. You're fifty-six and not exactly anonymous. Can you imagine the problems it would create for us if we tried something like that?"

Her towel fell off and he ran a hand along the inside of her right thigh, causing her to purr. "You rascal." She moved slowly away from his hand. "Besides, to be blunt I'm not a big believer in what the fairy tales call true love. Sorry if that sounds cold, but I can't help it. I have a theory: If you're lucky, it lasts for a few years. Then you're merely stuck with the wreckage."

"I could prove you wrong."

"You can do that without piling up the wreckage." She was holding the towel in front of herself with one hand, her face now soothing him with a genuinely caring smile. "I'm here whenever you want me, Doc. And I'm here because I want to be here, not because I'm obligated."

"I suppose you're right, honey girl." Rowland had recovered from his moment of fantasy, and now was sitting on the edge of the bed. "Besides, I'm going after Ron in a big way. I'm going to take him down. The last thing either of us needs right now is to have our—relationship be a part of all that."

"*You're* going to publicly attack Ron, Doc?"

"You're damn right I am." His face brightened at the prospect, and then grew serious. "Ev Lodge had me over to the White House yesterday. I tried to cut a deal with him on this Nakashitona bill. It didn't work. Things are getting messy real fast. Prime Minister Kanabayashi has already warned that if we push this too far, we could generate a backlash in Japan. He called the bill racist, can you imagine that? From the Japanese, the most racist society on earth! And who the hell has been pushing on trade, anyway? Not us. We've been pushed *around* on trade. They started selling off T-bills as soon as the bill passed this morning, and our stock market went down a hundred and fifty points! In one hour!"

Her eyes had narrowed. The towel was now back over her breasts. "So what's that got to do with Ron?"

"What's that got to do with *Ron*? Well, who the hell do you think pushed for cooperation with the Japanese on the Iroquois system? And who do you think was over there last week trying to kiss their ass? What do you think I'm going to do, let the blame for the crash of the stock market fall on *me*?"

Rowland shook his head, oblivious to her growing amazement, an expression somewhere between anger and bewilderment that was settling over her face. "Nope. The administration is going to pay. If the President had canned Ron like I told him to, the whole thing would be done."

"You told the President to *fire* Ronald?"

"What do you mean, *Ronald*? We're getting formal now, are we?" Rowland still had not picked up the scrutiny in her eyes, but now he noticed that she was dressing very quickly, ignoring him as she scurried about the room. "You in a hurry, honey?"

In what seemed an instant, she was dressed. Her hair was still wet, pulled back tightly into a bun. Her face had become harsh, businesslike. She pointed a warning finger at him, and spoke so coldly that he felt shaken in his nakedness.

"I told you to keep Ron out of this. I told you never to let my marriage get tangled up in it."

"Now what the hell are you saying? That I'm supposed to protect Ron because you and I are—are seeing each other? For the love of Pete, every damn reporter in this town protects him because he feeds them information. What are you telling me, that he sends his *wife* out to his enemies to protect himself, too?"

"I've had it," said Janet Holcomb, picking up her purse. "This has gone too far, Doc."

He called to her as she descended the stairs, but she ignored him. He began to dress, thinking he would follow her. But then the phone rang. It was Roy Dombrowski. His administrative assistant sounded deeply shaken.

"Doc, you've got to get down here. ABS wants to interview you live for a news update, and then replay you on the evening news. I've got a dozen other calls for interviews, but I think you should do ABS. They've been good to you in the past, and you need your best forum."

"What's going on, Roy?"

"Hell, the stock market's now down by about four hundred, and falling. And we just landed the marines in Eritrea."

"We landed the *marines*? Who landed the marines?"

"Hurry up, Doc! Don't even take a shower."

"Well, you don't have to worry about that," answered Rowland as he began grabbing his clothes. And then he laughed at himself, knowing he had said good-bye to Janet Holcomb for the last time, and focusing in on the new challenge. "Hold down the fort, Roy! The cavalry's coming!"

CHAPTER 17

1

The Eritrean Desert

Fifteen miles southwest of the Marine Corps position at Bera'isale, it might have been a scene from someone's cruelest vision of a living hell.

The sky was pure, azure and cloudless. It covered the Cuban armored column as if it were a blue gas flame fired by a hateful, smothering sun. They could not get away from it. It seemed to crawl inside their clothes, to shine from unseen windows on the ceilings of their vehicles. A craggy wasteland emanated in all directions from where General Abelardo Enrique Valdez rode inside his BRDM command vehicle, so desolate that the very land seemed dead. They passed wide, white lakes of salt where once the floor of the desert had been the bottom of the sea. There were moonlike scabs of lava, as large as whole cities, where volcanic eruptions had displaced the sea. And in between was the desert sand. It shifted this way and that between the lava and the salt, hosting small sticks of bushes and trees here and there, in other places becoming gashed with washed-out gullies that on occasion rose up to make small streams.

And now an invading army was stretched across this nightmare, from one end of the horizon to the other. A sickly yellow cloud of dust had risen above the Cubans as they made their way toward Bera'isale in a churning, struggling procession of tanks, self-propelled artillery, towed guns, trucks, and armored personnel carriers. They were moving carefully over the gullies and the sharp little ridges, keeping to a formation that made three long columns, spaced about a mile apart.

General Valdez rode at the head of the main body, in the center column. Two miles in front of him was the rear of his advance party. He had made the advance party strong and yet mobile, configured with a mix of T-64 and T-72 tanks, BMP combat vehicles armed with 73-millimeter guns and SAGGER antitank missiles, and several batteries of 122-millimeter and 152-millimeter self-propelled artillery that followed in the wake of the tanks and BMPs. Once the advance party was taken under fire by the Americans, Valdez would immediately deploy the artillery and provide a heavy barrage of covering fire for the tanks, who would then press forward in an assault. And by the time his lead tanks were heavily engaged, he would have fixed the Americans into their defensive positions, and discovered their weakest points.

And then he would deploy the main body of his attack. He would penetrate the American defenses, overwhelming them through his sheer numbers of tanks, artillery, heavy machine guns, and infantry soldiers, and either take their surrender or push them back into the sea.

Valdez had studied the American Marine Corps from their operations in the Caribbean and at Guantánamo Bay on his native island. He knew he would outnumber their reinforced battalion by at least ten to one, not counting the morass of

Ethiopian soldiers who thankfully had not yet deployed from their haven at Dubti, along the Awash River. The Ethiopians would only be in the way at this point. If by some miracle he was able to break through and again head toward Asmara, he would bring them forward.

But the Americans would have air superiority. Valdez would be backed by MIG 23 Flogger fighters, as well as HIP and HIND helicopters, all operating out of Mekele, but he held no illusions. These were the E and F models of the Flogger, developed by the Soviets for export. The aircraft, and their pilots, would be no match for the Americans. They would have done well against the Eritrean antiaircraft batteries, but they probably would not even make it to his battlefield. So it would be up to the SA-6s.

Valdez had brought six mechanized SA-6 surface-to-air missile systems from Addis Ababa, and now had placed them throughout the main body of the advancing Cuban division. A month before, six SA-6 systems had seemed almost superfluous to Valdez and his superiors as they contemplated the relatively simple task of fighting Eritrean soldiers. Within the past three hours, they suddenly had become the key to his survival. He had placed SA-6 systems at the forward and rear of the two columns on each flank. Two others were traveling near the center of the middle column, on each side of his long-range acquisition radar, which could pick up enemy aircraft eighty miles away. Each SA-6 carried twelve missiles, three of them mounted on rails, ready to fire at any time. That made seventy-two missiles, which could be fired out to a range of almost twenty miles. But if he ran out of SA-6s before the battle was resolved, Valdez knew he would be in trouble.

He had several platforms of SAM-9 missiles, mounted on trucks. In addition, many of his soldiers carried the shoulder-fired SAM-7 missiles. The SAM-7s and SAM-9s were infrared heat-seekers that operated without radar, and were most effective when firing at the tails of aircraft that had just dropped their ordnance. They were adequate against helicopters and slow-flying aircraft, but not against the kind of jets the Americans would bring. And they had a range of only about three miles under the best of conditions. Not only that, but they were frightening to shoot in the open terrain when under a direct bombing run.

He also had the ZSU-23-4 antiaircraft guns, which fired a 23-millimeter shell, and the M53/59 antiaircraft machine guns, which fired 30-millimeter bullets. Both were self-propelled, removing the requirement to set up the guns while under attack, and were spaced throughout his advancing columns. But they worked best when defending a fixed position where an aircraft's angle of approach was predictable. And neither had the range or power to knock out American aircraft, unless they scored a lucky hit.

And all of these systems would be shooting while the Cubans were moving forward, or even attacking the American ground forces, if Valdez was to be successful.

He had to take Bera'isale quickly. If he were stopped for too long in the desert by the air attacks, he would run out of water. And if he ran out of water, his men would die.

He felt at times that he was going mad from thirst. His lips had become prunelike and the skin on his hands was cracking from the salt and the heat. A mix of bewilderment and anger had been creeping up on him all day, from the moment he learned that the French had attacked the Soviet LST at Edd, and that the Soviets had turned away. He felt doomed, betrayed, foolish. *They had been shot at, and they had pulled back out to sea! The Russians! And the Americans had beaten them to Bera'isale!* It was beyond his understanding, after all he had been through. He felt used. He wanted to get it over with.

Valdez no longer dreamed of hotels in Asmara filled with whores and bubble baths. He could not even think clearly about what awaited him in his native land, if he ever made it back. Life had now dwindled down to himself in the desert, and an exit along the sea. He was not attacking the Americans as he advanced toward Bera'isale. He was fighting his way, like a frantic, smothering child, out of the oven of death. And he was going to cross any desert obstacle, and kill any living impediment, be it bird or hyena or American, that stood between him and the beach of his salvation. Bera'isale was his obsession, the only moment in his future. The rest of it could be sorted out later.

Far to the front he saw the contrails from the American fighters again, this time moving north to south. There were two of them up high, and then two others, much lower. It was hard to comprehend, but he knew that they were watching him. They could *see* him! For a moment he imagined that they were laughing as they peered through their scopes and surveyed the desperation on his filthy, unshaven face, and the wrinkles of dehydration on his cracked lips. And he himself saw nothing but the tiny, white pin stripes of their exhausts as they moved along the far, low edge of a burning sky.

2

Above the Gulf of Aden

One hundred fifty miles southeast of the Cuban column, five other U.S. Navy aircraft were flying at six thousand feet in a wide formation above the Gulf of Aden, heading toward Perim Island. An EA-6B Prowler and two F/A 18 Hornets, flying with an escort of two F-14 Tomcats in case they were intercepted by Yemeni MIGs, were putting out the lights along the southern coast of the People's Democratic Republic of Yemen.

They had begun with Aden International Airport and then moved quickly over to the military airfields at Al Anad and Sheikh 'Othman. In the space of ten minutes, from their flight routes above the sea, they had destroyed every radar system capable of tracking American aircraft, using single shots of the highly accurate HARM missile. The HARM locked in on a radar emission and followed it as if the missile and the radar were tied together by a string, and then blew away the radar antennae with a 146-pound payload.

In the backseat of the EA-6B, Commander Pete Kerlovic sat in an olive-drab flight suit, his gloved fingers touching the map that was strapped onto the kneeboard of his right leg. Through the sun visor on his flight helmet, Kerlovic was staring at the green screen of a computer. A small triangle had just appeared on the screen, which measured radio frequency on one axis and the azimuth to the target on the other. Kerlovic moved the cursor of his computer until it was over the triangle, and pushed a button as if he were playing a video game at home. And then he spoke on his voice mike to the pilot, Lieutenant Al Forrest.

"I've got a lockup on the BARLOCK at Perim," said Kerlovic, indicating the code term for that type of Soviet radar. "Come left twenty."

"Roger that." Forrest slowly eased the EA-6B to the left. "Coming left twenty."

"I'm holding him at sixty miles. Let's track in some."

Lieutenant Junior Grade Mike Luciano, the navigator, came up on the net. "I'm surprised Perim's still up, after the last three."

"They didn't even know what hit them," answered Forrest.

Luciano checked his scope. "I've got you at thirty-five, now."

"Shoot at thirty," said Kerlovic to Forrest. Almost immediately he added, "Ready to fire."

"Shoot the sucker," said Luciano.

"Here goes," said Forrest.

Kerlovic checked it. "There's one off the rail. Looks good." The missile flashed quickly to their front and disappeared, following the enemy radar emission with its own tracking system. Forrest pulled the EA-6B away from Perim Island, never coming within range of its antiair defenses.

Kerlovic watched his scope. In less than a minute the

radar from Perim Island ceased its emissions, causing the little triangle on the scope to disappear. He smiled wryly. "Signal's down. Sorry about that. We're done. Let's get back to the boat."

"Okay, guys," said Forrest, pointing the aircraft back toward the east, where the aircraft carrier *Roosevelt* was steaming. "Let's go get a cup of coffee."

3

Washington, D.C.

Inside the Pentagon Command Center, Defense Secretary Ronald Holcomb sat next to Joint Chiefs Chairman General Roger Francis at a long, U-shaped table, monitoring radio traffic and situation reports from around the world as the Red Sea crisis frothed over into a full-fledged battle. Just now Holcomb was talking to the White House, where an addled National Security Adviser Felix Crowell was ordering him to place limitations on the military's use of force against the Cubans. As the defense secretary talked, Crowell's instructions could be heard on a speaker in the command center.

"I say again," said Felix Crowell, "order the marines to hold their fire on the beach."

Holcomb's normally unreadable face was now taut with a wild, fearful uncertainty. He fidgeted, his small eyes unsteady as he shifted in his chair. He was trapped in a place that had no room for carefully staged meetings, secret maneuverings, or back-stabbing phone calls. He had to make a hard, clear decision, and he was unprepared to do so. To his left an increasingly angry General Roger Francis seemed ready to rip the phone out of his hand. And yet he hesitated to confront Felix Crowell, whom he knew was managing a delicate series of diplomatic negotiations with the leaders of other countries around the world.

Finally Holcomb quibbled, giving way to the general's unbelieving stare. "That's an impossible thing to manage, Felix. That's not an order I can give."

Crowell also seemed unnerved. It was his first operational crisis. "We're in contact with the Soviets and the Cubans through diplomatic channels right now," said Crowell. "Tell your people not to fire unless they're fired upon. We can't be put in the position of having started this. And if they're going to have to fire, get back to us."

Holcomb hesitated, and now Roger Francis did speak, sounding incredulous. "Get *back* to you? How are we supposed to get back to you if they decide they're going to have to fire?"

Holcomb now cut the general off. "What are we supposed to get back to you *for*, Felix?"

"You'll just have to. We'll have to reevaluate."

"Now, wait a minute," answered Francis, again cutting the defense secretary off. "Our men are supposed to wait out there to see if the Cubans attack them, and then if they do we're supposed to call the White House and ask for permission to let them defend themselves?"

"This situation is filled with international complexities, General, and we don't want any unnecessary casualties."

"It's a little late for that."

"I gave you my instructions."

"Does the President concur in these instructions?"

General Francis asked the question. Holcomb remained silent, wiped a hand through his long hair as he stared down into the table, avoiding the eyes of the handful of assistants, most of them military, who were listening with a rapt attentiveness.

"We haven't gotten him down into the grass on this one. He gave us the go-ahead with respect to the general direction we're taking."

"Well, I take my orders from the President," answered the general. "You're going to have to get him involved." But there was no time for that, and now Francis made up his mind. He peered at Holcomb with a look of pure disgust. "Gentlemen, let me solve this for you. I'll take full responsibility. I am instructing the commanders in the field to defend themselves against any—and all—Cuban advances."

Crowell's voice raised a full octave. He ignored the general, speaking again to Holcomb. "Ron, there's no time to argue about this! We don't know the intent of the Cubans. They've been avoiding contact with the French for weeks, and I'm sure they don't wish to fight us. All we know is that a Cuban column is heading toward the sea, and that *somebody* has put Americans in their way. Cuba recognizes Eritrea as a part of Ethiopia, as do the Soviets, and in their view the United States has put troops on Ethiopian soil. They're not in a state of war with us, and we don't want war with them. My instructions to you are to let them pass, unless they take our people under attack. And we don't want an incident like the one the French had earlier today with the Soviets."

"What about the Soviets?" asked Holcomb. "Have we heard anything from them?"

General Francis again cut both of them off. "None of that's even relevant anymore. Tell the Cubans you're talking with to stop *their* goddamn column! Things are moving too fast. We can't tell our marines not to defend themselves!"

An aide handed the general a paper with a fresh message on it. "Wait one—" Francis read the message, and almost shouted, "I was just informed by CINCPAC that a Japanese tanker in the convoy coming down from Yanbu' has hit two mines. Our people say it's sinking. In my view that's a hostile act. We're at war."

Holcomb sat silently, stunned. On the other end of the hookup, Crowell stammered briefly, and then resumed his insistence. "I don't know what to do about that. We don't have any reports. Whose mine was it? Soviet? Yemeni? I don't see the connection with the other thing. It's got nothing to do with it. You have my instructions on the situation with the Cubans."

"I say again," replied Francis, now having taken over

the military operation. "We're at war. Our people are going to fight."

4

The Red Sea

The Department of State could schmooze, cajole, and inveigle all the Cuban and Soviet diplomats in the world. Felix Crowell in the White House could argue all he wanted about the rules of engagement, and when the marines at Bera'isale could shoot. It didn't matter. Once the marines were ashore, no sailor, airman, or marine would hesitate to follow Mad Dog Mulcahy's order into hell, because to stop now would be to condemn their fellows on the beach to death, in the face of an advancing Cuban division. They knew it would happen, because it had happened before. On a beach off of Cambodia in the summer of 1976, two companies of marines were blown back into the water after the White House had declared the *Mayaguez* operation over and canceled their air support while the other side was still shooting. Forty-two men had died, some of them standing waist-deep in the waves, compliments of the stupidity, cowardice, and arrogance in Washington.

In the still, clear air above the Gulf of Aden the *Independence* strike group already were gathering at their rendezvous point thirty miles to the west of the aircraft carrier, circling as they "stacked up" in layers at different altitudes. There would be twenty-two aircraft in the strike. And then fifteen minutes after the *Independence* strike group attacked the Cuban column, a strike group from the *Roosevelt* would hit the Cubans again.

An E-2C Hawkeye early warning aircraft had already been launched from the *Independence*. The Hawkeye was now patrolling over central Djibouti, monitoring all aircraft launches in northern Ethiopia. The E-2C, which was capable

of automatically tracking up to six hundred targets at the
same time, and of simultaneously controlling more than
forty airborne intercepts, was watching along an axis that
would draw a line north of the Cuban and Ethiopian bases
at Dese and Mekele. Any enemy aircraft that moved beyond
that axis would be attacked. Also over Djibouti, ready to
move immediately into a second station over Ethiopia itself,
four flights of F-14 Tomcats were circling in separate orbits,
with a mission of intercepting and destroying any MIGs that
attempted to cross the "hot line."

From the time they were launched, the aircraft of the *Independence* strike group maintained strict radio silence. Eight
A-6E Intruders and eight F/A 18 Hornets straggled out to the
rendezvous point after being launched, and began orbiting at
their assigned altitudes in flights of four aircraft each. The
four F/A 18s and two EA-6B Prowlers that had been assigned
a "flak suppressor" mission also gathered, in two groups of
three. In little more than twenty minutes the entire strike
group was stacked up above the sea, waiting for the lead aircraft to pull away from its orbit and begin the mission.

Commander Ron Chambers, the strike group leader,
surveyed the aircraft below him as they arrived at the rendezvous point. Finally he had a full "off-count" of twenty-
two aircraft, and Chambers broke from the circle. He spoke
briefly to the ship, indicating he was on his way.

"Zulu Three Whiskey, this is Ranger One-eleven. Off
with twenty-two."

The other pilots saw Chambers's A-6E pull away and
they joined him at his altitude, moving automatically into
the formations they would use while flying toward the target.
And then Chambers made a slow descent, taking them
downward toward the sea. Soon they were all flying one
hundred feet over the water to avoid being detected by the
Cuban acquisition radar at the center of General Valdez's
advancing column more than a hundred miles away. They
kept tight formations in the order that they would go after
the Cubans. The flights of attack aircraft made four dia-

monds as they flew, with the A-6Es at the front and rear and the F/A 18s at the sides. The six flak suppressor aircraft flew near the front, just behind the leading diamond of A-6Es, three on each side of it.

Chambers's cryptic comment as he departed for the target had also served as a signal for Commander Ted Lawson, who commanded the U.S.S. *David R. Ray*, a destroyer operating with the *Roosevelt* battle group. The *Ray* was steaming in the Gulf of Aden, at that point more than a hundred miles from Perim Island in the Bab el Mandeb, but their mission was to destroy the guns on the island. Just after the French minesweeper *Andromède* had been attacked, the *Ray* had received "Rainform INDIGO" orders that directed it to prepare three Tomahawk cruise missiles for possible retaliation against the gun emplacements on Perim, which completely dominated the narrow straits. Lieutenant Roger McClure, the ship's tactical action officer, had then stationed a Tomahawk watch team in the combat information center, and along with Lieutenant David Levy, the ship's engagement control officer, had developed mission data that would bring each missile to within a few feet of the designated targets.

Lieutenant McClure had been monitoring the air strike group's radio frequency from his battle station inside the *Ray*'s combat information center. Now he turned to Commander Lawson, who sat in a raised chair, "fighting the ship" as he received a myriad of reports from different radars and other scopes inside the CIC.

"Sir, the *Independence* strike group is off with twenty-two."

Petty officers in blue denim uniforms stared intently at the radar consoles for every weapon system on the ship, making two semicircles around Lawson's chair inside the fluorescent brightness of the combat information center. Near him were the consoles for his most powerful missiles, including the Harpoon antiship missile, and the Tomahawk.

In the outer row was a gun console, a scope for the Phalanx close-in weapon system, which was a 20-millimeter anti-missile gatling gun, and one that directed the Sea Sparrow surface-to-air missile. To Lawson's right, a young petty officer studied the electronic warfare status board, and another monitored an antisubmarine warfare console. The mood was quiet, and serious. They all knew of the earlier HARM strikes against Yemeni targets, and were prepared for possible attacks from MIGs based in nearby Aden.

Commander Lawson answered McClure immediately. "Roger, fire the Tomahawks."

"Aye, aye, sir. Firing the Tomahawks." McClure spoke on a handset, and then reported back. "Firing imminent. Firing one."

They felt the ship tremble, and then heard a roar.

"Missile in flight," said McClure. "Missile status empty," he continued, verifying the launch. "Firing two. Missile status empty." The noises continued. "Firing three. Missile status empty." In a moment, McClure gave a further update. "Missiles look good, sir."

Lawson nodded approvingly. "Very well. Report the launch to Bold Spirit." Bold Spirit was the code name for the overall battle group commander, Rear Admiral Ward McCormick. Lawson let off a nervous smile. "And they damn well better be good."

The Tomahawks were all-weather cruise missiles, which could carry a thousand-pound payload hundreds of miles, and then drop it to within a few meters of its intended target. The three that had been launched from the *Ray* had been carefully programmed so that their internal guidance systems would follow just above the sea, and then over key terrain features on Perim Island itself, until they found the large artillery guns that dominated the Bab el Mandeb, and the two antiaircraft installations that would threaten the aircraft that had just been launched from the *Independence*.

Following Lawson's command, the missiles had appeared one at a time from their storage compartments belowdecks, popping up through doors that covered a matrix of twenty-four silos just in front of the *Ray*'s bridge. Each Tomahawk had roared upward into the air as it was launched, and then quickly dropped back toward the sea, settling into an approach flight to Perim Island from an altitude that was just above the water. At almost the same moment the *Independence* strike group neared the coast of Djibouti, the Tomahawks slammed into the remaining resistance on Perim Island, taking out the artillery and antiaircraft emplacements. There had been no warning to the Yemeni soldiers on Perim Island, except for the eerie commotion, like an incoming freight train, just before they died. Perim Island was now completely neutralized.

It had been less than ten minutes since Ron Chambers had reported his off-count to the *Independence*. The strike group was now over the coastline of Djibouti. Above the airfield at Faga, Chambers dumped a quick burst of fuel from his wingtips, causing two white streams of vapor to trail behind his A-6E. With that signal, each aircraft made a prearranged "weapons-armed" check, ensuring that their weapon systems were "hot," with the switches on. They then turned to the northeast and passed through the Bab el Mandeb, where the destroyed radars and guns of Perim Island now sat in helpless silence. Inside the Red Sea, above the nearest corner of a large island named Al Hanish Al Kabir, they made a hard, tight turn to the west, gaining an angle on the Cubans that would enable them to drop their ordnance down the length of the three armored columns.

Once they had turned, Commander Chambers activated the wing dumps of his A-6E again, a signal for the flak suppressor pilots to break ahead of the strike group. Immediately the two flights of flak suppressor aircraft accelerated ahead of the strike group, popping up high above the water and fanning out to the north and south, obtaining two wide angles on the Cuban column. They were still over the sea, sixty miles away from the advancing Cubans.

At the center of the Cuban column, the Cuban acquisition radar beamed immediately, picking up the strike group for the first time, and in seconds the Cuban SA-6 radars also were alerted and working to track the American aircraft. They did not comprehend it, but that was exactly what the Americans wanted: The harder the Cuban radars worked, the easier they were for the Americans to detect. In the EA-6B on the right flank, Lieutenant Joe Montoya's computer screen was now bright with seven triangles. The triangles were spaced on the screen according to the direction from the aircraft, and the emitting frequencies, of the radars in the Cuban column. It was as if he were watching the Cuban advance on television, so clearly could Montoya see where General Abelardo Valdez had placed his air defense missile systems. The flak suppressor aircraft had been tracking the Cuban acquisition radar, which was code-named Flat Face, from the moment they had passed over the weapons checkpoint at Djibouti. Their target sectors for the SA-6s had been agreed upon prior to taking off from the *Independence*.

Montoya placed his cursor over the right rear radar in the Cuban column. He had been jamming it with electronic countermeasures, forcing its Cuban operator to work his radar even harder. The harder it worked, the brighter was the signal Montoya saw on his screen. And now he punched its location into his computer, passing off the frequency and azimuth to one of his HARM missiles.

"I got the northwest Straight Flush locked."

Lieutenant Travis Jones acknowledged him. "Roger that. I'll shoot when we're feet dry."

The aircraft crossed over the Eritrean shoreline, and was now "feet dry." Jones pressed a button on his stick, shooting the HARM. "There it goes."

Montoya spoke again. "Missile's off the rail. Looks good. Shoot another?"

"Hold on. We'll race-track around and take another look."

The EA-6B pulled hard right, back over the water as it prepared to make a circle and come around for another run.

Near it, two F/A 18s had made the same maneuver. Miles away, on the southern side of the advancing strike group, three other aircraft had done the same thing. One of them had shot two HARMs, taking out the acquisition radar as well as an SA-6.

Montoya watched his screen. Within a minute the acquisition radar, and all six of the SA-6 radars, were destroyed. The Cuban missile launching systems were still churning toward Bera'isale, but they were useless. The American strike group had not yet come within range of the SA-6 missiles, and yet the Cuban radars could no longer track the incoming aircraft.

Montoya spoke excitedly into his voice mike. "Flat Face is down. So are the Straight Flushes. They're all down!"

Jones responded cautiously, still making his tight circle in the air. "Keep looking. Get a lock on anything that comes on your screen. They may have turned some of them off."

5

The Eritrean Desert

But they were indeed down. The reports came in to General Abelardo Valdez from all seven locations, shouted by his battalion commanders, their voices mad with fear. He and his commanders had not yet even seen an aircraft, or viewed so much as a contrail in the sky before them. For a moment he felt like surrendering, and then he realized that he did not even know how to give up. He grasped the handset of the radio that linked him with his headquarters at Addis Ababa, and screamed angrily, even as his command vehicle rolled forward toward the American defenses.

"We have lost our air defense! All of my radars are down! We are going to be slaughtered out here! I am going to attack! I say again, I am going to attack! I need air support! And where are the Russians?"

He stopped his vehicle for a moment, and then he did see the American aircraft, five miles to his front and moving with a rapidity that sickened him. They had come in very low and dropped payloads of Rockeye bombs along the axis of his advance party. Now they were soaring away from the Cuban column, moving upward and to the right and left, dumping chaff and flares from near their tails as they departed in order to counteract the heat-seeking SAM-7s and SAM-9s. Valdez saw four huge rolling clouds of dust and smoke where his advance party had been, and then the bright specks of flares lingering over his column like little birthday candles in the hot blue sky. The sounds of the air strikes reached him after that, rolling like thunder, peppered with smaller detonations from antipersonnel bombs that had broken away from larger canisters.

Before he had time to comprehend the damage and the terror, another four aircraft appeared, as if emerging from the ugly dust, and left a second trail of flashing explosions and curling debris much closer to him. Their screaming, high-pitched engines pierced the roar of the bombs as they, too, pulled away from his column. In their wake Valdez could also hear the sounds of some of his ZSU antiaircraft guns firing back at the attackers. But the aircraft were coming in so low and were so fast that it was almost impossible to hit them.

And then a third flight suddenly came right at him. He lay flat on the sunbaked earth, clutching a front wheel of his BRDM command vehicle, praying, whining, cursing, confessing his sins to a God he had forgotten, as the payload from one attacking aircraft laid a thousand-foot carpet of bombs along the middle column of the main body's lead elements. Another jet screamed overhead, dropping a second load farther back. The ground moved under him, pitching his body left and right as he clutched the wheel. The columns on each side of him were erupting with horrendous, echoing explosions that threw jets of dirt and salt and lava spewing into the air.

Almost immediately a fourth flight screamed past him a hundred feet off the ground, heading for targets in the column just behind him. The bombs shook the earth, piercing every membrane of his fear. He could hear his ZSU-23-4s firing more heavily now, as well as a few of his towed quad-12.7-millimeter machine guns. SAM-7s and SAM-9s fell through the air like Roman candles, having missed their targets. As the fourth flight of the American attack group pulled out and away, a blast from one of the ZSUs blew a hole in an engine on an F/A 18 Hornet. The aircraft fell slowly away from the others in its flight, losing altitude, leaving a black stream of smoke behind it as it headed back toward the sea.

No one cheered. But for now the bombing had stopped. For miles in both directions the desert had become torn and confused, heavy with clouds of yellow fog. The air was thick when Valdez breathed, like cigar smoke. Hot flares that appeared pink through the haze of dust floated down from the sky, mocking him as if they were souvenirs left behind by someone who had rudely crashed his party. From behind him he could hear the futile blasts of nervous gunners as they shot through the veil of dust that had enveloped them, trying to hit imaginary targets.

Slowly, Abelardo Valdez released his grip on the tire of his command vehicle. He rolled over onto his back and saw that the door just above him was gashed by a heavy piece of shrapnel from the bombs. The gash was more than a foot long, and three inches thick. *That close*, he marveled, again praising his new friend God. Any higher, and his communications would have been destroyed. Any lower, and he would have been dead.

He started to stand, and immediately fell on his face as if someone had tripped him. Then he looked down and saw that his left boot was mangled and torn, and that his foot was pumping blood into the unquenchable desert sand, matching the rhythm of his racing heart. He sat up in the hot sand and held his foot in both hands, trying to peer inside his boot. He saw only gushing blood, and raw meat. Squinting with curiosity and fear, he unlaced the boot, and pulled it off. Most of his foot stayed inside the boot.

Now I am going to die. "Alarcon!" There was no answer. He tried again. "*Alarcon!*"

His personal radio operator finally called back to him, opening up the command vehicle's door. "Yes, General!"

"Are you all right?"

"Yes, General." The sergeant's oily, pimpled face peered out at him. "All radios are up in the command vehicle, sir. The advance party has taken heavy casualties but is now firing artillery on the Americans. Lead battalion on the right has been hit very badly. I have no radio communications. The second battalion is moving past them, toward the objective. Lead battalion on the left has lost—" Sergeant Alarcon saw that Valdez was squeezing his mangled foot, trying to slow the bleeding. He reached inside the command vehicle and then brought the general a large first-aid pouch.

Valdez had calmed down. His cracked, dirty hands were now covered with blood. He nodded toward the first-aid pouch. "Get me a tourniquet. Quickly, quickly. And a cigarette. Light it for me and put it in my mouth. And tell all battalions to break formation and move toward the objective. There will be more air strikes. We are channeled between these two lava floes. We have no room to maneuver. Tell them to attack. There is no time to wait. I will be back on the radio in three minutes. But first I have to stop the blood."

6

Point Bravo

In the air above Eritrea, Lieutenant Mike Fortier and his wingman, Lieutenant Tommy "Sugar Bear" Canavan, were holding their F-14 Tomcats in an orbit at twenty-four thousand feet over their assigned station, Point Bravo, which was located between Manda and Assab. Their mission was to protect other American forces from attacking aircraft.

And now the E-2C early warning aircraft, which had been monitoring all takeoffs and landings at Dese and Mekele, broke into their radio frequency.

"Ripper one oh two, this is Lancer. You got bogeys coming in. Two-eight-zero at one hundred, angels twenty-two. Five-seventy knots, flight of two."

Fortier and Canavan immediately turned toward the incoming MIGs, which from the description of the E-2C were at a 280-degree bearing from his aircraft, a hundred miles out, flying at twenty-two thousand feet. Fortier peered at his scope and could not yet find the MIGs, so he called back to the E-2C, asking for more information.

"Bogey dope. I'm in a turn."

"Bogey now two-eighty at eighty, angels steady," came the response, indicating that the MIGs were already twenty miles closer. Fortier still could not find them.

"Bogey dope."

"Now two-eighty at sixty."

The F-14s and the MIGs were closing at a rate of twenty miles a minute. Canavan, flying Ripper 102, was just behind Fortier, off to his right. A minute later, Fortier finally picked up the MIGs on his radar screen.

"Roger, got a lock." He now called to Canavan. "Sugar Bear, you got 'em?"

"Roger, got 'em."

"Take the one on the right." Fortier immediately fired a Sparrow air-to-air missile toward the nose of the incoming MIG on the left, calling the code name of the Sparrow over the radio to indicate the nature of the weapon he had fired. "Fox one."

The Sparrow roared from a rail below him and within a second was traveling two thousand miles an hour. Fortier continued to head toward the nose of the MIG in case the Sparrow missed it, not wishing to give the Cuban pilot a shot toward his tail with one of its heat-seeking Atoll missiles.

The Sparrow missed. Now he could actually see the MIG.

He passed the information on. "Ripper one oh two, got a tally."

The MIG saw him, too. Its pilot fired an Atoll missile and pulled early, starting to head away from him, down low to where he could hide from the F-14 radar in the clutter of the desert mountains.

This guy's a nugget, thought Fortier when the MIG dove toward the desert floor. *New guy.*

Fortier did a quick jink to the left to avoid the Atoll, which went wide, screaming past him on the right. Then he put on his afterburners to chase the MIG. He quickly closed the distance and then fired a heat-seeking Sidewinder, calling "Fox two!" as he did so. The 'Winder hit the MIG broadside, just aft of its right wing. The aircraft blew apart in two large pieces, throwing a mass of clutter and debris into the cloudless sky.

"One oh two, Splash one," said Fortier exultantly. "Bogey going down."

Lieutenant Junior Grade Al Givens spoke into the voice mike from the backseat. "Shit hot, Rattler. He's gone."

Canavan called him from the other F-14. "Rattler, I'm engaged. I'm in the vertical."

Fortier could see Canavan's aircraft. "Roger, Sugar Bear, got a tally. I'm coming to you."

Canavan's F-14 and the other MIG were racing upward like jet acrobats in parallel vertical climbs, canopy facing canopy, each trying to get an angle on the other's tail so that they could fire machine guns, or let go with heat-seeking missiles if the other jet fell away from its climb. Fortier turned on his afterburners again and headed toward them.

"Sugar Bear, I'm coming from your nine o'clock."

"Roger, Rattler. He's starting to fall off."

The MIG was at the top of its climb, and now was losing energy, falling off to Fortier's left and onto its back. Then it rolled over, righting itself, and headed down toward the deck, repeating the escape maneuver of its destroyed wingman. It was picking up speed, hoping to open the distance between itself and Canavan's aircraft, and to turn quickly if Canavan came close enough to fire a Sidewinder missile. A quick turn could shake the heat-seeking Sidewinder.

Fortier had an angle on the MIG. "Sugar Bear, I'm going down with him."

In the midst of all this chaos, the E-2C interrupted, offering to refuel them, its radio operator calm as a weather forecaster. "One oh two, this is Lancer. I've got Texaco, zero-nine-zero at eighty. Say your fuel state."

Givens shouted testily from the backseat, sending the E-2C away. "Not now, Lancer, I'm engaged."

Fortier's F-14 was moving at more than a thousand miles an hour as he chased the MIG downward. He dropped below the MIG, now approaching the range where he could fire another Sidewinder. The MIG saw him and pulled upward, beginning another climb, rolling away from him at the same time. And then Canavan came back on the radio.

"I've got him, Rattler! Stay away, I'm letting a 'Winder go. Fox two!"

Fortier pulled up and away, preparing to make a second pass if Canavan's Sidewinder missed. And then he heard Canavan again. "Got a splash. Bogey's going down!"

The E-2C broke in, congratulating them in time-honored Navy fashion. "Bravo Zulu, one-oh-two and one-oh-seven. We've got a tanker inbound to Bravo. Your vector to new station is one-zero-zero at sixty. Shotgun two-oh-one and two-oh-five are engaged. We've still got bogeys over the Bull's-eye, but they're no threat at this time. They're holding clear of our hot line."

The Bull's-eye was the airstrip at Mekele. The Cubans and Ethiopians had just lost eight aircraft in ten minutes, and were now holding the rest of their MIGs away from the battlefield.

CHAPTER 18
WASHINGTON, D.C.

1

Sarah Myerson, the ABS Capitol Hill correspondent, was standing in the green grass under the baking August sun, waiting for Doc Rowland. Her camera crew had marked out a box of turf next to a small copse of trees in a park just across from the Cannon House Office Building, near the Capitol itself. The crew had then erected a wide, three-walled silver reflector to her front, in order to mirror the sun onto her tanned, pretty face, giving it a glow. A spotlight lit the place near a tree where Doc Rowland would stand.

Rowland saw her as he and Roy Dombrowski crossed Independence Avenue on their way from his office, and he immediately waved. Dombrowski caught his hand, his thin, professorial face apprehensive.

"Don't wave, Doc." And now Dombrowski moaned. "Oh, Christ, here they come."

Twenty other reporters now stood near the traffic light on the far side of the street, forming a wall between Rowland

and Sarah Myerson. They seemed cartoonish in their intensity, an energized mass of near hysteria, and Doc Rowland realized for the first time that he was, for that day, a Very Big Story.

He pushed through them, attempting to remain polite. Tape recorders were in his face. Other cameras peered through the crowd at him. His shoulders rubbed into them. The sweat from their hands and arms came off on his clothes and his face.

"Mr. Chairman, can you comment on the stock market crash? Are we heading for a depression?"

"Mr. Chairman, Mr. Chairman, do you have any comment on the possibility of our going to war over the Red Sea?"

"*Do you have any response to the President's allegations?*"

He waved to all of them, now finally inside their circle with the ABS crew. "Please, ladies and gentlemen, I'll be happy to talk to you at the right time. I've promised ABS I'd do a live network shot, and then I'll take your questions. *Please*, just hold your fire for a few minutes."

Sarah Myerson guided him toward the spot she had selected for the interview. She held a microphone in one hand. She looked pleasant, even mildly beautiful, in a bright red dress, with her dark hair pulled back, revealing a smooth forehead, wide brown eyes, and a full, pursing mouth. She ignored her colleagues, who now reached forward with boom microphones and small tape recorders, trying to pick up Rowland's comments for their own stations and newspapers. The ABS camera was rolling. The air was filled with a giddy tension. Was the country on the way to collapse? Was it on the way to war? Had Doc Rowland been the catalyst, or had he been the one to try to stop it?

Rowland grinned pleasantly back at Sarah Myerson, going over in his mind the answers he had already decided to give her, no matter what her questions might be. He was wearing yet another new suit, a white oxford cloth shirt, and his yellow power tie. This was a big moment, a compensation for the President's having left him to hang on the Nakashitona bill, a chance to explain himself directly to a few million viewers. He was going after Ronald Holcomb. He was going to pay the President back.

The line producer counted her down. "Okay, Sarah, ten seconds. Five, four, three, two, one—" He pointed at her and she came alive, exuding warmth and confidence. This was the big leagues, the sort of interview that literally made policy and ended up on page one the next morning. And Doc Rowland had her all to himself.

"Good afternoon, ladies and gentlemen. This is an ABS live news update. I'm standing with Congressman Doc Rowland, Chairman of the House Committee on Armed Services. Chairman Rowland is perhaps the leading expert in the Congress on defense issues, so maybe he can help us understand what's happening in the Red Sea today. He also was the author of the controversial Nakashitona Sanctions Act of 1991. That legislation, which passed the House earlier this morning, is already credited by many as sending a much-needed message regarding the loss of American technology to the Eastern bloc because of security failures in friendly countries. The bill is also being widely criticized as the catalyst for what appears to be a collapse of the stock market, and the further devaluation of the dollar in worldwide markets."

She smiled crisply to Rowland. "Mr. Chairman, thanks for being with us this afternoon."

"It's a pleasure to be here, Sarah."

Roy Dombrowski had chosen the live interview with Sarah Myerson because the producer of the show had guaranteed him there would be no hard questions, that it would be a benign forum that would allow Doc Rowland to explain himself. But now Sarah Myerson threw the first question as if it were a lance.

"Let me get right to the point. The stock market is down five hundred points, and it's only one o'clock in the afternoon! The dollar has fallen further against all major currencies. Chairman Rowland, there's a great demagogic appeal to your actions against Nakashitona Industries, but isn't something going wrong here? Aren't you throwing the baby out with the bathwater?''

Rowland squirmed a little, taken aback. ''Sarah, let's first identify what the problem is. I spoke for years against the idea of sharing our most precious technology abroad. I specifically argued against the sale of our Iroquois system to the Japanese. I'm not blaming the entire Japanese nation for what happened, but they clearly should have come up with a better way to protect the codes of this system. With all this renewed trade with the Communist bloc, the temptation was too great for some of these Nakashitona employees. The result was predictable, and then the question became what to do about it.''

She interrupted him, still smiling, but she was all over him. *From head to toe, like poison ivy*, he thought to himself as she spoke. ''The Japanese are taking your legislation as a national insult. They've even termed it racist and overly nationalistic.''

''Well, I know that,'' he explained, trying to appear patient and diplomatic. ''But it isn't racist or overly nationalistic, in my opinion, for a country to protect itself against the compromise of its most sensitive systems. It's the very basis of national defense.'' Rowland took on a well-practiced, wounded appearance. ''Sarah, if this was an American corporation, I'd be calling for strong action against them, too. So with all due respect to our friends in Japan, I say they're wrong. Now, I—''

She interrupted again, leaning forward and giving him that wonderful, disarming smile. ''The President issued a statement an hour ago holding you fully accountable for the crash of the stock market. Would you care to comment on that?''

''He did?'' Rowland's eyes narrowed and he took a deep breath, pushing his huge chest out toward the camera. He hadn't cleared the decks with Janet Holcomb a minute too soon. "Well, I would say this to my good friend the President. Doc Rowland didn't propose selling technology to the Japanese. Doc Rowland wasn't over there a week or so ago, begging them to go easy on us. This stock market problem is a direct result of the *Japanese* selling off Treasury bonds, to try and scare us out of taking the action we *have to take if we're going to look ourselves in the mirror and respect what we see*! Now, if the President has a problem with that, he should talk to his secretary of defense, who gave us the problem in the first place."

"Are you saying that the President should fire Defense Secretary Holcomb?"

"I don't get into hiring and firing of Cabinet members. I merely am saying that this secretary of defense has been in bed with a foreign government, and America is coming out the loser. Particularly when another country starts interfering in our domestic issues like this. In fact you could make the argument that a foreign nation is trying to interfere with the American political process."

"Are you making that allegation, Mr. Chairman?"

Rowland was rattled, feeling manhandled by the coolly smiling Sarah Myerson. "I said you could make the argument. Maybe some of you in the media can write columns about it, or have a talk show on it."

"But can't you see how the Japanese would become furious? A three-year suspension of an entire corporation, for the acts of a few employees in one subsidiary? Your legislation, if it's enacted, will cost Nakashitona Industries billions of dollars. Some are saying a minimum—a *minimum*—of five billion. It may even put them out of business. Is that fair?"

"Listen, the entire Congress considered that, and more than four hundred of them voted for my bill, Sarah. Let's remember that it's going to cost us billions of dollars to fix the damage that Nakashitona did to our national security."

"Sorry to interrupt you again, Chairman Rowland, but

we need to keep the facts straight for our viewers. The Japanese claim that we haven't clearly demonstrated that it was Nakashitona's leak that really compromised the system. They claim that they are being made the scapegoats, and that our own country, what with the spy cases of a few years ago, is responsible for most of the problem.''

He shut her off, fighting back his anger. "You call those *facts*? We've been through all that. We listened to it in committee hearings. I asked my colleagues for other ideas on the legislation. There's no merit to that allegation. But at the same time—"

"You are in trouble in next year's reelection campaign at home, for the first time in twenty years. Your opponent claims that if the legislation passes, it will cost your district almost a billion dollars in Japanese investments. That the backers of Akasaka Industries will refuse to go ahead with plans to build a major factory in Euphoria. Does that concern you?"

"Does it concern me? Of course it does, but I don't think that will happen." Rowland grew indignant, a device that had worked well for him on television in the past. "But the man you call my 'opponent' in an election that's more than a year away ought to be careful. If I have the power to drive Akasaka away, then maybe they came because of me, too. But anyway . . ."

He found himself stammering. The interview was slipping away from him like an empty, unmoored boat drifting out of reach of its crew. "Now, look. What I was trying to say at the beginning was that I met with the President on this yesterday, and I was very impressed with his concern that the legislation in its present form may be too severe. I'm not backing off on the issue, but as always, I'm willing to look for the best way to fix the problem."

Sarah Myerson's eyes flashed quickly now, as if she had been waiting for the opening. And she hit him between the eyes, as if her question were a baseball bat. "Mr. Chairman, is there any truth to the rumor that you offered to back down on the Nakashitona legislation if the President would fire Secretary Holcomb and make you secretary of defense?''

"Is that a rumor? I've never even heard that rumor." Rowland stared blankly at her, momentarily stunned and yet conscious of the camera's devouring eye. He felt betrayed, even cheapened. There had only been two men in the Oval Office when he had offered Ev Lodge a deal.

The President himself! Ev Lodge had twisted his comment, filled it with personal ambition, and fed it to the media. This was war, real war. With the President as a media source!

Finally Rowland recovered, carefully phrasing a response. "Sarah, I told you I don't get into hiring and firing of Cabinet members. And I *damn* sure have no desire to sit on the Cabinet of a man who would cave in to the Japanese and then try to blame me for his problem. You should know that.''

"I'm sure you would agree that it's a legitimate question, given that many of Secretary Holcomb's difficulties have emanated from your committee.''

"If it were true, I suppose it would be legitimate. But the record doesn't show any such thing. If you read the record, I think you'll see that Secretary Holcomb has been the source of his own difficulties.''

She glanced at her notes, moving to a new subject. "There is a great deal of concern in many circles regarding recent events in the Red Sea. We know that the French and the Soviets exchanged fire along the Ethiopian coastline earlier today, and that a Soviet ship was severely damaged. The American convoy taking Japanese and American tankers out of the Saudi port of Yanbu' apparently also has come under fire, or hit a series of mines, it isn't clear yet. The Soviet Navy has bombarded Massawa. And we are receiving unconfirmed reports that American naval and marine units may actually be preparing to fight the Cubans in the desert, in support of beleaguered French units. What's going on, Mr. Chairman? Can you share with us your views on the wisdom of such an undertaking?''

Now Doc Rowland cursed Ronald Holcomb with all his heart. Because he knew he could never question a military operation while young American troops were putting their lives on the line on a battlefield. In a few days he could. But so-called after-action reports were never effective. The President would have his propaganda machine in full gear, the newspapers would be showing combat footage, and those who were critical usually sounded like whining dogs, begging for attention.

''Sarah, this is a delicate moment. And I don't think any of us should be second-guessing policy while it's being executed. I'd be glad to talk with you once the operation is over.''

''So, you're saying at this point that we need to get behind the President?''

''He's the Commander in Chief.''

''Even to the point of backing his policy of using American ships to escort Japanese oil tankers out of mine-infested waters in a region that seems to have erupted in large-scale war?''

''Yes I do.'' Rowland had visibly sagged, so great was his disappointment. Sarah Myerson had beaten him on Nakashitona, and Ron Holcomb had whipped him in the Red Sea. ''Japan is our ally and our friend, Sarah. Nothing that's happened in the Nakashitona matter has changed that, although I must say I'm very sorry to see the actions of the Japanese financial markets, which could only have been taken with the knowledge of the government.''

She interrupted yet again. ''Are you aware that Navy Secretary Zara Boles took sharp issue with using our minesweepers in this fashion last night, claiming in a rare public disagreement with Secretary Holcomb that they do not possess the technology to deal with the sophisticated mines that have been laid?''

''Zara Boles said that?'' He caught himself. ''I'll have to talk to her. She's a good friend of mine. But for now

I'll have to side with the President. Let's not forget that the issue in the Red Sea is the right of all countries to navigate their commerce in international waters, Sarah. And we should be supporting that issue.''

''Well, let's talk about American lives instead of international navigation. If the Americans fight the Cubans in the Red Sea, what would you say to the families of those young men who are going to be killed?''

The reporters around them were churning. The air filled with sibilant whispering. The boom mikes and the tape recorders aimed toward Doc Rowland as if he were a bull's-eye. He felt that it was the worst moment of his life.

''Sarah, as I said before, this isn't a time for you to ask anybody that. These young men are doing their duty, and we need to slow this kind of talk down until they're out of danger.''

2

Ronald Holcomb sat at his desk, leaning back into his chair as if he were a limp mannequin. He had taken a fifteen-minute break from the command center, to relieve himself and to collect his thoughts. Finally the door buzzer sounded, and Hank Eichelberger stuck his balding head inside.

''You asked to see me, Mr. Secretary?''

''Come on in, Hank.''

Holcomb rubbed his face with one hand, as was his habit when under great stress. ''The marines are going to be attacked. Our convoy has lost all four Japanese tankers to mines. *All four!* I have to prepare a press statement for later today. I need your help.''

''No problem, sir.'' Eichelberger automatically took a seat at the couch next to Holcomb's preferred chair, and in moments the defense secretary joined him. ''You can give me the basics, and then I'll write it up and coordinate it with Sherm.''

Holcomb seemed stunned beyond belief. "We lost all four tankers. *All four!* I can't *imagine* how that could have happened. Not one American tanker was even touched! I don't know how to explain that to Tanashi. He's coming in next week, you know."

Eichelberger eyed Holcomb steadily, as if the defense secretary were in reality a pampered, zoo-kept lion, turned out into the wilderness—a wilderness that he owned. "You tell Tanashi to sit up and take notice."

"I don't understand."

Eichelberger tried again, now smiling slightly. "You tell Tanashi to stop messing with us, or we'll find a way to sink the rest."

"You've got to be out of your mind." For a long moment Holcomb sat quietly, as if waiting for his batteries to recharge after the day's events. Then slowly he began to stare at the former CIA agent with a new comprehension. He forced himself to swallow, feeling his face tighten with a new fear.

"What did you do, Hank?"

"I obeyed your orders. Sir."

"What do you mean?" Holcomb appeared on the verge of panic. The very master of press leaks and congressional innuendo had suddenly found himself lost like a suckling babe in the jungle of blood and death. "You did that?"

Eichelberger said it again, coolly and without emotion. "I obeyed your orders. You wanted to send the Japanese a message that they would understand, one that would cause them to pull back their horns and start dealing fairly with us."

"What orders? I didn't give you any orders."

"Let's put it this way, sir," said Eichelberger, knowing that even this simple conversation could well be recorded. "If the klieg lights ever go on over in the Congress, I'll tell the truth. And the truth is that the operation was carried out according to your desires. Desires you communicated personally, and orally, to me." Eichelberger read a different doubt on Holcomb's face, and reassured him. "Don't worry—it's clean. I guarantee. No fingerprints."

And now Holcomb stammered. "I—don't know what to say. I don't know what it would take to undo this."

Eichelberger was completely unfazed. He spoke to Holcomb as if the defense secretary had now regressed into childhood. "Come on, Mr. Secretary, chill out. Don't worry about it! In the fog of war, anything can happen. Write a good press briefing and it'll never even come up." Eichelberger took out his notepad. "You'll be glad you were so smart in a few days. In fact, whether you know it or not you're a goddamn genius."

Holcomb watched his trusted assistant secretary for a long moment, silently weighing his options. He had been told. Everything had changed. Now he was either an accomplice or an accuser. He either had to take action against Eichelberger, or support the clandestine operation by covering it up during his coming press briefing.

Holcomb's mind spun as he considered the whirlwind of congressional hearings and accusations that would accompany any attempt to publicize the sinking of the tankers. The press would want to believe Eichelberger. More than anything, they would want also to go after the President. They hadn't been fed any raw meat since Ev Lodge had taken over.

And actually, as he began getting used to the reality of what Hank Eichelberger had ordered, he rather liked it. In a way it was brilliant, if it was handled exactly right with the Japanese. Destruction of commerce was a language they could understand. Besides, there might be a way to deal with Eichelberger later.

Finally Holcomb checked his watch. "All right, Hank. Let's get the outline of this down. I've got to get back to the command center."

"I wouldn't be in any hurry," said Eichelberger. "This has been a bloody day, Mr. Secretary. And it isn't going to get any better."

CHAPTER 19
BERA'ISALE

On the beach at Bera'isale, Colonel Wild Bill Fogarty was preparing for the worst. And he knew it was going to come. Just now Captain Greg Bouttiere, one of his company commanders, was calling with new information on the location of the Cuban artillery that already was throwing heavy shells his way.

"Musk Ox, this is Burlap Charlie."

"Roger, Charlie, this is the Six. Go ahead."

Forgarty's knee burned as he knelt in the hot sand of the desert floor behind a three-foot rise of lava. On his right, Corporal Pinky Garst had just given him the handset to the PRC-77 radio that connected him with the ground units under his command. On his left, Sergeant Manny Archuleta, his other radio operator, was sitting comfortably against the lava as if it were a chair, smoking a cigarette and talking quietly to Admiral Ward McCormick's battle group operations officer on the *Roosevelt*. McCormick, the battle group commander, was asking for a spot report on the Marine Corps activities.

Fogarty would get to McCormick in a minute. Just now

he stared out toward the low hills to his west as he clutched the radio handset, and then at the flat plain just south of the hills, where a haze of smoke and dust sat like an unlucky cloud over the Cuban advance. The tinny sounds of faraway artillery guns echoed over him, mixed with the quick screams and loud explosions from 122-millimeter and 152-millimeter shells. The shells were impacting all around Bera'isale, some of them far in front of Fogarty, some a half mile off to the right or left of his marines, and some falling indiscriminately inside his perimeter.

The Cubans were trying a barrage, but they had put their self-propelled howitzers into position too hastily. They had set in without aligning their guns, and apparently were firing without forward observers who might make line-of-sight adjustments. They were free-tubing it from three or four miles away. The marines were taking casualties, but not in the numbers the guns were capable of inflicting. For that Fogarty was thankful. But the guns would get better if he gave them time. And after the artillery softened him up, the tanks would come, firing from much closer. If even a dozen tanks broke through, they could form a spearpoint that would literally wipe out his unit.

Captain Bouttiere commanded Charlie Company of the 1st Battalion, 5th Marine Regiment, which was the ground element of Fogarty's Marine Expeditionary Unit. Charlie Company had the central sector of Fogarty's three-company perimeter, and was closest to the enemy artillery. Bouttiere continued as Fogarty listened on the handset.

"Roger, Musk Ox. I've got the FAC up here and he's been talking to the Cobra. I think we've got a good grid on Fidel's art'y. They're behind a ridgeline out at about four-two-one-three, one-three-seven-zero. I say again, four-two-one-three, one-three-seven-zero. Direction forty-five hundred mils from my 'pos.' "

"How far out?"

"I'd say about six clicks," said Bouttiere, meaning six thousand meters. "Cobra says they're in a hasty line back there, just lobbing them over at us. They're in there sloppy, but the more they shoot the better they'll get. If we can get some iron bombs on them, Cobra can direct with Willie Peter."

Fogarty's map was laid out in front of him, on his hot little shelf of lava. He found the grid points, and traced their direction to his front. The Cuban artillery peppered Bera'isale with another barrage, several rounds again impacting inside his perimeter. Bouttiere and Captain Bob "Roadblock" Rivers, the forward air controller, were right on target, judging from the map. About seven kilometers to his west was a small ridgeline, no more than half a mile long. From the rate of fire, Fogarty judged that there were ten or more self-propelled howitzers crowded in behind the ridge.

"Roger that, Charlie Six," said Fogarty. "I'll get some counterbattery out there, but they've got good defilade. Kind of like hiding behind a building. That's a tough ridge to shoot in back of. We've got some Green birds coming in with the next strike group. Give me the FAC." Green birds were Marine Corps aircraft, which sometimes deployed on Navy aircraft carriers, and were highly skilled in close air support missions.

"Roger, Musk Ox," answered Bouttiere. "Wait one."

In a moment Captain Rivers answered. "Musk Ox, this is Roadblock, over."

"Roger, Roadblock. We've got some Green birds coming in with War Hawk. See if you can get a divert, and pass them over to the Cobra so they can take care of the art'y. I'm holding back the Harriers for armor, over."

"Wilco. Roadblock out."

Fogarty gave the radio handset back to Pinky Garst, who smiled gamely, his dark eyes rolling with a dreadful excitement, and put it immediately to his own ear in order to monitor the traffic. And then Fogarty nudged Archuleta.

"Get me the admiral."

Fogarty was sky-high on fear and adrenaline. He was

hopelessly outnumbered, and his men had not been able even to dig defensive fighting holes. But things were going alright, and once the artillery was taken out he would be able to fight until dark. Darkness was for him the key. The Cubans would be unable to match him in the dark, particularly with the all-weather A-6Es, which could bomb all night.

And they were going to knock out the artillery. He knew that Roadblock Rivers would already be talking on the air frequency to the lead pilot in the coming *Roosevelt* strike group. The fourth flight in that strike group, which was only minutes away, were Green F/A 18s. *Thank God for that*, he mused, taking back all the insults he had issued over the years to the "wing wipes" of Marine air for taking too much of the budget from the "grunts."

The interdiction bombing of the *Independence* strike group had already broken the Cuban approach, causing a mass of confusion in the advancing columns. The remainder of the attacking division had lost its unit integrity and was now scattered randomly, making its way past the burning hulks of hundreds of destroyed tanks, vehicles, and artillery pieces, and thousands of dead and wounded Cuban soldiers. But the Cubans were channeled along a narrow five-mile front, between two huge lava floes that pointed down toward the sea on either side of Bera'isale, like giant black tree roots lying on the desert floor. Their tanks and vehicles and self-propelled artillery were still several miles away from the marines. They were moving toward Bera'isale in a halting, stuttering disarray, the whole division still reeling from the air strikes and unable to comprehend any other way out except to attack.

The *Roosevelt* strike group was nearing the beach. After it made its run, Fogarty would bring in AV-8B Harrier jets, armed with laser-guided "smart" bombs that could be directed from the ground onto individual tanks and vehicles as the Cubans came closer. But until the jets came he had to hold back the Cuban attack by relying on four Cobra attack helicopters that were rotating off of the nearby *Saipan* onto the battlefield, and eight pieces of 155-millimeter artillery.

If the Cuban tanks came closer than three miles, the Cobras would be the first to go after them, with Hellfire missiles. For now, he was using the Cobras as spotters and fire support coordinators, to direct fire on such targets as the Cuban artillery behind the near ridgeline. The 155-millimeter howitzers could easily reach the Cubans, but they were capable of firing only three rounds a minute.

Archuleta pushed the handset toward him. "Admiral's on the net, sir."

For a brief moment Fogarty was thankful that Mad Dog Mulcahy was not controlling the operation, apparently having left the battle group for Hawaii. He would not have been able to hold back his anger at Mulcahy, and there was no time for that. He pressed the handset to his ear and heard McCormick's calm, flat voice calling him.

"Musk Ox Six, this is Bold Spirit, over."

"Roger, Bold Spirit, we're taking some pretty heavy incoming. One-five-twos and one-two-twos. But I think we're fixing that with close air. I need a sitrep on the Frogs and on naval guns. If Fidel gets his tanks moving before dark we're going to need some five-inchers shooting over our heads."

"Roger, Musk Ox," answered McCormick. "Be advised the Frogs just knocked out a Red blocking force to your Sierra. Fidel was trying to box them in with tanks and heavy guns. They've got a mech unit advancing toward Fidel's rear. They'll hit him with close air and then attack his flank."

McCormick now hesitated for a moment. "We're under orders from the Big Six in the Whiskey Hotel not to use naval guns at this time. He's vetoed *all naval surface action*. Ivan is off the coastline to your rear. We're standing him down, but the five-inchers are a no-go. And we've got ships all over the place. It looks like the convoy out there has lost four Jap tankers. Big ones. We're fishing people out of the water, and the whole Red Sea is a burning mess.''

Ivan was the Soviet Navy. The Big Six in the Whiskey Hotel was the person, probably Felix Crowell, in some cozy situation room in the White House who was now furthering their misery by holding back naval gunfire in order not to ''provoke'' the Soviet Navy. ''Roger, Bold Spirit. Tell Frog Six I'll buy him a beer when we're done. As for naval guns, I'm having a little trouble sympathizing. Ask the Big Six in the Whiskey Hotel if he'd be holding back naval guns if it was his ass on the line out here. Or his son's. Just kidding. But I may get back to you on the guns if things get worse. We're hanging in the breeze out here. I say again, we're in deep shit. Musk Ox out.''

Fogarty cursed softly. *The fucking White House. They toss us into hell, and then worry about the Russians.* Anyway, there was no time to think about it. They'd played politics with human lives for longer than he'd been a Marine. *What the hell do I know, I'm just a grunt.*

The Marine Corps 155-millimeter artillery gave off a crescendo of tinny booms as they fired at the ridge, but their trajectory was too flat and they shot over it, far behind the Cubans. The Cuban artillery screamed and crunched around him, thirty rounds landing inside the marine perimeter, their groupings growing tighter with practice. The marines were lying exposed, pressing their bodies into the rocks and gullies of Bera'isale as the artillery slammed into dirt and lava, saturating the air with shards of metal and rock. Fogarty scanned his perimeter and saw several Navy corpsmen running like monkeys, stooped low with their hands touching the ground and their Unit One medical bags hanging off their shoulders, or kneeling as they worked on wounded marines, even as the artillery impacted around them with its terrifying crunches.

Brave little squid bastards, he thought again, marveling at his Navy corpsmen. But they would be busy today. Fidel was definitely getting his range and distance sorted out.

Obviously, the Cubans now had a forward observer team either on the ridge or in front of it.

Finally off to his left, a mile to the south, he saw the *Roosevelt* strike group come in off the water, just above the ground. His men cheered, some of them waving fists into the air, and he cheered with them as the first group of A-6Es screamed past them and headed toward the Cuban column. They were small as bees in the distance, and yet they were the embodiment of power as he watched them in the glare of the merciless afternoon sun.

Fogarty pressed his handset to his face and keyed the receiver, calling Captain Doug Gerlach, another company commander. "Bravo, this is Musk Ox."

"Roger, Musk Ox. This is Bravo Six."

"Get those recon teams ready to go. There's a little hill about four hundred meters in front of your 'pos.' Send a squad out with them, but get them going as soon as the art'y slows down. We need the beamer out there ASAP."

"Roger that," answered Gerlach. "We're on our way."

Far to his front across the empty vastness of the desert floor, he saw quick flashes and dark explosions from the Rockeye payloads as the first strike group hit the Cuban main body more than five miles away. Then he heard the booms and the cracks of the detonations, and the rapid bursts of the ZSU machine guns firing back at the aircraft.

He found himself chanting, "Get some! Get some!"—a saying from two decades before. And to his south came the second flight from the strike group, moving fast and low into the rolling dust and smoke as if it were their very own protective screen.

His 155-millimeter howitzers fired another barrage at the ridgeline that hid the Cuban artillery, hoping to slow the Cuban guns or possibly to take out the forward observer teams as they awaited the Marine Corps air strike. Their rounds impacted in an open sheaf along the far ridgeline, raising spurts of dust and smoke into the air that he could discern with his field glasses. And then the Cuban artillery came again. The shells were impacting much more regularly around his perimeter. Their groups were very tight. And now it seemed they walked like giant, spumescent steps directly toward him.

Right at him, filled with dust and screaming metal and broken jags of lava. He lay flat, his voice emitting an involuntary, helpless whine. His lungs sagged and the energy left him as for that moment he surrendered himself to fate, no longer a colonel or even a marine, simply a child whose blood was going to melt inside the earth, helpless in the face of a power only God could control.

"Oh, Mama Mama Mama . . ."

The large shells screamed and exploded, first off to his right, and quickly formed a sheaf of ten explosions that erupted one after another, less than a second apart, landing behind him and moving farther toward his left.

The shell behind him landed less than twenty feet away. He felt his body move, floating for an instant as if giant burning pincers had grabbed him in a dozen places, shook him once, and then dropped him. He landed on his knees and for a moment tossed his head about like a water-soaked dog. Then he fell onto his face, limp and torn apart.

"Oh, Christ help me, I'm dead I'm dead . . ."

He looked over and saw that Corporal Pinky Garst was indeed dead, the young man's ebony face cracked open at the forehead by a large piece of shrapnel. Another barrage impacted over to his left. He took one more look at Garst and then dismissed the corporal's death, placing its reality back into a corner of his mind where he kept a long, bloody file of such irreversible tragedies. He needed a radio. He started to crawl toward Garst's.

He fell onto his face, then looked down and saw that his right leg was in tatters, gone from just below the knee, and that blood from his left leg had already soaked his jungle utility trousers. The blood was now dripping down the top of his boot. Inside his intestines, shrapnel stirred him like a large, dull knife every time he moved.

Well, that's that. I'm a goner.

Fogarty shook his head again and again, as if he had just been knocked down in a fight. Then Manny Archuleta was holding him as if he were a baby, the young corporal's own arms and shoulders gushing blood. Doc Perrone, his command group corpsman, was already running toward him. Perrone shoved Archuleta out of the way and pushed Fogarty on the chest until he was flat against the ground, and then ripped both of his trouser legs up to the crotch.

"Lay still, sir." Fogarty tried to sit up and Perrone pushed him again. "*Lay chilly,* goddamn it!"

"Don't give me morphine, Doc. I'll fall asleep."

"Okay, okay. But lay down!"

"Archuleta, give me your radio. And get Garst's over here, too. Doc, patch up Archuleta. His left shoulder looks bad."

"Colonel, if you don't lay down I'm going to hit you with morphine."

He compromised by turning over and laying on his face so that he could still see to his front. The third flight from the *Roosevelt* strike group emerged from the sea and flew past them, four F/A 18s loaded with eight tons of bombs apiece. The Cuban artillery came again, down toward the beach this time, near where an LCAC landing craft was offloading supplies.

Archuleta handed him Pinky Garst's radio and he tested it. It still worked. Doc Perrone rolled him onto his back, still checking for shrapnel holes. A tourniquet had already been expertly tied to his shattered right leg. Then Perrone rolled him back over onto his belly.

"We've got to get you out of here."

"Did you stop the bleeding?"

"In your legs, sir. But you've got a gut wound."

"I'll last for a while." He experimented, pushing the stump of his leg into the hot earth, thinking that it might somehow cauterize the mass of meat and veins that hung in tatters at its end. Looking sideways, he noted the uneasy look on the young corpsman's tanned and haggard face. "Take care of Archuleta, Doc. And then get out of here. You've got lots of people to take care of."

Bouttiere was calling on the radio, his voice now fervent. "Musk Ox, Musk Ox, Musk Ox, this is Burlap Charlie, Burlap Charlie, radio check, over."

"Roger, Charlie, got you Lima Charlie. Where's the FAC?"

"Are you okay?"

"I'm hit. My talker's a KIA. Where's the Green strike?"

"FAC's got him hooked up with the Cobra. Watch to your front. He's on the way. Are you okay?"

"That's affirm. Listen up. Burlap Alpha, Bravo, Charlie. I need a casualty count."

The company commanders came on the net one at a time.

"Alpha here. Three KIA, eight wounded."

"Bravo Six reports five KIA. Still counting."

"Charlie. We're okay. It's all been behind us. I think I've got two men hit."

"Get the LAVs up to your 'pos' and send your wounded down to the LCAC," said Fogarty, his eyes now scanning the horizon for signs of the coming air strike on the Cuban artillery. He could hear the light amphibious vehicles churning almost as soon as he spoke, moving forward from the beach area toward the rifle companies on the perimeter. Another artillery barrage came in, this time on the forward edge of the perimeter, near Charlie Company.

Captain Bouttiere came on the net immediately. "We got hit pretty hard that time. Get an LAV over here! Musk Ox, I'm giving you the FAC. I've got to go help somebody."

Rivers began speaking almost immediately. "Musk Ox, this is Roadblock. Cobra marked the target with a Willie Peter. The Green strike will be coming in to our front, right to left. I say again, right to left. It's on its way. We've got a Frog strike off the *Clemenceau*, coming in deep on Fidel's rear. They're holding for our Green strike, but you'll see them to your Sierra at about twelve in a few minutes."

Sierra was their south, toward the now-calm fortress of Assab.

And then the Hornets came in off the water just to his north, flying low and fast, one after the other, at an angle that was almost perpendicular to his lines. He cheered again as he watched the four jets disappear briefly behind one mountain and then again behind the far ridge, reappearing as they climbed rapidly back into the air, leaving flares and a huge roll of smoke and dust behind them. SAM-7 missiles arched and fell in their wake, and finally the artillery was silent.

Captain Rivers came back onto the net. "Roadblock here. Cobra reports the artillery is all down, at least for now. Nothing but crispy critters back there. Piece of cake. Are you okay, Musk Ox?"

He tested his stump, felt the blood leak from his abdomen, and lied. "That's affirm, Roadblock. Tell the Cobra to keep looking at that ridge."

Far off to his left, the French air strike began. Fogarty could see the rolls of smoke and dust deep in the Cuban rear as the Étendards broke up the remainder of the faltering Cuban advance. From what Admiral McCormick had told him, he knew that a French armored unit out of Assab would be attacking the Cuban flank near where the Étendards had hit it.

In the west, the sun was approaching the top of the mountains. Soon it would fall behind the Danakil alps, and night would come to Bera'isale as if a light switch had been turned off. Fogarty reached an arm out rather weakly in front of him, and measured the distance between the sun and the top of the mountains: three fingers, that was all. In three fingers the sun would disappear. And then he would be free.

The tanks were coming. He saw them to the south, directly in front of him, at the edge of the horizon. There were at least a dozen of them rumbling out of the clutter and the dust, now within a mile or two of his forward lines. Their big guns were firing and the ground began to shake again from their explosions.

He was feeling faint, but had not lost his concentration. Doc Perrone had patched up Archuleta and was now squatting over Fogarty, appearing almost motherly as he tapped a vein in his left arm and fitted him with a hit of serum albumin. He still gripped the radio with his right hand. And now he called Captain Gerlach again.

"Bravo, this is Musk Ox."

"Roger, Musk Ox. Bravo Six here." Gerlach had anticipated him. "We see the tanks. Recon is in place with the beamers."

"Roger. Break, break break. Roadblock, Musk Ox."

"This is Roadblock. Harriers are on the way. I've got recon on my freq. We're all set."

"Roger that. I guess I'll get me a good seat and watch." He felt weak, almost queasy. He started drifting a little bit, floating when he stopped concentrating. He was nauseated, and the inside of his head swayed even when he rested his chin against the lava on one clenched hand. But he didn't hurt yet. For the moment the trauma had numbed him. He knew that would come later, when the adrenaline wore off and his body started reacting to the damage.

If he survived. He looked over at the stiffening frame of Pinky Garst and for the first time allowed himself the luxury of a moment of sadness. But that would come later, too. *One more phone call.* "Burlap Six, this is Musk Ox."

Lieutenant Colonel Mike Anderson, the battalion commander of the ground force, answered immediately. "Musk Ox, this is Burlap Six."

"Roger, Burlap. You'd better start thinking about relieving me at my 'pos.' I'm okay for now, but if I start losing it, be ready to assume command."

"Roger that. Break. We've got a full load of medevacs on the LCAC, moving back to the Big Boat right now. You were smart not to risk a chopper. The art'y would have taken it out. Even now I think it would draw a lot of traffic."

"Once the Harriers work out we'll be clear for choppers.

I think Fidel is going to quit for a while if we stop the tanks. And they're too beat up to hit us in the dark. They'll have to regroup, and take care of their casualties. They must be in a real mess out there.''

He started feeling very dizzy. The big guns of the tanks were getting closer. His stomach now hurt, as if he were going to vomit, but his legs did not. He thought about that and for some reason wanted to laugh. For the first time, he wondered seriously if he might die. He knew that whatever happened, a part of him was dead. A way of life, a profession.

I can run all night. And I can run all day.

The Harriers rolled in one at a time, the six jets making a wheel as they orbited around his perimeter and out toward the tanks. They were flying low and then suddenly arching skyward, launching laser-guided bombs into the air. The reconnaissance teams on the hill in front of his lines were guiding the bombs onto incoming tanks with a laser beamer. And the tanks were blowing up or tilting onto their sides as if he were watching it on a video game at a penny arcade. The surviving tanks came ever closer, now directly raking the marine positions with large 115-millimeter shells and coaxial machine-gun fire. He saw several of his TOW missiles roar from their tripod launchers at the edges of the perimeter. And finally the tanks were silent.

In the west the sun touched the top of the mountains. Fogarty began to feel cold. Doc Perrone had hit him twice more with serum albumin. He could no longer feel the handset when Archuleta held it against his cheek. And then he could no longer see Archuleta. He did not hear the helicopters as they came to take the wounded, and he did not know they were carrying him on a stretcher up the tail ramp of one of his churning, faithful old CH-46s. The world had faded from him. He was dead.

CHAPTER 20

1

It was midnight in the Red Sea, but in Washington it was still late afternoon. Since early morning the Pentagon had been brimming with tension and activity, its hallways filled with rumors and speculation. And now its dimly lit press room just down the "E" ring from the River Entrance was packed with an overflowing crowd of reporters. More than a hundred of them filled eight rows of folding chairs that had been set out in the middle of the low-ceilinged room. Another twenty stood in an open space behind the chairs. An electric excitement had galvanized the reporters. They had been summoned for a briefing by Secretary Holcomb himself. And so they waited, speaking in hushed voices to each other and scribbling newly learned facts and insights onto their notepads.

"Ladies and gentlemen, the secretary of defense."

The lights from a half-dozen television cameras came on as Assistant Secretary for Public Affairs Sherm Novotny announced Ron Holcomb's arrival at the press conference. The lights followed Holcomb as he entered the room from the corridor outside. He walked briskly, his head down and his hands made into fists. A scowling General Bear Lazaretti preceded Holcomb as if he were the defense secretary's bodyguard, pointing here and there to warn reporters that they were coming too close to the secretary. Ribbons and stars gleamed from the general's dress blue uniform. There was an uncharacteristic stiffness in Lazaretti's movements, as if he were coiled to react.

The air filled with the sound of clicking cameras, and Holcomb stepped onto a small stage in front of a wall covered by dark, heavy curtains. The lights above the stage went on, brightening him as he moved toward a podium at a front corner, where Sherm Novotny had placed the formal text of Holcomb's press briefing. A large map sitting on a tripod dominated the center of the platform. The map stretched six feet wide and eight feet high. An equally large piece of white poster paper covered it, masking its details from the press.

Holcomb nodded to an Air Force colonel who stood on the far side of the map, holding a long wooden pointer in one hand. The trim, handsome officer worked in the Middle East/Africa Division, under the director for strategic plans and policy in the Joint Chiefs of Staff. Holcomb could not hold back a sudden thought that the officer looked rather like a younger clone of Bear Lazaretti himself, who had worked in that directorate before becoming Holcomb's military assistant.

At Holcomb's nod, the colonel stripped the covering off of the map, causing an immediate, sibilant chatter to fill the room. The map showed the land and water areas of the southern Red Sea and the western parts of the Gulf of Aden. It was filled with ship and unit indicators of varying colors: blue for the United States, red for the Soviet Union, green for the French, yellow for the Cubans, brown for the Ethiopians, gray for the Eritreans, lavender for the Yemenis, white for neutral merchant shipping.

Holcomb nodded again, this time solemnly, a greeting to the waiting reporters. His hands trembled slightly as he picked up his briefing papers, a measure of his nervousness and of the long day's tension. But they were behind the podium, unseen. His eyes were steady and his voice would be strong and certain as he addressed the cameras. He quickly swiped at a lock of hair that had fallen onto his forehead and then peered down at his carefully prepared opening remarks.

The remarks were the result of intense haggling among himself, Felix Crowell, and Secretary of State Richard Fumaro. Once the general administration position on the events had been agreed upon by those three, Holcomb's prepared speech had been given a "spin" by Hank Eichelberger. As a consequence, the remarks were a mix of bald truth, diplomatic half-truths, and what Holcomb had privately called "necessary, unconfirmable distortions." Nonetheless, they would become the government's official pronouncement on the day's action.

The photogenic Air Force colonel still stood erect and attentive. He began tapping the wooden pointer from place to place on the map as Holcomb addressed the reporters.

"Good afternoon," said the defense secretary. "As all of you know by now, American military units have been involved in a major engagement in the Red Sea area throughout the day. I believe it is important at this time to outline for you a chronology of what has occurred. First, by way of background, most of you are aware that a large Cuban force assembled more than a month ago near Addis Ababa, and made its way toward Eritrea, a nation jointly recognized by the United States and France. The Cubans have been leading an element of the Ethiopian Army that numbers more than one hundred thousand soldiers. Their evident purpose was to capture the major towns of Eritrea, to defeat the Eritrean Army, and to turn those cities over to the Ethiopian Army. Two nights ago—yesterday afternoon, our time—the Cuban force, which was of divisional size, invaded Eritrea, with an immediate mission of attacking key cities along the seacoast, and, it appears, of linking up with the Soviet Navy in order to establish a supply base on Eritrean soil. A few hours after the Cuban invasion—at about eleven o'clock last night, our time—a warship from the Soviet Union opened fire without provocation on a French Army unit that was operating in the coastal city of Edd. The French unit returned fire, seriously damaging the Soviet ship, and driving it away from Edd.''

Holcomb paused for an overly long moment, staring rather severely at the reporters, gaining their complete attention. ''I point out here that despite denials and counter-accusations from the Soviet Union, it is the position of the United States that the Soviet Navy was responsible for sowing a large minefield in the northern Red Sea two weeks ago. This minefield caused the disruption of commerce through the Suez Canal, and out of the Saudi Arabian port of Yanbu'. We have succeeded in some preliminary clearing of that minefield. Our navy was escorting the first convoy out of Yanbu' today as other activities developed inside Eritrea, and in the Red Sea itself.''

And now he trod softly on the Soviets, mindful that they had in many ways used the incident to deflect attention from their own domestic problems in the Ukraine, which were still hidden behind a press blackout. There was always a tomorrow in international relations, and soon the Soviets would resume their push toward warmer ties. ''I would also point out, however, that the Soviet Union has been most cooperative during the crisis of the past twelve hours. The President believes that, in the final analysis, this gives us a strong indicator of the ability of our two nations to work together, and to contain international incidents.''

Holcomb nodded again to the Air Force officer who stood next to the map, and continued. ''Shortly after the French were taken under fire at Edd, it became clear that the entire

Cuban division which had just invaded Eritrea had in fact turned toward the coastline, and was preparing to make an attack on one or more French positions. At almost the same time, a Japanese tanker under escort from U.S. Navy ships hit two mines in international waterways, and subsequently sank. Later in the afternoon, three more Japanese tankers under escort were hit by several other mines, and also sank.''

He hesitated for a quick moment, watching the faces of the assembled reporters in an attempt to measure their dismay at the fact that all four Japanese tankers had gone down. But Hank Eichelberger had been right: The overwhelming chaos of the entire day marked this as simply one more unpredictable catastrophe. Holcomb continued, using language that an unknowing Felix Crowell had insisted on inserting in the briefing. ''It is the position of the U.S. government that this minefield was separate from the minefield laid in the northern Red Sea, and that the mines were probably laid by the Yemeni Navy acting independently, in support of the Cuban attack.''

The room remained absolutely silent, except for clicking cameras and the persistent tapping of the colonel's pointer against the map. For all the usual talk of budgets and nuclear throw-weights and practice exercises with NATO, the reporters knew that this briefing was different, that there was death in the air.

Holcomb felt his own eyes widen and his heart race as he contemplated his next statement. His hands were now trembling so fiercely that he could not read the paper when he held it. He dropped the paper onto the surface of the podium, and grasped its heavy wooden edges to steady himself. He was going to lie rather blatantly this time, to cover Mad Dog Mulcahy's tracks and his own involvement in the Eritrean debacle. True, Mad Dog's career was finished, and many, including General Roger Francis, wanted the admiral to suffer a public humiliation. But Holcomb had convinced the President during a highly secure conference call that the administration would be embarrassed far more by an unending series of media stories regarding the admiral's insubordination than it would be if it simply took credit for the results on the battlefield, which on the whole were not bad. The marines had held their own against an entire division of Cuban soldiers. Naval air and surface units had worked almost to perfection.

And so Holcomb would "give the operation an administration face," as he had delicately put it to the President. He wouldn't lie. He almost never lied. He would merely package the facts, box them up and wrap them with a bright, optimistic ribbon. And anyway, his version could never be challenged.

He continued his briefing. "In response to these blatant violations of international law, and as a gesture of support to the French government after the Soviet attack on their units, the President directed that the Department of Defense implement Operation Justifiable Anger, a highly classified contingency plan known only to a few, even inside the JCS, which had been conceived some time ago as an option if the French were directly threatened by a large-scale Cuban ground attack in Eritrea. Justifiable Anger involved retaliatory action against certain targets along the southern coast of the People's Democratic Republic of Yemen and at Perim Island, and also called for a Marine Expeditionary Unit to occupy the town of Bera'isale on the Eritrean coast, near the French Army outpost of Assab."

They were buying it. He breathed deeply and his hands ceased their trembling. "I must emphasize that this occupation was *defensive* in nature, designed only to show our support for the French."

Having invented a military operation in order to protect both himself and the administration from a Pandora's box of cumulative humiliations from the media and the Congress, Holcomb now elaborated on its military execution. "Our forces put Operation Justifiable Anger into effect beginning at approximately noon, Eritrean time. The Marine

Corps unit at Bera'isale was subsequently attacked by a Cuban armored force ten times its size. Our young marines have fought valiantly, with air and other support from the *Independence* and *Roosevelt* battle groups, which have been operating in the western waters of the Gulf of Aden. Casualties have been heavy on both sides, but the Cuban attack has been crushed.''

And now, as he had promised, Holcomb finalized the fictional campaign, closing it down and making it disappear. ''Unless other events intervene, Operation Justifiable Anger has now been concluded. In the past few hours, Cuba and the Soviet Union have jointly petitioned for a cease-fire, in exchange for the immediate withdrawal of all Cuban military forces from Eritrea. The United States and France have agreed to this cease-fire, and it is now in force. As you know, it is night in the Red Sea. Nonetheless, our units have begun supervising the evacuation of Cuban casualties to the Soviet ship *Nicolaev* through the town of Beylul, which is halfway between the Marine position at Bera'isale and the French outpost at Assab. At the conclusion of the Cuban withdrawal from Eritrea, it is the intention of the United States to immediately remove all its forces from that country.''

There, Holcomb thought. Mission complete. History, and tomorrow's news, would show that the administration saw a problem, anticipated its enlargement, structured a response, executed it, and ended it favorably. Very clean. His voice was now steady, and his face serene as he peered commandingly at the reporters from behind his podium. ''I will now take your questions.''

''Mr. Secretary! Mr. Secretary!''

Twenty hands went up and thirty questions were shouted. Finally Holcomb pointed to Ed Loftus, a longtime Pentagon correspondent for NBS. The NBS camera was just behind Loftus as he spoke in a stentorian cadence. ''Mr. Secretary, do the French consider themselves to be at war with the

Soviet Union? And were we at any time in direct conflict with Soviet military forces?''

''The French will speak for themselves, Ed. From everything I have seen, however, they were acting in strict accordance with the Mandebaran alliance among themselves, Djibouti, and Eritrea, rather than in any offensive manner against the Soviets. They were taken under fire by the Soviets. Their actions appear to have been in self-defense and were not continued once the Soviet naval vessel pulled away. As for the United States, we have not at any time been in direct confrontation with the Soviets, and as I mentioned at the outset, we are pleased that the Soviets cooperated fully with us through diplomatic channels as the crisis unfolded.''

Holcomb pointed again, this time toward Ann Lehrmeir, a print reporter for the API news service. ''Ann?''

''Mr. Secretary, what happens now? Is this over, or do we consider ourselves now directly involved in the war between Eritrea and Ethiopia—or, as the Soviets might put it, in the Ethiopian civil war?'' She raised a finger. ''And I have a follow-up.''

''I already mentioned that it is the intention of the United States to withdraw its forces from Eritrea, once the Cubans do likewise. As far as we are concerned, the matter was unfortunate, and is resolved. That is, as long as the Cubans honor their commitment to immediately withdraw from Eritrea.''

She continued. ''My follow-up is this: You say the President directed this action.''

And now he told a truly bald lie. The alternative was to open an even greater Pandora's box that was worse than any of his previous fictions. ''The President was in full control throughout the decision making process.''

''In a way that's disturbing. Is there any connection between his decision to intervene in Ethiopia, and the fact that the polls indicate he's in trouble because of the sharp drop in the stock market? Isn't this a good way for him to show he's a leader, and that he's tough on the Communists, to make up for what appears to be an economy that's falling through the floor?''

''First of all, we did not intervene in Ethiopia. Let's be careful with our terms, here. We came to the aid of France, a good friend, when they were attacked by the Soviets in *Eritrea*, a country both of our nations now recognize. But secondly, Ann, I have known our President for twenty years, and I must tell you that he deeply values the life of every young man and woman who serves in our military. The President would never put our sailors and marines into a situation such as they faced today for his personal gain. The country knows he is a strong leader, and they will take his leadership in those other areas as well.''

Holcomb pointed to John Weatherford, another longtime Pentagon reporter. ''John.''

''Yes, sir. And I'd like a follow-up also. First, you haven't given us an exact casualty count for this operation.''

''We don't have it yet.'' Holcomb could feel the tension in the room collectively rise. ''As you might imagine, there is still a great deal of confusion on the battlefield. I can report, as I said before, that the marine casualties were high. Initial indicators show that the battalion on the ground lost more than forty killed, and more than a hundred wounded. The reports are still coming in. We also lost an F/A Eighteen aircraft to Cuban ground fire. Both crewmen ejected safely over the desert, and search teams are still trying to find them. A second aircraft is still unaccounted for, and may be lost. Two helicopters have been reported missing, one in the darkness after the cease-fire was agreed upon, and both are unaccounted for. Several landing craft were damaged or destroyed by artillery. As I said, we're still counting. And from all indications, Cuban casualties are in the thousands. Their armored division was absolutely decimated.''

Secretary of Defense Ronald Holcomb, who had never in his life heard the sound of enemy guns, then volunteered an estimate that reaffirmed forever his nickname among the fighting troops of America: Chicken Hawk. "I would say, considering the success of this operation, that these were acceptable losses."

Weatherford adjusted his glasses, squinting at Holcomb. "Could you explain the losses with the convoy?"

Holcomb examined the notes Eichelberger had prepared for him, then looked calmly at Weatherford and again lied through his teeth, but this time for himself. "As you know, we had cleared a sea-lane into and out of Yanbu', and were more than two hundred miles south of Yanbu' when a second minefield was hit. The convoy was being led by the *Lawrence*, a guided-missile destroyer, whose principal function was to protect the tankers against surface or air attack in the southern Red Sea and the Bab el Mandeb. It was not contemplated that mines would be encountered in this area. The beam of the *Lawrence* is forty-seven feet. The beam of the Japanese tankers, which are huge—they displace fifty thousand gross tons—is one hundred thirty-one feet. It appears that the *Lawrence* cruised through the small minefield, and that all four tankers, because of their wider beam, hit it along their starboard sides. These were quite powerful mines, and the tankers were sunk."

And then Weatherford asked him a question he had been waiting hopefully to hear. "Do you have any second thoughts about the warning of Navy Secretary Zara Boles when we sent our minesweepers into the Red Sea? You will recall that she was opposed to the move, claiming that we should not be risking American lives to protect Japanese commerce without much more careful preparation?"

Zara Boles did not know it, but she had actually insulated the government from further scrutiny. Her criticism made the sinking of the Japanese tankers seem inevitable, instead of having been an attack by a covert operations team somehow pieced together by Hank Eichelberger. Holcomb lifted his chin for the cameras and spoke with clipped authority. "In retrospect, Secretary Boles seems to have been absolutely correct. I will propose to the Congress next year that we increase funding for modern minesweepers. But we cannot undo this tragedy, and again, on balance, Justifiable Anger was a resounding success for our military.''

"Mr. Secretary!" It was a face he did not recognize. "Has the Japanese government expressed an opinion about this failure to adequately protect their tankers?"

"I am meeting with Foreign Minister Tanashi next week. The meeting has been scheduled for some time, regarding the Nakashitona controversy and other issues. I imagine the loss of the tankers will come up in the meeting, and I am confident that Minister Tanashi will be sympathetic to the efforts of our country to assist them in the Red Sea. And elsewhere.''

There was another face he did not recognize. "Sir, can you tell us why the press was not allowed on Operation Justifiable Anger?''

Holcomb swallowed back a stunned epithet and retained his composure. "The operation was executed on less than an hour's notice. When you examine the casualties, I believe you may reconsider your question.''

That was enough. It was deteriorating, and it was time to finish it up. "Thank you very much," said Ron Holcomb. And he strode immediately out of the room.

2

As Defense Secretary Ronald Holcomb walked quickly along the corridors toward the sanctum of his "E"-ring office, Corporal Russell Paynter was standing at parade rest next to his car, which was parked in front of the VIP arrival lounge at Hickam Air Force Base. It was noon in Hawaii. Paynter was Admiral Mad Dog Mulcahy's personal driver. The admiral's S-3 aircraft had just landed, and was now taxiing in front of the VIP building. Paynter came to attention as the aircraft shut down its engines.

The air was heavy with its tropical perfumes, a scent that

Paynter found malodorous. He had taken leave in his hometown of Lawrence, Massachusetts, when the admiral left
for the Red Sea, and it would be a few more days before
he again adjusted to Hawaii's aromatic winds. A slight wind
now brushed against his face as he walked toward the admiral, saluting him.

"Welcome back, sir."

Mulcahy lumbered toward him, dressed in his working
khakis, and perfunctorily returned Paynter's salute.

"Paynter, you goddamn killing machine. How was Massachusetts?"

"Very fine, sir." Paynter blushed slightly as he took
Mulcahy's briefcase. "I'm engaged, sir."

"To be *married*?" Mulcahy seemed incredulous. "What
are you, Paynter? All of twenty, maybe?" He climbed into
the right rear seat of the staff car. Captain David Mosberg
joined him in the car, sitting heavily in the left rear seat.

Paynter closed their doors, and then started the car. "Yes,
sir. I turned twenty in May."

"None of my business." Mulcahy peered out of the window, fighting back fatigue. "But marriage is kind of like
retirement, Paynter. Seems to me you'd like to try your
dick out a little bit before you hang it on the wall, up there
with your high school diploma and your football letters."

They were silent as the car made its way to the main gate
of Hickam Air Force Base and turned onto an outside road.
Mosberg and Mulcahy drifted in and out of sleep, having
traveled halfway around the world, from the *Roosevelt* battle
group to Diego Garcia, then to Subic Bay, and finally to
Hawaii, in less than two days. A few minutes later, Mulcahy
opened his huge, reddened eyes, and seemed to startle as
he stared out of the window.

"You missed your turn."

The car was indeed driving past the CINCPAC Fleet headquarters at Makalapa Heights. Paynter kept to the road. The
car passed over the top of Interstate H-1 and headed up a narrow, winding road toward Halawa Heights, the CINCPAC

headquarters of Admiral Jeff Davis Smith. The corporal seemed surprised at Mulcahy's comment, and then embarrassed.

"No, sir. Admiral Smith ordered me to take you to his headquarters as soon as you arrived, sir. I thought you knew, or I would have mentioned it, sir."

"Well I didn't!" Mulcahy was fully awake again. "I'll see Admiral Smith when I'm goddamn good and ready, Corporal. Right now I want you to take me home."

Paynter kept driving. He now seemed deeply afraid. He reached down on the front seat, and then handed Mulcahy an envelope. "Sir, these are orders from the secretary of defense, sir. I thought you had them, too."

Mad Dog snatched the envelope out of Paynter's hand and tore it open. He seethed as he read the letter, swearing softly under his breath and squirming in his seat as if it had suddenly become afire. The letter was addressed to Jeff Davis Smith.

To: Commander-In-Chief, Pacific
From: Secretary of Defense
Subject: Relief of Commander-In-Chief, Pacific Fleet

I hereby order you to immediately relieve the Commander-In-Chief, Pacific Fleet for cause, on grounds of insubordination, taking actions in excess of legal authority, and failure to exercise proper military judgment. I desire that Admiral Mulcahy be informed of my decision, under the conditions you and I have already discussed, immediately upon his return to Hawaii.

A stiffly saluting Marine guard waved them through Camp Smith's main gate. Paynter drove slowly, made a U-turn, and stopped underneath the archway in front of the entrance to the Pacific Command's headquarters building. General Rick Herrington, an Army officer responsible for operations on Admiral Smith's staff, was waiting for them. He smiled politely and saluted Mulcahy as the admiral stomped out of the car and headed for the door.

"Good afternoon, Admiral. Welcome back."

"Go to hell."

Mulcahy brushed past the dark, muscular officer and burst into the headquarters building. An elevator was waiting for him, and he entered it immediately. He paced like a caged animal as it ascended. When the doors opened he strode directly into Smith's office, ignoring the receptionist and the admiral's staff secretary as he made for the door to Smith's inner office.

Admiral Jeff Davis Smith was standing in front of a window, peering out toward the sea. He had watched Mulcahy's arrival, and was now waiting for him. The two men had been counterparts in their early careers, and competitors for decades after that. Smith had graduated from the Naval Academy two years ahead of Mulcahy. Both were surface warfare officers—ship drivers, in the parlance. Both had become known for their operational skills, from Yankee Station off of North Vietnam to the Gulf of Sidra off of Libya. But there the similarities ended. Mulcahy was a manipulative genius who had ridden Ronald Holcomb's career for years. Smith was a patrician in the style of the old South whence he came, more of a frustrated Nimitz than an ass-kissing imitation of Bull Halsey like the man who now fumed before him. And now it was clear even to Mulcahy that his political protector had turned on him with the viciousness of a rattlesnake. Mad Dog was in very big trouble.

The two men faced each other in the large room, surrounded by the memorabilia of Smith's career: plaques and pictures, boatswain's whistles and baseball caps, a tenure that had in so many ways paralleled Mulcahy's own. It was as if they were both at a wake after having grown up and lived in the same small community. Only one of them was viewing the casket, and the other was inside it.

"Mad Dog, would you like to sit down?"

"Why, is it time for tea? Knock off the bullshit, Davis. This is serious."

"You'd better believe it's serious. You ordered a landing without proper authority. We've got more than fifty marines dead on the beach. The Soviets are already exploring the possibility of retaliation in Central America. And one of the most promising colonels in the Marine Corps is dead."

Mulcahy paced around Smith's office, waving his hands into the air. "Goddamn it, think a little bit, Davis. We knocked the Cubans out of Africa. We may have knocked the *Soviets* out of northern Africa! They started it! They laid the mines! And then they *ran*, goddamn it, they ran! The region will never be the same again!"

"It wasn't your decision, Mad Dog. Forget the rest. You're relieved. You should be smart enough to accept that."

"I am." Mulcahy peered at his blander superior, the man whom he had never so much as called on the phone in more than a year. "Just don't ask me to apologize."

"No, I'm not asking you anything. I'm *ordering* you to keep your fucking mouth shut." Davis Smith had suddenly become ferocious. He walked toward Mulcahy, stopping just in front of him, actually intimidating the taller, stronger man. "You did what you wanted to do. You got what you wanted. It may even work out. But you killed some damn good people, do you understand that? You're not God. You're not even the President. Now, you listen. I'm your operational commander, Mad Dog, remember? And this is the deal. Do you understand? *This is the fucking deal!* We've managed to package up your little mess and make sense out of it. If anybody asks, you ordered your forces to execute Operation Justifiable Anger. Do you understand? That is, unless you want us to announce that you did it on your own, and that for the rest of your life the families of the sailors and marines who were killed should remember you as the Butcher of Bera'isale."

Mulcahy stopped his pacing at that thought. He was stunned by Smith's sudden attack, breathless at the label that hung between them. No, he was the Nelson of the Nineties, not the Butcher of Bera'isale. "You wouldn't do that."

Smith put a finger into the larger man's chest. "You keep your mouth shut, and in two weeks we'll have a nice retirement ceremony. Distinguished Service Medal. Parade. Foreign dignitaries. Speeches. Nice words for a career marked by aggressiveness and leadership. You talk, just once—even after you retire—and I'll reopen the matter. We'll have a public inquiry. I'll make sure a court-martial hangs your ass so fast you won't have time to say goodbye to your wife. Do you understand me?"

Mulcahy's arms hung limp at his sides. He managed to mutter a response. "I understand. But what does it get you?"

"Damage control." There was an intensity in Smith's body and in his stare that frightened Mad Dog Mulcahy. "But we don't need any new facts. Got it?"

"Well, you've got all the cards, Davis."

"You're damn right I do. And your man Holcomb has personally left you dangling." Smith tossed Mulcahy a copy of the morning newspaper clips. "So don't lose any sleep wondering whether I'll follow through, Mad Dog. You get cute and I'll bury your ass in hell."

Mulcahy sifted through the clips. Carnage covered every page. The fact that Holcomb had boxed things up so neatly, and then ordered Mulcahy's relief from command, said everything. He was a goner. But then he had expected that. He simply had relished the idea of being able to tell his story, to take full credit for smashing the Cubans and chasing out the Soviets. And now no one would ever know it was his plan. *His* plan! What was this shit "Justifiable Anger," anyway?

"A Distinguished Service Medal, huh?"

"And a parade." Smith folded his arms, scrutinizing Mulcahy. "A *big* parade."

A DSM. Hmmmm. And a parade. "Like I said, you hold all the cards."

CHAPTER 21

Doc Rowland had slept fitfully, dreaming through the night of lovers he once held. They melted together, joining each other as leering gargoyles—a round thigh, a perfect set of teeth, a springy, uplifted breast, brown eyes, blue eyes, blond hair, black hair, a full wide mouth, laughing, laughing. And then they pranced away from him in the dim light of a hundred little rooms, young hips flaring out from slim waists, arched shoulders delicate and uneven, faces hidden from his view. Their heads turned slightly as they entered the shadows. He called to them but they merely waved, soundlessly creeping out of his grasp. They were saying good-bye and he awakened feeling old.

He was up early. He showered and dressed and then sat at his kitchen table, drinking a cup of coffee and reading the front sections of the *Post*, the *Times*, and *The Wall Street Journal*. He had an hour before Roy Dombrowski would pick him up. Rowland read each paper carefully every day, a habit he had picked up during his first term in Congress. And he was not alone. The morning papers in Washington were like casting calls on Broadway, or casualty lists in the Pentagon. They announced on a daily basis who was surviving, and who was on his way to ruin.

At first it had amazed him at how avidly, and yes, how seriously, Washingtonians took their news. They devoured their newspapers every morning with the same ravenous appetite that Parisians reserved for their *croissants* and *café au lait*. They read the stories with great care. They savored and mulled over details and innuendo, considering carefully what had been said by government officials, what had been leaked behind the scenes, and indeed what had not been mentioned at all. They called their friends to discuss the day's stories. They traded secrets that they knew had not yet been printed, wondering when the facts would be discovered. They knew that every small detail in the news, every piece of gossip, could affect the workings of government and the immediate future of the nation.

The tidbits in the papers could also make or break the professional futures of thousands who had hitched their wagons onto different stars. Or the reputations of others who had garnered prized friendships. Or the status of those who lived for the prestige of sharing a favored dining or shopping haven, or being a member of the same country club. Which was, of course, why so many Washingtonians were news addicts in the first place, and why they paid such close attention. These were their very own stars up in the clear black sky, glimmering brightly for all to see. Or they were comets fading into oblivion, soon to be forgotten.

And that morning's editions were filled with shooting stars, not the least of them being Doc Rowland, chairman of the House Armed Services Committee. The renowned "guru of defense reform" was suddenly fighting off a new handle: a man of petulance, "the architect of economic collapse."

He couldn't help thinking of how the phone lines would be burning with gossip and fear this morning, and of rumors that Doc Rowland had lost his influence in the government. The front pages of all the major newspapers were covered with similar stories. BLOODBATH IN THE DESERT: U.S., FRENCH COMBINE TO STOP CUBAN ARMORED FORCE, read the lead headline in the *Post*, with two large official Navy photographs next to it, one showing hundreds of wrecked Cuban tanks and vehicles scattered in the desert and the other showing straggling columns of Cuban soldiers boarding the *Nicolaev*.

NAVY FAILS TO PROTECT TANKER CONVOY, lamented another, with a photograph inside the paper showing an aerial shot of a large tanker listing onto its starboard side, the air around it filled with black smoke. Those didn't hurt, but the others did.

PRESIDENT BLAMES HOUSE ARMED SERVICES CHAIRMAN FOR RECORD DROP IN STOCK MARKET, said one headline. Balancing the bottom of the front page, another story showed a small photograph of a frowning Doc Rowland entering his office, with a headline that said HOUSE ARMED SERVICES CHIEF DENIES SEEKING DEFENSE SECRETARYSHIP IN EXCHANGE FOR CHANGING POSITION ON LEGISLATION, MAY QUIT CONGRESS.

They were lying, lying! They had called their favorite reporters and told half-truths corroborated with other half-truths and he was choking on their dissembling, vicious attacks. But there was nothing he could do. It reminded him of Lyndon Johnson's story about the 1948 Senate campaign, when in the final days one of Johnson's aides had suggested that they start a rumor that his opponent liked to have sex with pigs. Johnson had insisted that no one would actually believe the man screwed pigs. *It doesn't matter*, said his aide. *He'll spend the rest of his life denying it.*

Allegations, lies, denials, dissembling, distortions, frantic deterioration into the rampant slinging of mud and shit: the Harvard shootouts. The President and his leaders could not solve the real problems that faced them. They could not balance the issues of national sovereignty and self-discipline that were being lost under an avalanche of foreign investment and the power that went with it. They preferred quietly allowing the Soviets—and the Chinese—to repress, or perhaps even slaughter, their own people in the name of "internal control" as long as relations remained reasonably on track. So they used their friends and even their foreign competitors to devour Doc Rowland for attempting the only truly selfless act he had made in twenty years: calling on the country to take the first painful step in bringing new balance to foreign affairs. And worse, they accepted a "small" measure of violence in a place no one had ever heard of, because it allowed them to pull a curtain over the other, more difficult problems that they could not face.

The President took decisive action when the threat emerged. And you are well off, America, as you trade your national freedom for a job.

And all the while they secretly whispered to the media, choking on the falsity of their formal, diplomatic existence, addled by jealousy and hate. And the media gave them their forum, always ascertaining beforehand that their allegations were borne out by facts if not the truth.

Well, that's the last time I'll ever get out front on a big issue.

Then Rowland turned to the Style section of the *Post*, and in one instant his heart did such a flip that he did not know whether to laugh or cry. For despite his "legendary sexual antics," as the article he stared at so cleverly put it, he had fallen in love with Janet Holcomb.

She gleamed at the camera, her smooth features covering a full quarter of the front page of the section, over a legend that proclaimed "Private Lives: A Woman of Passion and Substance." He had known that Style reporters were interviewing her for a feature, but now Janet had hit the big time. The reporter had asked about reports that she and Doc Rowland had been seen together several times over the summer, and she had coquettishly demurred. "Doc is a most charming man. I will admit that I was one among many who came under his spell. But in the end I think he was more interested in finding ways to go after my husband

than he was in having what you'd call a—relationship—
with me. Besides, I *am* married, and Ron is a wonderful
husband.''

So she had boxed him in. She had hurt his ability ever
to go after Ron Holcomb, and at the same time protected
herself. He accepted it immediately, and felt no bitterness
toward her. She was too smart, too connected and too attractive, and their relationship was too volatile in a town
that would now follow them both with bawdy, voyeuristic
delight.

It was over, he had known that when she stalked out of
his house. but he had underestimated her cleverness, her
ambition, her very chutzpah. What a job she'd done! He
found himself admiring her more deeply. She was more
ambitious than even Doc Rowland himself. That was probably the one, immutable trait that she and Ronald Holcomb
shared, the single bond that would always unite them. Not
that she would ever be faithful to Holcomb. She would
quietly move on to someone else.

And not that she hadn't warned him.

By ten o'clock Warner Haas had already called, telling
him that the Janet Holcomb story was all over the district,
and that the Akasaka project was on hold because of the
Nakashitona legislation, pending word from the Japanese.
Haas also advised Rowland to be looking for a new line of
work, something that didn't take him back to Illinois too
often.

Two nights later, Rowland sat in his office with Roy
Dombrowski watching the evening news as Rowland waited
for a series of votes on the House floor. The anchorman
was announcing the ABS ''Person of the Week.'' Rowland,
half expecting to be named for his part in a still-sputtering
stock market, looked up and saw an aerial shot of the Eritrean desert, littered with the carcasses of tanks and fighting
vehicles and artillery pieces. He reached for his remote

control, and turned up the volume. The announcer came back on the screen.

"This week, in the remote desert of the Horn of Africa, a Cuban armored division slugged it out with a combined force of American and French infantrymen, backed by carrier-borne air power. It was a bitter, bloody fight, a fight that very likely shouldn't have happened, a fight without a winner. What it yielded were casualties"—the screen now cut to pictures of dead Cuban soldiers, rotting in the desert, and of American marines being offloaded from helicopters and aircraft—"and questions."

The anchorman came back on the screen. "Why were the Cubans present in such force in Eritrea in the first place? Why did the President decide to execute Operation Justifiable Anger, and land the marines in the path of the Cubans? Who attacked first? How, indeed, could such a calamity have been avoided?"

The screen now showed a Soviet Aeroflot aircraft at the Havana International Airport, surrounded by a cheering crowd. A lean, grizzled soldier was carried off the aircraft as he sat erect on a stretcher. The crowd cheered wildly as the soldier was brought to Fidel Castro, who embraced him and immediately pinned a medal on his chest, to the roar of the crowd. The anchorman spoke in the background as the tape ran on the screen. "This man is perhaps the only one who really knows. General Abelardo Enrique Valdez commanded the Cuban forces in Ethiopia. He is a soldier of vast experience, beginning as a young man in Fidel Castro's revolutionary army. He has trained in the Soviet Union. And he is no stranger to Ethiopia and the Horn of Africa, having previously served there with great distinction during the Ogaden battles of the mid-1970s. The award you just saw pinned on his chest was his second Hero of the Republic of Cuba Medal, both of them awarded for heroism in Ethiopia. For more than a month, General Valdez led his armored forces—the largest forces ever assembled by the Cuban Army—as the spearhead of what apparently was to have been an attack on the major cities of Eritrea. Was this an invasion, or were the Cubans, in concert with the Ethiopian Army, attempting to restore order in a rebel province? To the Cubans, the answer is clear.''

The screen shifted to a close-up of Fidel Castro, who continued to embrace a weary General Abelardo Valdez with one arm as he waved the other into the air, speaking into a microphone to the animated crowd. A translator spoke flatly, interpreting Castro's harangue. ''We were asked by the Ethiopian government, a government recognized throughout the world and by the United Nations, to aid it in its attempt to put down an insurrection by rebels who had unlawfully taken over the major cities of the province of Eritrea. This was an internal crisis. The French and American governments then invaded Ethiopia. They provoked our forces, denying them access to the sea, and finally they viciously attacked them. General Valdez, and our brave soldiers, fought their combined armies to a standstill, forcing the Americans to agree to withdraw from Ethiopian soil. This is a great moment in the history of the Socialist Republic of Cuba.''

The anchorman reappeared on the screen. ''President Castro's rhetoric may be a little extreme, but the fact remains that General Valdez, who was seriously wounded in the battle—he lost a leg early in the fight—had not sought a confrontation with our forces, and indeed was maneuvering around the French position at Assab when the battle began. His division was heading toward the town of Bera'isale, apparently in order to link up with Soviet naval forces, when the Americans landed there. Who attacked first—the Americans or the Cubans—is not clear. But General Valdez did choose to attack the American position rather than to surrender once the battle began. Even after heavy carpet-bombing by American aircraft, he ordered his tanks and artillery to continue fighting, and his forces inflicted heavy casualties on our marines. The general continued to direct the battle until a cease-fire was negotiated among the French,

American, Cuban, and Soviet governments. Those governments have also agreed to a Soviet proposal for a multinational naval fleet that will immediately sweep the Red Sea of the mines laid there a few weeks ago by unknown forces.''

The anchorman now smiled, his angular face framed by perfectly blow-dried hair. ''Whatever the reasons were that brought about this unfortunate battle in a remote desert, and meaning no disservice to the courage of our own fighting men who were forced by circumstance to perform so courageously in a little town called Bera'isale, ABS News recognizes that General Abelardo Valdez, a man who apparently had no wish to fight with the United States, has emerged as the most enigmatic man from this truly enigmatic conflict. He is a man of vast military experience, undeniable courage, and is a hero in the eyes of the Cuban people. And for this reason, we have named General Valdez the ABS 'Person of the Week.' Thank you. And good night.''

Roy Dombrowski stared for a long moment at the screen as the news credits rolled. He appeared to be remembering something from far in his past. Finally he shook his head.

''What a week, Doc. I wonder how Holcomb feels about *that*?''

''No,'' said Rowland. ''I wonder how that colonel who died would feel about it?''

CHAPTER 22

Ronald Holcomb stood near the window behind his desk, staring out across the river toward the Capitol as if nothing spectacular had happened over the past four days. His hands were stuffed inside his trouser pockets. He leaned against the wall. Secretly he was wishing for a weekend lost long ago in the dust and dreck of Beirut, he and Janet inside the oily, odorous cabin on a steamer coming back from Larnaca. Those mad two days had been the only freedom he had ever known, and more than anything, he wanted to remember Janet as she was when she pulled him into the sagging, slept-in bed. Yes, for a moment he had broken the leash, floated on a cloud of passion, swayed above the earth in his very own orbit.

All that was gone, but strangely he knew that he had won Janet back from Doc Rowland. The Style section article had been her bittersweet love letter to him, a forgiveness and a reassurance all wrapped up together. She was telling him she might frolic with other men, but that her anchor was with him. And at forty-six, that was enough.

It was almost noon. A sharp, late summer chill had moved

into Washington the night before, and he could already see the trees beginning to go red and gold along the banks of the Potomac. The floor buzzer in the carpet outside his door sounded briefly and Holcomb turned toward it. General Bear Lazaretti stepped just inside the doorway and almost whispered.

"Sir, Minister Tanashi is outside. He has his entire party with him."

For a millisecond he panicked, unready to face the Japanese foreign minister. He looked quickly at Hank Eichelberger, who was studying his fingernails as he sat languorously on the nearby couch. Eichelberger almost barked, not even looking up.

"Make him wait, Mr. Secretary."

He turned back to Lazaretti, deferring to Eichelberger. "Check with me again in three minutes. And when you bring him in, I want it to be solo, Bear. Just him. And his interpreter, of course. Move the others into the reception."

"Yes, sir."

Lazaretti left the room, and Holcomb took his preferred chair, sitting next to Eichelberger. He would meet with Tanashi privately for a few minutes, and then would host an early luncheon for the minister and his official party in the secretary of defense's conference room, just next door. Already the conference room was filling up with Pentagon and State Department officials, most of whom were also invited to the luncheon. A receptionist from Holcomb's outer office was now leading the rest of Minister Tanashi's entourage along the "E" ring and into the room, to visit with their American counterparts.

Once their private chat was finished, Holcomb and Tanashi would enter the room through a side door that connected to his office, and form a brief receiving line. After that, they would take their places at the long table in the middle of the room, sitting across from each other as they dined. When the meal was completed, Holcomb and Tanashi would finish up by exchanging toasts, and giving each other a modest gift. Then the lesser officials in both delegations would meet throughout the afternoon in working-group sessions on key issues, while Holcomb would accompany Tanashi to the White House, for an audience with President Lodge.

This was probably the most important meeting of Holcomb's career. Tanashi had bullied him in Japan, refusing to budge an inch. And now the American stock market was down almost a thousand points, its worst dip since the Great Depression. Japanese newspapers were filled with photographs of the four sunken tankers, their insides belching millions of gallons of oil into the sea as American helicopters and ships gathered helplessly nearby. The Socialist party had enjoyed a sudden surge of support, and was calling for new elections as well as the end of the Japan-United States Security Treaty. The Soviets, having suppressed the Ukrainian dissident movement as the eyes of the world were on the Red Sea, were making overtures to the Japanese, stating their willingness to immediately return two of the four Kurile Islands they had captured at the end of World War II.

Holcomb had wanted to begin the meeting with a profuse apology for the loss of the Japanese tankers. But Eichelberger was holding his feet to the fire, insisting that he find a way to subtly use the sinkings as a warning. Holcomb felt enormously trapped. He had lied about the sinkings during the press briefing. Eichelberger knew it, and now had an unbreakable hold on him.

"Remember, Mr. Secretary," said Eichelberger in his high, piping voice. "I know what you're thinking, but this is the time to be strong. Believe me. I've spent most of my adult life in Asia."

The buzzer rang again and Lazaretti was at the door, watching him nervously.

"Sir, Minister Tanashi."

"Right." Holcomb forced a smile, and moved toward the Japanese government official. "Mr. Minister, so good to see you again."

"Ah, yes, Mr. Secretary."

They shook hands and bowed at the same time, an odd, hybrid ritual that had evolved over the years in order to satisfy both cultures. Tanashi wore his customary gray wool suit and a bland blue tie. His hand was thick and small inside Holcomb's, the palm toughened from hours on the golf course. He smiled politely as he bowed, and openly admired the size and decor of Holcomb's office as Bear Lazaretti led him toward a seat on the couch next to Holcomb's easy chair.

Holcomb recognized the tall young interpreter who had followed Tanashi into his office. It was the same young man who had interpreted at their dinner in Tokyo a month before. The slender young man represented a new generation of Japanese who knew only victory, and who had very little respect for a bumbling America. The young man self-consciously adjusted his tie and then his thick glasses, and finally, on the very edge of arrogance, bowed slightly to Holcomb, bending only his head.

"Mr. Secretary, good morning. I am Shunara, Minister Tanashi's personal interpreter."

"Yes, yes. I remember you. Good morning."

On a pedestal next to the wall across from Holcomb's desk was a bronze bust of General Douglas MacArthur. Holcomb had asked that it be placed in his office as a gesture to Janet, whose father had served on MacArthur's staff for two years during World War II. Tanashi studied the sculpture with interest before he sat down.

"General MacArthur. *Hoh hoh hoh.*" Holcomb knew that "*Hoh hoh hoh*" was not a laugh, but instead was a measure of Tanashi's interest, as if he were saying "I see, I see."

"Yes," answered Holcomb, not waiting for the question. He peered at Tanashi as he spoke, and then gazed expectantly at Shunara once he was finished. "My wife's father served under General MacArthur. During World War Two."

Holcomb had only briefly met the man, whom he considered to be a pontificating bore, but he immediately capitalized on Tanashi's interest. "Yes, I'm very close to him. He's had a profound impact on my thinking. And of course, he was very devoted to the general. MacArthur was a brilliant leader."

Shunara translated. Tanashi nodded as he listened. He was now sitting forward in his chair, his elbows on his knees. He lit a cigarette. Then Tanashi answered quickly, giving off a small laugh.

"We all served under General MacArthur," Shunara said, translating Tanashi's reply with a decidedly American accent. "And we are all better off for it, I think."

Holcomb eyed Tanashi with a look that was almost cunning, even unbelieving. He was conscious of Eichelberger's expectant stare from the seat just across from him, and continued with an unaccustomed bluntness. "Certainly Japan is. He could have turned your nation into one big rice paddy, but instead he spent years as your champion, helping you rebuild."

Tanashi listened, nodding slightly, and then gave Holcomb a long, animated reply. The foreign minister smiled politely as he talked, his voice warm and even respectful, peering directly into Holcomb's face. Shunara had furiously scribbled onto a notepad as Tanashi spoke. He examined his notes for a moment, and then continued.

"Yes, we owe a great deal to General MacArthur, and to your nation. And as you and I have discussed before, this is a time of great change for all of us. It is my wish personally, and I think I also speak for all Japanese, that we remain the closest of friends with the United States. At the same time, I have the duty of bringing forward the concerns of my government. We face two new problems, Mr. Secretary. I hope we are facing them together. The first is the legislation that would unfairly punish Nakashitona Industries. It is now almost September and the legislation has not been resolved. As you can see from the reaction on your stock market, our investors are very worried. They fear that your government will continue to take revenge on Japanese private investors for the acts of a few people. This causes them to seek investments elsewhere. The second is the quality of your military. Mr. Secretary, we in Japan have always greatly appreciated our friendship with the United States, and the protection that your military has given us around the world. But we feel also that we have paid for this protection. We give you precious land for military bases, in a country no larger than California, most of which is uninhabitable, where almost one hundred forty million people live! We help finance your bases. We have bought military equipment when you have suggested that we buy it. Your military has gotten careless. We had another fishing boat damaged during a naval exercise in Japanese waters just last month. And now we see, from the events two days ago, that our tankers were not safe traveling in an American convoy. This causes many people in Japan to question the need for an alliance. This last point I only make as a personal observation.''

The foreign minister eyed Holcomb playfully as his Shunara delivered his punch line. ''But just yesterday one of our politicians commented that the 'United States watchdog has become a Mad Dog.' ''

Tanashi now grinned, and spoke the words himself. ''Mad Dog. Ha ha ha.''

Holcomb visibly flinched at the double entendre, which combined Japanese vernacular with the wild antics of Admiral Mulcahy. ''Yes, I understand. We are very sorry for the incident you mentioned, and for the loss of your tankers.''

There were only four people in the room: Hank Eichelberger, who continued to stare expectantly at Holcomb, Tanashi and his interpreter, and Holcomb himself. Holcomb took a deep breath, measuring Tanashi as he searched for the right words. ''Again, the loss of the tankers was most unfortunate. And I hope we can resolve the issues you mentioned.''

Eichelberger squirmed in his chair and cleared his throat, as if admonishing him for his cowardice. Holcomb's pulse beat faster as he continued. ''But let me say something that I hope *you* will understand. This is supposed to be an *alliance*. American soldiers are not mercenaries, Mr. Minister. They don't protect you because of the money you're giving them, and they will not be used for someone else's profit.''

Shunara translated, and Tanashi nodded. Holcomb and the foreign minister stared quietly at each other. A large clock ticked in an alcove across from Holcomb's chair. They could hear jovial conversations in the room next door, where the reception was getting underway. And finally Tanashi uttered a question, his tone filled with uncertainty.

Shunara spoke again. ''Yes, we have always known that. I have studied American history. I recall the Colonial soldiers defeating the Hessian mercenaries during your Revolution. We have always known that you do not care for mercenaries. I am speaking of Japan's contribution on behalf of the alliance.''

Holcomb grew bolder. ''Yes, but so am I. And that brings up another interesting point. Many Americans are beginning to think that Japan's definition of an alliance means that America should protect Japan's investments around the world, in exchange for the privilege of working for Japanese companies here at home. I personally don't feel that way—''

Eichelberger squirmed again, now scribbling on his notepad, and then finally interrupted Holcomb. ''Mr. Minister, the secretary is a man of great patience and goodwill. He's been asked to communicate something to you on behalf of our government, and his respect for you and your culture is too strong for him to say it directly. So he has asked me to do it. The events of the past two months have angered a great many Americans. And if Americans believe they are being treated like a colony, they will fight. And we fight very well when our nation is aroused, Mr. Minister. Ask your father, if he is still alive. Or ask the Cubans.''

Tanashi stubbed out his cigarette as Shunara translated. He watched Eichelberger carefully as he considered his response. Eichelberger stared coldly back, until the minister dropped his eyes. Holcomb was panic-stricken. His entire professional career had boiled down to a meeting where a subordinate had taken the issue away, and pushed it in a completely different direction.

Finally the stocky, graying minister took out another cigarette and nodded, as if accepting an intellectual point. He spoke briefly, waving a hand in the air, and lit the cigarette. But now he was speaking to Eichelberger.

''Our nation above all knows the futility of war. It is a concept that has no place in the modern world.''

And Eichelberger immediately responded. ''Perhaps our nation is learning the futility of kindness, Mr. Minister. And besides, there are a variety of ways to wage war. Many Americans believe that your country has been waging economic warfare for more than forty years.''

Eichelberger paused, obviously forcing Tanashi to consider carefully his next point. ''And there are other, less visible ways to wage war.'' He held Tanashi's eyes as Shunara translated. Then he continued, nonchalantly tilting his head and waving one hand through the air, as if offering an abstract proposition. ''I, myself, find it interesting that the only ships lost in the Red Sea two days ago were the Japanese tankers.''

Holcomb caught the stunned expression on Shunara's face. He smiled quickly, rising from his chair and ending the meeting. He had decided that Eichelberger was a genius. ''Mr. Minister, you understand that my assistant's comment is not the government position. It also is only a personal observation.''

* * *

After the reception line and the luncheon and the wine, Ronald Holcomb rose from his seat directly across from Minister Tanashi and offered a toast. He spoke eloquently about the Japanese-American friendship, a tie that was becoming the most important axis of world cooperation. He spoke of the appreciation his government felt for the help of the Japanese government in resolving the occasional issues that caused friction between the two countries.

Minister Tanashi then rose and responded with his own toast, spoken from deep inside his heart. The Japanese foreign minister acknowledged that there were occasional points of friction between the two great nations, but expressed his belief that they could be dealt with on the basis of mutual respect. Then he ended with his wish that the United States and Japan might always be brothers on the earth.

After the toasts, the two men nodded deeply to each other, their eyes communicating a new, more profound understanding. Tanashi's gift to Holcomb was a small, portable color television set that ran on batteries, one of the principal exports of Nakashitona Industries to the American commercial market. Holcomb, against the advice of Bear Lazaretti but at the insistence of Hank Eichelberger, had chosen a miniature bronze sculpture of the flag-raising at Iwo Jima as his gift to Tanashi. Both men smiled as if sharing a private joke when they shook hands and bowed and said good-bye.

And that evening, after consultations with Tokyo, the Japanese government officially apologized for the "grave misconduct" of Nakashitona Industries, announcing its intention to pay reparations for any damages caused by the "criminal leak of technology to the Soviet Union."

CHAPTER 23

"You know, Roy, this may be the last time I ever come home."

"Settle down, Doc. This isn't over yet."

Two days had passed since the Japanese apology for the Nakashitona incident. Doc Rowland and Roy Dombrowski were on the way to Euphoria, Illinois, to face Doc's political executioners. They fell back into a moody, remembering silence as Dombrowski guided the new Chevrolet they had rented at the airport along the flat, straight roads of southern Illinois. The roads seemed to connect the farm towns together like narrow pipes, at the same time blocking off the farms neatly into square allotments.

They passed sparse treelines, narrow hedgerows made of briars and brambles, and quaint, tiny towns. Ripening cornfields seemed to stretch forever in the dusky, cloudless sky, dotted by distant farmhouses and reaching silos. It was peaceful and breathtakingly beautiful as Rowland watched the sun begin to fall, bringing the silos and the cornfields into brilliant focus against a rich blue sky. It all came back to him as he looked at it for perhaps the last time—swimming holes, King Corn carnivals, baseball played in pastures, watermelon eaten as he and childhood friends walked summer roads, the dust like powder between their toes. Norman Rockwell's America had indeed once existed, and it still extended all the way to the far horizon. But he was no longer entitled to be its champion.

Looking out at the rural vastness that had spawned him and shaped his early beliefs, Doc Rowland felt at once ashamed and rebellious. They had every right to judge him. But how could they even understand?

Dombrowski nudged him from his thoughts as they neared Euphoria. "Well, I probably shouldn't even say it, Doc. But this had better be the speech of your life."

"Don't I know it." Doc Rowland forced himself out of it, suddenly slapping Dombrowski on the shoulder as they pulled into the parking lot of Euphoria Community College. "Anyway, what the hell, Roy. If life was easy, it'd take all the fun out of it."

"I guess so. But did you have to pick *Euphoria*? Talk about walking into the teeth of the tiger."

"No, if I fix it here, it's fixed. And if I don't fix it here, it'll never go away, anyway. This is called getting to the root of the problem."

Dombrowski laughed, staring with affection at his long-time boss. "The *root*? No offense, Doc, but with the stories in the media over the last few days, I wouldn't use that analogy out here in farm country."

Doc Rowland tilted his head back until his face was pointing upward, and cackled hilariously. For a moment he imitated a rutting hog. "*Root root root*. You're right. The tiger it is, Roy. The teeth of the tiger."

They exited the car and began walking toward the college auditorium. The night had now become black and the air was brittle cold from an early September frost. Through tree branches that reached like vast cobwebs up into the sky, Doc Rowland could see a beautiful harvest moon, the first of the season, so full and golden that it made him want to cry. When he was a small boy he would sit on nights like these on the back porch of a white frame house on a farm six miles away from where the college now stood, and watch the harvest moon with a wonderment that bordered on sexual arousal. He used to think that the moon came closer, particularly in October, that it had special powers, that it lured the the field mice into the corn cribs and the quail into the rolling rows of milo. And hobgoblins into the meadows, to dance and chant and sing.

The harvest moon was for every living thing, not just people. His grandmother used to tell him that. It had a fecund, celebratory power. God's earth was yielding up its bounty, providing his animals sustenance to make it through the cold, dark months of winter. Corn came to the silo. Yeast rose, making beer. Red squirrels gathered walnuts, and packed their nests with freshly fallen leaves. Babies grew in the bellies of young farm wives who clung to their husbands for warmth as the first cold winds of winter chilled the inside of their homes. And Doc Rowland had watched the mellow beauty of that moon from the loneliness of his porch, entranced by the sadness and the joy that seeped from it across the evening sky like the juice of an overripe watermelon. And he had longed to fall in love.

Love, he thought, approaching the doors of the college auditorium. How many times have I tripped over those cruel wild briars and ended up rolling in their thorns?

Some group had hung a professionally made banner above the podium at the front of the auditorium, so that it would frame Doc Rowland as he spoke. The sign said EUPHORIA WELCOMES AKASAKA INDUSTRIES. Doc examined the sign as he climbed onto the stage and sat in his assigned chair in front of a packed and lively crowd. He immediately saw the handiwork of the Chamber of Commerce in it. They had made too many signs supporting him over the years for him not to recognize this renegade warning as their product.

There were no grand cheers for him as he took his seat. Nor did he call out into the audience and greet his myriad of "cousins," as had become his trademark over a quarter of a century of service in the Congress. The crowd became more lively once Rowland came on the stage. Brash, taunting whistles echoed off the walls. People stood and waved, presumably to each other. He thought he heard a few cat-calls. In the back of the auditorium he saw a handful of reporters, and two television cameras.

Warner Haas lumbered over, tall and gaunt, almost Lincolnesque with his dark suit and high boots and large, unhappy eyes. He shook Doc's hand rather formally.

"Any time you're ready, Doc."

"Well, you go right ahead, Warner. I'd rather talk than sit, you know that."

Haas moved to the podium at the center of the stage. He tapped the microphone a few times, testing it. The speakers in the auditorium clicked loudly when he tapped the mike, making sounds like gunshots, and the crowd became quiet. Haas greeted them stiffly, as if he were mildly embarrassed to be up on the stage with Rowland.

"Good evening, folks. You know why we're all here. Doc Rowland has asked to speak to the people in his district about—about matters affecting his job, and allegations that have been made. And the Chamber is happy to sponsor his talk tonight. We appreciate you all coming out on a weeknight to share this evening with Doc. Doc?"

Haas turned to Rowland, gesturing toward the podium. He was not smiling. The crowd applauded politely as Rowland stepped to the podium. There were a few more taunting whistles. Two college students standing at the back of the auditorium held up a sign: DOC ROWLAND IS A PIG. And the lights of the television cameras immediately came on, capturing their small protest.

There was no alternative. Doc Rowland was as trapped in his own way as General Abelardo Valdez had been in the heat of the Eritean desert. His only option was to attack, attack, attack. When the stories first broke, he had toyed with the thought that his time had come, that he should leave the Congress. But now he felt that if he lost this next election, he would surely die.

He turned it on, revved it up, reached down inside a place somewhere near his heart that stored the energy that sustained a champion. Immediately he gestured toward the protesting students. "Thank you, thank you. Now ladies and gentlemen, there's a few people in the back of this room that are holding up a sign saying I'm a pig. I'll tell you this: I've got nothing against pigs. Like a lot of people here tonight, I've raised a few pigs in my day. They're a smart, friendly animal. I know how to call them and I know how to slop them and I know how to slaughter them. And I've voted right for twenty-three years so people around here could *keep* slaughtering them. But I don't need any snot-nosed, pimply faced college kid who never watered cattle or slopped hogs in the dark of a cold winter morning calling me names, thank you very much."

How deeply Americans adored their underdogs, and how jealous they were of their power to forgive repenting sinners! Half the audience immediately applauded. This time the catcalls were in his behalf. In the back row, several middle-aged men pointed threateningly toward the door, and the students left the auditorium.

"Well, now, I appreciate that." Rowland scanned the people in the audience, aware that the television cameras were continuing to operate. He recognized many of the faces. He had helped most of them in one way or another over the decades; a VA check here, a Medicaid claim over there, a speech on the House floor congratulating this one on her retirement, a special letter to that one's son when he was appointed to West Point. He had voted for them, too: farm votes, Social Security pension votes, public works votes, national pride votes. And now there were just two little problems separating him from them: his lust for a certain woman, and their desire to be owned by Akasaka Industries.

And that was a good place to start. "For almost a quarter

of a century, you have called me your congressman. And I believe you have done well to call a man your congressman who, for that entire space of time, has met and fought with every President, legislator, bureaucrat, or sniveling lobbyist who has tried to take away our pride in our nation, our independence, or the way of life we all so deeply love right here in southern Illinois. Yes, if I may be permitted to boast a little bit, you have done quite well to have elected one of your own, who grew up with calluses on his hands not hardly five miles away from this very spot, who learned as a young boy the pride that comes with keeping your own farm going, the independence that is mixed like loam into our very soil out here, the beauty of a harvest moon such as the one that now hangs over the trees outside this auditorium. When I was a young farm boy, I used to sit on the back porch with my grandmother and watch that harvest moon and dream. And those of you who have supported me over the years have answered all my dreams. But at the same time, I think you all know that my greatest wish as I have worked in Washington has *always* been to help you—each one of you—find your own dreams, too.''

They were hushed and attentive. The auditorium was silent. Doc Rowland wiped a genuine tear from one eye as he stared out at people he had known for decades. ''I've been your voice. In many ways, I've been your image. And I know how it must feel when your image gets a little tarnished. But when you leave here tonight, do me a favor. Look up at that harvest moon and hold your wife's or your husband's hand, and think of how it feels to wish for love, and not to have it. We're all flawed. I'm no exception. I'm a twice-divorced man, you all know that. I've not been blessed with the kind of love that many of you know and feel. I've tried for it all my life, and I was trying for it again. I guess I was trying with the wrong woman. I failed. It was not a public matter until someone in the media decided to make it public. If my failure counts with you so strongly that you decide I'm not the man you want up in Washington, then I'll just have to accept that.''

Doc glanced almost melodramatically up at the banner that hung just above his head. "Now, let's talk about Akasaka Industries. I've been severely criticized for my position on the Nakashitona scandal. There have been rumors in the district that Akasaka might pull out of Euphoria if the legislation I sponsored in the House becomes law. The stock market tumbled by almost a thousand points in the three days after the bill passed the House. I've been criticized in a lot of editorials for being protectionist, and unfair.''

He held up that morning's edition of *The Washington Post*. "I don't know how many of you have been closely tracking the issue in the papers, but two days ago the Japanese government officially apologized for the actions of Nakashitona Industries. Why do you think they did that, ladies and gentlemen? Why do you think they apologized? I'll read you a little bit of what *The Washington Post* said about it in its lead editorial this morning.''

He spread the paper on top of the podium, and put his finger on the editorial page. "'The dramatic turnabout by the Japanese government marks a major victory for embattled House Armed Services Committee chairman Doc Rowland, who at times stood alone in his insistence that the Japanese accept responsibility for this major security violation.' "

Rowland leaned forward on the podium, now daring once again to resume his folksy, informal style. "*The Washington Post* said that. About *me*. I stood alone! I took on the Japanese! I risked my whole career, and the respect of all of you, the people I most love in the whole entire world. But I *won*, ladies and gentlemen, and the country is going to be better off for it!''

Now they were beginning to applaud. Light and hope were reflecting back from dozens of shining eyes. He gestured reassuringly to them. "We'll get our plant here, friends. Nobody's going to lose a job. And the stock market

will fix itself, you know that. The market gained alm
two hundred points today alone. *Today!* Hell, they n
even end up calling this the Rowland rally, by the time
over.''

They laughed at that, and he continued. "And with
apology, it will probably be possible to loosen up the sa
tions in my original piece of legislation. But the point i
had to hold on, to be tough. It was an issue of natio
pride. It was my responsibility as chairman of the Arm
Services Committee, and as an American. Many in Wa
ington doubted me. Many of you, I'm sorry to say, doub
me. But it worked. And to tell the truth, I don't know w
else you might want of the person who'll be pulling
lever for you in Washington.''

They were strongly applauding him now. Warner H
was by his side, putting a long arm around his should
Rowland leaned forward into the microphone one last tin
a hand briefly held over his face, pinching his eyes. "I h
you all don't mind, but this has been a pretty emotio
time for me, and I think I need to just go call it a day.

They were standing in front of their chairs, still appla
ing as he departed. Warner Haas remained at the mic
phone, echoing his thanks to Doc Rowland for his servi
his commitment, and his courage. And in the car, as tl
backed out of the parking lot, Roy Dombrowski shook
head in amazement.

"Remarkable, Doc. Terrific. It's all over. You turne
around on them. An absolute twenty-four–carat speech.

"Thanks, Roy," sighed Doc Rowland, staring up at
haunting moon and thinking of his grandmother. It seen
to him that her violet eyes shone down at him just th
and that her soft face was glowing with pride, making
moon a little brighter. "I'll tell you the truth, Roy. T
place is as deep inside me as my own brain and guts
turned it around because I meant what I said.''

CHAPTER 24
ONE MONTH LATER

1

It was a beautiful day for a parade.

Autumn was going golden all over Washington. The sky was surprisingly clear. A light, brittle wind had washed away the amber haze that had gathered over the city during last week's musky, hot Indian summer. The wind caused the flags on the tall poles down by the Tidal Basin to flutter and dance, pointing north. Another warm front was blowing in. Tomorrow there would be rain.

A parade was forming on the drying grass just beyond the River Entrance parking lot. Cannoneers had unloaded their ceremonial guns from drab, canopied army trucks and were placing them in line at the far end of the field, facing the river. When the time came, they would shoot their blanks off toward the water, delivering a nineteen-gun salute. Near the cannons the Marine Corps Band was testing its instruments, the horn players obsessively breathing into their mouthpieces to warm them in the chilled air, the clarinetists

wetting their reeds, the drummers experimenting with quick
snare rolls. Along the rear area of the parade field, fifty-
four soldiers, sailors, airmen, and marines were forming a
wide line, rigging wooden poles that held the flags of every
state and territory into sockets strapped onto them at the
waist. The white belts that held the flags made large Xs on
each man's back, so that from behind they looked like a
row of little toy soldiers.

Honor platoons from each service, including the Coast
Guard, were rehearsing in front of bleachers that had been
specially erected for the ceremony. The platoon formations
centered on a podium in front of the bleachers. At the
podium, key aides tested the microphones again and again,
moving large speakers here and there behind the bleachers,
and at the far ends of the field. To the right of the bleachers,
a tall scaffold had been erected for cameramen and pho-
tographers. Ropes near the base of the scaffold marked off
an area for the press.

It would be a grand ceremony.

A score of reporters were already wandering around the
edges of the field or lingering near the stands. On the roof
of the Pentagon, hidden sniper teams were scanning their
assigned sectors with field glasses and powerful scopes,
talking to each other on ciphered radios. In the parking lot,
secret service agents moved to and fro, identifiable, for all
their care, by their constantly searching eyes and by the ear
devices whose cords disappeared inside their collars. A
walkway was being cordoned off from inside the Pentagon
down to the parade area. Soon it would be manned by two
rows of soldiers, as if this were the exit from a church after
a military wedding. When the soldiers lined the walkway,
the police would stop all traffic into the River Entrance, and
on the road below. And then the dignitaries would walk out
of the Pentagon between the soldiers, across the emptied
parking lot and out to the parade field, beginning the ceremony.

Grand and glittering. But also routine, when you lived inside the prison of your own power.

Ronald Holcomb watched this preparation, as he had contemplated so many other events over the past three years, from his office window while he leaned against the wall, as if wishing to escape. Before, he had found such ceremonies distracting, a necessary nuisance. But this one was different. It was filled with danger but also with paybacks, and in a strange way it would make him free. He turned to Hank Eichelberger, who sat easily on the couch nearby, and nervously asked another question.

"You're sure there aren't going to be any problems?"

Eichelberger rolled his eyes, tired of baby-sitting Holcomb. "You and I and maybe ten other people in the whole world are the only ones who know. And the other ten people have no desire to go to jail."

"How about General Francis? He knows there was no such thing as Operation Justifiable Anger."

"Francis is a soldier. The battle's over. Anyway, he boxed up Mad Dog. That was what he wanted out of this. And he lost his chance to speak out a month ago when he didn't challenge your version. Calm down, Mr. Secretary."

"Rowland could get to him, and persuade him to speak out. You know, Rowland wants more than anything to control the government, to be a de facto prime minister, or even someday to be President. More than *anything*. More than he wants a family, or to be loved, or to have enjoyed the pleasures of this life when his time on earth is done. It is a purely personal ambition. Others in this town, I regret to say, have some of this as well. But you have to watch Rowland. Rowland will do anything to control the agenda of the government, to position it to where he can either take credit, or save it. I don't mean to sound bitter or trite, but that's the reality, Hank."

Eichelberger shook his head unbelievingly, and then laughed. "Rowland? Don't bullshit a bullshitter, Mr. Secretary. All Rowland cares about is getting laid. It's—other people who think like that.''

Holcomb ignored Eichelberger's pointed barb, continuing until the assistant secretary's face was filled with a new cynicism—the realization he was being toyed with. ''You may wonder why the President keeps listening to someone like Rowland, when he behaves so obscenely. That's easy. It's because Rowland has answers, and he knows how to get things done. Even when, sometimes, the wrong things get done, or the right things get done for the wrong reasons. Government requires motion, perhaps even more than wisdom. And there is a constant temptation to depend on those who know how to keep it moving, rather than demanding that it stay on any particular course. But I suppose that's the grand conundrum, isn't it?''

''Yeah,'' said Eichelberger, his narrow eyes now burrowing a hole through Holcomb. ''Now, why don't you tell me the last time the President listened to Rowland?''

''He let him take credit for Nakashitona, didn't he?'' Holcomb sat for a moment in the easy chair where he had held so many staff calls and conducted so many meetings, becoming conscious of the enormous power that attended his seat. He rubbed his hands gently over the arms of the chair, and then continued. ''We sank the tankers. *We* faced down Tanashi. And *Rowland* becomes a national hero for it!''

Eichelberger now shook his head, as if disgusted. Holcomb was again looking out the window, not even watching Eichelberger as he continued. ''We have to protect ourselves from him. Even more than from the media, because the media is in many ways simply his weapon. Not because they think he's right, but because he knows how to play to each reporter's own set of prejudices—where they were born, where they went to school, which issues they've championed and which they've attacked. We can never meet with him, or even talk with him on the phone, without someone else present. A witness. Someone you trust. When he is on the phone with you, he always has that aide of his on the other line, taking notes, in case he ever needs to go after you.''

Holcomb smiled almost warmly over to Eichelberger, as if he were a father. ''I'm glad I've had you for that. You know State, you keep good notes, you can be trusted.''

Now Eichelberger's eyes narrowed with acute suspicion. He was not being toyed with. There was more to it than that. Holcomb was too smooth to be talking like this. The defense secretary had a new agenda, and was fishing for something. Eichelberger was being set up.

''What's going on, Mr. Secretary?''

''What?'' Holcomb seemed distracted. Suddenly he stood up, and gestured toward the far end of his office, where a door went into his conference room. ''Well, shall we?''

A dozen people waited for them in the conference room, broken apart in family groupings. In one corner, Colonel Bill Fogarty's wife, Linda, and his two teenage children were standing with Major General Iredell Cox, the late colonel's division commander, who was wearing his dress blue uniform. Linda's eyes held a tragic pride as she peered steadily at the defense secretary. She was wearing a black sheath dress and a small black hat with a black veil. Her daughter, whom Eichelberger judged to be about sixteen, had a lanky gracefulness that in a few years would fill out into an uncommon beauty. But it was the son whose presence burned into Eichelberger's soul, back inside a spot he had not visited for many years. The boy, who was about fourteen, was dressed tastefully in a dark blue suit, a white oxford cloth shirt, and a red tie. But he seemed so sure of himself, and so conscious of both his mother's and his sister's pain, that it seemed he had grown into a man overnight. His face purposely held no emotion—not fear, not sorrow, not even awe at his surroundings. His flat gray eyes steadily held even Eichelberger's menacing stare. Eichelberger had seen that look before. It was the look of an accuser who was not afraid to die. The boy probably didn't even know it yet, but he had become his father's avenger.

In another corner, Janet Holcomb stood with General Bear Lazaretti and Colonel Dan Bittman, Holcomb's protocol officer. They were chatting airily as she drank a cup of coffee. And Doc Rowland stood next to the doorway with a wispy-thin Roy Dombrowski, ignoring the others as he vigorously flirted with a young, full-breasted Army sergeant who had been stationed there to take hats and coats and to control access into the room. A Filipino mess specialist carried a silver tray among them, refilling coffee cups and offering them cookies.

Eichelberger fought back an ironic grin as he and Holcomb made their way toward Janet. How very—Washington, he thought, to walk among three separate groups of whispering, mildly embarrassed people, who had been affected in such drastically different ways, and to see them now all quietly drinking coffee and eating cookies in the same small room. But here it was.

Holcomb and Doc Rowland even waved to each other! It was amazing, but it was not surprising. Because in government there was always a tomorrow, and there were always memoirs. And so the long knives never gleamed when failed assassins met. In fact, the knives were always thrown away, in favor of smiles and bright bouquets.

Or perhaps, he thought, nodding and waving back to Rowland and Dombrowski as they did the same to him, it was all illusion anyway. In this town of speeches written by someone else and issues that affected other people, perhaps even the hatred was not real. Perhaps it was simply the flip side of their very narcissism, a measure of self-love that had no real outward direction. Perhaps, after all the flailing was finished, they were left merely with a sense of disappointment, a lingering envy, but none of the bile that would have been present if they had truly hated enough to kill.

That was it, he decided. That was why he disliked all of them so deeply, and why his presence so often chilled them in return. He was a true-to-life knuckle-dragger, and they were at best intellectual assassins, who didn't even have what it took to personally pull a paper trigger. They even used secret surrogates on their staffs or in the press when they sought to murder reputations and mangle credibility so that they might push a pet issue, or attempt a leap to glory. But face to face, the knives would do no good anyway, because they lacked what it took to use them. And so they sipped coffee and nibbled cookies, smiling as they secretly seethed.

But they'd turn on people like me in a heartbeat.

Just in front of Eichelberger, Holcomb smoothed his tie and offered a hand to Janet, who seemed almost to gush in her fondness for his touch. Janet looked handsome and athletic in a brown tweed suit. Her hair was natural, falling loosely around her shoulders so that it framed her face. She seemed pleased with Holcomb, and yet uncomfortable being inside the Pentagon. Perhaps it was the memories across the room in Doc Rowland's hands and eyes that so stiffened her smile. Perhaps she among all of them *was* real, thought Eichelberger. Watching her, he understood Rowland's weakness for her, and her own need for something more than what her husband brought to her bed each night. She emanated a muscular sexuality, as surely as some politicians emanated power and some warriors reeked of death.

Holcomb seemed magnanimous as he gestured toward the room. "Well, are we ready? Mrs. Fogarty, can we escort you to the elevator?"

Linda Fogarty stared coolly at Holcomb as if remembering some conversation from a lifetime ago. Then she took her son's arm, and nodded politely. "We'll follow you, Mr. Secretary."

"Very good, very good. Well, we're on our way."

For a long moment, Bill Fogarty's son stared deeply into the defense secretary's face. He seemed to be searching, perhaps for some glimmer of why his father had died. And finally he spoke, unable to hold it back any longer.

"How old are you?"

"I'm forty-six. Why do you ask?"

The boy peered at Holcomb with the look that Hank Eichelberger had recognized a few moments before, and then spoke flatly, as if he were throwing the words into Holcomb's heart. "My dad would have turned forty-six last week."

In the hallway, under the watchful smile that emanated from General Eisenhower's portrait on a nearby wall, a small army of military and civilian aides surrounded them, offering last-minute updates on VIP attendees and the format of the ceremony. Hank Eichelberger and General Bear Lazaretti shepherded them along, conscious of the clock. The ceremony had been rehearsed down to the minute. Lazaretti addressed both Ronald and Janet Holcomb.

"Sir. Ma'am. The President is running right on time. He'll leave the White House in about eight minutes."

The small group stayed together on the elevator, and then entered the roped-off walkway, which now was lined with soldiers who brought their rifles to present-arms as they passed. They made their way down the steps of the River Entrance and across the parking lot, and then down another set of concrete steps that led to the parade field. As they walked they looked toward the parade field and saw that the bleacher seats were packed full of spectators, drawn mostly from the Pentagon itself, and from the congressional offices across the river. In front of the bleachers, secret service agents stood facing the crowd, their eyes constantly moving, their hands clasped together at the waist. They reached the bleachers and the Marine Corps Band played "Ruffles and Flourishes." At the sound of the music the crowd came to attention, and remained standing while they passed.

General Roger Francis awaited them at their seats just in front of the podium. His face looked ruddy in the chilly breeze. Bursts of wind lifted the lapels on his green dress overcoat. Francis sharply saluted the defense secretary, and then helped Linda Fogarty into her seat. Then Francis nodded to Ronald Holcomb.

"Are you ready, Mr. Secretary?"

"Yes, Roger. Go ahead."

Francis adjusted his cap and smoothed down the lapels of his overcoat. Then he walked up to the podium. Before him, the honor platoons of the different services stood at attention. Farther back, the flags of the states and territories flapped in the cold but gentle wind. Far to his right, the Marine Corps Band and the Army cannoneers also stood at attention. Nearer, the press cameras were busy on the scaffold. And behind him as he spoke, a thousand spectators sat patiently in their bleacher seats.

"Ladies and gentlemen, good morning. This is a day of special meaning for those in uniform. Because we are honoring the chairman of the House Armed Services Committee for his years of special service, a man who has been a great leader and a true friend of the common soldier. And at the same time, we are awarding the Medal of Honor to the family of one of our bravest officers, who died serving his country in the battle of Bera'isale. Mrs. Fogarty, to you and your family, on behalf of those who are now serving, I want to say how deeply we regret your husband's loss, and how much we appreciate his service to our nation."

The crowd politely applauded, and General Francis gestured toward Holcomb. "Ladies and gentlemen, the secretary of defense."

The applause was louder now, and prolonged as Holcomb stepped up to the podium and adjusted the microphones. "Thank you very much. Distinguished guests, General Francis, ladies and gentlemen. I am very pleased to announce that the rumors you have heard are correct: The President will be joining us for a short while today. He will be arriving in a few minutes. But before he does, I would like to emphasize that this is a day for a—*great* friend of our armed forces, Chairman Doc Rowland, and also for a very special American family. It was the President's desire to drive over here for a few minutes to personally participate in the Medal of Honor ceremony. I look forward to watching that ceremony, along with the rest of you, when the President arrives.''

A small smile now began to creep across Ronald Holcomb's face. It spread until he was grinning broadly, as if he had just heard a tantalizing, off-color joke. He could not suppress the grin, and for that moment he was glad that the crowd was at his back and could not see it. ''But again, before the President arrives, I would like to express my personal appreciation to a great American, by bestowing the Department of Defense Medal for Distinguished Service—the highest civilian award that can be made by the secretary of defense—on Chairman Doc Rowland.''

Holcomb turned toward the bleachers, and waved Doc Rowland forward. The remarks he made were his own, and the words were carefully chosen, filled with a double entendre that only a few would comprehend. But this type of irony was his special province, and Holcomb knew that most of those who knew of the internal battle of the past months would discern the meaning of his words. ''Congressman Doc Rowland has *actively pursued* the interests of the Department of Defense for many years from his position on the House Armed Services Committee. In fact, I think it's fair to say that he has given the department more of his—attention—than any other member of Congress. I can't recall a time in the last three years when Doc Rowland hasn't been readily available to us, *and to the media*, to give his opinion in national security deliberations. Doc was—*most thoughtful*—in holding hearings to obtain my views on a wide variety of matters, and I always appreciated his providing me a—forum. And I know all of you are familiar, from the newspaper accounts, with Doc's role as perhaps the key member of government during our recent difficulties with Japan over security leaks by Nakashitona Industries. I think it's—*fair*—to say that there would not have been a favorable resolution of that problem without Doc's—special efforts—on the matter.''

Holcomb gestured toward Doc Rowland, who now stood very near him, at the right side of the podium. In front of the podium, General Bear Lazaretti stood at attention, holding a gray velvet pad, on which rested the medal.

''Mr. Chairman, I give you my profoundest thanks for services rendered to our nation and to the Department of Defense, and it is my pleasure to award you the Defense Medal for Distinguished Service.''

From a separate microphone an announcer read the citation that accompanied the awards. The citation praised Rowland's diligence, intellectual brilliance, and dedication to country. Holcomb stood at attention before Rowland, and when the citation was read he pinned a medal on his lapel. Doc Rowland first fought back a visceral anger, and then a tear, and Holcomb knew that the chairman was not on the verge of weeping for joy. Feeling gallant, he shook Rowland's meaty hand and uncharacteristically slapped him on the back.

Rowland took the microphone for a moment, never one to turn away from a captive audience. ''Mr. Secretary—'' His eyes rested for one lingering moment on Janet, who turned her face away, pretending to stare out at the river. ''Other guests. Look, there's never been anything more important to me than the well-being of our fighting men. And this actually is a day to honor a true hero, not somebody like me who pilots a desk and fights with words.''

Rowland now gestured briefly toward Bill Fogarty's family as the crowd spontaneously applauded. ''Mrs. Fogarty, this day is no substitute for the loss of your husband, but I hope you know how humble I feel in the shadow of his memory. On behalf of the Congress, God bless you.''

Rowland then returned to his seat, accompanied by a thundering wave of applause.

The little ceremony had been perfectly timed. In less than a minute, sirens and flashing lights from a caravan of limousines at the River Entrance signaled the arrival of the President. The limousines stopped at the edge of the parking lot. A bevy of secret service agents burst out of cars at the front and the rear. They formed a watchful phalanx as President Everett Lodge strode quickly toward the podium along the grass, his endearing, loping gait a legacy of his upbringing in the great outdoors. The Marine Corps Band played "Hail to the Chief" and the honor platoons brought their swords and rifles to present-arms as those in the bleachers came to their feet to honor his arrival.

Two presidential assistants quickly and expertly turned the podium around, so that when President Lodge reached it he was facing the crowd. Holcomb had stood nearby, and now spoke into the microphones. "Ladies and gentlemen, the President of the United States."

The President received a prolonged standing ovation, and the cameras were busy on the scaffold. President Lodge waved warmly to the crowd and briefly hugged Ronald Holcomb before beginning to speak. There was a dramatic moment of silence as the President gathered himself. And then he spoke, in the folksy cadence that had so captivated his countrymen.

"Ladies and gentlemen, thank you very much. I am here for two purposes today. First, I'd like to join in with Ron Holcomb in thanking Chairman Doc Rowland for his years of—absolutely *brilliant* leadership over in the Armed Services Committee. Doc, we in the administration must truly thank you for your tough stand in the recent Nakashitona crisis, and for holding firm until a favorable solution was reached. I don't mind eating a little crow when I'm wrong, and in spite of what I said in the press, your tough stand turned out to be just what the doctor ordered, if you'll pardon the pun."

The President grew somber as the crowd chuckled at his play on words. "And second, it's one of my saddest duties, and at the same time a great honor, to be posthumously awarding Colonel William Fogarty, United States Marine

Corps, the Medal of Honor. Words cannot convey the sense of awe and respect I felt upon reading of what Colonel Fogarty accomplished, at the cost of his life. And to his family I can only say, I wish more than anything that I could give you back your husband and your father. I can't do that. But allow me to convey the deep respect that our country will always hold for him.''

Linda Fogarty and her daughter were now weeping softly. The President continued, now addressing the crowd. ''A few months ago, we were faced with a very grave situation in the Red Sea. I'm not sure the American people fully comprehend how severe that crisis really was, and how dangerous it was to our interests around the world. The Red Sea, as those of you here today well know, is one of the key commercial and military waterways of the world. It is the passageway into and out of the Suez Canal. It hosts the port that connects the Saudi Arabian oil pipeline to tankers that carry oil to our friends and allies. And early last month, it became clear to me and my advisers that the freedom of passage through this waterway was being endangered, both on land and at sea. Clearly, something had to be done.''

President Lodge paused again, his handsome, etched face somber as he surveyed the crowd. ''I take great pride in the improvements we have made in our relations with the Soviets over the past several years, and I have every confidence that they will continue. But these improvements have come about because the Soviets and their allies know we will not hesitate to defend our interests if they are challenged. Our interests were in fact challenged in the Red Sea, at sea in a number of ways by the Soviets themselves, and on land through the aggression of their Cuban allies and through their surrogates in Yemen and Ethiopia. It was a very serious crisis, and it is over because we, and the gallant French forces who joined us, decided to act firmly in defense of those interests.''

The President paused yet another time, nodding his head as if remembering a moment of torment. ''I want you to know that it wasn't easy making the decision to activate Operation Justifiable Anger, and to send our troops into Eritrea. We are not a warlike nation, and the loss of even one serviceman in the line of duty causes me a great deal of grief. But I came to the conclusion that such action was necessary. And in retrospect, I know the public opinion polls, as well as the many, many letters I have received, indicate a wholehearted support of that very painful decision by the American people. This military action has resulted in what I have termed the Lodge Doctrine, which states clearly, for now and into the future, that the United States will not hesitate to act if democratic movements in the Third World are subjected to external attack.''

Now the President's eyes lingered again on Bill Fogarty's family. The President was becoming deeply sentimental. His words grew soft, and his face had the demeanor of a pained parent. ''For many of us, words such as 'defending American interests' are just that—words, concepts, abstract principles to be applied as the world situation demands. But for our military people, those who must operate day in and day out on the edge of danger, such words take on a different meaning. Colonel William Fogarty was a man who understood the price of national defense, not in terms of billions of dollars but in terms of human lives, and of his own health. He was wounded in Vietnam as a young man. Last month he was wounded again in an Eritrean town called Bera'isale, as he directed the defense of a small Marine Corps unit under attack by a reinforced armored division. He was literally blown apart by an enemy artillery shell that landed almost on top of him. And yet he refused to be medically evacuated or even relinquish command until the enemy attack had been stopped and his men had received medical treatment. He lay on the ground in that small desert town, bleeding into the dirt from multiple shrapnel wounds, one leg blown off and the other one shattered, his intestines sliced apart by shrapnel, and continued to fight. His men were outnumbered by more than ten to one, and yet through

Colonel Fogarty's actions, they soundly defeated the Cuban attack.''

President Lodge gestured toward the Fogartys as he now addressed the entire crowd. ''There are many, many brave men and women who have worn the uniform, but ladies and gentlemen, I wish to say to you that Colonel William Fogarty is a man who uniquely served us all, to the moment of his death.''

Young John Fogarty felt giddy, watching the President only a few yards in front of him as he was enveloped by the applause that came from all sides. It was a thrill beyond measure to hear his father's name spoken from the lips of the President of the United States. And yet, there was something in the President's kind remarks that he did not like. He could not put a finger on it. He was too overcome by their power, and by the memories that the words had conjured up from a day that he wished had never happened. He struggled to fight back tears, and to appear strong despite the loss of his father, who had been like a demigod to him. The cameras were devouring him, picking him apart as if they were microscopes. He was afraid to smile or to frown, to touch a leg or even speak to his mother. Even the slightest motion that he made was accompanied by a hundred clicking shutters, and if he wasn't careful, the camera might lie. Or worse yet, it might tell the truth. What symbolic moments would the cameras capture to explain him on the evening news or in tomorrow's paper? What photograph would represent forever more his vision of his father?

Two tall, perfectly built Marine captains from the barracks at Eighth and Eye glided slowly up to him and his mother and sister, giving stiff, mechanical salutes and taking the two females by the arm. John Fogarty rose from his chair and followed them, now so overwhelmed by the ceremony and the appearance of the uniform his father had so proudly worn that if it were not for Bill Fogarty's memory he would have turned and run, all the way up to Arlington National Cemetery a mile away, where he could sit on the raw earth before his father's headstone and cry. But he could not do that. He had to be strong, for the memory of his father.

He walked slowly forward, stifling his emotions with great effort, until he was just in front of the President, flanking his mother on one side while his sister stood on the other. The crowd ceased its applause and now was hushed. The cameras were merciless in their noise and motion. Another Marine captain marched forward with the robotic glide reserved for ceremonies, holding the Medal of Honor on a velvet pad in both of his hands, as if it were made of fragile glass. He came to fierce, rigid attention just off to John Fogarty's side, between him and the President.

The announcer from the other microphone began to read the Medal of Honor citation, the most awesome words in the military lexicon now tying John Fogarty's father forever to a bitter battle in a piece of ash and salt known as Bera'i-sale. "*For conspicuous gallantry and intrepidity at the risk of his life, above and beyond the call of duty . . .*"

The citation continued, recounting the sudden emergency that called for the landing of the marines, the enormous odds they faced, and Colonel Fogarty's wounding by a fierce artillery barrage. At first he looked at the kindly smiling face of his President and mused, *I have traded my father for a piece of cloth*. But he quickly set that thought aside, remembering instead the other side of all that blood and dreck, the hours of waiting for word of their father and then the general showing up at their house in the middle of the night, dressed in his blues, how he had immediately known when he saw the general's face and how he had run out of the kitchen when he heard the horrible final words, into the bedroom where he had fallen onto his bed, clutching the picture of his father to his chest and crying so hard that he was heaving, twisting, shuddering with a dull overwhelming pain that he knew would never leave him, no matter how many lovers or wives or children he would ever hold with the same tenacity that he embraced that cold, empty glass frame.

As that memory stirred inside John Fogarty, the sterile, praising words of the Medal of Honor citation washed over the crowd. "... *refusing medical evacuation, Colonel Fogarty continued to direct the defense of Bera'isale, coordinating close air support, artillery counterbattery fire, and arranging for the evacuation by sea of those seriously wounded* ..."

He was coming to terms with his emptiness, but he did not know why he felt so angry. What was it that the President had said only minutes before? He strained to remember. *It wasn't easy making the decision to send our troops into Eritrea*, that was what Lodge had lamented to the adoring crowd. But why had he? Staring at the tall, etched man who now seemed almost in a mantra as the words told the story of his father's death, John Fogarty was struck by a new reality: This was the man who had killed his father, sent him to his death.

" ... *by his heroic actions, his calm and brilliant direction of his fellow Marines in the face of a vastly superior attacking force even to the moment of his death, Colonel Fogarty brought great credit to himself, and upheld the finest traditions of the Marine Corps and the U.S. Naval Service.*"

And now the President stepped forward, taking the hallowed sky-blue cloth of the medal from the young aide and awarding it to Linda Fogarty. The President was standing very close. He was only six inches away from John Fogarty. He peered kindly down into each of their faces, and then took John Fogarty's right hand inside both of his own, a sincere gesture of his thanks. The crowd applauded loudly behind them, and the cameras clicked and rolled. And John Fogarty could no longer hold it back.

"You killed my dad. Why? Why'd you send him in? Why?"

Lodge's face registered a quick moment of confused apprehension, as if John Fogarty were going to make a scene, screw up the ceremony, rain on his dad's very last parade. But the President also knew the power of the probing cameras, and his smile immediately returned. He expertly disengaged from John Fogarty, taking a step back and nodding slowly to him as if he were a shrine. And then he waved to the crowd as they continued to applaud. And the boy spoke again.

"Who cares about Eritrea, anyway? Who cares? What good did it do? Why?"

His mother leaned over from near his left shoulder and whispered, cutting him off. "Please, John. Remember your father. And don't make me cry right now."

His comment had been lost in the noise. The crowd was standing, continuing its applause. President Lodge studied John Fogarty's face for another moment, reading it with the expertise of a life spent gambling his future on other people's reactions to him. Then he stepped forward one more time and emotionally embraced the boy as if he were his own son.

The crowd loved it. A new wave of applause swept over the stands. And underneath its din the President spoke almost in a whisper as he clutched John Fogarty to him.

"Young man, we're honoring the memory of your father. He didn't ask that question, did he? He saw a reason. He went in and stopped a Cuban division in its tracks. That's what we're left with. Don't disappoint your mother, son. She needs your strength right now."

Lodge stepped back again, keeping his long arms on John Fogarty's shoulders for a moment as he looked deeply into his eyes. Finally the boy stared for a moment at the pale blue piece of cloth for which his father would now always be remembered. Tears filled his eyes, and he relented.

"I'm okay. I'm all right."

But he wasn't. And he never would be.

2

All day the wind had blown from the south, and now it had begun to rain. It was five o'clock in the afternoon. Outside the window of his office, Ronald Holcomb could see headlights moving south on Interstate 95, as if an army of glowing ants were coming out of the city over the Fourteenth Street Bridge. Below him, a few cars moved in the River Entrance parking lot, mostly limousines dispatching passengers after visits at State or on Capitol Hill.

The office was lonely and huge, and for that moment it was cold, and museumlike. It had never really been his. The presence of men who had preceded him, some great and some little better than him, still clung to the walls and the desk and the chairs. But, he thought with a measure of self-satisfaction, he had left his mark forever—on the government, on the military, in the office itself. It was a legacy that had grown an issue at a time, not blessed with any vision but at the same time not having fallen to disaster, either. A caretaker's legacy, developed as subtly as the worn spot on the carpet where he had walked so many thousands of times between his desk and his favorite stuffed blue easy chair, that throne from which he had presided over three years of staff calls and meetings.

A legacy that was threatened by Hank Eichelberger, one of the few men he had ever trusted.

He paced back and forth along the pathway he had worn, looking along the walls and in the alcoves at his favorite pieces of memorabilia and photographs from visits around the world. Suddenly he felt very small. He had positioned issues and dissembled, postured and obfuscated, for his entire adult life, but always for his own reasons, always at his own initiative. It troubled him that he had done so for Eichelberger, even if the end result had been stunningly favorable, at least for the moment. He had fallen into one of his own favorite traps: Convincing someone to lie for him on some small issue was the first, and usually the final, step in gaining complete control over the person. If discovered, the lies ended careers, put people in jail.

Eichelberger had assumed that kind of control over Holcomb. And the only answer was to find a way to compromise Eichelberger, on a completely separate issue. Once Eichelberger was brought to public scrutiny on another charge, he would have lost his credibility. He could no longer accuse Holcomb of knowingly lying about the sinking of the Japanese tankers. There was no record of their conversation on the day of the sinkings. Holcomb could claim that Eichelberger had never mentioned a covert operation, that as far as he knew, the tankers actually did run into a Yemeni minefield, and that Eichelberger was trying to drag down honest people with him.

There were a dozen such issues that would work. Eichelberger had been Holcomb's continual liaison to the odious underworld of covert operations for three years, which was how he had so easily set up the sinking of the Japanese tankers in the first place. The former CIA agent had been free to "solo" many of his missions, under very broad guidelines. He had sipped whiskey with corrupt dictators, arranged for weapons to be smuggled to rebel leaders of all stripes, delivered bombing missions onto Third World targets that had seemingly come out of nowhere and whose reality had immediately been denied. The trick was to pick one of those things that would neither involve Holcomb nor unduly harm the nation, and to arrange a way for a snippet of information to be made public. After that, some smart reporter would smell a Pulitzer Prize and go after Eichelberger like a duck on a june bug.

Holcomb sat in the big easy chair, once again deciding that he belonged on the throne. He had just the issue. Seven months before, Felix Crowell had directed an operation whereby defective artillery ammunition was sold to the Afghan government through an Iranian intermediary. The ammunition was designed to explode in the artillery tubes, killing the gunners. The Congress had not been notified. Holcomb had argued against the proposition, warning that it was involving the United States directly in the Afghani hostilities by intentionally killing their soldiers. The President had given his approval.

And Eichelberger had been the negotiator.

Holcomb knew just how to handle it. In a day or so, an unmarked manila envelope would appear at the home address of Alex Woodburn, an investigative reporter who already had won a Pulitzer. Inside the envelope would be a sterilized copy of the memorandum that summarized the White House meeting at which Holcomb had argued against the ammunition sale, and Eichelberger had been designated as the negotiator. Woodburn would take it from there.

Eichelberger was going down.

3

Hank Eichelberger walked swiftly down the "E"-ring corridor toward his office, passing the familiar paintings that marked the Air Force secretariat's hallway. His lanky legs moved so quickly that he seemed to trot. His hawkish face with its narrow, piercing eyes and tight frown peered straight ahead, acknowledging no one as he passed dozens of military and civilian office workers. Ahead, a young soldier wearing her dress blues was conducting a Pentagon tour for a group of twenty gawking tourists. He brushed past the group, nodding briefly to the soldier, who recognized him and shyly smiled.

"Good afternoon, sir."

"Afternoon."

He burst inside his office door. In the outer office, his secretary handed him twenty telephone messages. She started to explain the top few.

"Sir, Ambassador Qualtrough wants to know—"

He cut her off, swiping the messages out of her extended hand. "I'll be back out in a few minutes. Hold my calls."

Inside his office he sat for a moment at his desk, surveying the dozens of souvenirs and foreign decorations that adorned his own walls. He had come a long way since his early days as an enlisted soldier in the Korean War, a student in college and graduate student after that, and the frustrating and yet halcyon years operating with the Company in Vietnam. He had seen overconfidence ruin his government's posture overseas, and he had despaired as the weakness of its leaders destroyed its consensus on foreign policy at home. He had endured the woeful stupidity of the early Carter years, and the unpredictable policy swings of the Reagan administration. He had believed in Ronald Holcomb, and for almost three years he had supported him with every ounce of loyalty and passion he could summon. And they had done some good. A lot of good.

For *almost* three years. And in the past two months he had watched Holcomb fall to pieces when the chips were down. The young defense secretary had succumbed to his own vanity years ago, but that was tolerable as long as he listened, and dared in the way that Mad Dog Mulcahy and Eichelberger dared. It had worked! The Soviets were out of the Red Sea, and the Japanese had apologized for Nakashitona. At the same time, Holcomb had clutched twice with the Japanese, and then again inside the command center during the Eritrean operation. He had dropped Mad Dog like yesterday's fish. And he was getting ready to move on Hank Eichelberger, the old intelligence operative could feel it.

Their conversation that morning just before the ceremony had been strangely disconcerting. Holcomb was probing, rambling with his intellectual bull about himself at the same time he was invoking the menace of Doc Rowland. It had been confusing, but the final, nauseating smell of it was betrayal. The defense secretary had no loyalties, no close friends, not even a wife who stuck with him. He would not hesitate to dump Eichelberger.

One of those phony character assassinations, since they don't know how to do the real thing.

He thought about it some more, and pulled his Rolodex toward him from its place on a credenza behind his desk. Flipping through it, he found a number and stared at it for a while. His heart raced and his hands began to tremble slightly as he reached for the telephone. He dialed the number and then quickly hung up, and thought about it some more. Then he redialed.

A deep, almost irritated voice answered. "Morrissey."

"Yeah. Hank Eichelberger." Eichelberger hesitated, then spoke nervously, doodling on a yellow notepad as he talked. "Look, I've got no desire to get into the middle of this, but I've got something I think you'd be interested in. This is straight stuff. I know what I'm talking about. Ron Holcomb withheld information from the Senate during those hearings on the Red Sea debacle. He blew all that smoke into the air about the President's leadership during the Eritrean battle, and he knew good and well the President didn't order the Marines into Eritrea. He knows the administration's position on the matter was a cover-up."

The reporter's voice immediately became warm, his attention now rapt. "*A cover-up?*"

For the first time in days, Eichelberger's face broke into a smile. Bull's-eye. He had spoken the magic word.

"That's right. The Marines had landed before they even told the President. Eritrea was an accident. A mistake. But it worked. And they didn't want the President to look bad. And Holcomb knew." He rolled his eyes toward the plaques and memorabilia on his far wall. "There's a lot more to it than that. The whole thing has got a million holes in it. Maybe you ought to call up General Francis, and ask him point-blank if there ever was an operation called Justifiable Anger. That'll get it rolling."

"Wow." The reporter paused on the other end of the

line, finishing his notes. "Are you sure on this one, Hank?"

He carefully deflected that one. It wasn't his obligation to be completely sure. "A hundred percent on Justifiable Anger. On the other, I'm telling you what I've heard." He further enticed the reporter. "I haven't steered you wrong yet, have I?"

"No. No you haven't. Hank, I owe you a beer on this one."

"Forget it. Just don't get me tangled up in it."

"Can I call you back on this?"

"No, I'll call you in a day or so."

Eichelberger hung up the phone, and then started sifting mechanically through the stack of messages his secretary had given him. He was in a hurry now. It was getting late.

And he had other calls to make.